CW00539784

Handy for You

Book 2 in the All for You series

Adele Buck

Quiet Confidence Press

Also by Adele Buck

For John Jacobson, who's made me a better writer.

Chapter One

The dripping faucet was panic attack number seventy-three since Kari closed on her house. Or was it one-hundred and seventy-three? Or one-thousand and seventy-three?

"Why did I think this was a good idea?" she muttered, eyeing the trickle of water snaking from the base of the kitchen faucet down the side of the stainless-steel sink and into the drain.

A steady drumbeat of anxiety had plagued her since her first night under her first un-rented roof six months before. Everything leading up to it had seemed fine. Fine for a momentous occasion like being the first person in your immediate family to own property. Exciting, not panic-inducing. She had approached the decision with her usual calm deliberation, looked for a house that was a bit of a fixer-upper but not so much of a fixer-upper that she'd blow any fixing-up budget in the first few months. She'd found a realtor she liked, one who got her and didn't look down on her for looking for a mid-century ranch to actually live in instead of tearing it down to build a modern McMansion so close to the D.C. Beltway.

The search had yielded a short sale: worn and definitely shabby, but the important parts were well-maintained and it had a sunny back yard on a quiet street in one of the rabbit warren of neighborhoods in Rockville that hadn't yet completely succumbed to gentrification. The offer was accepted, the settlement date set, an enormous stack of papers signed, and she was handed a set of keys. Then a little gaggle of volunteers moved her limited possessions in. Sam, her niece, had put clean linens on the new bed Kari had put together with Allen wrenches and bags of screws. Kari set up her coffee maker for the next morning and dropped gratefully into those clean, smooth sheets with a smile on her face.

Then rolled to her back, her heart hammering, her brain racing. *What if I can't make the mortgage? What if something breaks? I had nothing to lose and now I have everything to lose.*

What have I done?

That first night was a century of fitful sleep, starting awake, then the thoughts scurrying like mice in a wheel, going nowhere, only generating a lot of movement and nauseating whirling.

Why did you have to leave me, Mor? Kari's lips had trembled at that predawn cry for her mother. *I wouldn't have been able to buy this place if you hadn't gone and died.*

Which was the most ridiculous thought of all. Her mother, in her nineties and in poor health, had slipped away a little more than a year before. There was no question of "leaving." She had died. She left Kari a small legacy that had tipped her bank balance to the level that enabled Kari to put together the down payment, and nobody but Kari had made the decision to actually purchase the house.

Sunlight shimmered on the slim trickle of water and Kari

looked from it to the backyard. Her shoulders eased a little out of their tense hunch. At least out there she had nothing to stress her. She had started to move some of the former owner's plantings around and made some judicious purchases of new plants of her own. A shady side of the house was shaping up into a beautiful hosta garden. She could see a paved patio area in her mind's eye. Maybe a grill for cooking outside on hot Maryland summer nights.

Enough. Her eyes snapped back to the sink. She needed to open the cabinet underneath at the very least, check and see if there was any water leaking down there. She took a deep breath and knelt, closing her eyes for a moment in a brief, formless prayer. Flinging the nondescript cabinet doors open, she felt the pipes. They seemed dry, but they were also cold. It was hard to tell. Getting to her feet, she tore a paper towel from the roll and ran it up the bend of pipe. Examined it. Breathed a sigh of relief.

It was dry. For now.

Getting to her feet, the backyard drew her attention again. That azalea she and Sam transplanted a few weeks ago looked wilting and thirsty. The thought of Sam gave her a different kind of pang. A guilty one.

Hell with it. Better to water the plants outside than try to deal with the water in the kitchen.

Kari was out there again, a hose in her hand, a fine spray of water dancing across the azalea she had transplanted with her sister.

Rob shook his head, rubbing his eyes, weariness welling up inside him. No, not her sister. Her niece. He had probably come off like a skeevy middle-aged jerk when he met them a few weeks back, saying he thought they were sisters.

He certainly felt like one when he found out he had guessed the relationship wrong.

But they *did* look like sisters. And apparently the two women weren't that far apart in age. Not to mention the fact they took his error in stride — as if it happened all the time — but dammit if he didn't feel like a jerk for stepping in it anyway.

And now he was compounding the skeeve by watching her out of his bathroom window, which had an unobstructed view of her backyard. If she turned her head, she might catch him spying on her. He should stop now. Go put that load of laundry that just finished the spin cycle into the dryer. Yes. He should absolutely do that.

Except…she wiped the fingers of one hand under her eye. Like she was crying. And then took a big breath, her chest heaving, as if she was containing some big emotion.

Something was wrong.

Rob was out of his house and approaching the fence that separated his property from hers before he had a coherent plan. So what came out of his mouth was the supremely inane, "Hey neighbor!" that he had cheerily used the last time he had stepped in it. Like he was Ned fucking Flanders.

Kari's head whipped around, her light blue eyes meeting his. She swallowed and a wan sort of smile flitted across her face, then she scanned around him. "Hey yourself. No dog today?"

"Um. No. Not my dog."

"Was it a loaner? A rental?" Her shoulders straightened and she lifted her chin, tossing her pale blond hair back from her face and he could see the effort she put into her casual stance. It made his heart hurt.

"No. My daughter's dog. My granddog, I guess you could say." He was babbling. It was criminal, the level of babbling he was committing. And yet, his mouth continued

4

to move. "He visits when my daughter—Mia—needs me to take care of him. It happens about as often as I had expected —a lot. But he's a good boy."

He had told Mia that getting a dog was a mistake when she was just starting her career, that her mother lived states away now and couldn't help. That he wasn't sure he could help as much as she might need. But Mia knew he was a soft touch. She had gotten Hugo anyway and, of course, left him with her soft touch of a dad every time she needed dog-sitting. And damn if he wasn't becoming attached to the mutt. No—not a mutt. Of course not. Mia hadn't been impressed by the #AdoptNotShop hashtag on her beloved Instagram. No, she'd decided to spend money she could have used better elsewhere to buy a purebred German Shepherd puppy.

Rob had been all geared up to be angry with his daughter's uncharacteristic fit of irresponsibility before he actually met Hugo, who instantly cut him down at the knees, all giant feet and lollopy ears. By the time Hugo was a year old, Rob knew he was basically done. The weapon? A German Shepherd pup. The guilty party? His daughter. One shot to the heart and it was all over. The stupid animal had him wrapped around his paw and Rob was not-so-secretly over-joyed every time Mia called him, starting the conversation with, "Daddy? Do you think you can take Hugo...?"

Kari was looking at him with a funny expression on her face and Rob realized he had been woolgathering. "Anyway. I'm sure Hugo will be back around sometime soon. If you want to see him. Sorry, I don't even know if you like dogs. But he's a good boy. Uh, I said that already, didn't I?" *Aaaand now we're back to babbling.*

She shrugged. "I've never had one, but they seem perfectly nice. Sam—my niece, you met her—she loves them."

"Never had a dog? What about a cat?"

She shook her head.

"Hamsters? Gerbils? Guinea pigs?" He was starting to feel a little desperate. "Lizards?"

She laughed a little, lightening the heavy feeling in his heart. "No. Never had a pet." She paused and eyed him uncertainly. "Was there something you wanted?"

He gripped the fence, the boards rough under his hands. He hadn't thought this through. He had barely met the woman, let alone know her. He couldn't ask about the distress that had been so obvious when he was spying on her from his house but had completely vanished as they talked.

"No…just…wondering if you're settling in okay, if there's anything you needed."

She shook her head, her blue eyes grave. "No, I think I'm good."

"Okay, then. I'll just…" Rob pointed a thumb over his shoulder, back at his house. "…Get back to laundry. Satur-day. Laundry day." Turning on his heel, he walked back to his back door, desperate to stop the verbal onslaught that seemed uncontrollable.

"Actually." Kari's voice stilled his steps. "Do you know a good, hopefully inexpensive plumber?"

Rob turned back to her, a thoughtful look on his face. "What sort of problem are we talking about? Serious?"

Kari looked at the spray nozzle in her hand. "I…don't think so? But I don't know. I'm really new to this home-owner thing. I don't even know if I should just ignore it."

His eyebrows went up. "Don't ignore it, whatever it is. Plumbing can be a pretty serious thing. Water getting where it shouldn't creates all sorts of problems. It can ruin drywall, create mold, even cause structural damage in the worst cases."

"Oh god." Kari's heart kicked, a sickening thudding in her chest. The panic was back.

"Want me to take a look at it?" Rob had moved back to the fence as they talked. Kari eyed him, her habitual suspicion of people who offered things threading through her.

"Are you a plumber?"

"No."

"A contractor?"

He gave a brief laugh. It made laugh lines fan out from his eyes and Kari's heart seemed to flutter instead of kicking this time. "No. But I've been a homeowner for a long time. And growing up, my parents had rental properties as investments. So my brother and I were free apprentices for my dad. Someone would move out, we'd paint, do basic plumbing, electrical, fix holes in the drywall—you name it."

Kari tried to assess whether or not she wanted to let him into her house based on everything she knew about him. Which was practically nothing. Divorced, a grown daughter, a "granddog." Probably her age or a little older. Dark brown hair going silver. Kind brown eyes and a sensitive mouth. Fit, in a rangy sort of way.

Attractive, if she was perfectly honest.

She bit her lip. "If you wouldn't mind, I'd be grateful. There's a leak from my kitchen faucet."

He walked to the gate that led to his driveway, let himself out. "Yeah, that could be a problem. Not something you want to ignore."

She shut off the tap and coiled the hose, meeting him at her back door, her shoulders tightening. "I did check under the sink to make sure it wasn't leaking there."

"Good thinking."

Opening the door, Kari moved to the sink and waved at

the faucet. The same gleaming thread of water slithered from the faucet into the sink and down the drain. Or was it worse than before? She couldn't tell. Strange how such a mundane thing could look so sinister.

"Ah. Yeah." Rob's hands landed on his hips and he peered at the faucet for a few moments.

"Bad?" Kari's stomach clenched.

"Not generally. That's usually a quick fix."

"…But?"

Rob waved at the sink. "That faucet might as well have cracked out of an egg at *Jurassic Park*." He grasped it and twisted it from side to side. "Stiff, too." Glancing around the kitchen, he added, "Not a lot of updates here generally, though, so I guess that's no surprise."

"I've only just moved in," Kari said, hating how defensive her voice sounded.

"I know." Rob held up two hands in a gesture of surrender. "I'm just saying I can fix it pretty readily with a few parts, or you could spend a little more money and I could update it to one with a pull-out spray nozzle. It'd make doing your dishes a heck of a lot easier." He waved at the counter with its dish rack, apparently noting the lack of a dishwasher among the cabinets that looked rattier than ever with him there to observe their shabbiness.

"You can do that?" she asked.

"Do what?"

"Replace an entire faucet? On your own?"

Rob grinned at her, an appealingly lopsided expression. "Sure can. It's not exactly rocket surgery, you know."

"Rocket surgery?"

"Yes. Don't you know I'm a renowned rocket surgeon? That's my day job." His face was solemn, but his eyes twinkled with suppressed humor.

Kari nodded. "I see. Master plumber, rocket surgeon. I'm starting to get the idea your accomplishments are endless."

"Too true. So. Want that new faucet of your dreams?"

That all-too-familiar panicky feeling trickled through her again. "Uh. How much would that cost, you think? General idea?"

He shrugged, frowning. "It would depend, for sure, on how grandiose your dreams about faucets are, but probably in the hundred dollar range if you want to go with a budget option."

An unfamiliar but welcome wave of relief crashed over her, making her weak in the knees. "Is that all?"

"Yeah. I mean, like anything else, you can spend big money on something if you have it and want to, but…a big money faucet might look a little out of place among the contractor's special cabinetry and the vintage vinyl flooring."

Kari nodded. "You sure I shouldn't call a plumber?"

He crossed his arms over his chest, looking both amused and a little wounded. "Don't you trust my skills?"

"I do." She was surprised to find that was the truth. Despite his tendency to run off at the mouth, he had a calm, non-showy way of carrying himself, of assessing the situation, that inspired confidence. "But you don't owe me anything…"

He frowned again. "I don't have to owe you. Let's shut the water off and head for the home center."

"Now?" He was ready to drop everything to help her? Kari, raised with her parents' insistence on self-reliance, had never experienced such open-handedness before. Something about his spontaneity made the offer especially compelling.

"No time like the present."

"Didn't you say you have Saturday things to do?"

"Nothing that can't get pushed to Sunday. Let's go get you the faucet of your dreams."

Kari's pale eyes were wide as she scanned the wall of faucets at the home improvement big-box store. "How do I decide?" She turned to Rob and he realized those blue eyes were almost level with his own. Good grief, she must be close to six feet tall.

How incredibly attractive.

Right. She had asked him a question. "Narrow it down to the ones you can afford. What's your budget?"

Her gaze swiveled back to the wall of fixtures. "I hadn't really budgeted for a new faucet at all. But...I guess if I can keep it around that hundred dollar mark you mentioned it won't break the bank."

"Okay." He rubbed his chin, the weekend stubble rasping against his palm. He pointed to a few fixtures. "Those are all good choices. I wouldn't go with that one." He pointed at another faucet. "I've had bad luck with that brand in the past. Wouldn't risk it."

"Okay, so between those..." She counted, fingers pointing at each option as she considered it. "Four, which one would you choose?"

"It's not about what *I* would choose. What do *you* want? What look appeals to you? What sort of features do you want?"

"Features?" Her face twisted into a funny grimace. "Like options on a car?"

"Sort of. Like that pull-out spray nozzle. How does that sound?"

A laugh puffed through her lips. "You know, I've never thought about it."

"About what?"

"About what I wanted in my house. I mean, aside from

furniture or decorative items. Stuff I could take with me when my lease was up. But everything else? The landlord chose it. Usually the cheapest thing possible, I guess. Whatever would just scrape by, get the water from the ground to the sink."

"Well…" A smile tugged at his lips. "Now you're the landlord. Um. Lady. Lady with her own land. You get to choose. What do you think you would like to have? In *your* house."

Kari's hand lifted to her chest and settled there, pressing against the thin cotton of her tee shirt. Rob swallowed, averting his gaze from her chest and turned to look at the wall of faucets, gleaming with finishes ranging from shiny chrome to brushed steel. She pointed at one model. "That one."

He followed the trajectory of her finger and tapped a unit. "This one?"

"Yeah."

"Why?"

"Because it's ninety-nine dollars — seriously, why do they do that? Why not round up to a hundred?" She readdressed herself to the wall of faucets. "And because it has a pull-out thingy with a spray thingy and it's brushed metal instead of shiny and it…has a brand name I recognize. Does that pass inspection, Professor?"

Her words felt like a soft punch of regret to his sternum. "Yeah."

"Why did your face just go all funny?" Her eyes narrowed, her expression concerned.

"Did it?"

"Yeah."

He shrugged. "Don't know." She could have no way of knowing she'd just inadvertently dusted off a dream of a lifetime ago. Bending, he found a box that corresponded with the item number of the faucet she had selected. "Let's get checked out and I can install it for you."

"You sure you're want to do it?"

He paused, looking sideways at her. "Don't you think I can?"

She waved her hands in front of her face. "Didn't mean to disparage your abilities. It's just...you're giving up your Saturday to do this for me. I feel guilty. I could always hire a plumber."

"Not an issue. I like doing this sort of thing." He hefted the box. "Need anything else while we're here?"

"I don't know." She looked up and down the wide aisle, then nodded at the box. "Will that have everything you need to do this? Or do we need to get additional pieces or parts or whatever?"

"I'll get some new supply lines. Otherwise, this should have everything we need. Except for tools, of course." He laughed at the sudden, stricken look on her face. "Which I have. Don't worry."

"Okay." She nodded toward the front of the store. "Let's get this show on the road, I guess."

And as Kari followed him to the aisle that held the other things he needed he realized that he hadn't helped a woman around the house in a very long time. It was a little scary how good it felt.

Chapter Two

"Are you sure you don't want some coffee or something?" Kari fidgeted, feeling useless. No, worse than useless. Useless *and* very aware of the long, male legs attached to the long, lean torso sticking out from under her sink.

Something clanked and Rob grunted and shifted his shoulders, which were propped on the edge of the open cabinet. It looked uncomfortable as hell.

"Or I could just shut up and let you get on with it," Kari muttered.

"Did you say something?" A thump sounded from under the sink. "Ow. Fuck."

Kari bit her lip and closed her eyes. Great. Not only was she taking advantage of her neighbor, now she'd injured him. She crouched and found him squinting at her, rubbing his forehead.

She grimaced. "I'm so sorry. Didn't mean to make you hit your head. I just wanted to know if you wanted me to make some coffee or something. I feel useless as heck just standing around while you fix my sink."

A weak grin slid across his face. "Coffee after noon? I'd be up until dawn."

So, he wasn't Scandinavian. Her mother would have offered coffee from sunup to sundown without thinking twice. "Anything?" Kari winced at the pathetic tone she couldn't keep out of her voice.

He dropped his head back and continued to fiddle with whatever he was fiddling with. "You really don't have to. I'm having a blast."

"Sure seems like it, what with the swearing and the traumatic brain injury."

"Well, if you could find an old towel or something to cushion my back, that'd be a help." His voice sounded distracted and there was another clank.

"That I can do." Kari hopped to her feet and nearly sprinted to the linen closet in the hall, stretching to the top shelf to find the store of towels she kept after they had gotten too threadbare for anything other than rags. Scooting back to the kitchen, she crouched next to him. "Towel."

Rob rocked his hips side to side to inch out from under the sink and Kari swallowed as his tee shirt rode up, exposing a strip of bare stomach. She'd estimated that Rob was a bit older than her forty-two years, but there was no question that he kept himself fit. She lifted her gaze to his face, heat flooding her face at the gentle curve of his lips as he tugged his tee shirt down. *I wasn't perving on you!* she wanted to protest.

But it wouldn't be one hundred percent true. Rob was a little awkward and a lot eager, but he was also generous and helpful. He dog-sat for his daughter. He was helping Kari with her plumbing. He didn't ask for anything in return.

And, if Kari was being honest, the man was cute. Seriously cute. As in silver fox matinee idol cute. As in Central

Casting could find him a job as George Clooney's cousin cute.

She offered him the towel and he twisted to lay it in the cabinet, settling back and inching under the sink again without a word. He took a wrench and applied it and a pair of pliers to the pipe, pushing them in opposition, grunting as the fitting gave way. This time, knowing his attention was on the plumbing, Kari allowed herself to appreciate the play of lean muscles in his arms, of the way his abs tensed under his tee shirt as the pipe gave way.

"Excellent." He set the tools down beside him and picked up another wrench, doing something else with it, then scooting out to get to his feet and pull the whole assembly out, absorbed in his task, seemingly not even remembering Kari was there.

Having Kari looking on while he worked was distracting as hell. Rob tried to cover by examining the old faucet, though there was no need. The thing was going in the trash. It should have gone there years ago from the look of it.

But he wanted something to focus on so he wouldn't think about the way Kari had blushed when he caught her looking at him. He wasn't too proud to admit he appreciated an admiring glance, but Kari was right here next door. He needed to be careful. He knew all too well that starting something would almost certainly be followed by ending something, and he wasn't about to have a next-door neighbor who hated him. Having an ex-wife halfway across the country hating him was bad enough.

"Problem?" Kari's voice squeaked a bit and he shook his head.

"No, but I'm glad you decided to get a new unit. This

thing is probably original to the house and wasn't long for this world. Now I just need to get the new one installed and you'll be right as rain soon."

"Rain. Great. More water. Maybe my roof will leak next."

"That's awfully pessimistic of you." Rob opened the box with the new faucet and laid out the parts on the counter. "Think about something happier. When we first met you mentioned you just got back from a cruise, right?"

"Yup. Caribbean."

"Sounds swanky."

"It was okay."

He lifted his gaze to her face. She was looking out the window at the backyard. There was something sort of wistful about her expression. "Why only okay?" he asked.

She sighed and looked down at her hands. "Just not my type of thing. Very hectic, very busy. Lots of people all the time."

He considered this as he settled the gasket and threaded the hoses through the hole in the back of the sink. He was a pretty gregarious guy, but even to him, that sounded like it might be a bit much. Kari had a much more quiet, self-contained vibe about her. "Doesn't sound very restful."

"No, it wasn't. Lots of activities too. I would have preferred to curl up with a book on a lounge chair or something."

"They don't leave you alone to do that if that's what you want to do?"

"Oh, they do. It's just that there's always something going on *around* that lounge chair. Games or parties or families with a lot of screaming kids. We docked in Nassau one day, and walking around the city is just one long string of people trying to get you to come into this shop or that one... Frankly, I was happy to get home."

What would make a woman who seemed as reserved as Kari want to do such a thing in the first place? "Why did you go if it wasn't your type of scene?"

"I won it at work. It's not like I spent money on the ticket or anything."

"Nice that you could find out it's not your thing without spending money on it, I guess."

"True." One corner of her mouth quirked up. "You're an always look on the bright side type, aren't you?"

He settled back down on the kitchen floor, preparing to stick his head under the sink again. "I suppose so. I try to be, I guess. I mean, most things in life aren't tragedies. Anyway, you got home from the stressful cruise to a nice quiet house and some relaxation, I guess."

To his surprise, Kari started to laugh.

She couldn't help it. It was perfect, somehow. And if she didn't laugh, she'd cry.

Nice quiet house indeed. She'd come home and before she'd even unpacked her dirty clothes, Sam had come over and asked Kari the question she'd been dreading since Kari's mother died, tearing the lid off of a lifetime of secrets and lies.

That had been two weeks ago. And Sam hadn't called since.

The tears did come then, with a suddenness that shocked her. Kari's mouth twisted and she clapped her hands over her eyes. The harder she tried to clamp down on the emotion, the harder her chest heaved, sobs wracking her lungs. Then there were arms around her, pulling her into a hard, warm chest, hands rubbing her back.

"Shh. What's the matter?" His low voice was right in her ear, soothing.

Her hands still pressed against her eyes, she took one deep, shuddering breath. Then another. Tears still trickled, but the out of control sobbing was over. She pulled her hands away from her eyes and set them on his shoulders. He stepped away at that, releasing her. She wished he hadn't. That brief bit of human contact, of comfort, had been like water on a thirsty plant. She took another breath, steadier this time.

"I'm sorry. I…I've just been under some stress lately." She lifted her gaze to meet his, swiping her fingertips under her eyes to get rid of the moisture. He frowned, concern etched into the lines around his eyes. "I'm okay. Really."

"You don't seem so okay to me," he said. His hand lifted and reached halfway between them, then fell.

She waved him away. "No. I'm fine."

"If you say so. Do you want to talk about it? How fine you are?"

She shook her head. No, she didn't want to talk to this attractive near-stranger about how she'd kept her mother's secrets and lies only to be found out by her only living relative. And maybe losing that most precious relationship in the bargain. Shame and embarrassment would swallow her whole if she did that. Pile her panic about home ownership on top of that horrible little story and he might run screaming from her house. And at the same time, it all seemed so pathetic. So small.

Avert your eyes, we don't talk about the madwoman next door. Seriously. She was a mess.

"Okay. Want me to continue to work on your sink? I'd leave you alone, but…then you wouldn't have any water."

She grimaced. "Please. Can we just ignore my awkward outburst? Pretend like it didn't happen?"

"If that's what you want." His expression remained grave.

"Thanks."

He nodded, then sank to the floor again and wriggled into the cabinet. "Not too much longer and I'll be out of your hair anyway."

She wanted to tell him she wasn't counting the minutes until he could leave. That she actually enjoyed his company. It had been an awfully lonely two weeks. And she was getting used to seeing his long, jeans-clad legs sticking out from her kitchen cabinets.

"Can I...make you lunch or something? As a thank-you?"

He lifted his head—carefully this time—and looked at her. "You sure?"

She nodded. "Nothing fancy. I have the makings for ham sandwiches. Some chips. Beer, even."

He let his head fall back and readdressed the pipes. "That sounds perfect."

Kari nodded and moved to the fridge, taking out ingredients and assembling two lunch plates, stepping carefully around his legs. By the time she was done, Rob had finished with the faucet, run down to the basement to turn the water back on (seriously, how had she not even known where the main water valve was? Why did she think she could own a house? Who was she fooling?) and they were sitting at the little table in her dining room.

He looked around, taking in her minimal décor. She had plans to paint every room in the house, but for now, all the walls were stark white. His gaze roamed over the framed art posters, the little chest of drawers with a piece of whitework embroidery laid on top, and back to Kari's face.

"That's a nice cloth thingy on the chest there. Did someone make it for you?"

Kari shook her head. "No. I made it."

His eyebrows went up. "Impressive."

"My mom was very keen that I know traditional Norwegian hand-crafts like *hardangersøm*. I grew up doing it. Now I mostly need to keep my hands busy doing something. Knitting, embroidery…always something."

He took a sip of beer, his dark gaze pinning her. "I take it back. That's not impressive. It's *very* impressive."

Kari's blush should be registered as a dangerous weapon. It made Rob think decidedly carnal thoughts that he had no business thinking. Better to get on more neutral ground.

"What do you do for work?" he asked.

"I'm an office manager and bookkeeper for a small publishing house," she said. "Nothing terribly exciting."

"My daughter would probably think it was very exciting," he said.

"She wants to be an office manager for a company that makes instruction manuals?" Kari's eyebrows quirked in humorous disbelief.

"Well, she wants to work in publishing. She's been trying to get editorial work for a while now. Doing some freelancing, but she'd love to go full-time."

"If we get an opening I can let you know since I'll be practically the first to know," Kari said. "Seeing as I'd be the one posting it. But there aren't a lot of jobs like that out there. And certainly not in this neck of the woods."

He sighed. "I know. I tried to get her to look into something more practical, but Mia's both hardheaded and a dreamer. It can be a bad combination." He picked up his sandwich and bit into it. A simple thing, a sandwich. But it had been a long time since anyone had made one for him. It tasted good.

"What do you do?"

"I'm the IT director for a computer game company."

"So you could not only fix my sink but my computer too? Wow."

"Does your computer need fixing?"

"No." An unexpectedly sly smile flitted across her face and he felt another bolt of attraction run through him. "Besides, you've already fixed my sink and all I've been able to offer you in return is a sandwich. I'd better not push my luck."

"It's a good sandwich. Also, don't underestimate the power of beer as a motivator. Anyway, I'm happy to fix your computer if something goes wrong with it. Or anything else."

She sighed and looked around the room. "There's so much to do. I hate all these white walls, but I don't even know how long it will take me to paint a single room. Or how much paint to buy. Or...anything, really."

"You've never painted a room before?"

She shook her head. "I'm the first person in my family to own a house." She laughed a brief, reflective laugh. "Like I said before, when you first suggested I get a new faucet it was kind of a shock to me to realize I could do that. That it wasn't up to the landlord to decide. That there is no landlord."

He sipped his beer, thought for a moment. "Yeah. That's one of the nice things about homeownership. But it's also overwhelming sometimes."

Kari's eyes went wide. "You feel that way too?"

He shrugged. "Sure. Sometimes."

"I thought I was just being a big baby. I finally got what

I wanted—a home of my own—and then I don't know what to do with myself."

Rob nodded. "It's kind of like when you're a kid and you can't wait to grow up and make your own decisions. Then you're an adult and you sometimes wish someone else would make a decision for you—because it's exhausting being in charge. And it's scary sometimes."

Kari stared at him, a pickle held halfway between her plate and her mouth. She blurted, "I've been terrified ever since my first night in this house."

"Terrified?" Maybe that explained the semi-hysterical scene in the kitchen.

"Well, not every second. But it's so unknown, all of it. What if something goes wrong, what if something breaks and I can't afford it? I didn't have much before, didn't have much to lose. Now…"

And she was all on her own. When Rob had first bought a house, he had been married and experienced in basic maintenance. First time homeownership with neither a partner nor experience would be incredibly challenging. He was starting to think that Kari wasn't, as she put it, "a big baby," but incredibly resourceful and brave. "What about your parents?" he asked. "Other sources of support?"

"My dad died about five years ago. Mom went a few years later. They never had much, but what my mother left me boosted my nest egg to enable me to buy this place."

"Siblings?"

"My brother Bjorn and his wife died in a car accident not long before my mother passed."

He stared at her. "Wow. That's…a lot of tragedy to be dealing with in a short time."

She swallowed, her throat working. "It was hard. Sam and I…" She swallowed and lowered her eyes. "Sorry. I'm not going to cry all over you again." Her face flushed again and Rob wished he could hug her or give her some other kind of comfort. She looked up again, meeting his eyes. "I don't know why I'm telling you all this. Hell. I've already confessed my fear about becoming a homeowner. What's one more confession? I don't think Sam's speaking to me now."

"Your niece, right? What happened?"

"She found out about a big secret that my mother had been keeping. A lie. And she found out I knew and hadn't told her."

There. She'd said it.

She waited for the earth to open up and swallow her.

Nothing happened.

"Why didn't you tell her?" he asked. He sounded curious, but not judgmental.

Kari shrugged and stared at her half-eaten sandwich. "I'm...not really sure. *Mor*—Mom—told me when she was really sick. Not long before she died. And then she did die. Sam and I were coping with a lot and it seemed wrong to put more on her emotional plate then. And then...it was like that overdue library book you have under the bed when you're a kid. You know the fine is only going to get worse the longer it sits there, but..."

"You just keep nudging it even further back with your toe."

"Exactly. The longer it went on, the worse it was going to be. How could I bring it up? How could I explain why I hadn't told her before? And I told myself there wasn't any way she could find out."

"But she did."

"Yeah." Kari pondered whether she should stop talking

about this now. *Oh, what the hell.* "She inherited property from her great-uncle in Norway."

"*Her* great-uncle?" He seemed to calculate something in his head. "Wouldn't that make him your uncle?"

"That's the thing. My father wasn't her biological grandfather. My mother was married to a different man and pregnant with my brother when they emigrated. The ship they were on sank. *Mor's* husband didn't make it. She and my dad had met and fell in love on the crossing and ended up living happily ever after."

Rob's eyebrows lifted. "That's quite the story."

"Yeah. One I should have told Sam without her having to drag it out of me."

"Hey." Rob's voice was soft and she looked at him. "How long are you going to beat yourself up over this?"

She half-shrugged. "Until Sam's speaking to me again, I guess?"

"What if she doesn't?"

Dread latched icy claws into Kari's belly and she pushed her plate away. "I can't even think about that."

"Is she the type to hold a grudge?"

"Not usually, but this situation isn't exactly usual either. And she's…she's all the family I have." *And what if I don't even have that anymore?* Kari felt scooped out and hollow at the idea. She was used to being responsible and reliable, but she wasn't used to being this *alone.*

"And you're all the family she has, too, right? I think she'll come around. You guys seemed really close when I met her."

"We are. Or we were. You weren't the first person to mistake us for sisters."

"Why don't you give her a call?"

"Because I'm a coward?"

"I doubt that." His eyes had gone all warm, making her feel funny and fluttery inside.

Kari slumped back in her chair. "Why is it so hard to believe? I've just told you that I am terrified of my own home and was cowardly enough not to tell my only niece— only living relative—about something huge that affects her."

"Being terrified of homeownership isn't cowardice, it's rational behavior." Rob said. "You're actually brave to take it on by yourself for the first time. And I think a lot of people would have done what you did regarding your mother's secret. It seems like you meant to tell her, but the timing was bad…and then I can't imagine how you would have brought it up."

"Hey Sam—remember my dad? Turns out he wasn't really your grandfather. Sorry about that, kiddo."

"I'm sure you put it more diplomatically than that."

"Only because she asked me point-blank if I had ever heard of *Mor's* first husband. By name. It let me off the hook. I didn't have to do the awkward lead-in to the horrible conversation."

His fingertip touched the back of her hand and the fluttering feeling in her gut intensified. "If you want my unsolicited advice, reach out to her."

She swallowed. She'd been so afraid of having her worst fear realized—of having Sam reject her forever—that she hadn't reached out. But *Mor* had avoided facing the truth for her entire life. Maybe Kari shouldn't be emulating her. "I'll think about it."

Chapter Three

Kari did the dishes after Rob left, marveling and feeling somewhat ridiculous at how luxurious something like having a new faucet could be. He was right. The pull-out spray handle was great. Drying her hands, she eyed her cellphone sitting on the countertop.

Don't really *be a coward. Send her a text.*

She picked up the phone and held it for a moment and letting it out in a rush. Unlocking the device, she opened her texting app and sent Sam a message before she could coward her way out of it.

Hey. Can we talk?

As olive branches went, it wasn't exactly the most eloquent, but hopefully it would get the job done.

Resisting the urge to stare at her phone screen and wait for a response, Kari stuffed it in her back pocket and wandered back into the dining room, gazing around at the blank, white walls. *It's your house. You can actually paint it whatever color you want.*

So what color did she want?

The room was an interior one without any windows.

So...something sunny? A soft yellow, maybe? Kari rotated in a slow circuit. Yes. Yellow would be good in here.

Wow. She'd made a decision.

Bolstered by this, she moved to the living room. There were windows here, but they faced north and east. So, more light but still...she turned and walked to the desk in the corner and fished out an old sketch pad and a package of colored pencils. With swift motions, she sketched an idea. A pale color on the walls—barely a color at all. Or she could leave it white and add some Scandinavian motifs over the doors and windows. Maybe she could cut a stencil...

Her phone shrilled in her back pocket. Kari's pencil skated across the page, her pulse jumping. Dropping the pad and pencil to her sofa, she dug the phone out of her back pocket.

A text from Sam. Just one word. *Sure.*

A tightness in her chest Kari hadn't even known was there loosened. She tapped the phone's screen. *Now?*

Ok.

The tightness snapped back. Kari swallowed, tapped Sam's contact information, raised the phone to her ear. Her hand shook. She felt like she might throw up. The phone barely rang and Sam's voice was in her ear. "Kari?"

Kari would normally say something smart-assy at the questioning tone of Sam's voice. Something like, "Got any other aunts?"

But not today.

"Hi, Sam." Now that she had Sam on the phone, she didn't know where to begin. She should have planned, had some sort of script or something. "How have you been?"

Sam didn't say anything for a few moments and Kari could hear her walking. It sounded like she was outside. "I'm...I'm okay."

A tiny trickle of relief made Kari's shoulders lower a

fraction of an inch away from her ears. "Good. Are *we* okay?" she blurted.

The sound of Sam's footfalls stopped. "We'll get there."

The trickle of relief turned into a torrent, rushing through her, filling that scooped-out hollow place inside her. "I am sorry I didn't tell you. I didn't know how."

"I know."

"How's everything else?"

"Good. Really good, in fact. I've started seeing someone."

"You have?" A pang of something—jealousy or loneliness or some emotion in between—shot through Kari. "Who is he? When did you meet?"

"Over a month ago. He hired me to take him out on the river."

Kari's brows drew together. Sam, a fly fishing guide, had always had hard and fast rules about dating her clients. As in, she didn't do it. Ever. "He did?"

"He did. And I can hear the disapproval in your voice, but don't worry. He's not my client anymore. Just my boyfriend."

"What's your boyfriend's name?"

"Graham. His family calls him Gray. He's a librarian at the university." Sam's voice went soft, unusually so for her. "He's a really good guy, Kari."

"Well, I'm glad for you."

A pause, as if Sam was working up to something. "I'd like you to meet him."

The lonely, jealous feelings tightening Kari's stomach and chest blew away, like a cool fresh breeze passing right through her. "I'd love to meet him. Why don't you find out when you guys are available for dinner and come over?"

"That'd be nice. Speaking of which, how's that good-looking next door neighbor of yours?"

"Rob? He's nice. He replaced my kitchen faucet today, as

a matter of fact." The memory of his shirt riding up as he emerged from under her sink sent a rush of heat to her cheeks.

Sam's voice went sly. "Is that a euphemism for something? 'Cause it sounds kinda dirty."

Kari laughed, feeling almost dizzy with relief that the conversation had taken this turn into normal territory. "One hundred percent clean, I promise. It was leaking. I asked him for a plumber recommendation. He told me he could fix it himself. He did. And there we are."

"Well, well. Maybe he can help you if you have any more…personal plumbing issues."

"Shut the front door, Samantha Halvorsen. He fixed my sink. Don't become one of those people who starts dating someone and then wants to pair everyone else off. I'm fine."

Sam laughed at that, a happy sound. "Okay. But…it feels good to be able to tease you again."

"It feels good to be teased. Let me know when you two can come over for dinner. I'll do my best to be the intimidating old hag of an auntie."

"Right," Sam said. "Because that's so you."

"It's a new look I'm working on. I'm heading for Crone Club."

Sam made a noise that sounded like *pfft*. "Right. I'll see when Gray and I can come over. And Kari?"

"Yeah?"

"Thanks for calling."

Kari swallowed around the growing lump in her throat. "Of course."

Adele Buck

Returning to his house, Rob tried to throw himself into his usual Saturday chore routine. Laundry into the dryer, some light cleaning, paying bills.

Oh, the exciting life of the single, middle-aged guy. A regular bachelor rave-up.

When had his existence settled into something so solitary? Helping Kari with her faucet might be the most social he had been in…was it months? It was. As a young man, he had been up for going out for a few beers, but hadn't been a part of the club scene. More like the Irish fiddle at a local folk pub night scene. Then marriage to Liz, having Mia, they had done domestic things. Birthday parties and outings with other families where the parents could team up and take turns making sure the kids didn't succeed in what seemed to be their endless quest to get killed doing something reckless. They had gotten sitters and had the occasional date night, too, growing rarer and then stopping as they grew apart and the marriage exploded so impressively it might have made for a Fourth of July fireworks display if it hadn't also been so upsetting.

The long process of unwinding the life they had made together, of dividing assets and finding new homes, of setting out careful plans and schedules for Mia had left Rob too tired and demoralized to date much immediately after the divorce. Not to mention, divorce doesn't exactly leave you in the best frame of mind for jumping back into the dating pool. Eventually, that pain had faded and he had gone out with a few women, but it was clear that their sights were set on marriage—eventually if not a lot sooner—and Rob wasn't about to put himself through that again. But those women had seen his single-dad-ness and his easygoing manner and assumed he was looking for another spin into married life, a new mom for Mia.

It always ended when they found out they were wrong.

He could do commitment. But he wasn't doing marriage again. And Mia already had a mom.

So he had stopped dating entirely. As a teenager, Mia had teased him about it. "Maybe if you issue a warning before the first date," she said. "Get them to sign a contract or something."

"Yeah, because nothing says, 'I'm an arrogant shithead who thinks all women want to marry me' like a pre-date warning that I have no intention of remarrying anyone ever."

"True. It's not a good look." Mia had looked thoughtful at that, her big, dark eyes going all somber and serious.

"Stop thinking about my love life, kiddo. That's an order from your old man."

"Not so old as all that. You should at least be able to have some fun sometime."

"It's not fun if it ends up hurting someone. So, for the time being at least, no dates for me."

But it was lonely, living this way, especially since Mia had moved out. And it was also kind of a cliché. A bachelor existence seasoned by the occasional poker night with a few people from work. Rob stuffed a new load of dirty laundry into the machine, added detergent, and turned it on. His mind turned back to Kari. Pretty Kari with her wide cheek-bones and pale blue eyes that met his so easily because she was almost his height. Kari who seemed so tough and yet had a deep well of uncertainty underneath her calm, self-assured manner.

He wondered if he could be friends with his next-door neighbor. That would be nice. Just getting to know some-one. They wouldn't have to go on dates. If they wanted to, they could hang out and never leave their own back yards. He could help her more with her home-improvement stuff.

Peering into his office, he nearly groaned at the pile of

paperwork and mail. He had a habit of tossing everything that came in in a haphazard pile, then clearing out the whole thing in one epic sweep. He got hardly any bills on paper anymore, so it wasn't like he was letting anything important go.

But it wasn't exactly an efficient system. He knew he should handle it differently. A different method might come with less guilt, fewer furtive glances into his office, followed by shutting the door and reassuring himself that tomorrow was soon enough.

Today finally was that tomorrow. The desk was a mess. So was the floor, for that matter.

Sighing, he settled into his chair and picked up a catalog. It was two years old.

This was going to be a long afternoon.

Feeling lighter than she had in more than a week, Kari put her phone down and picked up her sketch pad, frowning at the mark that had marred her drawing. Flipping to a new page, she re-sketched the motif she had in mind. Doing something creative, something that would make this house more her home, brought a small smile to her lips.

This is really mine. This house. I did it.

She tilted her head, examining her sketch, then held it up, imagining it over the front door, an extended version of it curving over the arched opening that led to the dining room.

Rein it in. First things first. She should learn how to paint a wall first. Suddenly, she wanted to make sure the dining room was painted before she had her first proper guests over for dinner. She wished she had thought of picking up some paint when they were at the home center. Kari wondered what Sam's new boyfriend was like. It had been a long time since Sam had dated anyone after her last disaster and this sounded pretty serious.

Maybe she should go back to the home center and get some paint.

Maybe Rob needed something. You know. Because she was going anyway. That was neighborly, right?

Or maybe she was being more than a little ridiculous. Collecting her keys and her purse before she could think about knocking on Rob's door, she marched herself out to her car and set out for the home center. Dodging contractor's vans and the other weekend warriors in the parking lot, she found a space and went inside to the paint aisle.

And froze.

How did anyone choose *anything* when there were so *many* choices? There were at least six brands of paint, each with their own chromatic rainbow, an infinite range of shades of every color. She had been thinking "soft yellow" and here were at least fifty of them. And which brand of paint? Did it even matter? She assumed it did.

Reaching a hand out, she plucked one card of paint samples from its place on the wall display and swallowed. Maybe she should just take all the likely ones home.

Of course that was what she should do. You couldn't choose a paint color for a room across town in this airplane hangar of a building, under these fluorescent lights. Kari nodded to herself and plucked yellow cards out of every brand display. Considering the thick stack of cards with mounting dread and feeling weird, she detoured to the plant area and selected an African violet to take home. It would like her sunny, South-facing kitchen windowsill. Standing in the line to pay, she flipped through the stack of paint chip cards. Some of the samples looked garish in the sunlight streaming through the glass doors at the front of the store, some were barely even a color.

Deep breaths, Kari. You got this.

How ridiculous do you sound? You're panicking over painting a couple of walls?

Smiling reflexively at the cashier, she paid for her violet and drove back home, carrying the plant back to her kitchen before going to the dining room and leafing through the cards. She had been right not to make a decision in the store. The light here did different things to the colors. The ones she had thought were too garish in sunlight now looked more muted in a room that didn't get much natural light. She laid the cards out on the table, nearly covering the surface, scanning over the collection.

This was trickier than she had thought.

Going into the kitchen, she got a roll of Scotch tape. The colors when placed on the table were definitely different from when she held them up to the wall. Setting her jaw, she taped each card to the wall, hoping that one of them would come to life like in a magical realism film, sprouting arms to wave at her and calling, "Me! You want me!"

No such miracle occurred. Her dining room was merely shingled with a multitude of cards sporting various yellow hues. It was overwhelming.

She took a breath, held it. Let it out. *No. Not overwhelming. Your house, your room, your walls. Your decision.*

She scanned the cards, reaching out to pluck the ones that pulled an immediate "no" from her off the wall and dropping them on the table. Now the neat row of shingled paint samples was more of a snaggle-toothed mess. Kari forced herself to ignore the urge to rearrange them back into tidy rows and just focus on the colors. She pulled another few cards off the wall. It was down to a manageable number now, but…the easy decisions were gone. The low-hanging fruit had been harvested.

She was going to need help.

The tap on the door was so soft, Rob almost didn't register it at first. He was trying to figure out what he should do with the paperwork from the HVAC company he had been given after the twice annual visit—file it? Trash it? He never seemed to know which things were worth saving and which weren't. Hence the piles that never seemed to get much smaller, even after he had gone through an attempted purge. And his office looked worse now instead of better.

Well, he could get rid of the siding salesman or religious proselytizer or whoever it was at the door and get back to his least-favorite task in the world.

Being an adult was so much fun.

But when he opened the door it was neither a salesperson nor a person offering copies of *The Watchtower.* It was Kari.

"Hi." Pleasure bloomed in his chest at the sight of her, only to be followed by worry. "The faucet's okay?"

"The faucet's great. More than great. Almost a pleasure to do the dishes."

"Almost?"

"Almost. It's still washing dishes, when all's said and done." Kari chewed on her bottom lip. "Do you have a minute, or is this a bad time?"

Pleasure bloomed in his chest. Helping Kari Halvorsen might be addictive. "Sure. I mean, no. Not at all a bad time. Come on in." Rob stepped back from the door and waved her inside. "I was just doing my least favorite task in the world, so you're saving me from it."

"Least favorite task? Let me guess. Cleaning the bathroom?"

"No, because when you do that at least you end up with a clean bathroom. I'm trying to figure out what to do with a bunch of mail and other paperwork that seems to just pile up on me. I can never decide what I need to keep and what needs to go."

"We can trade. You can clean my bathroom and I'll file your paperwork."

"You don't know how tempted I am by that offer. But what did you stop by for?"

"Paint." Kari glanced around the room, almost a copy of the one in her house next door. The entire neighborhood was made up of nearly identical ranch houses, all probably put up by the same builder in the middle of the last century. Rob was pretty sure he could navigate any of them blindfolded, even with the changes various owners had made over the years and the slight differences in size and floor plans to suit larger or smaller families.

"What about paint?"

"The stuff on the walls?" She pointed at his, which he had painted a soft beige when he moved in. "Your piece of handy-man-ery inspired me."

Rob resisted the urge to puff his chest out. "Really? Inspired? I like the sound of that. Inspired you to what?"

"Don't get too excited," she said, rolling her eyes. "I went back to the home center and got a bunch of paint chips for the dining room. I think I have it narrowed down, but I want a second opinion. But I don't want to take up too much of your time. Five minutes to help me pick a color. Also…I don't know how to paint. Walls. I mean, it seems straightfor-ward enough, but I'm sure it's not as easy as it looks. I was thinking maybe you could give me some tips."

Rob folded his arms across his chest. "No, it's not as easy

as it looks, but it's also not hard as you might be imagining. Not like figuring out whether or not to keep or toss my semi-annual HVAC servicing contract paperwork, for instance."

"Keep it." Kari's eyebrows quirked in a *do you really have to ask that?* expression.

"See? It's easy for you to say, but why?"

"Because you have a servicing contract. You keep records about contracts."

"How do you know this?"

She shrugged. "I don't know much about owning a home, but I do know about the paperwork about the lease on our office space. When we have workmen come in, I keep the records. If something goes wrong a short time later, it can be useful as leverage."

"Like what kind of leverage?"

"Like, 'You said you had fixed the thing and now it's three weeks later and the thing isn't working. Come fix the thing. And if you even think about charging me for fixing the thing you said was already fixed, I'm going to make your life unpleasant.'"

This side of Kari, the vengeful Viking Shield Maiden side, was more than a little hot. "Wow. I don't think I'd want to cross you."

One corner of her mouth tilted up. "That's why I make the extremely medium-sized bucks."

"I'm starting to think office managers are underpaid."

"From your mouth to God's ears. I'm starting to think I need to look at your unfiled paperwork."

"Paint chips are more fun."

She snorted. "Paint chips? Fun?"

He scooped up his keys. "When compared to paperwork? Definitely. Let's go."

Chapter Four

"Don't laugh," Kari said, letting them into her house, nerves making her belly flutter. "I have no idea what I'm doing here."

Rob's face assumed a comically serious expression. "No laughing. Got it." Following her into the dining room, he looked at the wall with its paint chips. Then looked back at her, his face puzzled. "What am I supposed to be finding not-funny?"

"Do people really do this? Tape up paint chips?" She hated the way her voice squeaked, her nerves made audible.

"Of course. How else do you think they get an idea of what the color will look like on the wall? Paint looks different in different light."

"It looked kind of…overwhelming when they were all up there." She waved at the dining table, with its heap of discarded chips, everything from neon chrome yellow to a color so soft it was a first cousin to ecru.

Looking at the pile, Rob's lips quirked up. He bit them together, dark eyes darting to meet Kari's. "Nope. Not laughing."

Kari folded her arms across her chest. "What's so not-funny?"

"Usually people have a little more of an idea of what they want than...every yellow possible. That's seriously impressive."

Kari's chest heaved and she flung her arms out, letting them slap against her sides. "See? I knew I was doing this wrong."

"Not wrong. Just...overambitious, maybe."

Kari massaged her temples, not knowing how to assess how ridiculous she was being. "Oh, that's me. Such an over-achiever."

"I get the feeling you sell yourself short." Rob turned back to the wall, with its taped paint chips curling off of it. "So, what do you want from me?"

"I've hit the wall. Literally, apparently. I can't decide between this group of colors."

He looked at them for a few moments, then swiveled back to her. "They're almost identical."

"I know. That's what makes it so hard."

He blinked. "You really think if you paint your wall this color..." He stabbed his index finger at one of the cards, pressing it against the drywall. "In six months you're going to be kicking yourself that you didn't choose this one?" He poked at another card. "You're not even going to remember the difference. You're clearly in the right ballpark for you. Eeny-meeny-miney-moe it and move on."

"Really?"

"Really."

"Okay." Kari tapped the paint chips in quick succession. "*Elle melle, deg fortelle, skipet går, ut i år, rygg i rand, to i spann, snipp, snapp, snute, du er ute.*" Her finger rested on a chip. "That one. I guess."

Rob stared at her. "What did I just hear?"

"You told me to eeny-meeny it."

"And you turned into the Swedish Chef."

"Get. Out." Kari pointed toward the front door. "I am *not* Swedish."

Rob laughed. Then saw her face and the laughter dried up. "You're kidding, right?"

"About not being Swedish? No. About getting out? Yes." She smiled to let him know she'd actually been joking.

"Where did you learn to do that?"

"Do what?"

"*Ergen fergen*," he said, his voice swooping in an exaggerated version of a stock Scandinavian accent that sounded — yes — just like the Swedish Chef.

Kari blinked. "I learned that at my mother's knee. Probably literally. It's a Norwegian counting rhyme. Like eeny-meeny."

"That's right. When I met your niece she teased you about whining for your mom in Norwegian." He had heard Sam say "*Mor*" and asked, "More what?" Kari suppressed a laugh at the memory.

"Yeah. My folks emigrated here when they were younger."

"So you said. You speak fluent Norwegian?"

"No." Kari's face went hot. "I understand a lot more of it than I speak. My parents used it as a sort of 'private language' between them. But I internalized a few things."

"Things like a counting rhyme."

She thought about it. Why had she remembered it so easily? "It's the kind of thing that gets repeated in context. And rhymes are easy to remember by design."

"I suppose. So. We going to go get your paint?" Rob turned a grin on Kari that made her swallow hard.

"We?" Kari struggled to get her breathing back under control. She felt like she was twenty again. And she was more than twenty years away from twenty. *Get yourself under control.*

Rob's face fell, erasing the eager grin and Kari felt awful. "I'm sorry. That was presumptuous," he said.

"No!" Kari waved her hands in front of her face. "No, I was just surprised."

"Surprised? Why?" His eyebrows lifted.

"You have your own life, your own stuff to deal with. I'm intruding on it with my being a neurotic home-owning newbie who has no idea what to do with any of this." She waved her hands again, this time taking in the interior of the little house. His gaze tracked around the area she indicated, coming to rest on the sketch pad she had dropped on the couch.

"You draw?" He pointed at the pad, his eyebrows lifting.

"A little. I was thinking of doing some Scandinavian motifs on the walls. I was sketching some ideas out."

"May I?" He angled his head toward the pad, his eyes on her face.

She liked that he didn't just walk over and pick it up. Didn't assume anything. Maybe that's why she kept opening up to him.

"Sure."

Rob moved to the sofa, lifted the sketch pad. A lovely, simple motif of flowers and scrollwork sketched in blue pencil adorned the page. It was simple and solid, but comfortable somehow. The kind of adornment that seemed suitable to a Northern climate. Stark, but it reminded you of spring. In fact, it reminded him of *something*, but he couldn't put his finger on it.

He looked back at Kari, whose foot seemed to be trying

to drill into the floor, her sneaker-clad toe swiveling into the hardwood in a nervous motion. "This is beautiful," he said.

"You think?" Her anxious expression eased a touch.

"I do." He glanced around the room. "Where would you put it?"

"Mostly over doors and windows." She strode across the room and stood beside him, sweeping her hand to indicate the arched entry to the dining room. "Like there. But also maybe a modified version there." She turned and indicated the front door and the area over the picture window. "I could pick out pieces of the motif and recombine them for different purposes." She took the pad from his hands and paged back. "Like this."

A mark on the page marred the motif she showed him. As if someone had bumped her arm. "What happened here?" he asked.

She craned her neck to look at the page, then her eyes flicked down to the floor. "Sam texted."

"She did? That's great." Rob took in Kari's averted gaze, the tense set of her face. "It's not great?"

"No, no. It's good." Despite her blithe words, her eyes looked haunted.

"What's the matter?"

Those haunted eyes flicked up to meet his gaze, then flicked away again. "Sam has a boyfriend. And...I didn't even know."

Damn. There was that sheen of moisture across her eyes again. He hated seeing it. "How long have they been seeing each other?" he asked.

"A month? I mean...it makes sense. We talked a couple of weeks before my trip, and then when I got back..." She waved a hand to indicate the topic she obviously didn't want to re-hash. "You know. Her life wasn't on hold just because she wasn't speaking to me. Which I understand. But I've never *not* been in her life. And this seems serious." She took a deep, shuddering breath and said in a rush, "So I invited them over for dinner."

Comprehension flooded through him and he wished he could hug her again. Wished he had the right even to ask. "Hence the sudden need to paint your dining room?"

She shrugged. "Maybe? I've wanted to paint since I bought this place. It needs color. Life."

"So let's give it color. And life."

She gave him a hard look. "Let's? As in you and me?"

"What's wrong with that?"

She shifted, her gaze ranging around the room, not meeting his eyes. "You want to do this with me? It's not your house."

He spread his hands out in front of him. "I got caught up in your enthusiasm. Consider me your assistant. If you want to."

She pinned him with a hard stare. "Why are you so invested? You hardly know me."

That stopped him. Why *was* he so invested? "Um. I like you?" It was the truth. A little too close to the bone, but he found he didn't care just now.

Kari's eyelids fluttered, her face going blank for a moment. "Uh. I like you too," she said. That shouldn't have triggered such a warm feeling in his belly, but it did. "But I'm starting to feel like you're doing me too many favors."

"How many is too many?"

"When the ledger is firmly balanced on your side. You've fixed my sink and helped me sort my paint situation. I've made you a sandwich."

"I'm not worried about that."

"I am. I come from a long line of people who don't get beholden."

"Okay then…" His brain whirred into overdrive, seeking

something that would balance her ledger. "File my paper-work? Since you seem to want to do it so much."

"What?" Kari gave him a suspicious look. Which he guessed he deserved.

"I mean…You know what to do with furnace receipts and…mail." It was true, after all, pathetic as it might sound. He was useless with paperwork. What he should file and what he could safely throw away. Liz had been good at that stuff and disdainful of his uselessness there. Maybe that's why he hated it so much.

She folded her arms over her chest. "Mail frightens you?"

"I don't know what to toss, what to keep." Her face remained stony. "It's true," he said, throwing his hands up. "Maybe that sounds pathetic to you, but it's true."

She nodded. "Okay. Fine. I deal with your mail trauma and you teach me how to paint a room."

"Deal."

"I am so glad I brought you with me," Kari said, her eyes wide as she surveyed the cart. He had started by measuring the room to gauge how much they'd need. Then he followed it up with knowing what sort of paint to get—Kari could have handled the indoor/outdoor distinction, but would probably have frozen, at least initially, in trying to decide what finish to get.

"Eggshell," he said. "If we were doing a kitchen or bath-room, something a bit glossier and easier to wipe down, but not for the dining room."

Then he had known to take the can to the paint counter and have them custom tint it based on the color on the paint chip. She probably could have figured that out too.

But then he had filled the cart with paint trays and rollers and roller covers and brushes and blue tape and a tarp and…her eyes had pretty much glazed over at that point. She barely knew what she had in there.

"Wow. That's a lot of stuff." She looked at Rob, who was looking at what he had collected, a crease of concentration between his eyebrows.

"Yeah. Don't worry. This stuff isn't very pricey. And it's not so bad when you do the other rooms. You're not going to need to buy another roller or tray, for instance. Just the covers."

"If you say so."

They started for the registers and Rob snapped his fingers. "Forgot something I need. Go ahead on and get checked out."

Kari did, collecting her bags from the cashier and waiting for him by the exit. He joined her with a single bag in his hand. "Ready to go?" He asked. She nodded and they went out to her car. Before she could get it started, he handed her the bag.

"What's this?"

"Housewarming present."

"What…" opening the bag, she found a small plastic container of designer paint—periwinkle blue—and a set of fine brushes.

"To do the motif in your living room. If that's not the color you want I can take it back right now and get something you like better. But I wanted to surprise you."

"No. It's perfect." Kari resisted the urge to clutch the little pot of paint to her chest. "So sweet. Now I just have to cut a stencil."

"I have a better idea. Let's swing by my office before we go home." Puzzled, Kari let him direct her to a nondescript office building only a short detour from their route home.

He darted inside and returned minutes later, a case in his hand.

"Is that a bomb? Are you going to blow my house up? You look like someone out of a James Bond movie with that thing."

Rob lowered his head, looked up at her from under hooded eyes. "Fox...Rob Fox." And suddenly she couldn't breathe because she was laughing too hard. Laughing at his horrible Sean Connery impersonation, and laughing because his name was Fox. Of course it was. A silver fox named Fox. It was all too perfect.

"I'm going to have to work on my international super spy cred, I see," Rob said, settling back into the seat and fastening the belt.

"It's...original." Kari wiped her fingers under her eyes to capture the tears that had leaked out while she was laughing. "Rocket surgeon, master plumber, and now international man of mystery."

"I have to say, I prefer to see you cry that way than the way you did earlier today."

Kari's face flooded with heat and she started the car. Also, was that only this morning? It felt like they had known each other for months now. How was it even possible that she was so comfortable so quickly? "I'm sorry about that."

"No worries." Rob waved a hand. "I raised a daughter. I don't melt around tears. Although I thought I would some-times when she was in her teens."

Kari piloted the car out of the parking lot and thought as she drove. "You're a really good guy, aren't you?" she said finally.

Rob shrugged, slapped his hands on his thighs. "I try?"

"You going to tell me what's in the bomb briefcase?"

"It's another surprise."

"Okay. You're one for one on surprises so far, so I'll allow it."

"You're a guarded person, aren't you?"

"Aren't most women?" Kari let her eyes cut sideways to him for a second before returning to the bumper of the car in front of her.

"I don't know. I don't seem to know a lot of women these days."

"I find that hard to believe." Kari couldn't keep the dry note out of her voice. See above, silver fox.

"That sounds like a compliment. Is it a compliment?"

She gave his profile a quick glance before returning her attention to the road. "It might be."

The sidelong glance Kari slid at him while giving her almost-compliment arrowed straight through Rob, pulsing through his body. The idea that Kari might find him attractive was more than a little arousing.

And she lived right next door.

On the other hand, Rob's disastrous marriage and his equally wretched post-divorce dating life hadn't given him much confidence in his ability to successfully navigate an adult, functional relationship. He prided himself on being an honest, self-reflective guy and what was the common denominator to all of those disaster stories?

Him.

And, as he had noted, she lived right next door.

He could just continue to enjoy her sense of humor and her companionship. He could teach her what he knew about being a homeowner. They could be friends.

That sounded like a much better idea than having sex with her, having a good time for a while, discovering that despite being upfront and honest about not wanting to get married again that would be a sticking point, and then having the whole thing explode spectacularly.

And still having her living right next door.

Just the idea of going out back to barbecue or mow the lawn and being met with her retreating back and a slammed door was enough to tamp down the arousal he had felt just a moment before.

"I suppose it's probably too late in the day to start painting," Kari said, sounding disappointed.

Rob checked his watch. "Yeah. We can move the furniture if that makes you feel any better. It'll put us one step ahead of the game tomorrow morning."

Kari laughed. "What a treat. But you don't have to help me if you don't want. I can do it. There's not that much furniture in there and none of it is large."

"No, I really do want to," he said.

"Okay. If you really want to."

"I do. Besides, I can patch any areas that need it now and let it dry overnight." He considered what he had observed of her so far. "Why do you find it so hard to accept help?"

Her eyes cut to look at him, then returned to the road ahead. "Do I?"

"Well, either that or you want to keep score when you do accept it."

Kari shrugged. "It's at least partly a family trait. Now I guess it's a habit. Especially with people I don't know very well. Though I admit, I have to keep reminding myself that you and I really only just met. You're a very comfortable person to be around. Mostly."

"Mostly? Why only mostly?"

"I'm going to plead the Fifth on that one," she said,

pursing her lips. She kept her eyes on the road at this, avoiding his gaze.

Rob wondered if her fraction of discomfort had anything to do with the half-admission of attraction she'd made. Well, if he was going to continue to pursue the just-friends approach, he'd best not know if she was attracted to him. If she was, it would make her harder to resist.

And dammit, he really *liked* her.

Chapter Five

Rob paused, swallowing and taking a few deep breaths in the bright morning sunshine before rapping on Kari's front door. She had invited him over first thing for breakfast before they started work. He shifted his grip on the black case he had collected from work the day before.

Her smile when she opened the door was reassuring. So was the smell wafting through the house when he followed her inside. Coffee, bacon, and...

He nearly moaned. "Oh. Pancakes. I haven't had pancakes in I don't know how long," he said as she poured him a cup of coffee in the kitchen.

"You'll have them in a few minutes. Have a seat." A covered glass bowl steamed with already-made pancakes and another batch was starting to bubble in a skillet on the stove. Kari grabbed a plate and lifted the lid off the bowl. Rob seated himself at the little banquette at one end of the kitchen. She had set it with cloth napkins and silverware. A butter dish and jug of maple syrup sat in the middle of the table.

"Real maple syrup. The good stuff," he said, laying a napkin on his lap.

"The only stuff," she replied, laying a plate in front of him with a tidy stack of pancakes flanked by several strips of bacon.

"A woman after my own heart." He laid his hand on his chest and rolled his eyes at the ceiling and Kari laughed, an easy, lighthearted sound. She moved back across the kitchen to keep an eye on the next batch of pancakes. Rob put butter and maple syrup on his, the butter disappearing swiftly into the surfaces of the cakes, the syrup trailing lazily down the sides of the stack. The first bite was pure heaven and Rob really did roll his eyes now.

He chewed and swallowed. "Damn, Kari. This is…"

"A just reward for helping me so much."

"I told you I don't need a quid pro quo."

"Hush. Let me do a nice thing for you when you've done so many nice things for me." Her voice slid across his skin like silk. I needed to feed my sourdough starter anyway." Kari slid into the seat opposite him, her own plate piled with food.

"Sourdough?" Rob asked around a mouthful.

"Sourdough buttermilk pancakes."

He swallowed. "Good grief. No wonder they're so fabulous."

They settled into a companionable silence as they ate, Kari hopping up at one point to flip the last batch. Rob had seconds, eating far more than he usually did and enjoying every bite of maple sweetness and bacon saltiness.

"That. Was. Tremendous." Rob leaned back in his seat, rubbing his stomach. "I haven't had a breakfast like that in years."

"Glad you liked it." Kari collected the plates and moved to the sink to wash up.

"Want me to help with that? Or I can start the prep work in the dining room."

"I'm good here, thanks. I have this fabulous new faucet." She shot him a friendly smile over her shoulder and Rob's heart gave an unruly thump.

Collecting his case, Rob took it into the living room. The sketch pad with Kari's motif ideas was still on the coffee table. She had erased the stray mark that marred one of the drawings and had added more ideas on subsequent pages. Using his phone, he snapped photos of each page, then opened the case and took out the portable projector inside and connected it to his phone. It took a little experimentation, but he was able to set the projector up to point at the arched wall over the entrance to the dining room.

"What's going on in here?" Kari asked, wiping her hands on a towel as she came into the room.

"Your 'stencil.' Of a sort." He pointed at the motif projected onto the wall. "You can use that to guide your painting. Like doing a pencil outline, but no need to erase anything."

Kari turned and regarded his handiwork. "Very clever," she said, giving him a slow clap that was muffled by the dish towel.

"Not at all. Mia likes home improvement shows. I've seen this kind of thing done more than a few times."

"You watch home improvement shows with your daughter?" Kari turned bright eyes to his face.

"Yup. I've always tried to make sure I have a handle on what she watches. It started because I wanted to monitor what she was taking in—you know, when she was a kid. Now I just like to know what she's interested in so we could have stuff to talk about that isn't just school or work or things like that." It had been a while since Mia had come over for dinner and TV. A pang of loneliness made his next breath a little shaky. Seeing Mia grow up and become independent was his greatest pride and greatest sorrow. Pride for her, sorrow for his selfish self.

"That's really sweet."

He blinked, coming back from his wayward thoughts. "Home improvement shows are a damn sight better than Disney princess knockoffs. Mia's of an age where Disney wasn't making many of the princess movies when she was at the prime age for them. I wish she had been able to see *Frozen* when she was a kid, for instance. That movie had some great messages for girls."

She waved her hands in front of her face, the dish towel flapping. "I take it back. You follow Disney princess movies even though your daughter is an adult? That's not just sweet. That's adorable."

"Pretty hard to miss *Frozen*. I'm far from the only adult who has seen it."

Kari raised her hand. "I've never seen it."

The look on Rob's face at her admission was priceless. His mouth hung agape for a moment, then he slapped his own cheeks, as if to revive himself from shock.

"You've never seen *Frozen*?"

"Nope."

"But you're Scandinavian."

"So?"

"It's…" He waved a hand. "You've got to see this movie. That's all I'll say."

"Okay, I'll look into streaming it."

"Or you could come over to my place sometime and watch it. I have it on Blu-Ray."

"You just keep surprising me." Kari shook her head,

unable to resist the smile that tugged at her mouth. She wondered if he had an entire collection of Disney movies. "Sure. That sounds like fun."

"Maybe after we finish up with this?" He turned and waved at the painting apparatus sitting on the tarp-draped dining room table. "A suitable reward for a hard day's work."

Was he...flirting with her? He looked back at her and Kari examined his eyes. They didn't seem overly warm or coaxing or sensual. Just friendly.

"Okay." She resisted the urge to say, "It's a date." Because it obviously wasn't and joking about it seemed like it would make it weird.

Rob showed her how to change the images he had taken of her sketchbook and position the projector until the motif was lined up just so. Then he set her up with the stepladder he'd brought over from his house the day before and went into the dining room, sanding the areas where he'd spackled the various nail holes from hanging pictures and other small imperfections on the dining room walls.

Kari resisted the urge to watch him, instead getting her supplies set up on the stepladder's little shelf and examining the placement of the projected motif on the wall. Deciding it was what and where she wanted, she selected a fine brush and started applying paint to the wall in delicate strokes. She lost herself in the task for a while, enjoying the meticulous work, trying different brushes for different purposes. Realizing she'd need to move the ladder before she attacked the next section, she leaned back to assess the effect.

"Beautiful." Rob's voice was low and appreciative behind her. She capped the little pot of paint and grinned down at him.

"You think so?"

"I really do. You could hire out to do this sort of thing, you know."

Kari scrubbed at her forehead with the back of her hand, conscious of the still-wet brush in her fingers. "Right. I'm so sure. But I have to say I like it."

"I'll convince you later. I want to get these walls rolled."

Kari stepped down the ladder and looked into the dining room. He had painted the edges of the walls and they glowed pale gold, the paint still glossy and wet. "Wow. It already looks so different."

"Different good?" Rob's face was anxious, the skin around his eyes tight.

She met his eyes and smiled. "Different beautiful."

Rob hadn't been aware of how much he was hoping she liked what he was doing until he asked.

Her glowing face said everything and every cell in his body seemed to bask in her praise. He hadn't chosen the color, but it seemed his current happiness apparently depended on her approving of his application of the paint.

"You really like it?" he asked.

Her eyes roamed over the color that ringed the dining room walls as she replied. "I do."

"Well, then. I'd better get to rolling." Rob walked back into the dining room to recheck the spots he'd applied spackle to, smoothing a hand over the walls prior to pouring paint into a pan and loading the roller with practiced strokes. Raising the roller to the wall, he ran it in an easy W, then repeated, filling the space with an even layer of paint. The rhythmic nature of the task should have been soothing, but he was all too aware of Kari, who had returned to the ladder in the dining room's doorway, her long legs outlined by skinny jeans.

The slicking sound of the paint on the roller didn't help. Barring the faint squeak from the roller itself, the soft, wet sound of paint being applied to the wall sounded like sex, pure and simple.

Focus on the squeak.

Yeah. Sure. Not with Kari's legs in his peripheral vision and the intimate, slick sound of the paint in his ears. Besides, the squeaking sounds could be bedsprings creaking. How long had it been? His hand paused and he blinked, maneuvering the roller over the wall in studied, steady strokes. It didn't matter how long it had been since he had been with a woman. He was a disaster at relationships. He knew this. Besides. Kari wouldn't be interested in a middle-aged wreck like him.

Also, Kari was special. He wasn't going to screw up what looked like a promising friendship. Or even worse, make things weird with his next-door neighbor. He focused on the paint, watching the pale sunshine color blossom across the dining room walls.

Yes. He could do this for her. He could fix her sink. He could paint her dining room. He could keep her at arm's length...crap.

He had invited her over for a movie night. Tonight.

The thought of Kari's legs tucked up on his sofa for movie night made his wrist wobble across her dining room wall. He redoubled his attention to the task at hand. He glanced over at the ladder where she stood. He couldn't see her face, but he could imagine the concentration as she traced out the motif she had designed, the delight as it bloomed on the walls as she painted.

Up, down. The swaying motions of painting soothed him

now. The room emerged as a golden wheat field, ready for…
what? Bodies to roll in?

Good grief.

His imagination needed to take a break. He put the roller
in the pan and stood back from the wall he had finished
painting, scanning for inconsistencies or other flaws.

"Beautiful." The voice in his ear made him start. Kari.
Next to him. Looking around the room with a dazed expression that made his imagination spark again. "I can't believe
it. You're done."

"It's not a very big room." Rob's voice sounded rusty,
even to his own ears.

"But it looks bigger now, somehow. I can't believe I
didn't just run in and paint every room in the house immediately." Kari bounced on her toes, then spun and flung her
arms around his neck hugging him tight. "Thank you."

His arms went around her. A reflex. As was the deep
inhalation that mirrored her own, almost a sigh. Her body
felt so soft and warm against his, so *good*.

"Thank you," she murmured again. Then, before he
could muster up the willpower to pull away, she stepped
back, still looking around at the room.

That's right. The room. She had hugged him because
he'd painted a room.

For a few moments, he realized, he had some sort of silly
schoolboy fantasy that he had done her some huge service. A
knight's quest. A dragon slain. But no. He had merely
painted a room for her.

Something anyone could do.

The change in the dining room was a *miracle*. With the color
on the walls, Kari could now envision the rest of the rooms

in the house, all blossoming to life like flowers blooming in a time-lapse movie. A pale green in her bedroom. Sea-glass blue in the bathroom. Terra-cotta for the kitchen.

And the living room, the first room anyone saw, with its austere white made rich by the Scandinavian motif picked out in cornflower blue.

"Come see what I've done." Kari wheeled and strode back into the living room, Rob right behind her. She was coming down off her high a bit now, feeling a little awkward about that hug. He'd hugged her before, when she had broken down in the kitchen. But that had felt like an almost perfunctory thing. A person needed comfort. Hugs were comforting. A hug was administered. As soon as she started to pull herself together, Rob had retreated.

This exuberant expression of joy felt like it had crossed a line, gotten more personal. And his body had felt so good—too good—when he'd hugged her.

"What do you think?" She waved at the arch over the entry into the dining room, watching his expression. No, she definitely shouldn't get more personal.

Rob was friendly and attractive, but he also didn't seem like he wanted anything more than friendship from Kari and she had no interest in making a fool of herself over a guy who wasn't interested. She was too old for that nonsense. A lifetime of a few relationships developing out of occasional dates from guys who didn't consider her to be too tall, too intimidating, or too…whatever left her less than enthused about the idea of romantic relationships in general.

Rob's gaze scanned the motif, his eyes warming and the corners of his lips lifting. He looked sideways at her. "This is great. I might need to commission you to do something in my house." Oh, she wasn't going to fixate on that expressive mouth. No, most definitely not.

Because sex? Great in theory. Occasionally great in reality. But usually? A huge disappointment. Guys who seemed to be sweet and attentive on a date who turned out to be clueless in the bedroom were all too common. Kari's own fingers or her small collection of vibrators were far more reliable sources of pleasure.

And besides, if she came to climax by herself, it logically followed that she had the bed all to herself after. She could stretch her entire all-too-long-for-most-guys body out and not have to share with anyone else. She didn't have to try to make herself small to accommodate someone who thought that at least sixty percent of the mattress real estate was the minimum of his fair share.

"What are you thinking about?" Rob's voice intruded on her internal monologue and she felt heat licking across her cheeks as if someone had applied a match to her face.

Kari cleared her throat. "Just getting ahead of myself a bit. Colors I want in other rooms. You've inspired me."

"I have, huh?"

Oh, crap. Now his crooked smile seemed flirty and interested. Completely at odds with his platonic-friendly attitude of a few moments earlier.

"Sure. You have all the handyman skills I should acquire. That's inspiring, right?"

"Sounds more like a job than an inspiration when you put it that way," Rob said, his gaze scanning the wall they faced as if it held some sort of secret code he could unlock if he only looked at it hard enough.

"Nah. For someone like me, it's definitely inspiring." Kari bumped his shoulder with hers, earning another sideways smile.

"Someone like you?"

"Someone who always called the building manager or landlord or whoever and only hoped they'd give a crap. As opposed to being able to even consider doing it myself."

Rob tilted his head, seeming to concede the point. "So, what's next on your home improvement quest, fair maiden?"

"Fair maiden?" She snort-laughed. She couldn't help it.

"Fair Maiden Who Slays Her Own Dragons. I thought the whole thing was too long to put on the business card."

She bumped his shoulder. "Says the guy who has Rocket Surgeon, Master Plumber, and International Man of Mystery on his."

"Well, if I'm being modest." His dark eyes twinkled with humor.

Kari folded her arms across her chest. "I think the next thing isn't about my house but yours."

"Mine?"

"Yes, yours. You have a mountain of mail for me to sort. Or so you claim."

"Oh, I don't claim anything. The mountain is real."

Chapter Six

The mountain was *so* real.

Rob insisted they clean up everything at Kari's house before going over to his. All brushes rinsed, paint cans sealed tight and put away, the tarp folded up, all other paraphernalia gathered and set aside.

Which was ironic, given the disastrous state of his office.

"Look, here's the thing," he said, his hand on the knob, his eyes not quite meeting Kari's face. "Mostly I just open the door, toss the thing in my hand inside and close it. It's not pretty."

"Let's see it, Fox." Kari folded her arms across her chest and Rob remembered how good that chest had felt pressing into him.

Not the time for that. Not that there ever would be a time. Rob took a deep lungful of air and opened the door.

Kari stepped into the room and did a slow perusal of the disaster. He wasn't sure when it had tipped from "manageable but messy" to "total shit-show." But there it was. And her reaction showed on her face. He was ready for her to shake her head, say, "Nope. Not doing this. Not doing any of it you weird hoarder," and walk out.

Instead, she gave him a long, silent look. It stretched out, making him want to fidget. Then it stretched further and he wanted to dig a hole and bury himself in it.

Then she broke the eye-lock and scanned the chaos and said, "Got a recycling bin and some file folders?"

"Sure." Bemused, Rob went out back and fetched the big blue plastic recycling bin that sat there. When he got back to his office, Kari was already sitting cross-legged on the floor, sorting things into piles.

"Why on earth would you save so many catalogs?" she asked, dumping a pile of them into the bin with a thump.

Rob shrugged. "I don't know. It all just got out of hand somehow. Easier to open the door, dump, and run."

"Easier still to deal with stuff as it comes in. Sort everything right over the recycling bin. Toss the things you're never going to open." She shot a minatory glance in his direction and he gritted his teeth. She was right. He could see how a simple change in his habits could have made this mountain of mess never have happened. If he was still with Liz, she would accuse him of doing it to make work for her, pouting extravagantly while she dealt with it. And her was Kari, just…dealing with it.

"I guess so. It's just…"

She held up a catalog and he winced. "Are you really shopping out of the Victoria's Secret catalog?" She glanced at the label. "Or, more correctly, if Miss Mia Fox wants the VS catalog, don't you think she gets it at her own place?"

"True."

"What about any of these?" She fanned out a collection of catalogs, none of which he had ever opened.

"Nope."

"Are you ever going to do any catalog shopping? Ever?"

Rob hadn't considered this before. Catalogs, like the weather, just came. "I guess not. I'm not a shopping guy, and if I need something, I use the internet."

"Grab your laptop. You're going to start un-subscribing to all of them."

"You can do that?"

"Sure you can. Why are you so surprised?"

Rob shrugged. "I hadn't thought about it. Let me get my laptop. I think it's on the coffee table."

She gave him another one of Those Looks. "You sure this is your office?"

"No, I'm beginning to think we're in a hardwood floored, centrally heated and air-conditioned dumpster."

She nodded. "Get your laptop. You're about to become catalog-free."

Feeling sheepish, Rob went into the living room and fetched the computer. He brought it back and settled on the floor across from Kari, his knees protesting as he lowered himself. "Ugh. This is no way for an old man to sit." Fishing his reading glasses out of his breast pocket, he slid them on.

"You can't be much older than I am, if that." Kari rolled her eyes and returned her attention to the stack of catalogs and other junk that was in her lap.

"I'm forty-eight," he said. "If you're close to that, then I'm a unicorn."

Kari tilted her head, considering him. "I'm forty-two. That's not so far apart." She squinted. "Do I see a horn on your forehead?"

Rob blinked. He had recalibrated his estimate of Kari's age a few times, partly based on her relationship with her niece. At first, when he thought they were sisters, he figured Sam was in her late twenties and Kari was in her early to mid-thirties. When he'd been told they were ten years apart, he'd adjusted Kari into her late thirties. At most.

This was going to take some thinking about.

Kari shook her head, amused. One of these days, her age would catch up to her. It had happened to her mother. *Mor* had been youthful-looking and vital, fooling people into thinking she was much younger than she was for most of her life.

Until she got sick. Then she went downhill so fast, considerations of her looks were left for Kari as she sat by her mother's bedside, clutching the hand that was wasting as fast as the rest of the body it was attached to. Suddenly, *Mor* was unrecognizable. Gone was the older mother who had attended Kari's school events, the quality of her skin making her the envy of women younger than she was. Gone was the old woman whose spine was straight and whose light blue eyes still glittered with health. In illness, her skin showed every year with compound interest, her spine bent with fatigue, and her eyes dimmed. As if a vengeful god had taken back *Mor's* unearned gifts and repaid her with interest.

Then the old woman's secrets had poured out and Kari had been left with yet another unlooked-for legacy to bear all on her own. One that she had bungled with Sam. But maybe she could retrieve it. Anxiety welled in her at the thought of the dinner she'd host at some point.

In her newly painted dining room.

That thought made her smile, gave her a tiny sliver of confidence.

"What's that smile for?" Rob's voice intruded on her thoughts.

"Just that I'm happy I have a nice dining room now for that…maybe stressful dinner with Sam and her new guy. Thank you."

"You're welcome. Now, what was responsible for the entire *telenovela* drama that played out on your face before the smile?"

"What?" Horrified, Kari tried to remember what she had been thinking about only moments before. *Mor.* Of course. "Just...remembering the tangle my mother left me in with Sam." She bit the inside of her cheek.

"But that's going to get fixed. You guys will figure it out." Rob's voice sounded bracing. She wondered if this was a thing he did for his daughter, this "buck up little buckaroo" act.

"Maybe." Something he said made her sit up straighter. "Wait. How do you know how a *telenovela* works?"

Rob laughed, smoothing his hand over the computer in his lap. "I don't. But Mia watched that show that was modeled on *telenovelas* —the one about the romance novelist in Florida?"

"And you watch it with her. Like the home improvement shows." Kari suppressed a smile. "I can't even deal with how cute you guys are. Anyway." Wrenching her brain back to the job at hand, she told Rob about the website he could sign up for to unsubscribe to catalogs en masse.

Far better to keep this...whatever it was...on catalogs and paint colors and far away from anything resembling that heart-meltingly domestic picture.

After taking a break for lunch, they spent the next hour or so tidying, with Rob entering the seemingly endless names of the various catalogs he didn't want into the web form. Slowly, Kari's oasis of order in the surrounding chaos spread. When the piles of papers she deemed he should keep, set out in tidy piles around her, reached a critical state, she demanded file folders and he found a box of them in the closet. She labeled each one with a careful, tidy hand that somehow managed to convey her personality. It reminded him of the motifs in her sketchbook and on her wall.

And now that personality, in the smallest way, was inscribed in his own home.

He swallowed hard at that thought.

Next door. Romance equals disaster. Romance with someone next door is disaster on a scale you have never imagined.

Kari got to her feet, placing the neat stack of folders on the otherwise empty desk. "That's a start," she said. There were still piles of unaddressed paper in the corners of the room, but Kari had gotten him past the roadblock of getting started to undo the mess he created.

He stole a glance at her. She was pressing her hands to the base of her spine and arching her body to ease an ache in her back. Swallowing, he returned his gaze to his laptop. That image of her—back arched, breasts rising up, eyes closed and going internal with some physical sensation— wasn't going to help him in his quest to keep her at arm's length.

No, it made him want to get her far closer. He wanted to offer to massage away those aches. To have her join him on the sofa, leaning back in him while he dug his thumbs into the knots, easing the pain out of tight muscles.

Nope. Shut that right down. He stared at his computer screen as if it was his job.

Sighing, Kari bent her back one way, then the other, feeling the stretch move into the sides of her torso. Her lower back ached. But the desk was clear. If Rob wanted to, he could actually use it.

It was a victory, of a sort. Not on par with the way he had fixed her sink or shown her that painting a room was a bit more involved than she had thought, but a victory nonetheless. She opened the almost empty filing cabinet and set the file folders in it. Straightening, she glanced around the room. "We've made a lot of progress." It wasn't anywhere near organized, but it wasn't a disaster zone anymore. And when he hauled out the almost-overflowing recycling bin full of catalogs and other detritus, there would be room to maneuver in the small room.

Rob was still sitting on the floor, his reading glasses making him look annoyingly nerd-attractive, apparently enthralled with whatever was on his laptop screen, but he looked up and gave her a weak smile. "I can't begin to thank you for what you've done."

Kari leaned on the desk, ran her fingers through her hair. Even her scalp felt tired. "Seems very mundane compared to what you've helped me with over at my house."

"See, I was thinking the same thing...but in reverse. I think you know what I mean." Rob twizzled two fingers back and forth.

"So." Kari heaved a sigh. "You helped me do a thing I couldn't do and I helped you do a thing you...supposedly couldn't do."

Rob's dark brown eyes held hers. "No, not supposedly. You broke the logjam of whatever was making me do whatever I was doing. I have my office back."

"It just seems so easy."

"For you. Painting a wall is easy for me. Replacing a faucet is easy for me."

"Stop being so rational. And how does someone so rational manage to end up with that many unwanted catalogs?" Despite her skepticism, his appreciation for her help was starting to make her feel warm. It was cozy, this mutual aid.

"Enough. I surrender." Rob waved a hand in the air and then extended it to her. "Help an old man up?"

"Old. Right." Kari remained where she was, hands on her hips.

He laughed, his head bowing, shoulders shaking, looking as tired as she felt. He looked up again, and his dark eyes seemed to freeze her in place.

"Okay." He clasped his hands in his lap. "How about I make you a cocktail in exchange for helping me up off this hard, goddamn, other curse-words-I-shouldn't-say floor?" He closed his laptop with one hand and raised the other to her.

Kari looked at his extended hand, nodded, and put her palm in his, hauling him to his feet. "I suppose I should have asked how extensive your bar was before taking you up on that offer. But now that I'm in no position to bargain, I suppose I should just roll with it."

Rob set his laptop down on the desk, then rolled his shoulders and rocked his head from side to side before looking at Kari again. "I'm thinking we need a French 75."

"A French 75?" Kari blinked. Rob suddenly seemed far too worldly. Far too…much.

"Yes. Champagne—or sparkling wine. Gin. Simple syrup. Lemon juice. Any issues with any of these?"

Kari blinked and shook her head. "No issues, just…you have simple syrup? What *is* simple syrup anyway?"

Rob raised his clasped hands above his head, stretching to one side, then the other, his face contorting. Then he let his arms fall to his sides. "Simple syrup is just dissolved sugar in water. I like cold brew coffee straight from the fridge, but with a little sweetening. Granulated sugar doesn't dissolve in cold water…so. There you have it. I always have simple syrup on hand."

Kari thought furiously. "And the Champagne?" *Who has Champagne just hanging around?*

"Sparkling wine. Not necessarily the real stuff from France. Mia loves it." His eyes met hers again. They seemed so dark, so infinite.

Oof. Right in the feels. Again. "You keep sparkling wine on hand for your daughter."

"I do. And also for any occasion that seems to merit a celebration."

A laugh sputtered out of her. "Throwing away a bunch of catalogs and filing other stuff merits a celebration?"

"Honey, you have no idea." Rob's dark eyes lit with laughter.

"Oh. No. I think I have some idea." Kari suppressed a smile, thinking about how he had painted her dining room. He'd made it seem so easy. But dealing with his junked-up office had been easy for her. It was right in her wheelhouse, after all. But…he had told her that painting a room was in his wheelhouse.

And he was just so fun to be around. Even dealing with a mundane task like this. He was funny. He was comfortable. He was…

Kari shied away from that thought. No. He'd shown no interest in anything other than friendship. She wasn't going to make a fool of herself here.

Chapter Seven

"To...homeownership." Rob tapped his champagne flute against Kari's and her eyes smiled at him over the rim as she took her first sip. He wondered if she was smiling at the slight hesitation, the almost-stammer in the brief toast.

He had almost said, "To us."

Because they were such a good team. They were becoming friends. Yes.

Kari raised her own flute. "To neighbors who make a great team." He brought his glass against hers again, creating a brief, musical *chink* when they met. Her sentiment was a lot closer to the one he had almost voiced, but it managed to keep the necessary distance between them.

He'd made the right call. He knew it. Why did it feel so disappointing?

"Do you like it?" He pointed to the cocktail.

"I do." She took another sip, looking around his kitchen. "Wow. This is inspiring and depressing all at the same time."

"What is?"

"The cabinets. The countertop. The flooring. All of it.

Mine is so shabby, but it will take me forever to save up for a renovation."

"Don't hurry. Living in a house without a kitchen is the worst. And I did most of it myself, so it took a while."

Her eyes went wide. "How long?"

"A little over four weeks. Eating at restaurants all the time got old fast."

"Expensive, too."

"Yep." He leaned his hip against the countertop, remembering how amazing it had felt when the countertop installers left and a final few tasks were all that stood between him and cooking in his own kitchen again.

"Maybe I'll just be happy about my new faucet. For now. Until I get up the nerve and the cash for the renovation."

"Solid plan," he said. "So…what was with that look you gave me?"

"Look?" Kari's face showed nothing but honest bafflement.

"The look before we dug into the chaos in my office. The silent one that, when combined with folded arms and serious eyes, made me want to dig a hole and bury myself?"

She colored, sipped her drink. "I call it 'weaponized silence.'"

"Come again?"

"A specialty of the Halvorsen family. I don't even know I'm doing it sometimes. We're very comfortable with silence. When it's used on someone who isn't…" She gave a slight flourish with her hand, as if to say he could finish the thought for himself.

"I see. Noted. It is, indeed, a weapon. Now, how about that movie?"

She flinched. "You sure you still want me around?"

"Why not?"

She shrugged. "You helped me yesterday. Then again today."

"And you helped me."

"I just don't want to mess up any plans you might have had for the rest of today."

"You're not messing anything up." In fact, the idea of her going back to her own place sounded lonely. Which was ridiculous. He was used to being alone. He mostly liked it, in fact. "Unless you have something you need to get back to and you're just being polite?" He hoped it wasn't the case. He'd hate it if it was.

She shook her head. "Nope. No plans. Watching paint dry, maybe."

"Riveting stuff. I think you'll enjoy the movie more."

She followed him to the living room, sitting on one end of the sofa as he rummaged through his collection of discs to find *Frozen*. When he had it playing, he sat on the other end of the couch. It would have been weird and inappropriate to sit any closer to her. But he wanted to.

He wanted to very, very much.

He consoled himself by watching her reactions to the movie rather than the movie itself. After all, he'd seen it more than enough times. When it began, she watched with a sort of polite skepticism. But as the story unfolded, she grew more and more rapt. When Anna purchased her new clothes, Kari pointed at the screen and smiled.

"The motif on her dress!"

"Yeah. It's kind of like the ones you drew."

By the time the movie had swept to its conclusion, Kari was curled up on the sofa, her shoes off and her feet tucked under her, as at home as a cat might be, eyes riveted to the screen. Sighing and leaning back as the credits rolled, she said, "I can see why you wish this had been around for your daughter when she was a kid. I really thought it was going to be yet another 'guy saves the girl' story."

Rob grabbed the remote and turned the tv off. "Yeah. But instead, she gets saved by her sister."

"Girl power." Kari briefly raised a fist into the air, then rubbed her hands across her face. She picked up her phone, which she had left on the coffee table. "Ugh. This girl has to take herself home and get ready for the week."

"If you have to." He hated the idea of her leaving. Which was silly. She was right next door. He could see her whenever he wanted, practically. "Thanks for everything today."

"No, thank you." She rose, pocketing her phone and giving him a weary smile. He saw her to the front door where they both stood, a slightly awkward silence stretching into fully, completely awkward as they looked at each other, then away. Kari's eyes fixed on the door and he opened it, reaching past her to get to the doorknob. He was close enough to kiss her. Close enough to smell her shampoo or soap or whatever lingering sweetness that made him want to discover its source, trail his nose along the arch of her neck, sift her fine hair through his fingers.

She swallowed as he straightened, the open door an invitation and a rejection. "I guess I'll see you around the back yard."

That was right. *Next door. Disaster. Focus.*

"Yeah. Or I could really teach you how to paint a room instead of just doing it for you."

Her face brightened. "You'd do that?"

And just like that, all his resolve crumbled. "Sure. Next weekend? Saturday?"

73

"You're on." Kari's heart gave a little hop-skip in her chest. She knew she could see Rob whenever. They lived literal yards from one another. But having an actual date on the calendar made her happy somehow.

"I'm just angling for another one of those amazing break-fasts," he said, a sly smile crinkling the skin around his eyes.

"You get all the breakfasts. For all time." The words were out of Kari's mouth before she realized what they implied. Her face flamed. "I mean…"

"I know what you meant." Was that a tiny hint of disap-pointment on his face because she hadn't intended a double entendre? Or was it her overactive imagination?

"Anyway. Thanks again." Kari bit her lip, unsure of how to retrieve the moment.

"No, thank *you*." Rob's returning smile was warm.

Kari gave an awkward little wave and stepped through the doorway, self-consciousness coursing through her as she walked the short distance to her own front door. Letting herself in, the self-consciousness dropped away as she saw the motif over the entrance to the dining room, and the sunny walls beyond and smelled the sharp scent of curing paint. She wrapped her arms around herself, doing a little dance of glee, sneakers squeaking on the hardwood.

She was doing it. She was making this place her own. Just like she'd imagined when she had first toured it with the realtor.

In the midst of her little celebration, her phone chimed in her back pocket. Pulling it out, she saw a text from Sam.

Dinner — next Sunday work for you?

Kari swallowed hard and sat on the sofa, stroking a finger over the phone's screen. Sunday. Her chance to repair her relationship with Sam. Meet her new boyfriend. Make a new start.

No pressure on one dinner at all.

Swallowing hard, Kari tapped out: *Absolutely. Anything the new guy doesn't eat? Allergies?*

A pause. Then dots pulsing on the screen. *Nope.*

Great. Come at 6. I'll serve him lutefisk. Kari chuckled as Sam responded with a swift "vomit" emoji.

Come on, Kari typed. *How often does a guy get offered fish preserved with lye?*

Sam's response was a pithy, *Never. And he never will.*

You must really like him, Kari typed, a wistful smile stealing over her face.

I do.

Good. See you Sunday at 6.

Kari set her phone on the table and glanced at the motif again, hoping it would give her that same zing of joy it had when she entered. But its power had leached away. In place of the giddy joy was pure nervousness now.

After Kari left, Rob busied himself with putting away the Blu-Ray disc, washing up the champagne flutes they'd had their cocktails in, and other small, non-urgent tasks.

None of them served to erase the memory of Kari's blush. What was it about the wash of pink across her cheeks that reminded him that he wasn't just Rob a handy neighbor, or Rob a dad, but Rob a man with a definite appreciation for a pretty woman?

Whatever it was, it sure worked. He'd had to slam the lid on the urge to kiss her so hard, he was pretty sure the urge had a concussion.

He should be backpedaling away from any more home improvement projects, cozy breakfasts, and movie showings. He should be putting some polite distance so they could continue to coexist next to each other.

Instead, he was looking forward to Saturday already. In fact, if they were going to paint another room, she should really pick out the color and get the paint sometime this week. He should go with her, make sure she got the right thing.

He shoved the last wet load of laundry into the dryer and started the machine going. It was a more productive thing to do than sinking to the floor and lying there until someone with more of a brain told him off for having so little self-control.

While he was having these useful thoughts, his phone rang. Mia's ringtone. Digging the phone out of his pocket, he didn't try to hide the smile in his voice. "How's my grandpuppy?"

"*Daddy.*" Mia's mock-exasperated voice rang in his voice. "You used to ask how *I* was doing."

He paced into the living room. "That's what happens when you become a parent. You get kicked to the curb for the offspring. Ask me how I know."

"Well, that's actually why I'm calling…" Mia's voice trailed into a coaxing note he was all too familiar with.

"How long does Hugo need to stay with me?"

A sigh gusted into his ear. "Can I drop him off on Tuesday evening and pick him up on Saturday afternoon?"

"Sure." He remembered his plans for Saturday. "I might be next door on Saturday, though."

"Next door?"

"Yeah. My new neighbor. I've been helping…her with some home improvement stuff." *Shit*. He shouldn't have paused. Mia jumped into the breach with both feet.

"Her? Is she nice? Is she pretty? Is she good enough for my dad?"

"Mia. She's a friend." He could just as easily have said, *Yes, she's nice. And oh, yes she's pretty. But your old man isn't good*

76

enough for her. I'm terrible at relationships and unfortunately you almost had a ringside seat for most of the evidence.

"Friend is a good place to start…" Mia's voice held the same coaxing note it had when she thought she needed to talk Rob into taking Hugo for a few days.

Rob's hand sliced through the air, even though Mia wouldn't see the gesture. "And that's where it's going to stay. You know my history."

"I know you've never found the right woman for you. That's what I know."

Her optimism was as heartwarming as it was maddening. "How is it that I raised a daughter who thinks that Hallmark Christmas movies are instruction manuals? Some people just aren't cut out for relationships, kiddo."

"Da-ad."

"Nope. End of conversation about Dad. I'm happy to take Hugo. Stay for dinner on Tuesday when you drop him off."

"Oh, I'm sorry. I can't. Rain check?"

Rob refrained from asking what her plans were. Just like he needed his boundaries, she needed hers. Her space. But damn, it was hard seeing her all grown up sometimes. He missed being needed for more than dog sitting. Missed the way she'd unconsciously lift her hand for him to grab when they went places years ago, relying on him to take care of anything and everything. "Rain check, sweetie. See you Tuesday for grandpup drop-off."

"You got it. Thanks, Dad."

"You owe me."

"I'll never even make the interest payments."

"No, you won't. But that's what being a parent is. I love you, kiddo."

"I love you too. Bye."

Rob stuffed his phone in his pocket and stared at nothing

for a while, wondering what his life would be like if he could just be the guy his daughter thought he was.

On Monday morning, Kari stared at the pile of invoices on her desk and her list of auxiliary tasks for the week. The pile that wasn't going anywhere until she paid them and the list was…the list. Usually, she dove right into tasks like this, not because they were fun or interesting, but because they were finite. Something you could draw a satisfying, straight line through when they were complete.

This morning, though, her job just seemed dreary. Or maybe it was the blank walls of her tiny little office. She spent almost as much time here as she did at home—why had it never occurred to her to do more than put a couple of framed snapshots of her and Sam on her desk and call it a day? Maybe, like with the anonymous apartments she had always lived in, she just didn't see the opportunity.

"Daydreaming already?" Sapna, one of the company copyeditors, stood in the doorway, her dark eyes glowing with humor.

"You caught me." Kari pushed her hair back from her forehead.

"Ambitious. I usually wait until at least Wednesday after-noon to let my brain drift. But I suppose you get a pass. You're always doing everything. What's on deck now?"

Sam consulted her list. "I have to corral people to bring in treats for the quarterly coffee social. I'm trying to come up with someone who hasn't done it in a while."

Sapna's dark brown eyes glinted. "I can only imagine. Trying to get anyone outside the usual suspects is probably a big pain. Especially the guys."

Kari winced. Sapna was way too perceptive. "I was also

thinking about how painting a couple of the rooms in my house this weekend kick-started me into thinking I should have decorated here a little more.

Sapna looked at the walls. "Our cubicles are decorated like mad, but I think that's because the cloth walls invite pushpins." She waved at Kari's office, bracelets tinkling down her arm. "This, not so much. But you probably shouldn't try to paint your office. The Man wouldn't be pleased."

"No." Fred Logan, President of Monocle Press and otherwise known as The Man, wasn't the kind of person to appreciate a painted office wall. "But I could at least get some art posters in frames or something. Anything to jazz this up." Kari waved at the white blankness surrounding her, unrelieved by even a window.

"True." Sapna looked from the walls to Kari. "So, big fun in the new house. Painting walls." She gave a sarcastic "woohoo" and made crowd-cheering noises, pumping her palms toward the ceiling, bracelets sliding down her wrists.

"It was fun, actually. My neighbor helped out. He fixed my kitchen sink too." And how on earth could just remembering a man with his head stuffed under her sink make her feel tingly?

Sapna arched a perfectly groomed eyebrow. "You're smiling. Is 'fixing a sink' a euphemism for something?"

Kari groaned. "Not you, too."

"Am I being unoriginal?" Sapna grinned.

"Sam — my niece — made references to my...personal plumbing when I told her about it." Reminded of Sunday's dinner, she bit her lip. "Speaking of which, when you brought Raj to meet the family, what was it like?"

Sapna looked confused. "Are we talking about you bringing your plumber to meet Sam or something else?"

"Something else. Sam has a boyfriend. The first one in a

long time and it's apparently serious. I'm having them over for dinner on Sunday. I'm…nervous."

"Ah. You need a bozo buffer," Sapna said, folding her arms across her chest and leaning on the doorframe.

Kari blinked. "A who and a what now?"

"Someone to break up the dynamic." Sapna held up one index finger. "You and Sam know each other really well." She brought her other index finger up to meet the first. "Sam and new guy know each other really well." She drew her fingers down and away from each other, then stopped. "That leaves a weak side to the triangle: you and the new guy. You need someone else to balance things out. Make the triangle into a square."

Kari almost winced at how fast her mind flew to Rob. "Is that fair to the other person—what did you call it?"

"Bozo buffer. Don't ask me why. It's my mom's term for it. But it does help defuse that weird dynamic, so it's not like it's unfair to the bozo in question. You just end up with a nice, normal gathering. Got anyone in mind?" Sapna's eyes grew sly and her lips, painted with a bright matte magenta lipstick, drew into a wide grin. "The plumber?"

"He's not really a plumber." Kari said, her brain whirring. "Just a guy who's good with his hands."

Sapna hooted and Kari's face heated. "Not like that," she mumbled, propping her elbows on her desk and dropping her flaming cheeks into her palms.

"Or not that you know yet. Right?"

Kari lifted her head from her hands and pointed at Sapna. "No. And I don't plan on knowing. He's nice. He lives next door. He has a life. I have a life." *And he's not interested in me.*

"Fine. But nice and lives next door sounds like a great recipe for someone who can be a perfect bozo buffer."

Kari considered Sapna's words. She wasn't wrong neces-

sarily. But actually asking Rob was a whole other considera-
tion. She could imagine the awkward conversation.
*Remember that embarrassing and stressful thing I told you about?
It's gathered steam and become a potentially embarrassing and
stressful dinner with the only remaining member of my family and
the guy she's apparently really serious about but I had never heard of
before.*

There had to be a better way. A different person. An
entirely different bozo buffer.

"Ready for me?" Rob's help desk manager, Sandra, stood in
his doorway.

Rob glanced at his computer and nearly smacked his
forehead. He'd been dreamy and distracted all morning,
even missing the little calendar notice that should have
alerted him of his biweekly meeting. "Absolutely. Come in."
He waved at the little round conference table at the other
end of his office and got to his feet. "Have a seat. How's the
general status?"

Sandra nodded. "General status is good. We're
reducing our response times on average, closing tickets out
faster."

"Excellent," Rob said as they both settled into chairs.
"And how are the new hires settling in?" The company had
recently hired three new help desk technicians, which meant
a lot of training for Sandra and her more senior staff who
mentored them.

"Seem to be okay." But Sandra's dark skin creased
between her eyebrows.

"And…"

Sandra shook her head. "Nothing I can put my finger on
yet. Just an intuition. You know I've had my fair share of

nitwits who didn't take either me or the job seriously at first."

Rob nodded. Sandra was his best manager. And she was a Black woman in charge of a sometimes fractious, often immature team of mostly young, mostly male, mostly white employees.

"You let me know the instant something doesn't feel right. I have your back. Whatever you need."

"I know. I can handle it. Maybe it's nothing."

Knowing Sandra wouldn't thank him if he pushed the issue, Rob decided to move on. "How are Brenda and Trin's teams doing?" he asked, naming her subordinates who managed the Los Angeles and Austin teams, respectively.

Sandra nodded, her usual brisk, no-nonsense demeanor returning. "Good. Their weekly numbers are on track. Good response times, good feedback. There was a little malware incident in L.A., but Brenda's team has got that under control."

A strange, hectic noise was rising outside Rob's closed office door. "What the heck is going on out there?"

Sandra got to her feet, opening the door, then glancing over her shoulder at Rob. "Nerf battle. Time to play bad cop."

Rob saw a bright orange foam projectile sail past his door. "Let me see if there's tickets waiting." He got to his feet and went to his computer. Only one trouble ticket was open, and it was assigned to one of their most senior employees. Rob had no doubt the guy was off taking care of it, but he walked to the doorway to be sure. Yup, that particular help desk employee was nowhere in sight, probably in the office of the employee with the issue.

"Do what you think is best, but there's nothing really going on right now. If you don't mind them goofing around a little, I don't care. Just as long as it settles down when another ticket comes in."

Sandra shrugged and shut the door, moving back to the table to sit again. "If they want to act like fools for a few minutes, that's on them. But they better be back at their desks by the time our meeting is over."

Rob nodded. He had no doubt that if the help desk bullpen wasn't quiet by the time he and Sandra finished their meeting, there would be a whole different kind of hell being raised. And he would have Sandra's back if that hell needed raising.

Chapter Eight

Thursday evening, Rob found himself sneaking glances out the front window of his house, waiting for Mia's little car to pull up. When it finally did, he grinned. Hugo looked enormous sitting in the passenger seat, ears pricked and tongue lolling. The dog waited patiently while Mia unbuckled his harness from the contraption that attached him to the seat belt—his "car seat" Rob had joked when Mia had first shown it to him—and the dog walked at Mia's side to the front door, not ranging around or pulling on his leash.

"Dad, we're here," Mia called as she opened the front door. "Your grandpuppy is ready for his visit."

"And granddad is ready for his grandpuppy," Rob said, coming into the entryway and dropping a kiss on Mia's cheek before he sank to his knees and rubbed Hugo's head. "Who's a handsome boy? Do you take after your granddad?"

Hugo panted and squeezed his eyes shut, haunches thumping to the floor.

"Seriously, Mia. He's looking great. And obedience training looks like it's going well, too."

"Yeah, we're working hard at it." Mia trailed a fingertip between the dog's ears and Hugo looked up at her, mouth closing, attentive to her voice.

Rob unbuckled Hugo's harness and took the tote bag Mia transported the dog's things in when he visited. "No change in the routine?"

"Nope. He's had a little separation anxiety lately, but I'm hoping that's a phase. I have his crate in the car. I've been crating him again at night, which seems to help."

"Dogs like their dens," Rob said. "Let me help you get it out."

Following Mia to her car, Rob wondered at the strange, almost wistful tone that seemed to come and go as she spoke. He knew better than to press, though. Mia would clam up if you tried to get her to open up before she was ready to talk about a thing. Instead, he wrestled the folded crate out of Mia's car and brought it inside, setting it up in a corner of his bedroom and lining it with the fluffy blanket Mia had brought from her apartment. He patted the blanket and looked at Hugo, who had followed them. "Nice place to sleep for you while you're here, Hugo." The dog stepped readily into the crate, turned in a circle, and dropped to lie down, heaving a huge sigh. "Yeah. He's going to be more comfortable with his own spot. Thanks for bringing it, honey. That couldn't have been easy to wrangle on your own."

"No biggie. Thanks again, Dad." Mia hugged him around the waist, hard.

"Oof. You're welcome." He patted her back, trying to think of a sly way to broach the topic of her odd manner when the doorbell rang.

"You expecting someone?" Mia looked up at him.

"Nope. Probably someone selling siding."

"Then go send him about his business, Pops."

"Aye aye, Admiral." Rob gave an exaggerated salute and Mia groaned.

"Dad. You're such a dork."

Kari fidgeted on Rob's doorstep, wishing she had thought to get his cell phone number last weekend. But no. He was right next door, so why should she need his number?

Well, she needed it because she wanted to see if he was willing to be her "bozo buffer" on Sunday evening. And she'd prefer to be shot down over the phone. Much less humiliating than in person. But no. She had tried to think of a different alternative for days, but Sapna was right. Rob was the perfect candidate.

For bozo buffer.

She needed to think of a better term. Fast. Now. Before the door opened.

Rob opened the door. *Oh.* She hadn't remembered quite how handsome he was. And the smile that lit his eyes gave her that tingly feeling again.

A curly head popped out from behind him. *Oh, crap. Huge mistake.* Rob hadn't mentioned a girlfriend. Kari's molasses-slow brain took in the woman's unlined face. A girlfriend... maybe half his age?

Kari's smile froze on her face as the whole scene careered into a slow-motion train wreck.

"Hi!" The petite, curly-headed brunette darted around Rob, sticking her hand out. Kari extended her own hand, her reactions seeming slow compared to the tiny woman before her. "I'm Mia," the pixie said, and comprehension washed over Kari.

"Oh!" Kari's hand engulfed Mia's. Now the young woman's face seemed perfectly familiar from the photos of her that littered the house. *His daughter, fool.* "I'm Kari. It's so nice to meet you. Rob's said so many great things about you." Of course he had. She was his daughter. Mia was going to think she was the worst kind of suck-up.

Mia's gaze scanned Kari's face, her expression unreadable as she withdrew her hand. "You must be the mysterious new neighbor."

Kari's laugh sounded brittle in her own ears. "Not so mysterious. Clueless, yeah. Your dad's been a big help."

Mia poked Rob in the belly and he responded by giving what looked like a very practiced, very over the top impression of having been stabbed, grunting dramatically as he bent over, clutching his stomach and groaning. "Yeah, Pops is good people." At that point, a black and brown furry face peered around from behind Rob's legs. Mia pointed into the house. "Hugo. Back inside, boy."

The dog gave Kari an inscrutable look before retreating back into Rob's house. "How about we all go inside," Rob said. "Are you having problems with your house?" he asked Kari as he retreated backwards into the entryway.

Before Kari could try to calculate how embarrassing it would be to ask Rob if he'd come to dinner at her house in front of his daughter, Mia said, "I gotta get going, Dad. I'll see you Saturday to pick up the furball. Thanks for taking him for me."

Rob bent to kiss her on the cheek. "No problem. But I wish you'd stay for dinner."

"No time. Rain check." Mia pointed at him with a fierce look. "And be sure to feed yourself before you get hangry. You know how you get."

"Yes ma'am." Rob performed an exaggerated salute. "Have fun doing...whatever you won't tell me you're doing."

A pang went through Kari at their interaction. Their banter reminded her of how she and Sam had been in happier times.

"Don't worry. I'll tell you later. I don't want to jinx it."

"Thanks. Now I'm even more curious."

Mia stuck out her tongue. "Suffer. Just like you made me do on my tenth birthday."

"It's not my fault you're gullible."

"Yes, it is. Genetics."

"Oof." He reprised his stabbed act, but this time he seemed to feign a flesh wound, not a mortal one.

"The truth hurts, Dad." Mia turned and gave Kari a brief wave and an enigmatic look. "Nice to meet you, Kari." She bent to thump her palm against the dog, who had come out again and was leaning into her legs, looking up at her with what must be canine devotion. Kari didn't know much about dogs but Hugo's gaze seemed…soulful. Intense. "Be good for granddad, fuzzball." And with that, she was off, walking to a tiny subcompact parked at the curb.

"Wow," Kari said as they watched Mia drive away. "She's…"

"A tiny tyrant," Rob said, affection suffusing his face as he stepped back into the house, ushering the dog inside and waving for Kari to follow.

Kari stepped over the threshold. "I was going to say, 'very self-possessed.' But you know her best."

"Both are accurate."

"What happened on her tenth birthday?"

He turned to face her, a sheepish look on his face. "I convinced her she wasn't getting the bike she wanted so desperately. Which of course I had bought for her. She was more furious than gratified when her birthday rolled around and there it was."

"Ouch."

"Seemed like a good idea at the time. I guess she's scarred by the experience," he said dryly.

"Completely. Very badly-adjusted young woman you got there," Kari said, piling on the sarcasm.

"Anyway." Rob folded his arms across his chest. "What can I do you for?"

Kari paused, his closed stance throwing her off.

"We're still on for Saturday, right?" he asked, his voice carrying an anxious edge.

"Oh! Yes." Kari, focused on Sunday's dinner, had almost forgotten about Saturday's painting appointment.

"Decided what room you want to paint?"

"Um. Yeah." It was her bedroom. And now that felt awkward. In fact, the whole interchange seemed to be spiraling into a black hole of awkward.

"Care to share what room?"

"My bedroom?"

"Was that a question or an answer?"

"An answer." Kari took a deep breath. "But I have another favor to ask you." She felt her mouth skewing in an apologetic twist.

"Seems dire, if you're making that face. What is it?"

Kari exhaled her response in a rush. "Come to dinner on Sunday?"

Crap. Crap, crap, crapshit. This was why he avoided even becoming friends with single women. It always went there. Then it went ugly. He opened his mouth to try to let her down easy, but Kari went on, her words tumbling out.

"Not a date." Her cheeks were flushed. Beyond pink, definitely red. "It's just that I'm having Sam and her new guy over for dinner. And I need a bozo buffer."

"Bozo buffer?" He couldn't help the startled laugh that erupted from his lips.

"Oh, God." Kari's hands clapped to her flaming cheeks, then slid up to cover her eyes. "I'm so sorry. I'm terrible at this."

"What is 'this'?"

"I don't even know. Don't worry. I'm not asking for a date or anything. Just someone to…"

"Buff bozos?"

"I'm sorry," she said again. "I can't believe I said that. It's just my colleague's term for someone who is invited over to make an awkward dinner less…awkward."

"Sounds like fun."

"I'm sorry," she said. He wished she'd stop saying that. "I —I'll leave. I've made a mess of everything. I understand if you don't want to paint on Saturday. Or have anything to do with me ever again." She extended a hand, palm out, her face averted as she turned to go.

He touched her wrist. "No, Kari. Stop." She paused, looking from his hand to his face and he withdrew. "I want to teach you to paint. And I'd be happy to buffer bozos. Can I bring anything?"

Kari, whose eyes hadn't left his face, frowned. "You're… willing to do this?"

He shrugged. "It's dinner. I've met Sam once. It seems pretty low-stress."

"Even knowing what you know about our history?"

"Isn't that what I'm supposed to be there for? So that doesn't come up?"

Kari grimaced. "Uh. Yeah. I guess that's the idea."

"So, when do I show up with a bottle of wine and a dampening effect on overly personal conversations?"

Kari's eyes widened, the color in her cheeks ebbing. "Six?"

"Sure. Red or white wine?"

"What?"

"I'm very good at bringing the wine. Red or white?"

"Oh. I don't know. I was going to make pot roast."

"Red wine, then."

Kari's shoulders sagged. "I don't know why you're being so nice to me."

"I like you." Apparently, blurting out whatever came into your head was contagious. Kari's eyes were wary now. "Don't worry. I'm not propositioning you." Though he was aware of a perverse sense of disappointment threading through him to know that she hadn't been asking him for a date.

Make up your mind, Fox. Either you want her or you don't.

And you do, but you know why you can't act on it. Remember. You're a dating disaster. She lives next door. Bad combination.

Kari swallowed, her throat convulsing. "Thanks. I owe you."

"Not at all. You're feeding me, right?"

She laughed. "Yeah. That's kind of the point of dinner."

"And here I was, thinking it was about avoiding awkwardness."

Kari waved a hand as if bidding farewell to something receding in the distance. "That ship has sailed. Rest in peace, the idea that my life can be free of drama or awkwardness."

Rob laughed. "See you on Saturday morning to go to the home center and pick out paint?"

"Eight if you want breakfast." Kari made finger-guns with both hands and winked.

"You're on." Rob opened the door for her and she slipped out, still looking a little sheepish. As he was flipping the deadbolt, his phone buzzed in his back pocket. He pulled it out. A text from Mia.

I like her. You should date her.

Kari fled back to her house as if the hounds of hell were on her trail. Or the hounds of awkward.

And awkward was probably a circle of hell that, if it hadn't been invented yet, definitely needed to be invented. And it definitely had hounds. But instead of striking terror, they probably made you cringe in embarrassment.

She'd prefer the terror.

Back inside her own walls, Kari's rapidly thudding heart slowed. Her eyes scanned across the motif she had painted over the archway to the dining room. The blue symbols were like a talisman now, a shiny stone you kept in your pocket and rubbed your fingers across for luck.

Get yourself together, Halvorsen.

Another cringe-hound hit her full in the chest. She had to let Sam know there was going to be one more at her dinner. Digging her phone out of her pocket, mentally composed a text. Swallowing hard, she typed.

Hey Sammie. Neighbor Rob will also be at dinner Sunday, just FYI.

Sam must have had her phone near at hand, because her response was almost immediate.

Oh? She appended a "thinking" emoji.

Kari's heart sped up again. Crap. She had been so focused on finding a bozo buffer, she hadn't considered how it would look to Sam. She wanted Sam to like him and if her niece thought he was a missed love connection, that wouldn't go well. She glanced at the motif on the wall, then the glowing color of the dining room, the alterations to her home giving her an idea.

Yeah. I owe him. He's helped me with a few things in the new place. Is that ok?

92

Dots pulsed and Sam's answer popped onto Kari's screen. *It's your place. Your dinner. Your call.*

That was right. To a point. She had invited Sam and Graham to build bridges. But Rob was there as a sort of wall.

He's been great, she typed. *I really do owe him.*

Great. Look forward to getting to know him. Sam's response made Kari breathe a little easier until dots pulsed across her phone's screen again. Kari braced for a question or innuendo.

But no, Sam just sent a winking emoji.

Chapter Nine

On Saturday morning, Rob opened his front door and ushered Hugo into the house after their walk. The dog was definitely going through an anxious phase, as Mia had said. He hadn't destroyed any of Rob's things when he was at work, but on Friday Rob had come home to a stuffed toy that Hugo had played with peacefully for over six months, now pulled to pieces, stuffing and scraps of fabric strewn across the living room.

"I think you're going to spend at least part of the day outside, boy." It wasn't due to be a very hot day and the side of the house would provide shade if needed. Rob took the dog to the fenced yard, making sure there was a bowl of water and a few toys for him to play with.

Hugo was romping around with his half-inflated ball when Rob double-checked the latch on the gate and took himself over to Kari's. Eight o'clock on the dot. The door opened just as he remembered Mia's text.

I like her. You should date her.

Something must have shown on his face because Kari gave him a funny look. "What's up?" she asked.

"Nothing. Just my daughter being little miss busybody." He stepped into the house and followed her to the kitchen. He inhaled deeply, a savory, spicy aroma turning up the corners of his mouth. "Sausage?"

"Yeah. From the Dutch market." Kari picked up a spatula and turned the sausage patties in a pan. They were practically the size of hamburgers. "How do you like your eggs?"

Rob's stomach rumbled and he patted it as if to soothe a slavering beast. Which he guessed it was. "Over medium. Yum."

"Grab yourself a cup of coffee and have a seat. It'll all be ready soon." She cracked eggs into another pan and Rob did as he was told, appreciating the way she tidied up after herself as she went, never pausing, never not doing something. Efficient, her lovely long fingers handling tasks with liquid grace. Within minutes, he had a loaded plate in front of him.

"I could get all too used to this," he said. Kari's eyes locked with his for a moment and the coffee cup she was lifting to her mouth paused for the barest second before he went on, talking a little too quickly. "Getting fed like this, I mean."

"Ah." She nodded and sipped, her face remaining neutral.

Crap. He'd just stepped in it, he was pretty sure.

"Do you know what color you'd like in your bedroom?" Crap again. He'd meant to turn the conversation to more neutral territory. But...*bedroom*. There it was. And yes, right on cue, Kari's cheeks were turning pink.

"I found a really soft green. Something peaceful. My bedroom furniture is white, so...it seems like it would be a good contrast." She dug in her pocket, pulling out a paint chip. "This."

"Nice. Is there a lot of furniture?"

She shook her head. "No, just the bed and a chest of drawers. Two nightstands. I already took out the lamps and the few knickknacks I keep in there."

That was just like what he had already observed of her. She thought ahead, was tidy and methodical. And her possessions were minimal, apparently.

"I'm guessing you've been something of a rolling stone in your life."

"What do you mean?"

"You haven't gathered any moss. No mess. Nothing extraneous." He waved at the neat kitchen. Barring a couple of things she had needed to make breakfast and a toaster, the counters were empty. None of the usual plethora of mixers, bowl sets, and other kitchen miscellany that so frequently never found a home inside overcrowded cupboards. The other rooms he had been in were similarly free of clutter. Whereas his house…he almost cringed at the difference, remembering the swamp of catalogs and other paperwork she had purged for him.

As if she could read his mind, her eyes narrowed and she said, "You're not hoarding lingerie catalogs again, are you?"

He waved a hand. "No. I've been sorting my mail over the recycle bin just like you said I should."

Her face relaxed and she winked at him before returning her attention to her breakfast. The wink disconcerted him far more than it should.

I like her.

You should date her.

Damn his adorable, meddlesome, maddening, good-hearted daughter anyway.

If he had met Kari even ten years ago when he still had hope that he could have a functional romantic relationship with a woman, he would have leaped at her, a bouquet in one fist and his heart in the other, both on offer.

But those days were over.

Rob seemed unusually quiet this morning. Quiet and no-nonsense. Kari found she missed the awkward babbling, the unselfconscious dad-jokey Rob of last weekend. They finished their breakfast in silence and Rob helped her with the washing up before they got into Kari's car and made for the home center. This time, Rob didn't fill her cart with as many items as before and she didn't feel so at sea with the things he did tell her to buy. She snagged a couple of free paint stirrers without prompting, causing his eyebrows to lift and his lips to curve in a smile. His approval to her tiny demonstration of having learned something from their last trip shot warmth through her chest and her heart seemed to trip over itself.

Loading the bags of supplies into the trunk of her car, she said, "Everything okay?"

"Sure, why do you ask?"

"You're...quiet."

He paused with his hand on her open trunk lid. His eyes slid sideways to meet hers, then looked straight ahead and he slammed the trunk shut. "Mia."

They got into the car and buckled their seat belts. "You're worried about her?"

This time, he didn't meet her eyes. "Not as such. She's just making me think."

"About what?" she asked. He looked out the passenger window instead of responding. "Or shouldn't I ask?" she added quickly. She started the car and backed out of the parking spot, her pulse hammering, feeling like she'd somehow overstepped some sort of boundary she wasn't even aware existed. But of course he would protect his relationship with his daughter. "I'm sorry. I shouldn't have pushed."

Rob rubbed his hands on his thighs. "No. It's fine. To be honest, my issue with Mia is that she's pushing me about you."

"Me?" Kari's mind went blank and she was happy for the need to pay attention to the road and the traffic and the other drivers. Because...*what?*

"Yeah. You. She texted me after she met you."

Kari forced herself to keep her eyes on the road. Hands at ten and two. "She...did?" Mia had been self-possessed and almost businesslike. What would she have been pushing Rob about?

Oh. Of course. She didn't approve and Rob's primary focus was his daughter. And that was absolutely the right priority for him to have. But it stung.

Kari swallowed hard. "She doesn't like me, does she?"

"What?" Rob's sharp tone startled her from her steady focus on the car ahead of hers. She glanced at him and then ahead and gasped, her foot slamming on the brake pedal in response to the red lights blooming in front of her. Her chest collided with the seat belt and one hand abandoned its clutch on the steering wheel to land on her sternum.

"I'm so sorry," she said, looking from the car ahead of them to him and back again. "Are you okay?"

"I'll survive a sudden braking with no impact," he said dryly.

She swallowed. "Good. Okay." Sure. All she had to do was drive home and...spend the entire day with him.

Then dinner tomorrow.

Oh, yes. This was great. His daughter disapproved of her and now he felt obligated to help her paint her bedroom.

"Please tell her we're just friends. I'd hate for anything to be…well, more awkward than it already is."

He paused before replying. "If that's what you want."

Well, there it was. She didn't want anything more than friendship from him. It was probably for the best. It would make it easier to put an end to Mia's well-intentioned meddling.

…So why did he feel disappointed?

His phone chimed and he dug it out of his pocket. "Mia's on her way over to pick up Hugo."

Kari kept her eyes on the road, showing him nothing but an inscrutable profile.

"She doesn't dislike you, for what it's worth. She'll be glad you and I are becoming friends."

Kari swallowed, her shoulders relaxing a fraction as she pulled up in front of her house. "I can bring the stuff inside if you have to get Hugo ready."

"What, pack up his jammies and his sippy cups?" Rob remembered getting Mia ready to go to her mom's when she was little. The memory of her solemn little face gave him a pang.

Kari shrugged, her arms loaded down with the paint can and a bag of supplies. "Never had a dog, so don't really know what it entails."

He grabbed the other bag and shut the trunk. "Just need to put a couple of his toys in a bag, fold his crate up. He's got food and bowls and stuff that stay at my house. And if one of his toys ends up not going home with him, no biggie. He'll probably be back at my place for a few days before the month is out."

"It seems like he's almost as much your dog as he is

hers."

"Sort of."

"You two have a good relationship—you and Mia."

"We do. She was a good kid. She's turned into a good adult. I'm proud of being her dad. Liz and I weren't a good married couple but we managed to raise a great daughter somehow."

"That couldn't have been easy."

"Easier than being married and fighting all the time. Liz doesn't like me anymore and I don't exactly have warm and fuzzy feelings about her, but we both prioritized Mia, so it worked out."

Kari led him to her bedroom. It was small and sunny. She had already stripped the bed, but they would have to move it into the center of the room and remove the other furniture. He told her this and she nodded, darting around him and cutting him off as he started for one of her bedside tables.

"I'll get that," she said.

Puzzled, he moved to the other side of the bed and lifted its mate. Kari hustled out of the room with the table, her chin tucked to her chest, cheeks flushing.

What the…? Sudden realization broke through his confusion. She must have something in the drawer of that nightstand. Something personal. Intimate, even. And why shouldn't she?

Trouble was, it was giving him ideas. Pictures rolling through his head that had no business being there. It felt invasive and creepy.

Shut it down. He followed her to the other bedroom, which held no furniture, only a few cardboard boxes. He set the nightstand down against the wall and followed Kari back to her bedroom to move the dresser and shift the bed. He wished the task was more mentally challenging—something to chase those images out of his head. But no. As stripped-down and uninviting as the bare mattress might be, it was still a bed. He felt a little better when they tossed a tarp over it, obscuring the shape of the furniture. Another text from Mia told him she was at his house, ready to get the dog.

"I'll be right back," he said after showing Kari how she should tape off the baseboards and the window and door frames. Hurrying over to his house, he found Mia sitting on the doorstep. "You could have let yourself in, kiddo."

"I know. I was just enjoying the sunshine. It's finally getting warm." Mia stood and dusted off her rear. "How's my boy doing?"

"Hugo's fine. So's your dad." He winked at Mia and unlocked the house.

She rolled her eyes. "I can see you're fine. What'cha doing over at Kari's house?" Her voice took on a singsong quality like the k-i-s-s-i-n-g schoolyard taunt. "I hope I'm interrupting something."

He gave her a level look. "You are. I'm helping her paint."

Mia wrinkled her nose. "Darn. But you like her, don't you?"

"I like her too well to screw things up. So get your button nose out of my business, cupcake." He tapped the nose in question and Mia turned an exasperated expression his way. He saw a shadow of her mother in that look. Her features were such a blend of his family's and Liz's that she was usually just Mia. But occasionally, she channeled her mother completely.

"Probably better that you take it slow anyway. I know how you are." Leave it to Mia to ignore him. He picked up Hugo's leash and walked to the back door. The dog came bounding at Mia, crashing into her legs and rubbing his face on her jeans in long sweeps, groaning with pleasure.

Something about what Mia had said nagged at him. "Wait a minute. What do you mean you know how I am?"

She looked up from rubbing Hugo's ears. "You're impulsive, Dad. I'd be willing to bet that ninety-nine percent of your dating issues were you rushed in too fast."

He snorted. He had scrupulously kept his dating life to the weeks he didn't have Mia when she was little, and even when she was a teenager he had only introduced her to a couple of the women he had gotten more serious about. "How would you know anything about it? I just always picked women who got the wrong idea."

Settling her hands on her hips, Mia straightened and pierced him with a look. "And how did they get that idea?"

Kari pressed the last strip of blue tape onto the window frame and opened the window. All too soon it would be air-conditioning season. Today might even be the last day she could get away with open windows.

In fact, the weather was warm enough that Kari went into the second bedroom and rummaged in her chest of drawers for an old pair of shorts. Slipping these on, she heard Rob let himself back into the house. "All set with Hugo and Mia?" she asked, stepping into the hallway.

He froze for a second when he saw her and she looked down at the shorts. "Yeah," she said. "They're ratty. But I won't care if I get paint on them."

He cleared his throat. "No formality in painting. Yeah. Got Hugo's crate loaded into Mia's car and the granddoggo is back with his mom. Ready to get started?"

"Sure." She watched while Rob stirred the paint and doled some of it into two smaller pots. He handed her one of them with a brush.

"You can start to cut in around the baseboards. I'll take the ceiling."

"I haven't taped that yet."

He gave her a wink. "I don't need it."

"You don't?"

"I'm that good, sweetheart." *Sweetheart?* His cheekbones reddened and he coughed, moving across the room to set up a ladder. "Don't load your brush with too much paint. At the same time, you shouldn't be able to hear it rub against the wall too much. If you can, it's too dry."

"Got it." She knelt and applied a long stripe of paint to the wall. "Will the tape really keep the paint from seeping onto the baseboard? One of the things I love about this house is how pristine the natural wood trim is."

"That's why we got the good tape," he said, his brow furrowed in concentration, his arm extended to apply paint to his corner. "If you pressed it down well, you should be fine."

"Good." They worked in silence for a while, with the creaks of the ladder being the only sounds. Reaching the door, Kari was finally able to stand to paint around the frame and realized her knees were throbbing. "Ow." She rubbed her bright red kneecaps. "I can see why you took the ladder job."

Rob paused in the act of moving the ladder and winced, seeing her knees. "Maybe the shorts were a bad idea. Jeans aren't much padding but they're better than nothing."

"I have a better idea." Kari left her painting things on the floor and went to the backyard, fetching the padded kneeler she used to weed the flower beds. Bringing it inside, she waved it like a banner. "This'll help."

Rob nodded and returned his attention to the wall he was working on. Kari frowned, wondering what was making him so moody.

Chapter Ten

Rob had thought he had a good idea of what Kari's legs might look like. Turns out, jeans—even skinny jeans—were far too concealing for any real idea. Rob hadn't ever thought of himself as a leg, ass, or breast man. Kari's legs might have him rethinking that policy, though.

Though her ass in that ratty old cotton looked pretty good to him too. And—

Shut. It. Down. His forehead was damp. It was just warm in here. That was all. Which meant he had to work quickly so they could start to roll the walls before the cut-in edge dried too much. Just a few more feet and he could get to the rolling. And get the hell out of here. Away from temptation.

Back to rattling around in his own house. Mere yards away. Where he would probably be plagued with calls or texts from Mia asking why he wasn't dating the perfectly nice single lady next door.

Who, he reminded himself, had made it clear in the car that she didn't want anything more than friendship. So. That should be the end of it.

He completed his part of the cutting-in and looked to see where Kari was with her part of the task. She was only a short way behind him, just a few feet to go. He got down from the ladder and looked at what she had done. It was nice, even work. Unsurprising, considering the good job she'd made of the motif in the living room.

"Did you study as an artist?" he asked.

She looked up from her crouch at the baseboard. "Why do you ask?"

"Your sketching. The nice job you did in the living room. You seem to have a gift and you handle paint well."

Her mouth tightened as she dipped her brush and swiped color along the wall. "Thanks. I took as much art as I could while I was in school. I've enjoyed it as a hobby ever since."

"That's it?"

"That's what?" She didn't look up from where she was connecting the line of paint at the baseboard.

"You've never done more with it?"

"How should I?" Rising to her feet she waved her free hand down her legs. "Voila. No housemaid's knee."

Rob's jaw tightened at her calling attention to her legs. "I mean...like I said. You're gifted. You have an eye and...I don't know."

"That's sweet." She picked up her paint pot. "Rolling now?"

"I'm sorry. Did I offend you?"

"No." The tightness in her face told a different story.

"I think I did. But—"

She held up a hand. "I'm not offended, but can we not do the whole, 'Oh, that is really nice, you could make so much money from doing that artistic thing' conversation? Because the economics don't work. I've done the math."

With effort, Rob swallowed the spurt of defensive irritation that had swelled up when she lifted her hand. "What do you mean?"

"Sorry if you meant something else, but when people find out you can knit or draw or do...basically anything creative, they immediately want to know why you don't do it for a living. And it's usually not practical. Like, at all. The economics are totally skewed."

Almost in spite of himself, Rob was intrigued. "What do you mean?"

"Just one example? Say I knit someone a pair of socks. I use a thick yarn, which means they knit up fast. Maybe I can do them in a weekend if that's pretty much all I do. The skein I knit them from costs twenty dollars. Which is cheap, if you want good yarn."

"Twenty dollars for a pair of socks?" Rob's mind reeled. He bought his socks in a five-pack at Costco for ten dollars.

Kari nodded. "You're not even factoring in my work. One sock? Maybe six hours of work. Two socks? Congratulations. Your handmade socks are now over a hundred dollars at just minimum wage. Even if you use the cheapest yarn possible, the labor costs mean that everyone's cute comment about how you could quit your job and do this for a living are totally bananas." Her hand sliced down in a gesture of finality. "I'm a good office manager and I make okay money. I do that for a living. I craft and do art for love."

She was right. He hadn't thought it through. He wondered what it might feel like to be on the receiving end of Kari's art created for love. He'd be willing to bet it felt fantastic.

"Can we roll the walls now?" Kari asked with forced brightness. She had forgotten how exhausting this conversation was. The whole, *Oh! You can do this creative thing!* Followed by an immediate demand that you abandon your actual career in pursuit of some artistic pipe dream.

"Sure."

Rob's instant capitulation made Kari tilt her head. "That was easy."

He shrugged. "Mia wants to be in publishing. I've heard her stories. And she doesn't even want to be on the writer's end of the industry. Getting into the editorial side can be hard enough."

Kari reflected on the flood of applications they got at work for every rare editorial opening. "True. Sorry if I sounded defensive."

"No, I get it. Let's get that color up." Rob poured paint into two roller pans and showed her how to load the roller and get started by painting a big W, then filling in with easy strokes until the coverage was nice and even. Kari moved to the opposite wall and started rolling. It was incredibly satisfying, seeing the soft green blossom across the wall's surface. And the repetitive motion was soothing.

The wet sound of the thick paint reminded her of sex, though. It had been such a long time. So long since she had given up on the idea of dating or relationships, just let that part of her life fall away as her friends paired off and she... didn't. And with no relationships, no sex. Just a ménage with Buzz and Vibe, her favorite vibrators she kept in her nightstand drawer.

The last lover she'd had was...good lord. Had five years just passed like that? She and Max had had a nice relationship. It was casual, they enjoyed each other's company. The sex was nice. Not mind-blowing, but he had been considerate and attentive and knew where the clitoris was. Then he got a new job in Seattle and that was that.

Slick, slick, slick. Her roller ran across the wall, rhythmic and lascivious. She glanced over her shoulder at Rob, his back to her, seeming to be completely focused on his task. Her gaze dropped to his ass and she swallowed and turned around again, bending to load more paint on her roller.

She had no business thinking about his ass or any other of his body parts. But damn, it was a nice ass. His old, faded jeans rode a little low on his hips. No high-waisted "dad jeans" for dad-jokey Rob Fox.

Great, now she was completely worked up and flustered from the sound of paint and the sight of a nice ass. At least she had managed to get to the nightstand where Buzz and Vibe lived before Rob did. That would have been just perfect, having the drawer slide open and dump them on the floor, silicone bouncing off the hardwood. The perfect metaphor for her nonexistent love life and the way she seemed to slide from one awkward moment to the next with this man.

She reached the end of the wall she was working on and realized Rob had started painting the last wall. "Wow. That went fast."

"Small room. You can start pulling the tape up if you want."

Glad for something to do that didn't involve watching Rob's backside, she bent and pulled at the edge of the tape. It came up in a long, satisfying strip, the sloppy bits of paint that had dripped magically peeled away from the baseboard.

"Wow. This is great." Kari balled up the tape between her hands and bent to get the next strip. "It looks fantastic."

Rob made a funny sound in his throat.

Great idea, genius. Ask her to do something that requires her to bend over a lot. He tried to keep his eyes rigidly fixed on the wall in front of him, but he ran out of wall to paint before she ran out of tape to take up. Swallowing hard, he poured the excess paint back in the can and stripped the roller covers into a trash bag.

"I'll just take these to rinse in your utility sink," he told her and then fled to the basement where he got the roller pans and brushes cleaner than they had any right to be. Mia's words floated through his head as he rinsed a brush. *You're impulsive, Dad. I'd be willing to bet that ninety-nine percent of your dating issues were you rushed in too fast.*

Could she have had a point? Granted, when he was dating he had been juggling fatherhood and his job. The relationships had had a weird rhythm to them—intense for a week when Mia was at her mom's, then on hold the next week when his daughter was with him. Had that exacerbated whatever issues he had with picking women? Had it given them the wrong impression? What kind of impression was he giving Kari?

He was pensive as he went back up the stairs and rejoined Kari in her bedroom. It looked fresh and more personal, somehow. "What now?" she asked.

"Well, you can either watch paint dry or I can take you out to lunch. Can't move the furniture back in until the paint has cured."

Her brows pinched together. "Does that mean I can't sleep in here tonight?"

"You might not want to. It will probably still smell like paint."

"Ugh." Kari's nose wrinkled. "I hadn't thought about that. I guess it's the couch for me."

That's right. She doesn't have a bed in her guest room. "Would you get any sleep at all? I mean, you're almost as tall as I am."

"One of my few extravagances was getting a couch long enough for me to stretch out on," she said. "Naps. Naps are important."

"Still not the best way to sleep for a whole night," he said, an idea that was either wonderful or terrible taking shape in his mind.

She waved a hand. "I'll be fine. But let *me* take *you* out for lunch."

"Let's get everything tidied up, at least."

"You know, if I hadn't seen your office last week, I would find your commitment to keeping my home improvement projects neat very impressive."

"And…since you have?"

"I just find it very confusing."

"I'm a deep and complex individual," he said, taking two corners of the tarp while she did the same at the other end of the bed.

She glanced at him as they started to fold the big sheet of plastic. "Oh. Really?"

"No. Shallow and inconsistent. Ask my daughter if you don't believe me."

"I doubt she would say anything of the kind."

"Maybe not. She did tell me I was impulsive, though." Which, he realized, stung coming from his daughter. He'd tried so hard to give her stability. Had he failed somehow?

"Are you?"

"I guess I was. For a long time. Not sure if I am now. The circumstances haven't come up for many years."

"What do you mean?" She took the folded tarp from him and held it against her chest.

"Dating. Women."

"Ah." She looked pensive. Suddenly, he realized it was

possible that there was someone in her life. She had never mentioned anyone, but he also hadn't asked.

"What about you?" he asked.

Her eyes flicked up, then down. "I'm definitely not impulsive."

He gritted his teeth. "I meant dating, but that's probably none of my business."

"Oh, no. Haven't for years." She stooped to pick up the paint can and he stared at her.

"Really?"

"Why's that so surprising? You just said the same thing about yourself."

"Yeah, but somehow...I don't know." He waved a hand at her. "You're..."

"Too tall."

I was going to say sexy. "Too tall for who?"

"For most men. They seem to like women who are about Mia's size, even if they're taller than I am. And if they're shorter..."

"You're not into them?"

"No, that's not it at all. Usually they're not into me. And sometimes they're too into the height—kind of a fetish thing." She stuck her tongue out. "Guys who are into 'Amazons.' It's kind of gross."

"How so?" God, he hoped his appreciation for her height wasn't gross.

"They do things like tell you that they're into being dominated after you've exchanged about five words."

Rob spluttered a surprised laugh. "Really?"

She nodded, a cynical look on her face. "Yeah. It's like, dude, I'm okay with being able to see the top of your head. But you can keep your sexual preferences to yourself until we've known each other for five minutes, okay?"

"Guys really do that?" Rob's mouth dropped open and he shook his head.

Kari nodded, remembering. "Oh, yes. And I have friends' stories from the online dating world that would probably curl your hair. Another reason I don't date is because I can't cope with the idea of what kinds of messages I might get in response to putting that I was almost six feet tall in my profile. 'Amazon' would be the least of it, I'm sure."

"It's unoriginal, too. I would have said Viking Shield Maiden," Rob said. But at least it was clear from the set of his eyebrows and the tilt of his mouth that he was joking.

"Yup. That's me. Totally scary."

"Put a broadsword in your hand and leather armor— never mind," he said as she started to laugh. "Now I'm just as bad as those other guys."

"But see, you managed to know me for a week or so before you busted out your leather armor fantasies. That's a little…less unacceptable?"

"Oof." Rob reprised his stabbed-in-the-gut act. The funny little gesture warmed her, reminiscent as it was of his routine with Mia.

"Let me get this stuff put away before this thing slices my fingers clean through," she said. The wire handle on the paint can was digging into her hand.

"Let me get that," he said, taking the can from her. "Ow," he said, cradling her hand and raising his eyebrows at the thin, angry red line that striped her fingers.

"It'll fade," she said, pulling back her hand and curling and uncurling her fingers, uncomfortably aware of the zing his touch had sent through her. "I'm starving. Let's get something to eat, huh?"

"Sure." He cleared his throat and they finished getting the painting things put away in silence, the awkwardness stretching between them like something elastic and sticky.

"Any idea of where you want to go for lunch?" If Kari hoped her words might magically re-set them back to the moment she had pulled her hand away, the hope died a swift death at his solemn gaze.

"I'm not picky. And Mia would probably say I'm ten minutes from going from merely hungry to what she calls 'hangry' and not responsible for my actions. There's a diner downtown that does good basic stuff if you're into that."

She shrugged and stuffed her fists in the pockets of her shorts. "Anything you like. It's on me, so if you want to go crazy, now's your chance." The weak joke also fell flat. God, her feelings were getting out of control.

He nodded. "Diner it is. I'll drive."

They headed for the front door where Kari paused and turned to him. "I still have your projector. Did you need it back?"

"Do you want to use it for something else?" He eyed her warily. She wondered if he thought she was trying to sever ties with him by giving it back.

"I'd love to. I was thinking about doing some other stuff in the kitchen. But doesn't it belong to your company?"

A tiny smile tugged at the corners of his lips. "Don't worry about it. We have three of them in our inventory and I don't think we've ever had more than one in use at a time. Keep it as long as you want."

"As long as I'm not going to get you in trouble."

He leaned toward her as if to whisper secrets in her ear. "It's okay. I'm the boss."

"Ooh." She laid a hand on her breastbone, feigning being impressed.

"Not gonna lie. It's good to be I.T. king."

She laughed outright at that. "I'm imagining you with a crown made of circuit boards."

And just like that, they were back to their easy companionship.

Chapter Eleven

"...**A**nd then she put her hands on her hips and with all the dignity an eight-year-old girl can muster, she said, '*Daddy*. I was being *sarcastic*.'"

Kari's mouth dropped open. "She didn't. At eight years old?"

Rob picked up his hamburger and nodded, grinning at the memory and proud of his daughter. "Yup. I should've known at that moment that she would end up working with words. The kid was precocious. She probably would have told you that herself at that age."

Kari shook her head. "Sam had her moments, but...I don't think I can imagine her saying that at eight. At twelve? Probably. At thirty-two? Absolutely." She took a bite of her sandwich, then shook her head, chewing.

"Did you and Sam grow up close?" Rob asked. "You seem as thick as thieves." Having shared some of Mia's greatest hits, he was eager to know more about Kari and her niece.

Kari looked up from her lunch with a wry grin. "I was

ten when she was born, so I've known her all her life. We were around each other a lot. My parents and Bjorn — my brother — and his family lived in the same little apartment building. Bjorn and his wife both worked and they dropped Sam off with *Mor* a lot. I'd come home from school and there'd be Sammie, coloring at the kitchen table. She and I have had our ups and downs, especially when each of us reached the teen years, but now we're very close. Or we were." Her face went apprehensive at that, and she put the potato chip she had been about to raise to her lips back on her plate. "Thanks for coming to dinner tomorrow. It means a lot."

An emotion Rob couldn't name pressed against his sternum. Something like longing and sadness and hope all twisted together. "I'm happy to help. You'll be okay, you and Sam. You know that, right?"

Her mouth twisted. "I hope so. I can't bring myself to count on anything, though. I'm afraid I'll be disappointed."

"She wants you to meet the new guy, right?"

Kari nodded, her eyes large and solemn.

"That sounds pretty big. Relax. If you can."

"Right. I'll get right on that. If I can figure out how."

He almost blurted, *Let me help you out with that.* It surprised him how much he still wanted to say it. He had thought his years without dating and without sex had slowly leached most sexual impulses out of him — or at least made them easier to control. And after all, he was forty-eight. But Kari had him thinking like, well, not like a teenager. He wasn't thinking about how he could gratify himself. He was thinking of how lovely her face would look all flushed and relaxed, her soft, pale hair spread out on the pillow, her lips curving into a satisfied smile.

These were thoughts he would have to shut down if he was going to implement his other idea.

"I was thinking about your bedroom situation—the paint smell," he added quickly.

She looked at him, eyebrows quirking in curiosity.

"Come over to my place. You can spend the night in Mia's old room."

"Mia's room?" She leaned back, the vinyl diner booth squeaking.

"Yeah. It *was* her room, that is. It's a guest room now. Not that I ever have guests. A guest room in theory, you could say. You could make the theoretical real. Imagine the power." Dammit, he was babbling again. But he hated the idea of her spending an uncomfortable night on the sofa. He could do this thing, make her life that little bit easier.

She frowned. "It would feel funny, staying in your daughter's space."

"It's not hers. She has her own place now. There's not so much as a Barbie left." He remembered the wistful pang he felt when he realized what a clean sweep Mia had made of the room when she got her first real apartment. But that was Mia for you—all or nothing.

"I'd hate to ask it of you. It seems invasive."

"You're not asking. I'm offering."

"Are you sure?"

"Let's put it this way. I don't know that I would get a minute's sleep thinking about you trying to make do on your sofa. You'd be doing me a favor."

She shot him a skeptical look. "Right."

"Really. Unless you don't want to, of course."

Kari considered his offer. It was tempting. Really, it was too tempting. A few minutes ago, something like heat had seemed to flare in his eyes, causing a corresponding rush of warmth to run through her. Now his face held nothing but friendly concern.

Or maybe she'd just been imagining that interested look. Wishing it into existence because she was attracted to him.

She thought about the picture he drew: her trying to get comfortable on her sofa when she was used to sprawling across her bed. He was right. It wasn't going to be great. In fact, it was going to make for a downright uncomfortable night. There was a difference between a two-hour nap on the sofa and trying to spend an entire night on it.

"If you really mean it, then yes, thanks. It's very nice of you."

"I do mean it. I'll just pop some sheets on the bed and it will be all ready for you."

"Turn down service and everything," she said.

He mimed a flourishing little bow. "I'll find a mint and put it on your pillow."

"I know you're kidding but somehow, that's the most adorable sentiment ever." Kari finished her sandwich and caught the waitress's eye. The waitress nodded and rifled through the check folders in the pocket of her apron, pulling one out and laying it in front of Kari. She turned to get her wallet out, putting her hand down on the folder when she saw Rob's arm snaking across the table out of the corner of her eye. "Don't even think about it."

"But…"

Kari looked at him, making her mouth a straight line and letting her gaze bore into him. Rob met her eyes and lowered the hand that hovered over hers. Warmth from his palm permeated the back of her hand. Kari swallowed.

"Your 'weaponized silence' doesn't scare me, Kari."

Kari's gaze skittered to the side. "I'm still buying lunch." She had to keep this about practicalities, otherwise her feelings might spill out and make everything horrible and messy. And probably ruin everything.

Rob's hand squeezed hers. "Okay."

"What are we doing?" Kari's voice was barely a whisper. Her eyelids slid closed, the darkness welcoming and terrifying in equal measure, Rob's hand squeezing hers again just the littlest bit.

"Kari."

"We're not talking about lunch, are we?"

"No." Rob's voice was husky. "I think we need to talk about how attracted I am to you. I should really have mentioned it before I offered Mia's room to you. Not that I had anything planned. Honestly. I was only offering a bed. For sleeping. I know you only think of me as a friend." Kari's eyes flew open as his words continued to tumble out. "But you should know. In case it makes you uncomfortable. I don't want you to be uncomfortable."

"Rob. Shh." Kari lifted her free hand. "I'm not uncomfortable. Well, I am. But not because I only think of you as a friend."

"What?"

Kari's cheeks flamed. "You're really attractive," she admitted in a tiny voice. But god it felt good to finally be able to say it.

"*I* am?"

"You own a mirror, right?"

He shrugged. "I'm a forty-eight-year-old dad. I haven't dated in almost a decade. I've gotten to a point where I don't really think about it."

"A decade?"

"Yeah. Turns out I was bad at dating. Or bad at being in relationships. Or just picked the wrong women. So, I quit dating. It just wasn't worth it. Too much of a distraction from raising Mia. But then this beautiful Viking Shield

Maiden moves in next door and I find myself thinking inappropriate thoughts because painting a wall sounds…" His cheeks reddened.

"Like sex," Kari finished. "You thought so too? It was driving me nuts today."

Rob's eyes slid closed and he chuckled softly to himself. "So where do we go from here?"

"You're asking me?" Kari gaped at him a little.

Rob shrugged. "I don't have any bright ideas, but I was hoping you might."

"You mean other than acting on it? Seeing where it goes?"

"Not the best idea."

Her head tilted and she gave him a curious look. "What do you mean?"

He winced. "I like you. I want you to keep liking me. So that's probably the worst kind of idea."

"Why?"

"I mean my past—the breakups were always ugly."

One corner of her mouth quirked in a tiny half-smile. "Oh. I see. You're an incurable optimist."

"Well, we're both here, both single."

"True. But who says we have to launch into a full-scale romantic relationship right away?"

"So you *do* have an idea."

Kari shrugged. "Be friends. Feel our way forward. Don't rush things. And don't play out the ending before anything has started."

Rob rubbed his face, his unshaved weekend cheek rasping against his fingers. Trouble was, he did want to rush things. "Mia did say I was too impulsive. And now it looks like the damn kid was probably right. Again."

"Sounds disconcerting, having your child be that perceptive."

"You have no idea."

She considered him for a moment. "We can also be really awkward at each other. That seems to work well for us."

"Oh," he said, "I have a lot of practice at being awkward. I'm expert-level awkward. Nationally ranked."

"I'll try not to compete. I think I can be satisfied with second-banana-level awkward."

"Okay, I'll just enjoy my seat on the awkward throne all alone," he said.

She tilted her head. "What does that throne look like?"

"It's made of silly putty and upholstered with banana skins, actually. So, hand over that second banana."

"Cute." She eased her hand out from under his, opening the check folder and glancing inside before closing it around a few bills she took from her wallet. The waitress walked past and Kari handed the folder off. "That's all set," she said to the other woman with a smile.

"You keep up with that level of smooth and you're not even rating second-banana awkward," Rob said, already missing the soft skin of her hand against his.

"Your standards are very low, you know that?" she said, getting to her feet.

"I don't know. I think I'm more discerning the older I get." He rose and walked with her out of the restaurant, letting his hand come to rest at the small of her back as they reached the door and he opened it for her, finally allowing himself to stake a tiny claim. "Speaking of which, have I made things so entirely awkward that you're going to suffer on your sofa tonight? I promise not to try anything funny if you want to stay in the guest room at my place."

"What if *I* tried something funny?" Her light blue gaze

slid sideways at him and seemed to pin him where he stood, one hand holding the door of the diner, his eyes locked with hers. As many lectures as Mia had given him on feminism and as much as he agreed with her, it somehow hadn't occurred to him that Kari might take initiative in that way.

The thought sent a secret thrill down his spine. "Is that your idea of taking it slow?"

"It might be my idea of making it awkward. You never know."

"I think I just might like your idea of awkward."

Kari's heart thudded and her stomach did a funny little ripple around her lunch. She didn't know how to do this anymore. It was like being a teenager again, figuring out which actions registered as flirting and generated interest and which ones fell flat. She was still a little in shock to know that Rob was attracted to her. And it was nice to know that he wasn't one of those who expected her to dominate him, mistaking her height for the person she actually was.

Rob let his hand fall away from her back as they walked to his car. Getting in, Kari glanced at them where they wrapped around the steering wheel. They looked strong. Capable. His right hand had a faded scar across his knuckles.

"What happened there?" she asked, touching the scar with a light fingertip.

He glanced at his hand, a wry expression going across his face. "Oh. That. That is one of the souvenirs from the Keeping Mia Alive file. That child seemed determined to either kill or maim herself at every turn there for a while."

Kari's eyes widened. "What did she do?"

"That time? Tried to take a header out of a whale watch

boat up off the coast of Massachusetts. I'm still not sure how I managed to get that scar, but flailing and grabbing at a six-year-old can cause some damage."

Kari's eyes widened. "I guess so."

"I'm also sure it took a few years off my life, but those scars are mostly invisible." He shot her a sideways glance and a wink at that, but Kari still felt the impact of his words. He had a special relationship with his daughter. And Kari still felt wary about Mia. Rob claimed that the young woman "didn't dislike" Kari. That wasn't the same as liking Kari or of approving if she and Rob decided to act on their attraction. Not the same thing at all.

"How's Mia's job search going?"

"I think it's still stalled out. She does get freelance gigs from time to time from writers she knows through the internet, but it's not enough to keep her afloat full time."

"What is she doing in the meantime?"

"Waiting tables." Rob made a face. "She tells me the money's good, but you hear all these stories about how horrible the restaurant business is for women and, well, I worry about her."

"I hate to break it to you, but just about all businesses are horrible for women," Kari said. But her heart had squeezed a little when he admitted that he worried. Even if Mia didn't like her, Kari felt warmly protective of his bond with his daughter. Which meant if Kari was threatening to it at all, she would have to back off entirely.

Rob pulled up in front of his house and turned off the engine. His fingers drummed on the steering wheel, but he didn't otherwise move. Kari steeled herself. This was it. He was reminded of Mia and Mia didn't like her and they were going to have to move back into "just friendly" territory because Mia had to come first. She told herself she was okay with that.

She didn't believe herself at all.

He took in a breath and let it out in an explosive exhale. "I'm trying to figure out how to tell you I want to keep spending time with you without it seeming overwhelming or intrusive," he said.

"You are?" Kari blinked.

"I am. And clever guy that I am I realized that by telling you I could tell you. Words are funny things. Useful in all sorts of contexts."

Kari laughed, a short, choked sort of sound. "We could keep working on your pile of paperwork."

Rob shook his head. "No. No more organization. No more home improvement, at least for today. What would you like to do that's just fun?"

Fun. Her life recently had revolved around moving and unpacking and then flat-out panicking about the weighty responsibility of owning the house. When had she last done something that was just purely fun?

The words came out of her before she could even think. "It's been an age since I've just sketched."

"Sketched. As in drawing?"

She nodded. "That's not exactly a fun group activity, though."

"Doesn't matter. I have an idea. Go get your sketching stuff and meet me back here in ten minutes."

Chapter Twelve

Rob rummaged through the hall closet that held all manner of things he didn't know what else to do with. An old tennis racket slipped and knocked against his elbow. He bit back a curse and rubbed the sore spot, seeing what he was looking for in the back corner. Grabbing the cardboard tube, a plastic case, and a tote bag, he detoured into the master bathroom and tossed a container of sunscreen into the tote. Moving to the kitchen, he added a couple of water bottles and a half-package of cookies. Lastly, he went to the basement and got a couple of folding chairs, blowing dust off of them before he hauled everything out to the car. Kari was just locking her front door as he closed the trunk on his motley collection of stuff.

"Where are we going?" She had a large pad of paper under her arm—bigger than the one she had used to create the motifs she painted on the wall—and a package of colored pencils in one hand.

"It's a surprise," he said, opening the passenger door for her with a little flourish.

"It's a good thing I trust you," she said, seating herself in the car. The statement made a tiny bloom of pleasure unfurl in his bloodstream, coursing throughout his body. He couldn't remember the last time he had enjoyed getting to know someone like this.

"Are you a generally trusting person?" he asked, sliding behind the wheel.

"No. Not at all." The bloom transformed to something more effervescent, more insistent. So. Her trust was not lightly given. It was special.

It was for him.

"Well, I hope your faith is justified with where I'm taking you." He started the car and about twenty minutes later he was paying the entry fee at a state park in Gaithersburg.

"I didn't even know this was here," Kari said, looking out the window as they wound their way around to a little parking area near a large swath of grass that sloped gently away from the lake that was the centerpiece of the park.

"It's a nice little gem. Does this look like it will provide inspiration enough?" He waved at the lake with its scattering of canoes and kayaks, the trees, the edge of the water where a couple of small children played, their parents nearby on a blanket, finishing what must have been a family picnic.

"More than enough. Thank you." Her fingertips gently skimmed his forearm and Rob almost forgot how to breathe. "But what are you going to do?"

"I brought my old fishing rod. I'm going to drown some fake worms."

Kari's face lit up in a way that was completely unexpected. "You fish? You and Sam are going to get on like a house on fire."

"She fishes?"

"She more than fishes," Kari said. "She's a fly fishing guide."

Rob whistled. "That's a really big deal. I'm just a guy who plonks weird rubber creatures in the water and doesn't expect the fish to get fooled much. Fly fishing is on a whole other level."

"She'll just love that you appreciate the water. She was a weird kid about water of all kinds. Drove my mother crazy."

Rob, about to unbuckle his seat belt, paused. "Why?"

"The shipwreck. *Mor* was terrified of water."

"Don't take this the wrong way, but your family history is very odd." Rob reached into the backseat and snagged a worn, faded baseball cap, clapping it on his head. It had the Maryland Terrapin reared up on its hind legs and read, "Fear the Turtle" in block letters over the creature's improbably snarling face.

"You have no idea," Kari said, unbuckling her seat belt and grabbing her art supplies. Rob got out of the car and opened the trunk. When she joined him, he handed her a tote bag and a folding chair. A shipwreck, secrets, strange legacies—it wasn't as if she'd trade her life for someone else's. She just wished sometimes that everything was a little *simpler*.

"Snacks and seating," he said, pulling components of a fishing rod out of a cardboard tube and assembling them. "Oh. And sunscreen."

"Thank you. Nice forethought," she said, amused at the Coppertone and the half-package of Oreos and bottles of water. In truth, she was still full from lunch. But it was a sweet thought.

"Let's get you set up, Marie Cassatt. I'm looking forward to seeing what you can do with a set of pencils."

She eyed him with approval as they walked across the

grass. "Nice. Most men would have said Picasso or Monet or someone like that."

"Never forget I have an outspoken, opinionated, gloriously feminist daughter who has handed me my ass on a nearly daily basis ever since she was tiny."

She nodded. No, she couldn't forget Mia. Even if she wanted to. And she didn't want to. Maybe they could get to know each other a little. That might be nice. Rob's affection for his daughter made Kari curious about who Mia was, unfiltered by Rob's pride and adoration. The person who inspired all that parental love.

Kari stopped a few yards from the shore, far enough away to get some perspective while Rob continued walking to the edge of the water. Rubbing sunscreen on her skin, she mentally framed her composition, a tall tree on the on the opposite shore of the lake to anchor the upper right, the little dock jutting into the water to form the lower left of the frame. Rob shot her a grin, setting down what she figured was a tackle box and doing something with his rod. Rigging it out, she supposed.

Smiling to herself, she opened her pad to a fresh page and pulled out a pencil.

Rob brought his arm back and cast, the reel sizzling as the line fed out, the wobbly, bright red worm landing in the water with a fat *plop*. There was almost no chance he'd get so much as a nibble, but that wasn't really the point. The sun was warm on his skin and the sound of a pair of children happily running around and making up some sort of game was pleasant. His breath caught in his throat as a great blue heron soared overhead. Someone in a canoe pointed as the bird drifted past, a silent ghost in the sky. Even the kids' voices halted until it disappeared somewhere to Rob's left where the shore curved out and the trees blocked it from his vision.

His reel ticked over as he brought his line in for another cast as the kids' chattering returned and canoes and kayaks glided over the water. He wondered what Kari was sketching and even if she would share it with him. Mia flat-out refused to show her poetry to him and he swallowed his pride and respected her decision even if his curiosity nearly ate him alive.

He smiled as he cocked his arm back and cast again. They were a lot alike, Mia and Kari.

I like her. You should date her.

Cheeky little Mia. Pushing at him even when she had no idea she was doing anything at all.

Rob continued to cast, surprised at one point when something tugged at his line, then unsurprised again when his hook came up empty. Could be anything or nothing. Time went away. That was the point of fishing, as far as he was concerned. It was a form of meditation. Like painting a wall. A repetitive motion, breathing steadily, watching what unfolded in front of him. Color spreading across sheetrock, the sun traveling across the sky.

"Ahem." The voice at his elbow made his arm jerk up against unexpected resistance. Turning his surprised gaze back to the tense line and the bowed rod, he tugged again, expecting a dead weight that would tell him he'd "caught" a branch, a root, or piece of garbage.

The line tugged back, a sure indicator that whatever he had was not mere dead weight. "Holy crap. I've actually caught something."

"Holy carp, you mean?" Kari's voice sounded amused, but he was too wrapped up in reeling the fish—yes, he was sure it was a fish now—to do anything other than huff a distracted laugh. The fish jumped then, a bright splash of water and coiling of muscle sheathed in iridescent scales. Rob laughed, reeling the tired fish in.

"Hey buddy. I'm sorry. I never even meant to hook you," he murmured to the glistening animal, its sides heaving, gills gaping. Releasing the hook from the fish's cheek, he lowered it back into the water, hovering his hand beneath the fish's body until it revived and darted away with an angry flick of its tail.

Rob stood, shaking water from his hands, to see Kari curled around her sketch pad, eyebrows drawn together, pencil moving with a furious speed. "Can I see?" he asked.

"One minute," she said, her teeth biting down on the corner of her lower lip. The action was unconscious and sexy as hell. He wanted to bite that lip, suck it into his mouth and release it slowly. Would she moan? Or was she the silent type? Would he have to interpret her reactions from tiny cues?

Somehow, he thought that was the way Kari would be in the bedroom. The thought made his breath shallow and his throat tight.

Oh, he had no business thinking those thoughts.

Why not? His inner demon prompted.

Because he'd determined he was no good at relationships.

But the woman he'd spent the last couple weekends who was starting to turn her sketch pad for him to examine, her eyes a little shy and maybe a little proud, might be giving the lie to that theory. He turned the idea over in his mind, forcing himself to think about the thoughts he always avoided. He did have good platonic relationships. He had one now with Kari. But those breakups had been so explosive. So hurtful. Maybe he was just afraid of being hurt. Of hurting Kari. Both ideas were awful. He looked at the pad.

With just a few strokes, she had caught the moment where the fish came out of the water, swinging toward his outstretched hand. His face was surprised, mouth open slightly. Or maybe that was just because he had spoken to the fish as he took it in.

"You're really good," he said.

"Thanks." She ducked her head, her fine hair falling across her cheeks, veiling her face.

"That can't be all you did." He wanted to take the pad from her hands, to leaf through her work and linger over it, but he wouldn't be so presumptuous.

"No, it isn't." She flipped a page back and handed him the pad.

Kari didn't look at the sketch. Instead, she looked at Rob's face as his gaze swept over it. His eyes scanned the page, taking in the whole scene: the lake, the heron overhead, a kayak in the distance, the sweep of green grass down to the water. And then his gaze sharpened. He looked at her, his eyes smiling, lines fanning out from the corners.

"You drew Mia there with me."

She nodded. She had drawn a young version of Mia, the little girl as she was in some of the photographs in Rob's living room standing beside him, tiny hands holding a fishing rod, a miniature duplicate of her father.

"She's...she's always with you. So it seemed right somehow."

"Always with me?" His brows drew together.

"You always talk about her. She's always present in your mind."

His mouth twisted in a sheepish smile and he looked back at the drawing in his hand. "Sorry."

"No, don't apologize. It's sweet. Your relationship is so nice. I miss my dad. We had a different way between us, but I miss him. I like seeing the two of you together." Her father had been a quiet, shy man—pretty much the opposite of gregarious Rob. But he'd supported her the way Rob supported Mia. She always knew he loved her.

"Nice of you to say."

"It's the truth."

"Can I buy this from you?" Rob looked from the pad to her face, his expression eager.

"What?"

"Pay you money. So I can have this. Frame it. Put it on my wall."

An absurd, nervous laugh—perilously close to a giggle—rose up out of Kari's chest. "Why would you want to do that?"

"Because I like it and I want to look at it."

Kari goggled at him. He looked sincere, but he had to be pulling her leg. "It's just a sketch."

"And people frame sketches and put them on walls all the time. It's called hanging art. I'll give you whatever you want for it."

"I told you I don't make things for money."

In fact, she remembered quite clearly that she had said she did it for love.

He squinted at her and she had the prickly, uncomfortable feeling that he had remembered her exact words too. "I don't want to insult you or make you do anything you don't want to do. I just really, really like this."

He was serious. It was finally sinking in. "If you really want it, you can have it."

He looked from the drawing to her face. "Why won't you let me pay you for it?"

"I wouldn't even know where to begin to explain why."

"Try anyway."

She huffed a frustrated sigh. "First of all, it's just an amateur sketch. Second of all, it makes me feel weird to try to put a price tag on something I enjoyed doing so much. Third of all...I have no idea how to value it."

"How about we stop by the big craft store on the way home and look at frames. I'm not paying you less for the art than the frame it should go in. That will at least give us a point to start from."

"I can't believe you're serious about this," she said, covering her eyes with one hand.

"Absolutely serious. Let's go."

Chapter Thirteen

"There." Rob stepped back from the wall, letting his hands drop to his side and looked at the framed sketch with satisfaction. "Perfect."

"You're unbelievable," Kari said, her hands over her eyes for what had to be the twentieth time since he had brought up wanting to buy the sketch from her.

"No, you're talented and you need to suck it up and stop fighting the idea," Rob said. They had found a pre-made frame with a mat at the craft store. Rob had made Kari sign the sketch before framing it and deciding that it should take pride of place over an armchair in his living room where a generic print he had been given by some relative had once hung for lack of anything else that was the appropriate size to go there. This was perfect. The print could be consigned to a hallway.

Kari still had her hands over her eyes. "Somewhere inside me is a fifteen-year-old girl who's convinced you're actually teasing me and you're going to say, 'Psych! Just kidding!'"

Rob pulled at her hands, peeling her fingers away from

134

her face. She let him do it and looked at him, a half-exasper-ated, half-amused look on her face. "Don't look at me," she said.

He took her shoulders and turned her toward the wall with its new artwork. "Okay. But look at that and tell me you don't think it looks great.

She heaved a sigh, her shoulders moving under his hands. Reflexively, he dug his thumbs into the tight muscles at the base of her neck, stroking out the tension. She let her head sag forward and a little groan of relief leaked out of her. Rob's pulse picked up, aware of the smell of her—sunshine and clean laundry, sunscreen and warm skin. He resisted the urge to pull her back against his chest, to bury his nose in her hair, to trace the length of her neck with his lips.

"See? It's good isn't it?" He didn't know if he was talking about the sketch, the impromptu back rub, or the so-bad-they're-good ideas that were running through his head.

"The sketch is okay. The fingers are magic, though."

Magic. The word shot through him, an electrical thrill of sensation. His hands slid down her arms, around her waist, and she leaned back into him, her head slowly tipping back to rest on his shoulder. They stayed that way for a few breaths. She just felt so unbelievably good in his arms. So right. The silky fineness of her hair a tickling softness on his neck, her belly rising and falling under his palms with every breath.

"We should probably—" she began to turn and lift her head at the same time as Rob's face turned toward her, and their lips brushed, noses bumped, and his hands weren't at her waist, but cupping her cheeks, fingers sliding into her hair and they were kissing. Her lips tasted like the Oreos she'd eaten in the car as she teased him about hanging her "amateur hour" on his wall.

135

Now the teasing was of an entirely different nature. Her head slanted and he followed her example, their lips moving and exploring, moving even closer until Kari's breasts pressed softly into his chest, her arms winding behind his neck, his hands sliding down her back to pull her even closer. She moaned, a tiny sound deep in her throat and her fingers moved up the back of his neck, into his hair, causing currents of electricity to run from his scalp to his toes and every sensitive, neglected place in between.

Somewhere in the back of Kari's mind was a little voice saying this was probably a bad idea.

Somewhere in the back of Kari's mind was a voice plagued with ignorance that needed to shut up. Because kissing Rob was *wonderful*. Who knew bumping noses and almost drawing away in awkward embarrassment could turn into this warm, thumping need, this press of bodies and searching lips?

Well Kari sure knew it now and that little voice could go to hell, especially with Rob's tongue teasing at the seam of her mouth, requesting entry.

Oh, yes. With a shuddering breath, she parted her lips and met his tongue with her own, licking and teasing, even more tangible evidence of his arousal pressing into her pelvis.

He pulled back with a little shudder, his eyes heavy-lidded and his breath coming hard. Kari forced herself to loosen her grip on the back of his head, her fingers easing out of his hair. But instead of pulling further away, Rob took one of her hands and pressed a soft kiss to her palm, sending a jolt of sensation through her.

"We should be smart about this," he mumbled into her hand, his breath hot against her skin.

"Can we be stupid first and smart later?" she asked.

He chuckled, his mouth still pressed to her palm, his breath huffing warmth against her skin. Then he folded her hand in his and brought it to his chest, meeting her eyes, huge black pupils starting to contract. "I like you too much to be stupid, Kari."

"I like you too, but being a little stupid isn't such a bad thing. Is it?"

"There's stupid and there's stupid. I haven't dated for nearly a decade because I was bad at it. I don't want you to end up hating me."

"There's that going for the ending before the beginning again." Irritation welled in Kari, combining in a toxic stew with sexual frustration, making her voice snap.

Rob smoothed a hand down her shoulder. "No, just learning from history. I jumped in feet first. Always. Too fast, too little thought. I'm not saying no. I'm saying let's slow this down."

Kari tamped her annoyance down. He had a point, as much as her hopping libido wanted to argue. After all, her ignorant, back-of-the-brain voice had said something not too different just a few minutes ago. Maybe that voice wasn't so off-base after all.

She hated the voice. She wanted to be stupid. She wanted to be the irresponsible teenager she had never been. She'd been careful Kari, sensible Kari, get the best grades you can and keep your head down Kari. The first-generation kid who had to make her parents proud. Then to get a good job so she could take care of herself. Then to be the daughter who had to care for her dying mother.

She sagged back a little, conscious of his hand still at the small of her back, still pressing her to him. It gave her

Adele Buck

courage, the little evidence that he wasn't repulsed by her. Maybe he even still wanted her.

His hand pressed more firmly against her back, the other evidence he wasn't repulsed by her hard against the front of her body.

"What's the issue?" Kari swallowed, her throat resisting.

"Me." Rob's eyes sank closed.

Rob took a deep breath. How to explain this without sounding like a presumptuous jackass?

I'm never getting married again.

Kari's wide, pale blue eyes were expectant, waiting. He supposed she would say he was beginning at the end. She'd be right.

And what exactly did Kari want? She was forty-two, had just bought her own home, no long-term relationship. Putting those factors together, maybe she wasn't interested in getting married either.

The thought was blinding in its novelty.

"What exactly do you want from me, Kari?"

Her eyes dropped to his mouth. With her free hand, she traced his lips with her fingertips, the barest touch, almost tickling. "Right now? I was enjoying kissing. It's nice to get wound up over something that is pleasurable instead of something that's stressing me out."

"So that was it? Just scratching an itch?" Perversely, the idea irritated Rob. He released the hand that he had been cradling in his and she gave him a little smack on the shoulder.

"No. I also like you. You're kind and funny and helpful and I enjoy spending time with you."

"Funny?"

"Well, you do tend toward dad jokes. But I'm not lactose intolerant, so I can handle the cheese."

"Of course I tell dad-jokes. I'm a dad." He'd never considered that telling dad jokes could be appealing. But Kari was different from anyone he'd ever met before. Special.

"I haven't forgotten." She frowned a little at that, and she pulled away a little. "Maybe it was a bad idea."

He smoothed his hands over her shoulders, stilling her retreat. "What's the matter?"

Her eyes flicked toward the drawing, then back to his face. Her lower teeth raked over her upper lip.

"Use your words, Kari." Glancing at the sketch, light started to dawn. "Is it something about Mia?"

"I just…no. I've never dated someone with a child before. I don't want to do something wrong."

Rob tugged her to the sofa and sat on it, pulling her down with him. "It breaks my heart a little bit to say it, but Mia's an adult. I don't know what kind of concerns you have about her as a factor in my life, but you might as well come out and say them."

"I just…" She huffed out a breath. "Okay, fine. She didn't seem to like me much. I know how close you two are. That seems to be the makings for a bad situation."

Rob blinked at Kari for a few endless moments. "You thought she didn't like you?"

"Well, she seemed very…reserved around me."

"She is reserved with people she doesn't know well yet."

"So she doesn't dislike me?"

"Why are you hanging on to this notion? I told you she liked you."

"No, you said she didn't dislike me."

"And?"

Kari blinked. "There's a world of difference."

"Good grief." Rob leaned over and picked his phone up off of the coffee table. Tapping at his texting app, he scrolled until he reached the message he wanted. "Look at this and tell me my daughter dislikes you."

I like her. You should date her.

Kari stared at the words as if they were written in a language she didn't recognize. The header in the texting app showed clear as day that the message was from Mia, complete with an avatar of the young woman snuggled up to her dog.

"This is about me?"

"Of course it is. Look at the date and time stamp."

Kari looked. The evening she had met Mia. The day she embarrassed herself to the ninth awkward circle of Hell and back. She'd been worried all this time for literally *nothing*?

"She was matchmaking based on less than five minutes' acquaintance?"

"Why not? You had convinced yourself she loathed you in the same time period."

Kari handed the phone back to him. "Somehow that seems more reasonable. Single dad, only daughter…"

"This isn't a Greek tragedy and Mia's an independent sort anyway."

"And yet she's trying to meddle in your love life."

"My so-long-dormant-it-might-as-well-be-dead-and-buried love life, yes. If we were two Barbie dolls, she'd be banging us together yelling, 'Now, kiss.'"

Kari cringed a little at *banging*, but the image still brought a smile to her lips. "Does she do this often?"

"Never."

"*Never?*"

Rob shook his head. "Nope. Never. Not that I've been blessed with beautiful next-door neighbors with household repair needs before now."

"Beautiful?" He said it with such a matter-of-fact air. As if it was the most obvious thing in the world. Kari's face burned and she looked at her hands folded in her lap. Rob's fingertip traced her cheekbone.

"Your blushes are lethal, Kari."

"Oh. And here I just thought they were embarrassing. Guess you *can* die from embarrassment. Or someone can." She lifted her gaze and was reassured by the smile lines fanning out from the corners of his eyes.

"You don't think you're beautiful?"

"I'm not exactly young."

"Not the same thing. I'm not young either."

No, but dammit, why did silver temples and stern, black-framed reading glasses make men look distinguished and sexy? Her pale blond hair camouflaged the gray that begun to thread through it, but it also looked less vibrant than it had. She was equally sure that when she needed reading glasses, they would just make her look like a frump.

"Take it from me, you're beautiful and that's that." He pinched her chin gently, then let his hand fall away. She missed his touch already, wanted his hand back on her.

"So where does all this leave us?" She hated to have to ask, but couldn't not know the answer.

He rubbed his jaw and considered her thoughtfully. "Well, you were supposed to spend the night here."

That was right. The paint. She had forgotten. Disappointment welled in her. She'd pushed too hard. It was the couch and back to a friendly distance for them, she was sure.

"I was," she said.

"Well if you still *are*," he said, his eyes never leaving her face, "let me ask you this: do you want me to make up Mia's bed?"

The question hung in the air between them. It shimmered and pulsed. Kari looked as if he had said something shocking. Had he completely misread the situation? His brain scrambled to go over what they had said, how she had reacted.

Her hand reached out, soft and warm, covering his. "You mean it?"

He turned his hand over to clasp hers. "I mean it. I'd like you in *my* bed tonight. If you want to be there. But only if you want to be there. And—" *Crap.* "I don't have any protection. I don't suppose you…?"

Her face twisted in a rueful smile. "If you insist on condoms, we can get some later, but…" Her eyes rolled toward the ceiling, but for once she didn't blush. "I never thought I'd be grateful for cysts."

"Cysts?"

"Painful, awful things. And I've had an IUD for four years because of them."

Comprehension flooded through him. "Oh. And…" He hated to ask this, hated to think about it, but hated the alternative more. "You've…you've been tested?"

She nodded. "You?"

"A million years ago, but that's still since my last, well. Encounter." He was pretty sure it was his turn to blush and from the sly, wicked smile on Kari's face, the heat in his cheeks was showing. "Hey. You knew what you were getting into. Dad jokes and awkwardness."

"I hold up my end of the awkward bargain, I think." Her voice was soft, not teasing. Just commiserating.

"Well, aren't we just perfect for each other?"

And the scary thing was, he really meant it.

Back in her house, Kari rummaged through drawers to get clothes for tomorrow. She dithered over pajamas. She didn't usually wear anything to bed, but was she being presumptuous?

Just put them in the bag and keep going.

Moving to the bathroom, she grabbed a toothbrush and toothpaste, a hairbrush, and various other odds and ends, shoving them in the little duffel with her clothes and the book from her nightstand. Going over what she had packed, she nearly smacked herself. She was going to be right next door. If she needed something that badly, she was going to be able to come over and get it.

Walking past the open doorway of her guest bedroom, she waggled her fingers at one of the nightstands. "Bye Buzz, bye Vibe." She giggled a little in anticipation and at her own silliness. She needed to settle down. Putting a hand on her stomach, she took a deep breath, then another. That was better.

Wait.

Speaking of Buzz and Vibe, she strode to the nightstand standing in the middle of the nearly empty room and pulled it open. A quick rummage and she tossed another item into her bag, then zipped it closed.

She locked up her house and hurried next door, feeling conspicuous, as if the neighbors she didn't even know yet were all peering out of their windows and seeing her bag and her red cheeks and coming to the all-too-correct conclusion.

143

Chapter Fourteen

Rob floated the comforter over the hastily re-made bed. The sheets were smooth and tight, the bedroom tidied. He wasn't the kind of guy who cluttered up every room in the house, reserving his one unrestrained mess for the office. Here it was a book on the nightstand, a pair of reading glasses on top. A framed picture of him and Mia on the dresser. He considered that, thinking about Kari's expressed concern about his daughter's feelings, and decided to relocate the photograph to the living room.

Mia wouldn't care—quite the reverse, she'd be cheering the two of them on.

But he was pretty sure that even Mia's photographic presence in the bedroom would have a dampening effect on Kari's feelings. Rob rubbed his hands together, nervousness zinging through his belly. What else? He gave a surreptitious sniff of one armpit. He...thought he was fine? But after a day of painting in a warm room and fishing? He probably wasn't.

Just a quick shower. He should be able to get in, lather up quickly, and get out and dry in less than five minutes. Darting to the bathroom, he turned on the water and shucked off his clothes. Stepping into the hot spray, he had just enough time to wet his hair and begin to lather his chest when a noise made him freeze.

"Hello?" Kari's voice, outside the bathroom door.

"Just taking a quick shower," he called, rubbing the soap under his armpits and across the back of his neck.

"You have me at a disadvantage." Kari's voice floated through the half-open door. "I should have showered myself."

He turned to face the spray, hanging his head and letting the water flow over his shoulders and neck, cascading off his hair. Closing his eyes, he gathered his courage. He had meant to take things slowly, to tease and discover, to peel layers away.

But it seemed like all his plans were meant to be jettisoned today.

He turned again and lifted his head, slicking his hair back with one hand. "You could join me," he offered. "If you want."

A long silence, and his half-hardened cock started to soften.

"Really?" He couldn't catch the tone of Kari's voice over the noise of the water.

"Really." He cleared his throat. His voice had gone all tight. He almost sounded like a teenager.

Another silence, and then he could see her form vaguely outlined behind the shower curtain. He rubbed the back of his neck, waiting, half turned on, half flooded with anxiety.

Pale fingers hooked around the shower curtain, drawing it aside slowly, as if she was waiting for him to change his mind. His hand on the back of his neck stilled and Kari stepped into the tub, the one long leg and her half-apprehensive expression making his breath stop. He held out a hand and she took it to support herself as she stepped all the way into the little enclosure that suddenly seemed a whole lot smaller.

A nervous little smile quirked her lips and her free hand hovered as if ready to cover herself. As if it could. He tugged her a little closer and she came without hesitation, stopping mere inches away. He swallowed, feeling like he should reassure her somehow—yet feeling like he needed reassurance too.

How did this used to go?

He settled his hands on her hips. "Beautiful."

Kari almost laughed. *Me?* She wanted to say? *Look at you.* Rob was toned and fit, his belly only slightly less than flat, his broad chest sprinkled with dark hair peppered with the occasional silver strand, just like on his head.

"Why are you looking at me like that?" she asked.

"Am I looking at you in a way?" he asked.

"Yeah. You're…fit. And I'm…" *Soft, sagging, succumbing to gravity* she wanted to say. Maybe a few other choice words starting with S, if she could think of any.

He turned her away from him, pulling her back against his body, the warm spray from the shower spilling over his front and sliding down her back, his delicious lips and rough stubble pressing into the nape of her neck. She shivered and his arms came around her, one hand cradling her belly, the other weighing one breast, pinching gently at her hardening nipple. "Sexy," he said. "Soft." He bit where her neck joined her shoulder. "Just right."

Make me feel this way and I don't care how I look, she thought. Every sensation—the water, his hands, his mouth—all flowed through her and coalesced in a bright heat between her legs. It had been so long since she felt this urgent, needy throbbing with someone else. She could have laughed, but instead she gasped as he shifted against her, his cock hardening as it rubbed against the cleft of her ass. The hand on her stomach drifted lower, sliding through her pubic hair, long fingers finding the hood of her clit and circling gently.

"Like this?" his hot breath in her ear made her shiver.

Her breath hitched. "Harder."

He chuckled, increasing the pressure and the speed and Kari's knees trembled. Normally, she was as far from a hair trigger as they came, but the warm water, the unexpected feeling of safety in Rob's embrace, one of his hands rubbing her clit and the other continuing to tease at her nipple—*oh.*

"I've got you," he murmured. Then he pressed a kiss to the side of her neck, tongue exploring the sensitive nerve endings there, and everything in Kari flew apart into bright, spangled shards of light and shivering energy.

She realized he really *did* have her. She sagged into him, one of his arms supporting her weight, the other hand pressing against the place where ecstatic shivers continued to radiate outward. She straightened, swallowing hard, and turned in the arm that still encircled her, winding her arms around his neck and spearing her fingers into his wet hair.

"Thank you," she murmured against his lips.

"My pleasure," he said. She could feel his smile against her mouth.

"You have that backwards."

"No, I don't. I'm just glad to know I still know how to do a thing or two."

"If you've lost a step, I want a time machine to go back to when you were doing this regularly."

But not to share. The thought came out of nowhere, flattening her with its sudden vehemence.

"Or maybe I can just get back in practice now," he said.

She leaned back, pretending to consider. "Oh, if you must."

"Cheeky." He must have grabbed the soap from behind her back because she felt strong hands sliding across her rear, slick, massaging the muscles and making her sag against him again.

"Not fair. You've been all give so far." She picked up the container of shampoo and dribbled some into her palm, scrubbing her fingertips into his scalp, massaging and exploring. He groaned and tilted his head back into the spray when her fingers slowed, rinsing himself clean. Lifting his head and blinking the water away, he soaped up his hands again and smoothed them up the front of her torso, lifting her breasts and running his thumbs across her still-tight nipples.

"Still giving," she said, rubbing the soap between her own palms.

"No, this is taking," he said, his eyes on the slide of his fingers over her skin, then gulped as she grasped his cock with her soap-slick fingers, his eyes sliding closed. "Be gentle on an old man."

"Hardly." She gave his shaft an experimental squeeze, gratified at the way it throbbed against her palm.

"No, really. I don't bounce back the way I did when I was younger. Pace yourself." He switched their positions, putting her back under the spray, letting water stream over her shoulders and down her front. She closed her eyes and wetted her hair, smiling when she felt his hands shampooing her. He didn't do that thing some men did: heap her hair on top of her head, rendering it a snarled mess. Instead, he concentrated on her scalp, combing his fingers gently through her hair as she rinsed.

"Ready to get out?" he asked.

"Right behind you," she said, suddenly shy about cleaning her armpits in front of him. Which was absurd. But there it was.

✿

Rob stepped out of the shower and snagged his towel from the rail. *Crap.* Kari needed one. Drying off quickly and wrapping the terrycloth around his hips, he darted to the hallway to get a spare from the linen closet. He heard the water shut off and was back just in time to hand her a towel as she pulled the shower curtain aside.

"Thanks." She lifted the towel to her hair, the movement making her breasts move in a mesmerizing way.

"Sure." Pulling the towel from his body, he rubbed it across her belly, wrapping it around to dry her hips, her ass, sliding it down her legs, his mouth going dry when his face was mere inches from the triangle of pubic hair, the curls darker gold than her straight, fine hair.

"Hello down there." Rob looked up at Kari's face, flushed from the warm water, her hair a delicious, tangled halo around it.

"Hello yourself." Levering himself to his feet, he lavished a little more attention on her breasts with the damp towel while she laughed and reached for his comb, tugging it through her tangled locks. "That's enough tidying your hair. I'm just going to mess it up again," he said, taking the comb from her hand and laying it on the counter.

"Someone's urgent all of a sudden." Kari's eyes danced with mischief.

"Someone's got some unfinished business."

"I see." Kari's eyes drifted down and her lips curled up.

"Among other things." Yes, his erection still throbbed. But he also wanted her warm, soft skin against his again, her almost-as-tall-as-he-was length plastered against his body. Grasping her hands, he walked backwards, across the hall to the bedroom, tugging her after him. A small duffel sat on the bed. He released one of Kari's hands and lifted the duffle. "What's in the bag, little girl?"

Kari's eyes traveled from the duffel in his hand up his arm to his face. "Clothes. Mostly."

"Mostly." He let an eyebrow quirk upward.

"Yes, mostly." Her mouth went prim, but her eyes danced with humor and innuendo.

"All right, then." Rob let the duffel drop to the side of the bed and pulled Kari into his arms, his eyes sliding closed with pleasure as his cock was trapped between his body and hers. *Yes.* This was what he wanted.

Well, not quite. He wanted the hot, slick slide inside her. The very thought was enough to make his eyes roll back in his head. He tugged her back to the bed, sitting on the mattress and lying back, pulling her down on top of him. A fit of nervousness hit him, and he looped a strand of damp hair behind Kari's ear.

"How are you doing so far?"

She gave him a startled look. "After that shower? Are you serious?"

"Just thought I should check in."

Her eyes narrowed. "How are *you* doing?"

"A little nervous, to be honest." Despite their promising start, he was worried that something would go awry, that he'd fail to please her, maybe even hurt her. It had been so long.

"Ah. Anything I can do?" That tiny, crooked smile that he was getting used to reappeared.

He considered their relative positions. "How do you feel about being on top? At least for a start?"

The smile broadened. "Just fine. One minute."

She stood and he lifted his head. "Where you going?"

"To get the Mostly."

She crouched by the bed and the sound of the duffle zipper being opened made him rise up on his elbows so he could see what she was doing. She stood, a tube of something in her hand.

"Scootch back." She popped the tube open and squirted something into her hand.

"What's that?" he asked, inching back until he was all the way on the bed.

She showed him the label, her eyebrows lifting.

He squinted. "Lube? Did I not do something right?"

"You did everything right. But, like you, I'm not twenty-five anymore. I'm not even thirty-five anymore."

A sudden doubt smacked him in the chest. "I thought you said you hadn't been with anyone for years. Why…"

She frowned. "A girl doesn't need to be with a *person* to need lubricant."

He remembered her furtive grab of her nightstand and his face heated with embarrassment. "Ah. Of course. I'm sorry." Great. He was already screwing this up.

"Yeah." She held his gaze as she applied the lubricant to herself, her fingers stroking between her legs in a way that made Rob's throat close and his mouth go dry. It was intense and erotic, that look, those fingers.

He cleared his throat. "Care to put some on me too?"

The band of tension that had constricted Kari's chest from the moment of Rob's question eased and she took a careful breath, reaching for the lube. "Sure. Warm or cold?"

He shuddered. "Warm. Definitely warm."

She squirted more lube into her palm and brought her

hands together until it had absorbed the heat from her hands, then slicked it over his hard length, savoring his indrawn breath.

"Damn, that feels good."

"Good." Kari circled the head with her thumb, coating him entirely, then snagged a tissue from the nightstand and cleaned her hands. Her heart hammered harder and her breath was tight again, but this time it was from anticipation, not apprehension. "Ready?"

"Be gentle with me." His words were flippant, but his expression held the same anticipation she felt, but maybe with the slightest tinge of anxiety.

"I'll do my best." She straddled his hips, gripping his cock and positioning it at her entrance, sinking down by slow degrees, her eyes sliding closed. Her hips came flush with his and she swallowed, her body adjusting to the welcome invasion.

"You okay?" Rob's voice was low, tight.

She nodded, unable for the moment to speak. She opened her eyes again, looked down at him. His hands were hovering around her hips, seeming unable to decide where to put them, what to do with them. She laced her fingers through his, gripping his hands, palm to palm, and began to rock in slow undulations.

Rob's eyelids lowered halfway and a muscle in his jaw ticked. His fingers flexed as she rolled her hips, squeezing her hands. "God. Kari. Oh." His breath hissed again.

"Too much?" She leaned over him, teasing his lips with hers. "Not enough?"

He released one of her hands, wrapping his arm around her waist. "Just right, Goldilocks. Just right. Don't stop. Are you okay?"

"More than okay." Her body had adjusted to the sensation of being filled, stretched, gloriously *fucked*. Rob started moving with her and she found she could take him even deeper, sliding her knees further apart, one hand holding his, the other planted on the mattress over his shoulder. His hand on her lower back and butt encouraged her to move faster and she tried, but couldn't keep up with the pace he seemed to want.

"I'm sorry." She was panting now. "I can't...too fast."

"How about we..." He tightened his grip on her back and rocked his hip in a suggestion. She nodded, and they rolled over, Kari's legs wrapping around his thighs. His stubble scraped her cheek and he began to move more quickly than Kari had been able to, thrusting into her in a rhythm she had to focus to keep pace with. Then a quick-ening of his hips and a final thrust that seemed to stop time, his muscles rigid before liquid relaxation flowed through him.

"God, Kari. I'd meant..." His breath was hot in her ear. "You should have been better taken care of...I should have..."

Kari hugged him with arms and legs, kissing his neck. "You took care of me in the shower. If you're keeping score, we're square."

He lifted his head, squinting down at her. "I still feel like I owe you one. Or two. Or something."

Kari toyed with the silver hair at his temples, swallowing back the emotion that threatened. "I could...take a rain check. If you wanted to do this again sometime."

Chapter Fifteen

She wanted him again.

Rob wanted to cheer. Maybe he deserved a parade.

Kari sure deserved a parade. More than a parade. Good grief, she'd rocked his world, blown his mind.

And he had...questioned her integrity at the most vulnerable of moments.

Maybe he deserved a pillory, not a parade.

He eased out of her and moved to lie beside her, scanning her face for any clue to her feelings. Her eyes were watchful, her hair a pale tangle on the pillow and across her face. He teased the wayward strands away, tucking them behind her ear. "How are you?"

Her face softened. "You keep asking that."

"I keep being interested in the answer. The conditions are variable. This is new to both of us. And I wasn't the best guy today. In fact, I'm pretty ashamed of myself."

One eyebrow arched. "You had a bad moment," she said. "But we're square. You weren't considering all the variables. Like you said, this is new for both of us." She sat up, slid off the bed, and walked to the bathroom, her previous self-consciousness apparently a thing of the past.

Rob rolled to his back, plucking tissues out of the box and cleaning himself up. He heard the toilet flush, then water running. He glanced at the time just as his stomach rumbled. "Dinner?" he asked as Kari came back into the room.

"Yes. I'm starving," she said.

"Well, let's get dressed and see what I might be able to rustle up." Rob grabbed a clean tee shirt and a pair of gym shorts from a drawer and put them on. Kari crouched on the floor, rummaging in her bag, her back a tempting expanse of smooth skin. Rob wanted to run his fingers across it, trace every bump of her spine. To hell with being dressed.

Reluctantly, he resisted the urge and left her to find clothes. He headed for the kitchen, smiling as he passed her framed sketch on the wall. Kari on his wall, Kari in his bed...it was a lot all at once. If he had considered such a thing yesterday, he would have backpedaled away from the notion so fast he would have left skid marks.

So why did it feel so right today?

He shook his head at his own thoughts. *Leave it. Just enjoy it.*

In the kitchen, Rob found that a can of tomato soup and the makings for grilled cheese sandwiches were the best he could do in terms of a meal. Kari ambled in, back in her shorts and tee shirt. Rob was about to comment on the way the shorts made her long legs look fantastic, when he noticed she wasn't wearing a bra. Her breasts swayed, nipples poking through the soft cotton.

Rational thought just wasn't in the cards after that.

"Jesus, woman. Warn an old man if you're going to do that."

"Do what?" Kari's eyebrows quirked.

"Waltz around my house all lanky and gorgeous and not wearing underwear."

Kari snorted and glanced down at her chest. "Bras are the creation of the devil."

"Hm." Rob moved closer, until they were nearly touching. "They also say that idle hands are the devil's playground..." He hovered his palms suggestively around her breasts and Kari laughed, swatting at his hands.

"Later. There's a different part of my anatomy that needs satisfying now. And that would be my stomach."

He lifted the can. "Soup and grilled cheese or ordering in, I think those are our options."

"Soup and grilled cheese sounds perfect. Amazing. I love it."

"Are you always this easy to have around?" Rob put the can down and slid his hands around her waist, pulling her to him. He was still astonished at how perfectly her body lined up with his, and the ease between them he wasn't sure he had ever felt around anyone else.

Kari tilted her head, a tiny smile curving her lips. "I don't know. I'm always around me. I find myself pretty easy to deal with, but that hasn't always been the consensus opinion from everyone else."

"Who are these cretins? Never mind. If they hadn't been cretins, you wouldn't be here."

Kari's mouth stretched into an uncertain smile. Rob was falling awfully easily into a very...couple-y rhythm. With anyone else she got along with this well, she would have been thrilled. But with the history Rob had, she was slightly worried.

"What's with the furrowed brow?" he asked, stroking a thumb across her forehead.

"No furrows," she said, pulling out of his arms. "Let me at the bread and cheese. You heat up the soup. A feast."

"A nice division of labor," he said, but now *he* had a definite crease between his eyebrows.

Kari moved to the counter where a half a loaf of wheat bread and a bag of deli-sliced cheese were lying. "Butter and a frying pan?" she asked. Rob supplied her with what she asked for without a word, silence stretching between them.

Kari assembled two sandwiches and heated some butter in the frying pan while Rob opened a can of soup and poured it into a saucepan. Kari bumped his hip with hers when they arrived at the stove together, giving him a little sideways smile as she put the two sandwiches in the pan to toast.

His smile in return was tight, absentminded.

Fighting the urge to just throw up her hands and go back to her house, paint smell be damned, Kari was about to ask Rob how his office decluttering was going just to put them back in more neutral territory — when the sound of the front door opening and closing made her stiffen.

"Dad?" Mia's voice rang through the house.

"In the kitchen," Rob called out.

Oh, crap. Kari looked down at her chest. The ancient tee shirt she was wearing draped way too softly and easily across her breasts that were far too obviously not supported by a bra. She folded her arms across her chest as quick footsteps pattered from the front door toward the kitchen.

"Hi Da—" Mia paused for a second in the doorway, her eyes scanning from Rob to Kari and back to Rob, bright smile getting brighter and taking on a sort of manic edge. "Kari, hi."

"Hi Mia." Kari tried to match the younger woman's smile

wattage and gave a tight little wave while keeping one arm wrapped around her. And all the while trying to figure out how she might get past Mia, down the hall, into her… father's bedroom…and put on a bra.

Yeah, that wasn't happening.

"Hey kiddo." Rob ambled over to Mia and hugged her, bending to press a kiss to her forehead. "What brings you over?"

"Nothing urgent," Mia said, backing out of the room. "We can talk later. I didn't know you had a guest."

Rob followed her, his voice trailing back into the kitchen. "You sure?"

"I'm sure. You have fun. Bye, Kari!" This last seemed to be tossed at velocity as Mia and Rob said a few more murmured words and Mia hustled out of the house, the front door closing softly behind her.

Rob re-entered the kitchen, a funny smile on his face. "I don't think I've seen her exit a conversation that fast since when I tried to have a talk with her about puberty when she was twelve."

Kari slapped a hand across her eyes, then peered at Rob through her fingers. "I don't know what to do with myself just now."

"Do what I always do with Mia. Get comfortable with being uncomfortable." Rob stirred the soup and shot her a resigned grin that made her want to dissolve into the floor.

"That would take a hell of a lot of work," Kari said, flipping the grilled cheese. "Note to self: wear a bra at all times. Wear a bra to bed. Shower in a bra. Wear a bra over a bra."

"Stop." Rob abandoned the soup and took Kari's shoulders in his hands. "Mia's an adult. She even wanted this to happen, remember?"

"I don't think she wanted to walk in on the aftermath and have it shoved in her face like that, though." The entire scene was so inappropriate, Kari wanted to curl up in a ball and let the ground open up and swallow her whole.

"There was no shoving."

"Well, she walked in on what must have looked like a pretty cozy scene, me hanging out in your kitchen without supportive undergarments. She must have been pretty uncomfortable."

"She wasn't uncomfortable."

"She bolted out of here fast enough."

"She told me she didn't want to intrude."

"How could I have made her feel like an intruder in her own home?" The rising tide of guilt sloshed through Kari, threatening to drown her.

Rob's fingers flexed, giving her a gentle shake. "Stop. This isn't her home anymore. Lord knows she took everything she owned out of it when she got her first place, just to make it clear that she was grown and on her own. Didn't even leave so much as a Lego for me to step on barefoot in the middle of the night. Hugo has spent more nights here than she has since then and he's not even two years old."

The roiling in Kari began to ebb a bit as she considered Rob's words. She had been thinking of Mia as a child—the little girl she sketched in her imagination, standing next to Rob at the lake's edge. She wasn't. She was a young woman with a life of her own and probably a love life of her own.

On second thought, Kari couldn't decide if that made things better or worse.

***

"Seriously. It's okay." Rob turned from Kari's guilt-stricken face, turned the stove off and plated the soup and grilled cheese. Emotions ping-ponged through his body. So much had happened so quickly. Friendship and laughter and camaraderie had turned into lust and excitement. And among it all, the chilly moment earlier in the kitchen sat like lead among the whirl.

They took their meals to the little breakfast nook and sat. Kari took a tiny bite of sandwich, a tiny sip of soup.

Rob dunked a corner of his sandwich in the warm soup and bit into it, the taste making him realize how hungry he really was. He kept himself from immediately wolfing everything down, but just barely, while Kari picked at her meal.

"Eat," he said. "You told me you were starving."

"My stomach is kind of jittery now," Kari confessed, but she did spoon more soup into her mouth.

This whole...whatever it was that he was doing with Kari was a little more complicated than he had counted on when it started.

"Does me being a dad bother you?" he asked.

Her light blue gaze flicked up, surprise evident on her face. "Bother me? No. Why would you ask that?"

"This seems like a bit of a heavy freak-out based on one visit from my kid."

"It's just...new to me."

"It's new to me having some woman bedeviling my life and blowing my mind in bed. Or it might as well be."

She gave him a level look. "What was dating like when you did date? When she was a kid?"

"Liz and I had fifty/fifty joint custody. One week on, one week off. So I would only go on dates when Mia was with her mother. It made dating awkward, trying to pack everything into every other week."

"Mia never met anyone you were dating?"

"Not really. A couple of women when she was a teen, right before I stopped dating entirely."

Kari rolled her eyes. "Oh, so now this is even more

weird. I'm the *first* woman she's seen you with in about ten years?"

Rob reached across the table and covered one of her hands with his. "Mia. Is. An. Adult. Trust me, back in the day, I didn't want to come to grips with that reality. But I did. And you know what? I like my adult kid. She's a pretty great person. The last few years I've been sorting out who I am without her around. It's nice not to be responsible for someone else. Do I miss her? Sure, sometimes. Sometimes a lot. But that's what you do when you're a parent. Your entire job is to make sure that you help them grow and develop into people who, when they're out on their own, they are independent and strong and don't need you. And she doesn't need me. At least, not like when she was living here half the time."

Kari gave a little nod, her chin coming forward. "I guess I get it intellectually, but emotionally...I try to imagine my dad dating and my brain fritzes out."

"But your parents never went through a divorce or separation, right?"

She nodded again. "Yeah. They were always crazy for each other."

"Whereas Liz and I just made each other crazy. Divorce isn't great. In fact, it's awful and I don't recommend trying it. But Mia always knew we were better off apart and she also knew that whatever Liz and I said or did or thought, we both love her very much. It's the only thing Liz and I could ever agree on, even though we disagreed about how to go about accomplishing it. A lot."

"Mia's pretty lucky, then."

"I hope so. Finish your dinner and I'll take you out for ice cream."

Kari shot him a wry smile. "I'll be sure to put on a bra first, though."

161

Kari winced as her bra band snapped against her back. Served her right, she guessed. Shoving her arms back into the tee shirt, she pulled it over her head, smoothing her hair back from her forehead as her face emerged from the cotton.

Ice cream. This whole situation was half adult movie and half teenage sock hop date. And half awkward she didn't even know what to do with it because being braless in the presence of the adult daughter of the guy she had just had sex with.

That was too many halves.

Rob popped his head into the bedroom. "Ready to go?"

Kari picked up a sneaker and sat on the bed to put it on. "Almost."

He propped a shoulder against the doorframe. "Still freaked out?"

She tied her laces and picked up her second sneaker, trying to put her finger on what bugged her about the scenario. "I guess I'm wondering why *you're* not more freaked out. Your dating hiatus is a lot longer than mine, after all."

Rob thought for a moment, rubbing his jaw. "I don't think it has anything to do with the dating hiatus. I think it has a lot to do with the fact that I'm comfortable with being a dad. And I know Mia. You don't, so you're reacting to a generic scenario, not a person."

Kari paused in the action of looping a shoelace, her stomach plunging toward her toes. "God, you're right. I'm sorry. That's kind of shitty."

Rob waved a hand. "Like you said before, this is new for both of us. But it does raise the question: how long was your dating hiatus?"

"Five years."

"And why did your last relationship end?"

"His job. Moved across the country."

"I can't believe you haven't dated since," Rob shook his head, a flattering look of wonder spreading across his face.

"I think you're rapidly becoming biased," Kari said, getting to her feet and joining him at the doorway.

"No, I have assessed the data and found the conclusion inexplicable. You're smart, determined, beautiful —"

"And also over forty, very tall, and usually very solitary. Not exactly a successful dating profile to put on one of those apps or anything."

"Did you ever try that? The dating app scene?"

Kari shuddered. "No. Unlike you, I'm not into tech. I mean, I do the basics. I'm not a total Luddite. But dating was never important enough to me to sign up for a service or anything. And some of the stories I've heard sound like Stephen King wrote them."

"And dating just wasn't on my radar at all until a certain Viking Shield Maiden moved in next door."

"My bad. Should I just go spend the night on my couch?"

Rob threaded his fingers through hers and pulled her to the front door. "Bite your tongue."

"Ouch. Can I bite something else?"

He shot her a wicked smile. "I'll draw up a list."

Chapter Sixteen

"So, tell me," Rob said as they left the chill of the air-conditioned ice cream parlor for the warm June evening. "What did you want to be when you grew up?"

Kari eyed him sideways, her shoulder-length hair fluttering in the faint breeze. The spoon in her mouth paused, then she drew it out in a measured way that made his brain skid sideways into carnal territory. "What makes you think I wasn't keen to be a bookkeeping office manager extraordinaire?"

"I'm sure you're excellent at what you do. But few of us actually get jobs doing what we thought we would when we were kids."

"What brings this on?"

"Mia. She's been crazy about books since before she could read. She would bring her board books to us and insist we read them to her. When she started reading, I was convinced she had memorized certain books and was just repeating from memory. Then we got her a new book and she sat down cross-legged on the floor with it spread across her lap and started sounding it out right away."

"How old was she?" Kari's face held a sort of wistful expression.

"Four."

"No wonder you didn't think she was reading yet. That's early."

Pride surged through Rob, and he reminded himself he hadn't done anything to earn that. That was Mia's accomplishment, not his. "Yeah. And as soon as she learned that people had written them, that they didn't just occur spontaneously, she started writing her own little books. Illustrating them and getting Liz and me to staple them together so they were actually bound volumes."

"I'll bet they were cute."

"Adorable. At any rate, she graduated from simpler stuff, like 'This Book Is A List Of Animals' to actual stories. She kept her second grade class spellbound with a serial she wrote about a girl who turned into a horse and totally rolled with her new horsey life. I always figured she'd move on like most of us do—figure out something else to do, to give in to life."

"But she hasn't."

"No. Her passion has changed. She realized at some point that she didn't want to write her own stories anymore, but she loves helping make writers make better stories. And she's really good at it."

"So she's on the same path she was on since she was tiny."

Rob nodded. A cold trickle of moisture on his hand alerted him that his ice cream was melting down the cone. He slurped at the melted sweetness, then made a passage around the base of the scoop with his tongue, catching Kari's expression as he tidied his dessert. Her pupils were blown wide, her tiny smile speculative.

Well. Now he was getting all sorts of ideas about where else he could apply his tongue.

He cleared his throat. "Anyway. I was curious. About your childhood dreams."

Kari took another spoonful of her double-fudge chocolate and held his eyes as she drew the spoon out of her mouth and swallowed. "You really want to know?"

Oh, she was killing him. He wanted to know anything and everything about her right now. And he wanted to start with her mouth. "Yeah." His voice rasped in his throat.

"A singer."

"Not an artist?"

"Different kind of artist, but yeah. I had some sort of idea of being a classical singer. Maybe opera. My parents' luxury was a small stash of records."

"Can you sing?" He nearly winced. He hadn't meant to be that blunt, but Kari nodded as if he hadn't just stuffed his foot in his mouth alongside a lick of pistachio.

"Yeah. I can. I used to play those albums over and over, trying to get my voice to sound like what I heard. But I had no notion of how expensive and uncertain that sort of path would be. And my parents didn't have money for private lessons or connections to that world or any other or…much of anything. So, like you said, I gave in to life. I moved on. I had a talent for organization, I'm good with numbers. I found a place where I could be valuable."

Rob nodded, his throat tightening. He knew all too well what it was to have a dream that didn't survive the harsh realities of life.

"What did you want to be when you grew up?" she asked.

The look of shock on Rob's face at her question surprised Kari. He had to be expecting this—wasn't this what this sort of getting-to-know-you back and forth was all about?

He made another circuit of his cone with his tongue, sending shivering heat through her body—good grief, was one bout of good sex enough to short circuit her brain forever?—and looked back at her, his big dark eyes pinning her to the sidewalk.

"I wanted to be a history professor."

"Like, college?"

He nodded. "I would have had to get a Ph.D. I'd just started my master's program which could have led into that."

"And then what happened?"

His mouth tightened, then softened. "Mia happened. Liz got pregnant and we had to adjust."

Kari's head rocked back. "Oh. Not planned, then?"

He laughed softly. "No. We weren't married. We were young. Having a kid was the furthest thing from our minds."

Kari nearly laughed aloud at that. "Can I tell you something?"

He looked at her, his eyebrows crimping together. "Of course."

"My parents were *never* married."

He blinked, but didn't question her further.

"Mom had Bjorn—my brother—after they survived the shipwreck. He was her husband's son. She had married in Norway. Not a love match. Mom and Dad met and fell in love on the voyage. When Mom's husband didn't survive the wreck, Mom and Dad told the authorities they were married. They were terrified of being separated in a new country. But since they had told everyone they were already married…they felt like they couldn't *get* married."

"Not even in secret?"

"At first, I'm sure they could have, but it would have been difficult. New country, new rules, who do you trust to ask these kinds of questions? I think later it might have become one of things they realized they didn't need. I didn't learn about this until just before my mother died, but somehow it didn't surprise me. So, when you say that you and your ex weren't married and therefore didn't expect Mia…" She shrugged. "It doesn't faze me. But my experience isn't exactly common."

"True. But nice to know other people's lives throw them curve balls. At any rate, Liz and I got married in a hurry, she had Mia, and our lives re-centered around raising her."

Kari took another spoonful of ice cream, considering. "You couldn't go back to your original plan? Go back to school?"

Rob chuckled, shaking his head. "Getting a degree—especially an advanced degree—and having a kid are both net negatives, economically speaking. I needed to make money. We needed to have insurance for Liz's pregnancy and Mia's delivery. Not to mention the eighteen-plus years of actually raising a kid. I took my college minor in computer programming and parlayed it into my first I.T. job. Like you, it turned out I was good at it. And here I am." He flourished his ice cream cone as if to indicate some vast kingdom.

His light tone danced over some deeper truth of dreams deferred or dead and she remembered that funny moment when they were buying her faucet and she'd called him "Professor." Kari's heart twisted. She was so used to burying her own desires under the grinding reality of need: the need to make rent. The need to pay bills. And now, the need to pay a mortgage. Panic seized her throat at that last, recurrent thought, the responsibility of owning a home.

Relax. Millions of people pay mortgages. It's not so different from rent.

Except it was. She *owned* those walls she had painted. She was responsible for that plumbing. Even the plants in the yard were counting on her to come through with water if there was a drought.

She glanced at Rob, who had worked his way down to the cone, cracking it between his teeth and looking thoughtful as he moved down the street. They had walked away from where his car was parked in unspoken mutual accord, past the shops in the downtown area. Expensive-looking little boutiques mixed oddly with national chains in the streets ringing the central square, anchored by the library and a paved area with a fountain where kids in bathing suits played in the summertime.

"Where did you live before you bought the house?" Rob asked.

Kari blinked at the suddenness of the question. "Why do you ask?"

His eyes glinted with humor and he looked at her side-ways. "You just seemed to appear from nowhere. One day the house was empty, the next you're there transplanting azaleas and cracking wise with your niece in the backyard. I have a little of your family history now, but I feel like I know young-Kari and now-Kari. What about in-between-Kari? Where did you go to school? What's your history?"

She shrugged, plastic spoon scraping against the card-board, transferring the last of the chocolate goodness to her lips. "Born and raised in Rockville. One of those late in life 'surprise!' babies. I got a two-year associate's degree at Montgomery College. I worked as a secretary. I got a certifi-cate in bookkeeping, got a few different jobs, finally got the job I have now seven years ago. Oh, and I moved around a bit, and lived in an apartment building about a mile from our neighborhood for the last ten years."

Rob cracked another piece of cone between his teeth, chewed it, swallowed. "Huh. If it weren't for the six years between us we might have met at a football game or something in high school. Funny thing to think about, isn't it?"

A little thrill ran through her at the idea of meeting a younger version of Rob. Both of their lives might have been entirely different.

Rob couldn't account for the startled look on Kari's face, but then she tossed her cup in a trash can and sucked ice cream off her thumb and he forgot to wonder. His entire attention fixed on that thumb, those lips, the hint of tongue as she pulled her hand away from her mouth.

Jesus. He hadn't felt like this since...when? He didn't know.

It wasn't that he felt like a teenager. Thirty years hadn't melted off of him—and nor would he want them to. In fact, the very idea of being a teenager again made him shudder. No, it wasn't that sort of hormone-induced wildness that would flare and retreat seemingly at random all those years ago. What he felt now was an intense, steady sensation of being drawn to Kari, with each detail he discovered about her only making the feeling stronger.

And with that tractor-beam feeling came the intense desire to not screw whatever this was up.

"You okay?" Kari asked.

"Sure, why?" he said, well aware that he was lying. Of course he wasn't okay. How could he be okay with this realization? He was the king of screwing things up with women. He'd never done anything *but* screw up things with women.

"You were staring."

"You're something to stare at." He winked and popped the last bit of ice cream cone in his mouth.

She snorted. "At least I'm wearing a bra."

"I knew something was missing."

"The opposite of missing, actually." Kari rolled her eyes.

"You know what I meant."

She smiled a little. "Yeah, I did. I'm still mortified about that, though."

"I'm sure Mia didn't care. If she even noticed."

"Oh, she noticed. Many woman would."

"How?"

"Keeping your arms wrapped around yourself the way I did is like the universal signal for 'I'm not wearing a bra and I should be and I'm embarrassed by that fact.'"

"Universal?"

"Universal for people who need bras. We have our own language, you know."

"I think I read a science fiction book about that in the eighties."

"It's not science fiction. It's stone cold fact."

"I always knew women were mysterious creatures."

She rolled her eyes again. "Mia lets you get away with saying stuff like that? Weren't you bragging how she made you a feminist?"

"Touché. She'd gut me for that one. Never tell her I said it, okay?"

"It will be our secret until I need leverage. I may blackmail you with it one day."

"Cruel."

"Maybe. But fair. I will only blackmail for good."

"Isn't that impossible?"

"I guess we'll have to find out." She shot him a mischievous look, one eyebrow arching. It gave him a sort of twisting, yearning feeling.

"Anything else we should do while we're downtown?" he asked.

"Hm." She glanced at the library. "Maybe we could get a movie. Something I've seen that you haven't. Like a cultural exchange."

"Why are you looking at the library?"

"Because they have DVDs." She gave him a look that said he should know this obvious fact.

"They do?" Rob had hardly been to the library since Mia was little.

"Yeah. Your tax dollars at work."

"That's kind of awesome. But I don't even have a library card."

Kari's sneakered feet stopped and she stared at him. "You don't. Have. A library card?"

Rob's eyes wandered upward, his face heating. "Um. Nope."

"Good grief. We're fixing that immediately." She grabbed his arm and dragged him across the street to the library.

He laughed and opened the door for her, waving her in. "After you."

She gave him a fake stern look and went inside. He expected hush and stasis. What he found was a soaring room, light and open, a staircase curving around a circular wall opposite the entrance. And people everywhere.

"Huh. I'd thought libraries had gone the way of the dodo."

"Only because you haven't been inside one for years, I'm guessing."

"Guilty."

She shook her head. "Bad assumption. And a huge waste of money. Come on."

He followed her to a desk where she told a librarian about his shameful lack of library card. The woman didn't seem to be as scandalized as Kari was, merely checking his ID and issuing a plastic card with a bar code on it. He slid it in his wallet and looked at Kari, who was regarding him thoughtfully.

"I know you're up on Disney, but how are you on classic movies?"

"Um. I've seen *Casablanca*."

"That's it? What about classic screwball comedies?"

He stuffed his hands in his pockets. "Blank slate."

"Good." Turning on her heel, she led him to the media area, scanning the spines of DVD cases until her face lit up. "Aha." She pulled one off the shelf and showed it to him. "*His Girl Friday*. Perfect."

"Weren't you giving me guff about feminism? That title sounds off."

"Don't judge anything by its title. Rosalind Russell plays a journalist who is so good she...well, that's a spoiler. I mean, it's definitely not perfect feminist material, but it was also the 1940's." She handed him the case. "Go ahead. Give that shiny new library card a test drive."

Kari settled into the corner of Rob's sofa, butterflies fluttering in her stomach as he put the DVD into the player. The last time they'd done this, she'd sat on one end of the sofa and he was on the other. But now that they were... something more than friends, would they curl up together? Kari realized she hoped they would. Sex had cracked the isolated shell she had been living in for the last few years and she wanted touch and closeness.

But she also wasn't really sure where this was going or

what it was at all. It was strange to know what he looked like without clothes on, to know how he smelled and how his mouth tasted, and to wonder if wanting a cuddle was a bridge too far.

She reviewed all the little touches and sweet teasing he had indulged in since they had gotten out of bed and tried to tell herself she was being silly to wonder.

It didn't help, somehow.

Rob stood and grabbed the remote from the coffee table, starting the movie. "I always forget how the credits were so brief in these old movies," he said, sitting beside her, his hip touching hers. "This okay?" he asked, hovering his arm over her shoulder.

She nodded, not quite trusting her voice at the moment. His arm settled on her shoulders and he pulled her against him. She leaned a little, not quite relaxing into him.

Where is this coming from?

Why did this feel intimate in a way that having him *inside her body* did not?

She swallowed and vowed to focus on the movie, trying to ignore how solid and warm his body was against hers. Ignoring the thought that they would be sharing a bed tonight. To sleep in.

Maybe just to sleep. Would that be such a bad thing?

A bark of laughter from Rob made her realize that, far from focusing on the movie, her brain had drifted. Rosalind Russell had just thrown her purse at Carey Grant and he ducked, not pausing in his rapid-fire banter as the bag sailed over his head. Kari smiled a little and let herself lean into Rob a little more. He kneaded her shoulder and she sighed.

This was just so *nice*. Rob chuckled at the movie and his laughter reverberated through her body.

Stop overthinking everything.

She slid sideways a little so she could rest her head on

his shoulder. He toyed with her hair, the light touch at the back of her neck making her shiver. Her eyes slid closed, soothed by the touch and the rhythmic dialogue. She wasn't sure when she'd last felt this relaxed, this cared for, or this hopeful.

Chapter Seventeen

Rob wasn't sure when Kari fell asleep. She had been a bit stiff when they first settled in to watch the movie, but had become increasingly relaxed. Relaxed enough to nod off and sleep through the sirens and shouting on the screen towards the end of the movie. When it was over, Rob tried to ease her to a lying-down position, but that woke her. Her head jerked and her eyes flew open.

"Good grief. I can't believe I did that," she said, her hand rubbing her chest.

"Why not? You've had a big day. It was a movie you've seen before. Not surprising at all that you'd nap."

She looked sheepish. "I hope you enjoyed it at least."

"I did. Very funny. Dated, but funny."

"Yeah. A movie from the '40's is never not going to be dated."

"True." Rob's phone buzzed and he looked at it. "Text from Mia. Wants to know if it's a good time to talk."

Kari shot to her feet. "You should talk to her. I'll go get ready for bed."

"Are you still embarrassed about earlier?"

"I will be embarrassed about that until I'm eighty-five." Kari hustled out of the room, red-faced but smiling, and Rob shook his head, tapping Mia's contact information.

"Daddy." Mia answered.

"How long do you want me to keep him?"

Silence on the other end of the line. "How did you know?"

"You always call me 'Daddy' when you ask me to take Hugo. You don't need to butter me up. You know I love that mutt."

"Um. Well, here's the thing."

"Spit it out kiddo."

"The last time you took him? The thing I didn't want to tell you about for fear of jinxing it?"

"Yes…" Anxiety spiked through him. Was something wrong?

"I was interviewing for an editorial assistant position. And I didn't think I'd get it, so I didn't want to tell anyone. But I got it."

"Honey, that's great news. But what does it have to do with Hugo?"

Another pause. "The position's in New York."

"Ah." Rob's stomach dropped to his toes. He always knew Mia might move away someday. He had thought he was prepared for that to happen.

He'd thought wrong.

Mia went on in a rush. "I have a place to live already lined up. Corinne—you remember my friend Corinne from college? She's got a place in Astoria with two other girls and they're looking for a fourth for the last bedroom. But the lease says no dogs."

"So you want me to take Hugo indefinitely."

A long pause. "Yeah."

He could picture his daughter, winding a curl around her finger and wrinkling her nose, her classic fidget when she was nervous or unsure. He wished she was here so he could hug her, reassure her. Maybe even reassure himself.

"I know this is crappy timing, Dad. And if I can get a different living arrangement in a year or so maybe I can take him back."

Rob laughed a little and shook his head. If he had wanted a dog of his own, he would have gotten one. But now...no, there was no choice. He was going to have to do this. "When do you need me to take him on?"

"Not for another week," Mia said.

She made it sound like a long time. "Damn," he muttered. "I have to go to out of town for an overnight trip right after that. For work. He's going to have to go to a kennel while I'm gone." He blew out a frustrated breath. It was one thing to take advantage of him for occasional dog sitting. This was next level.

"Oh." Mia's voice was small and he felt like a heel. "He's never been to a kennel before."

"I know. But what else am I going to do? Jeez, I wish you hadn't blindsided me with this."

"I'm sorry, Dad. Really. But it's the opportunity of a lifetime."

"I can see that. Okay. We'll talk further about this later."

"Say hi to Kari for me. I'm glad you're dating her."

"How do you know we're dating?"

"She was in your kitchen with no bra on. I'm pretty sure that's more than just being friends."

"Damn. She was sure you'd caught that. She was mortified."

"Tell her it just makes me like her even more."

"It will probably only make her more mortified."

"Bras are evil. She's a smart lady. But I knew that already. She picked you."

"Take your flattery and go, kiddo. We'll talk tomorrow when I've had more time to get used to the idea of having a dog."

"Thanks, Dad. I love you."

"Love you too. Congratulations on the job," he said.

"Thanks."

Rob stood for a long time after the call ended, staring out his front window at the darkening street.

Kari slid into the bed and picked up her book, Rob's voice murmuring in the other room. He was far enough away that she couldn't hear the actual words, but he sounded agitated. Kari wondered what could be working him up so much. Mia hadn't seemed like she was in trouble or upset when she'd come over earlier.

The unmistakable cadence of a call finishing met her ears and then...silence. Kari wondered if she should go out, find out what was wrong.

Or maybe she should just mind her own business. Yes. That was probably the right thing to do at this point. She hastily opened her book when she heard his footfalls in the hallway and pretended to read, looking up when he entered the room, running his fingers through his hair, his expression exasperated.

"Everything okay?" she asked.

"Not particularly." He sat heavily on the bed, the mattress bouncing.

Kari put her book down, nervousness fizzing in her veins. She'd been right before. Mia didn't like her. "What's the problem?"

"It appears I'm about to have a dog."

Kari tried to process this. Failed. "What?"

Rob lay back on the mattress and his head landed in her lap, eyes squeezed closed. "Mia's moving to New York. She has a new job. She can't take Hugo. So doggy granddaddy is about to be a doggy daddy."

"Oh. Wow." Kari studied the stressed lines of Rob's face. His brows were drawn together, his brow furrowed. Without thought, she ran a finger over his forehead, then pulled it back. "Sorry."

His eyes came open. "Why?"

"I don't know. I just feel like I should stand back when it comes to you and Mia."

His hand came up, wrapped around her wrist, warm and gentle. "That felt nice. You can keep doing it if you want." His eyes closed again.

She wanted to. She let her gaze wander over his face, the dark hair threaded with silver that sprang back from his forehead and temples. Reaching a tentative finger out, she traced it over one eyebrow, then the other. He took in a deep breath, held it for a bit, then let it go. She stroked his forehead as if she could iron out the grooves there. He smiled a little and the lines relaxed a bit. Emboldened, she let her fingers trail down his cheeks, massaging the hinges of his jaw with gentle pressure.

"God, Kari. That's amazing."

A stuttering laugh escaped her. "I'm hardly doing anything."

One eye slitted open and he squinted at her. "You're doing everything. Do you know how long it has been since someone has touched me like this?"

She faltered, her hands hovering over his face. "Um. No? Like what?"

His eyes closed and he sighed a tired laugh. "Comfort. Caring. I didn't even know I needed this. And here you are."

Tears prickled Kari's eyes. His words brought her back to her mother's last illness, the long days of watching her slip away and the realization that came with it: Kari would never get the kind of caring that only her mother could give her again. She stroked Rob's face, smooth skin and harsh stubble under her fingertips.

His hand wrapped around her wrist again. "Hey. Are you crying?"

"No. Yes. Maybe."

He sat up, pulling her against him, rubbing her back with one broad palm. "Hey there. What's wrong?"

Kari sniffed. "I thought I was supposed to be comforting you."

"It can work both ways. Did I upset you somehow?"

"No. I was just missing my mom. And that sounds ridiculous."

He leaned back, wiping under her eyes with his thumbs. "No. It doesn't. Of course you miss her. She was your mom."

"I mean, I miss my dad too. But I've had more time to get used to him being gone..."

His hand cupped her cheek, warm and comforting. "Hey. It's been a long, emotional day. Let's get some sleep. You've got another big day to face tomorrow."

"Oh, that's right. The dinner." Kari's stomach did a nervous flutter. Sam. Her new boyfriend. And now this new dimension to her relationship with Rob...it all seemed complicated now.

Rob rubbed her shoulder. "Sleep. We'll tackle tomorrow in the morning."

Rob woke up in the middle of the night with a start, heart racing. Something was off. The bed felt funny. Then he remembered.

Kari.

Her soft breathing on the other side of the bed was deep and regular. Rob re-settled himself on his side, eyes straining in the darkness to pick out her form under the covers. It felt strange to be sharing a bed with someone after so many years. Not bad, necessarily, but strange. He rolled onto his back and stared at nothing, wide awake in spite of his slowing heartbeat.

Maybe they shouldn't have taken this step. His original reasons for ignoring his attraction to Kari were sound. He liked her. He didn't want to fuck things up with her. And now he liked her even more and wanted to fuck things up even less.

Mia would tell him he was being defeatist, focusing on an end that was not inevitable. But Mia was an eternal optimist. Look at her going off to New York to pursue her dreams. And leave him dealing with her dog, possibly for the rest of Hugo's life.

The echoes of the past were all too easy to see. New relationship, suddenly moving fast. And then being responsible for a life. It wasn't perfectly parallel, thank God. He and Liz had mistaken youthful attraction for love and only after a few years did they finally come to the galling truth that they didn't even *like* each other very much. And a kid was a thousand times more everything than a dog.

But it was parallel enough to leave him sleepless and staring at the ceiling in the middle of the night.

And what was he going to do with Hugo during his business trip? The dog would just have to go to a kennel for once. Which…good grief. He was going to have to research kennels, find a good one, make a reservation, and actually drop that poor, already stressed out animal off in the hands of strangers.

But that was later. He had Kari's dinner to go to tomorrow. For now, he was going to have to be the...what? Boyfriend? The word sounded ludicrous, applied to a forty-eight-year-old man.

He glanced over at the shadow of Kari's sleeping form and something inside him twisted. She was counting on him. She trusted him. She'd shown him how much she trusted him today in more ways than one. His jaw tightened.

He didn't care what it was called. He wasn't going to let her down.

Chapter Eighteen

"**R**eady to get your bedroom back together?" Rob snapped the dishcloth he had used to dry the breakfast dishes between his hands, raising an eyebrow suggestively.

"Not if you're going to whip me with that towel, I'm not."

"I wouldn't." He looped the damp cloth over her head and down her back, pulling her against him with it and giving her the lightest of kisses. It was the first spontaneous-seeming thing he had done all morning. His usual burble of jokes and offhand comments had dried up and his normally easy smile had been replaced with a mouth bracketed with lines and shadows under his eyes. He looked like he had slept like hell, if he had slept at all.

Guilt surged through Kari. She had slept so hard that she'd hardly moved all night, stiff yet rested on awakening at the sound of the curtain rings rattling across the rail as Rob got into the shower. Instead of following him in as she had done the day before, she had stretched and rolled over, noticing how the light in his bedroom was almost the same as it was in hers. It made sense. The rooms were ridiculously similar. Their houses were ridiculously similar, even though Rob's was larger — a three-bedroom to her two.

When he'd emerged from the bathroom, a towel wrapped around his waist, wet hair slicked back from his forehead, Kari's breath had caught in her throat. Then she noticed how tired he looked and carnal thoughts had fled.

Well, not quite fled. But they'd been suppressed.

Kari had pulled into herself a bit, retreated into a kind of concerned watchfulness. She wasn't sure what was making Rob tense, but she didn't want to add to it. And she had her own issues to think about. She needed to go grocery shopping, set up the meal, get her house tidied.

Oh, and yes, as he had mentioned, get her bedroom squared away again.

She examined Rob's face again, her eyes scanning the dark smudges under eyes and the tense set of his lips. She feathered a finger down the line that curved from his nose to the corner of his mouth. "Has Hugo put this here? Or me? Or something else?"

His eyebrows went up, then he laughed softly and sighed. "Everything. I woke up in the middle of the night. Thinking about everything. Mind racing, to be quite honest."

"And there I was, dead to the world."

His thumb traced her cheekbone and his eyes softened. "I was glad you could sleep."

"It's not a virtue. I can sleep through just about anything."

"I've noticed."

Kari looped her hair back over her ear, face flaming with furious heat. "I'm sorry."

"For what? Not being awake when I was?" Rob's face

softened further, a tender smile tugging the corners of his mouth up.

She shrugged. "Maybe?" Had he not been able to sleep because she was there? The thought made her feel awful. "Anyway. I'm awake now. Can I help?"

"I don't think so." His eyes slid to the side. "Wait. Maybe you can. Can you take Hugo for an overnight visit in a couple of weeks?"

A chill seized her stomach. "You know I've never had a pet before, right? I don't know how to take care of a dog."

"Shh." His hands came up to her shoulders, the dish towel dropping to the floor. "No. I'll find a kennel to board him. It's just one night."

God, she was the worst person in the world. "No. I'll have time to learn how to take care of him."

"Only if you're sure."

"I'm far from sure. But I want to help. You've done so much for me."

He cupped her jaw with his hands, tilting her chin so she would meet his gaze. "I haven't done any of this because I wanted anything from you."

"I know." She swallowed, rested one hand on his chest. "I want to do it, though."

"You sure?"

"No. But I want to try. God, that sounds so melo-dramatic."

"No, being responsible for a life is a big deal. I get it."

Panic skittered through her. "Responsible for a life. Oh. I take it back. Now it doesn't seem melodramatic enough."

Rob folded her against his chest, pressing her cheek to the worn cotton of his tee shirt. "Look. I'm sorry I've been weird this morning. This is all just…new to me."

"New to me too," Kari said.

Tenderness exploded in Rob's chest. He stroked Kari's back. "Good grief, I feel like a teenager."

"How so?" Kari's voice mumbled against his neck.

He searched for the right words. "I don't know how to do this. I don't think you know how to do this. But we're doing it. Just like teenagers. Feeling our way. And we're... not teenagers."

She chuckled weakly. "No. Definitely not teenagers."

Rob gathered himself. "So. Since we're definitely not teenagers, maybe we should...talk about things?"

Kari rested her forehead against his shoulder, her nose poking into his collarbone. "That *would* be the adult thing to do."

Fear shuddered through him. Fear of what he felt, what it meant, what it might mean. What Kari might or might not feel. "Or we could defer the conversation. We have a lot to do. Getting your house back in order. All of that."

"*We* have a lot to do?" Her head came up.

He realized he'd assumed she would want his help. Not cool. "Well, I'll help you if you want the help."

She looked at him for a moment, brows drawn together, then gave a decisive little nod. "Right. Getting my house in order. Dinner party."

"Exactly." He released her and bent to pick up the dish towel. "What time are you expecting them again?"

"Six." She rubbed her belly as if it contained a flock of butterflies.

"Not a problem." He grabbed a small notepad and a pen off the counter. "What do we have to accomplish in..." He consulted his watch. "Ten hours?"

Kari took the pad and pen from his hands. "Let me. I'm the organized one." She tapped the butt end of the pen against her teeth for a moment, then slashed two horizontal lines across the paper. "Three categories of stuff that needs doing. One, get my bedroom arranged and normal again." She made some notes. "Two. Clean. Three, groceries and cooking. I'd planned to do a slow cooker meal, so that should actually come first."

"The last shall be first, then. Do you know everything you need to get?"

Kari nodded. "I've made this recipe a zillion times. Never make anything for guests that you're making for the first time."

"I've only ever had people over for burgers on the grill myself, but that sounds like a good strategy."

Kari's only response to this was an eyeroll.

"What? You've never had ten sixth-grade girls over for a birthday party sleepover?"

"Stop being adorable." She didn't even look up this time, writing a list as rapidly as her pen could cross the page.

"Adorable?" His mouth twisted as he tried to resist the smile that wanted to take over his face.

She looked up from her list-making, light blue eyes pinning him in place, pointing the pen at his chest like a blade. "You absolutely know that the idea of you voluntarily wrangling ten hormonal thirteen-year-old girls is next-level bullshit cute. Don't even try to deny it."

"It was terrifying," he admitted. Mia had been a late bloomer and her serious drama had been deferred for a couple of years. But several of the girls in that party still gave him nightmares. He had expected them to still be children.

He had been right and wrong about that. They were like lethal children with wild mood swings and alarming opinions expressed in loud voices. The next year had been Liz's watch for Mia's birthday and after that, birthday parties were declared too "childish." A dinner with a couple of very close friends was deemed more sophisticated and Rob was able to sigh with relief and easily foot the bill at a moderately priced restaurant, delivering the two other girls back to their homes for the evening and enjoying a quiet movie at home with Mia to round out the night. It was a nice tradition. He wondered if she'd come home to continue it this October when she turned twenty-six. God, she probably wouldn't. His heart squeezed at the thought.

"Okay." Kari straightened, ripping the top sheet with her notes off the pad. "Battle plans. Grocery first. Then, get the roast started. Then rearrange my bedroom. Then clean." She gave him a speculative glance. "You don't have to help with all of this, you know. Or any of it."

If she'd co-opted him into all her plans, he might have balked. Perversely, her giving him an out made him want to be involved in everything. "Nope. I'm in. All the way." He knew how nervous she was about reconnecting with Sam, about meeting the new boyfriend. "What's the boyfriend's name, by the way?"

"Graham."

"And what does he do?"

"He's a university librarian."

"And here I thought I was a geek."

Kari swatted him, a weak slap against his shoulder. "Behave."

"I will. Let's go."

Kari picked up a set of tongs and turned the big hunk of chuck in the frying pan, the meat sizzling as it met the hot metal. Browning the roast was the key to this dish and it only took a little bit of time before throwing it in the crock

189

pot with the vegetables and herbs. A gentle tapping from the dining room gave her a secret smile. Rob had noticed that she hadn't yet put the art back up on the walls. She had only gotten so far as to set each piece down on the floor below where she wanted it to hang. So he'd offered to do it for her.

She finished browning the roast and turned off the gas before transferring the meat to the crock pot. Next, a quick gravy to go over the whole thing and leave it to simmer until dinner time. She added the ingredients, stirring as it thickened, then poured the gravy into the slow cooker and settled the glass lid on, giving it a pat. "You do your thing and I'll check on you in a few hours."

"You always talk to your appliances?" Rob's voice came from the doorway, making her jump. "Sorry. Didn't mean to scare you."

"I only talk to my appliances when I think I'm alone. It's a certifiably goofy habit."

"I get it, though. Easy to start talking to the appliances or the dog or the television when you're on your own all the time."

He did get it. The thought sent a little spark of nervous happiness through her. They had such different backgrounds in so many ways, but at the same time they were so compatible. It was all too easy to let herself just lean into it.

But those dark shadows under his eyes were still there, even though his casual smiles had returned. She had to remember not to just let herself lean on him. If nothing else, Sam would lose her mind. Sam had always taken Kari's parents' messages on independence and self-reliance a little too far in Kari's opinion. And she would think less of Kari for accepting so much help.

She gave herself a little mental shake. There was still a lot to do before her guests arrived. Accepting his help was just good sense. She joined him at the doorway to the dining room and peeked in. "Oh, wow. It looks so great in here. Thank you."

"I just tapped in a few nails and re-hung your stuff. Definitely not rocket surgery."

"And you would know, being that world-famous rocket surgeon." But the color made the artwork pop in a way that it hadn't when the walls had been plain and white.

"Time to do rocket surgery on your bedroom."

She nodded and he followed her to the newly-painted room. The smell had almost completely faded, but it was hot and stuffy, and Kari opened a window to let fresh air in. When she turned back, Rob was examining the bed, visually measuring the distance between it and the wall. Without a word, she joined him and they heaved it backwards, stopping short of actually letting the headboard touch. "The paint may still be a bit tender for a day or so," Rob said. "Don't want to screw up all that hard work."

Kari nodded and went next door to the guest bedroom and carried a nightstand back to set it in place. Rob followed with its mate and set it down on the other side of the bed. They shifted the dresser back in together and when Kari fetched fresh linens, Rob helped her make the bed, pulling his side of the top sheet into a tight hospital corner.

"I always kick those out," Kari confessed. "Half the time I sleep with at least one foot hanging out from under the covers."

Rob shook his head. "Not me. I like having my feet all snugged up."

Kari shuddered. "I'll bet you like those weighted blankets too."

"I've never heard of this but it sounds intriguing."

The conversation reassured Kari a little. Too much compatibility would be disturbing.

Rob looked around at the walls. "No art to hang in here?"

"Not yet." Kari looked at the smooth expanse of pale green. "This is restful for now. I'll have to decide carefully on what I might want in here."

"Why don't you make something yourself? It would be just what you wanted."

Kari tapped her chin, thinking. "Hm. Maybe I will."

Rob helped Kari clean for a while longer before she shooed him out, telling him to go take a nap. "You've got circles under your eyes and I feel guilty. Get some sleep and let me scrub my toilet in peace."

He kissed her on her forehead and went without an argument. His house seemed quiet and empty. Setting the alarm on his phone, he stretched out on top of the bed and was asleep almost instantly. When the alarm went off, it dredged him up from a dark, dreamless void, and he blinked in confusion at the angle of the sun. He hadn't slept that long in the middle of the day, well, ever in his adult life unless he was ill. He sat up slowly, turning and putting his feet flat on the floor, his hands on his knees, trying to pull his conscious mind together.

His stomach rumbled. He had forgotten to eat lunch, but he only had a half hour to pull himself together before going over to Kari's for dinner.

You're going to get hangry, Dad. He could practically hear Mia's voice in his ear.

I'm about to have dinner, kiddo.

He could also practically see her skeptical look. *Sure. Right. Have a granola bar anyway.*

Ignoring the daughter in his head, he heaved to his feet,

padded to the bathroom, and turned on the hot water. He washed, then shaved and brushed his teeth, examining his face in the mirror. The dark circles Kari had noted were still there, but much fainter. He didn't look like he was about to keel over because he'd only had a few hours of sleep followed by a few more hours of staring into the darkness. The hot water had revived him almost as much as the nap.

Returning to the bedroom, he snagged a button-down shirt and chinos from his closet. He doubted if Kari expected him to dress up, but considering the occasion, he almost pulled one of his rarely-worn ties from the rack. But no. That would look like he was trying too hard. He huffed a little laugh when he realized that instead of being Kari's support as she met her niece's boyfriend, he was now in a mirror image situation. Though he had met Sam once before, it probably hadn't been for more than ten minutes, at most. She was a virtual stranger to him, aside from what Kari had told him about their relationship. And Sam was important to Kari, therefore he wanted Sam to approve of him.

Returning to the bathroom to check in the mirror, he gave a little nod at his reflection. About as good as it got for an almost-fifty guy, he guessed.

Time to meet the family.

Chapter Nineteen

Kari circled her little dining room table, setting out silverware and napkins and trying to settle the nervous whirligigs and firecrackers in her stomach. But her pulse gave another jump when the doorbell rang and she took a moment to breathe, her hand on her belly, before she moved to the front door and opened it. Sam stood there, next to a bespectacled, bearded man with sandy hair.

"Come on in, Sammie." She gave her niece a brief, stiff hug before turning to the man. "You must be Graham. Welcome." She didn't know whether to shake his hand or hug him, so she opted for the more formal gesture. But not without a spate of awkward half-waving her hands around in the air while she decided.

Well, it wouldn't be an evening at her place if it didn't come with a side of awkward.

Graham had slate-colored eyes that crinkled appealingly as he smiled and shook her hand, acknowledging the embarrassing moment. "Call me Gray. It's nice to meet you." He inhaled deeply. "Whatever you have cooking smells amazing."

"Thank you. Old, reliable pot roast recipe."

He hefted a cloth grocery bag. "And Sam made a lemon pound cake."

Kari's mouth watered as she took the bag from his hands. "Oooh—the buttermilk pound cake recipe?"

Sam nodded, her dark blue eyes glittering with appreciation. "The very one."

"Well, come on in. Rob should be here any minute." She ushered them into the living room where Sam stopped, a smile spreading across her face.

"Your doodles." Sam pointed at the motif over the dining room entrance.

"That's more than a doodle," Graham said, his eyebrows rising.

"What Sam means is I used to doodle Scandinavian motifs all over the margins of my school notes and grocery lists and any piece of paper I could get my hands on," Kari said. She moved over to the bookshelf and pulled out a volume, offering it to Graham. "Like the stuff you see in Carl Larsson paintings."

Graham took the book from her hands, studying the cover. "Larsson? Ending in -son? Wouldn't he be Swedish?" He shot Sam a sly look.

"Oh, you've trained him already." Kari's nervousness redoubled in the face of this tiny bit of unspoken communication between them. They had created an entire relationship and she hadn't even known. "Have a seat, guys," she said as the doorbell rang again and she moved to answer it.

Rob was there, in a crisp green plaid cotton shirt, his hair still a little damp from a shower. He smelled delicious, like clean laundry and spicy soap and...him. "Hey there," he said, hoisting a bottle of wine in each hand. "Am I late for the party?"

"Right on time." And right on cue, the nervous flutters increased yet again.

"You look gorgeous." He kissed her on her cheek, heated by his compliment. She'd dug out a casual tunic dress in a bright print that she'd bought a few years ago and hardly ever worn. She had also put on mascara and lipstick in a fit of nerves.

"You're not so bad yourself. Come on in and meet Sam and Gray."

She reentered the living room and made quick introductions. "Rob, you want to come back and open one of those bottles?" She felt brittle and too bright. Chirpy, even. Not herself.

"Sure." Rob's gaze settled onto her like a weighted blanket. Perversely, it made her want to kick her feet out, free her arms. In lieu of that, she walked through the dining room to the kitchen and set the bag with the pound cake on the counter. Then she leaned on the counter, breathing deeply.

"You okay?" Rob set the bottles of wine on the counter next to her.

"Just...so much change. So fast."

"You and me?"

She swallowed, nodded. "And Sam and Gray. They're already exchanging wordless inside jokes. And I didn't even know he existed before last week." She inhaled again as Rob's hand settled on the small of her back. "I just feel like everything is happening so fast. Like everything's been frozen for a long time and now all of a sudden it's melting. Changing. Turning into a flash flood."

"What do you want me to do?"

She squeezed her eyes shut. She had to get through this.

She was being ridiculous. What could he do for her? *Think.* "Open wine? Pour wine?"

His hand moved up to her shoulder, tightened his fingers with the briefest pressure. "I can do that. And you can do this. Things are changing, yes. But does Sam seem happy?"

She nodded. "I think so." She opened her eyes and turned to peer through the dining room into the living room. She could see Sam on the couch, leaning over the Larsson book. She couldn't see Graham's face, but she saw Sam's expression as it turned up to listen to something he said and her glowing smile made Kari's heart squeeze. She nodded again. "Yeah. I think she's happy."

"Well then. Let's go get to know Gray."

Rob eyed Kari nervously as he opened a bottle and poured wine into the glasses Kari retrieved from a high cupboard. "You're ready?" he asked, voice low to keep their conversation from the younger couple in the living room.

She nodded, picking up two glasses. "Yes. Sam and I will move beyond everything. You and I will figure out what we're doing. I'll come to grips with the fact that I actually own this place."

That's right. He tended to forget that the very fact of homeownership gave her the heebie-jeebies. He picked up the other two glasses and nodded toward the living room. "Okay then."

Her chin came forward. "Yes." She nodded, seeming to try to convince herself.

Rob set the glasses back down on the counter and turned to face Kari, placing his hands on her shoulders. "You don't sound like you're ready."

"I *have* to be. I love Sam. And she's all I've got. I have to make it right."

You have me too, he thought but didn't say aloud. "You won't be able to make anything right if you're forcing it. You need to find a way to relax."

The shoulders under his hands sagged. "I don't know how to do that right now."

He mustered what was probably a cheesy grin. "Yeah, we don't have time for me to relax you the way I did yesterday. Plus, if we snuck off for a shower, I think that would be a big giveaway."

Her mouth pursed sideways. "Thanks a lot. That's the kind of statement that is the opposite of relaxing."

"But now you're irritated at me instead of stressed about the situation with Sam. So…win?"

"Way to throw yourself on the grenade there, Mr. Fox."

"I'm a giving sort of guy." He picked up the glasses again. "Back into battle. Just be yourself. Sam loves you too. You guys will get through this."

She sighed and straightened her shoulders. "Yes." She marched from the room and Rob followed. Sam and Graham were sitting on the sofa, poring over a coffee table book of some kind. They both looked up as Kari and Rob entered. Graham closed the book, straightening the slipcover and setting it down before standing to take the glass of wine Rob handed him with murmured thanks. Rob examined the couple with the practiced eye of a father who had had a few young men brought home for his inspection.

Graham was dressed almost identically to Rob, in the workaday business casual uniform of button-down shirt and cotton pants. He had an earnest air, black-rimmed spectacles, a neatly trimmed beard, and slightly shaggy hair. And when he looked at Sam, the soft expression in his eyes was what Rob would want to see in any suitor of Mia's. He was besotted. Proud.

Preliminary verdict: decent guy. Dad-approved.

Rob glanced at Kari, who had handed off her second glass of wine to Sam and was standing talking to her. Sam was saying something about a job interview and Kari was reacting with enthusiasm. A little too much enthusiasm. She glanced at Rob and he leveled his palm at the floor, dropping it down a couple of times in a "tone it down" gesture. She swallowed and looked back at her niece, her smile dimming back from its klieg-light glare to a more normal wattage.

"So that's how it is?" Graham's soft voice recalled Rob to the younger man's presence.

"How what is?"

Graham gestured his wineglass at the two women. "Halvorsen women. They're pretty amazing if my experience holds up."

"Um. Yeah." Rob took a gulp of his wine. Crap. Was he that obvious? This evening was supposed to be about Kari getting to reconnect with Sam, for her to meet Graham. Not about Kari and Rob. "It's really early. And Kari's mostly nervous about making sure she repairs her relationship with Sam. Not sure if she's ready to go public about us." But if Sam was as perceptive as her new boyfriend, she'd probably figure it out too. And the pair was sure to compare notes after the evening was over.

Graham smiled as Sam turned to him, holding out her hand to draw him into the conversation with her aunt. "I was just telling Kari about my interview with the River-Keeper's Alliance." Graham responded to her gesture and Rob moved to join the rest of the group, feeling like a third wheel somehow, even though that math didn't work out. He shoved down a swell of irritation at the feeling.

Kari's smile was now like an eager, dancing flame, natural and unforced. "Sam's almost finished with a master's degree in water resources management. She has a professor who hooked her up with an interview with an environmental advocacy group and it sounds like it went very well."

Rob raised his glass. "I think this calls for a toast. To Sam Halvorsen, may she get the job of her dreams."

The group clinked their glasses together and a rush of near-giddiness flooded through Kari. Her interactions with Sam were different, but with Rob's presence as ballast, she could see that it was possibly because Sam was excited about the job interview and nervous about her meeting Graham and not necessarily because Kari had kept *Mor's* secret.

Maybe things weren't as broken as she had feared.

Kari caught Rob's eye and he winked as he sipped his wine, sending a zing of energy through the parts of her that had previously just contained raw nerves.

"So," Sam gave Graham a sidelong glance before looking at Kari and Rob, making Kari wonder if a more serious announcement was on the way. *Too fast. Too soon.* "You guys seem cozy."

Kari coughed and color flamed on Rob's cheekbones.

"Rob's been over here a lot. Helping me with the house." Kari indicated the dining room. "I didn't know how to paint a wall, for instance. But he helped."

She glanced back at Rob, but his cheeks were still red. And his eyes were hard. "Yeah," he said. "It all started with the kitchen sink and ended with paint."

Ended? Kari's brain whirled. "Um. Could you give me a hand in the kitchen while I plate everything?" she asked Rob.

"Sure." But even in agreement, his voice was clipped.

"Sam, feel free to put on some music." Kari strode through the dining room and into the kitchen. Out of immediate earshot of her other guests, she asked Rob, "Are you *mad* at me for some reason?"

His jaw clenched and he put his wineglass down on the counter with a snap. "I don't know. Are you *ashamed* of me for some reason?"

"What?" Kari fought to keep her voice from rising. This was the last thing she expected tonight.

"I'm just your handyman? Jesus, Kari. If that was the way you really felt about me, maybe you should have told me first."

Anger and embarrassment welled up in her. "That wasn't what I meant at all." But she could see how he took it that way. Shame and defensiveness mixed in her belly, a toxic brew.

"Then why did you basically contradict Sam when she inferred that we were seeing each other?"

"Weren't you the one worried about 'giving us away'? Wasn't that about not telling them that we're together?"

"No." Rob's jaw clenched. "It was about not having sex with them in the house."

"For crying out loud, I thought I was keeping the focus on them. Tonight was about them." Why was he flipping out like this? His extreme reaction wasn't the calm, measured Rob she thought she knew. At all.

"There's room in people's heads for more than one thought at a time," he rasped, the anger in his low tones unconcealed. "And both Sam and Gray seemed to think that our being together was a good thing. I guess you're the only one who disagrees."

"I don't disagree." Kari's voice started to rise and she slapped a hand over her mouth. Taking a breath, she removed her hand and whispered. "I also didn't know how *you* would react to me taking us public without talking to you about it first. Maybe *you* would be ashamed of *me*."

"That's horseshit and you know it."

"I don't know it. I know you didn't date for ten years."

"And I broke that streak very consciously. For you. I have your art—signed by you—hanging on my wall. And you think that means I would be *ashamed* of you?" Rob's fists settled on his hips.

Kari flung her hands wide, exasperated. "You didn't exactly run out and tell Mia. She basically inferred it too. I don't know how your mind works."

"Well I obviously don't know how yours works if you take what I've done and boil it down to that conclusion."

Kari closed her eyes, pinched her lips together, trying to figure out how this had gotten out of hand so quickly and completely. "Okay. Can we start over? I'm perfectly happy to march in there and tell them that yes, we're seeing each other. That it's very new. So new that I was nervous about talking about it. Would that help?"

"Help what? Help get through the evening or help things long term? If there is a long term?"

Ice shot through Kari's veins. "Hopefully both. I'm sorry. I didn't mean to hurt you."

"Okay. Fine. Apology accepted."

But he didn't look any happier.

Rob helped Kari portion the meal and plate it up, but anger still simmered through him.

This was exactly what he'd been afraid of. Everything going off the rails and them living right next door to each other, forced to see each other all the time no matter how much it hurt.

Kari shot him a nervous look and picked up two plates, carrying them into the dining room without a word. He had two choices right now. He could go home, leave Kari to explain what had happened, or he could make the best of the rest of the evening.

He did what he always did when he was in a moral quandary: he thought about what kind of example he would have wanted to model for Mia when she was a kid.

Dammit.

Gritting his teeth, he followed her with the other two portions. Graham and Sam came in as he was setting the plates down on the table. Sam commented favorably on the wall color as they sat down.

"Yeah. Rob did it all in here when I was doing the motif in the living room." She shot him another nervous glance, exasperating him. What did she think he was going to do?

Then he remembered that he'd been one short, sharp decision away from just walking out the back door and leaving her swinging. The realization shamed him. He looked across the table at Graham. The younger man's brows were drawn together and he was looking at Kari, but his expression smoothed when he met Rob's eyes. The change in his face seemed to say, "I don't like any of this but it's none of my business and I'm staying out of it."

Rob picked up his fork and took a bite of roast, nearly moaning out loud at the tender, savory meat. Absurd as it was, he wasn't sure he could stay mad at Kari and eat food this good. He swallowed. "Delicious, Kari."

"Thank you." Her face relaxed just a little and the other two chimed in with praise for the meal.

"Kari's always been good at anything creative," Sam said. "Cooking, drawing, painting, music, knitting, *hardanger...* Anything."

Kari ducked her head. "I don't know about *anything*. I know I enjoy creating something out of ingredients or paint or yarn. What about you, Gray? Do you have hobbies?"

203

Graham looked at Sam, warmth in his expression. "Well, fishing obviously. I enjoy hiking as well. But I don't have a creative bone in my body, I'm afraid."

"Kari got all the creative genes in our family too," Sam said.

"Untrue. You tie flies," Graham retorted. "She's been experimenting with some original designs, too."

Kari's face glowed with pride. "That's great, Sammie. What a neat accomplishment."

Sam shrugged. "Some traditional patterns just weren't working on some rivers. I had some ideas about why. That's all. No big deal."

Rob chewed, a smile spreading across his face as he watched this byplay, shoveling another bite into his mouth. His daughter's voice seemed to resonate in his ears. *Dad, I told you you should have something to eat before you went over. Hangry again.*

He almost let his hand slam into his forehead. That was why he'd flown off the handle at Kari. His blood sugar level was probably hovering somewhere around his toes. Add his impulsive nature to that and bingo, he'd overreacted.

He looked at Kari. She was looking at Sam with pride and affection, her expression open and relaxed. She seemed to feel his gaze on her and she glanced at him, her face going taut.

Nothing for it but to try to row back to normal interaction. "You work at Montgomery University?" he asked Graham.

"Yeah. I'm head of technical services in the library," Graham said.

"Rob is the head of I.T. for a gaming company," Kari said. The anxious look on her face as she made the attempt to connect them almost broke Rob's heart.

Graham's fork paused between his plate and his mouth

and he shook his head at an apparently common misconception. "Not at all the same thing. We have an I.T. department too. Library technical services are the things you — hopefully — don't see as a patron. Cataloging. Acquisitions. That kind of thing. Stuff that happens behind the scenes so you can get what you need."

"And you're in charge of all that?" Kari's gaze flicked from Graham's face to Sam's. Rob read the message there. *Impressive.*

Graham chewed, swallowed, shrugged. "It's a small department."

"Being in charge of a department is a big deal, no matter the size," Rob said.

Graham's head lifted and he looked Rob in the eye. "Being responsible for people is always a big deal."

Point taken. "You're right." He glanced at Kari. She swallowed and looked at her plate.

"We are seeing one another. Rob and I," she said.

"And I was kind of a jackass about it in the kitchen," Rob said, reaching out to wrap his hand around hers. Kari looked up, her mouth falling open in surprise.

He wanted to kick himself for his thoughts earlier.

He'd been ready to chuck everything because she'd had a moment. His throat went tight. He squeezed Kari's hand and looked at Sam. She was regarding him with an interested frown. "Why were you a jackass?" Sam asked.

"Because I deflected when you asked about us. I hurt his feelings." Kari poked at her food with her fork, her eyes on her plate.

"You going to be a jackass again?" Sam asked.

He smiled at her fierce expression "No ma'am."

"Good."

Chapter Twenty

After dinner, the little group sat in the living room, savoring Sam's pound cake and drinking decaf. "I'm going to have to disagree with you, Sam," Rob said. "Kari may be a creative mastermind, but you definitely have it going on where baked goods are at."

Kari nodded. The cake's texture was perfect, the flavor the right balance between tart and sweet as it spread across her tongue.

Graham gave Sam a look of pride, then glanced at Kari, his light eyes shining behind his glasses. "It's true. She made me *julekake* a couple of weeks ago. It was amazing."

Kari's eyebrows shot up. "You made *julekake?* But it's not Christmas."

Rob's bewildered face swiveled to look at the rest of the group. "Is this more Norwegian insider talk?"

"Norwegian food," Kari said.

"You haven't told him about *lutefisk* have you?" Sam asked with a sly smile.

Kari shook her head. "No. I don't want to scare him. But he told me to do eeny-meeny-miney-mo to make a decision and was a little taken aback when I busted out *elle melle, ðeg fortelle* instead."

Sam laughed, and Kari realized it was the first time in over a month she had heard that sound. A pang of time lost shot through her at the same time as a surge of elation.

"If you ladies have had enough of your inside jokes, I'd like to know what kind of baked goods I'm missing out on," Rob said with a long-suffering air.

"Bread," Graham said. "With cardamom and candied fruit and nuts."

"Fruitcake?" Rob's brows scrunched together and his nose wrinkled.

"No. Most definitely bread," Graham corrected. "Delicious. Sam's informed me that there will be no more until Christmas, though." He laid a hand over his heart and looked at the ceiling, the picture of a wounded man.

"But...I still don't know why you made Christmas bread in June," Kari said.

"It was a thank-you," Sam said, darting a pleased glance at Graham. "Gray's brother is an attorney. He's helping us with the Norwegian lawyer. To sell the farm."

"You're...selling Litengård?" Kari's throat closed and she set her plate down on the coffee table.

"I have to," Sam said, her face the picture of helpless woe. "I can't afford to keep a farm in the U.S., let alone one in another country."

Kari nodded, numb. Sam inheriting the farm had been what started this mess in the first place. *Mor's* family had lost it in a debt to Sam's real grandfather's family, the Johannasens. *Mor* had married Einar Johannasen on the assurance that he would return the farm to her family. Instead, he had taken her to America and his family had kept the farm. Einar's brother, Sam's great-uncle, had left the property to Sam upon his death, apparently in a fit of conscience.

Kari had known and accepted the farm was Sam's. And that meant she could do as she liked with it. So why did it hurt so much to know she was selling it?

"Are you okay?" Sam asked.

"Sure," Kari said with a brightness she knew sounded forced and off.

Sam pushed the last little morsel of cake around her plate. "I should have consulted you. Before deciding to sell."

Kari shook her head and picked up her coffee. Her throat was dry. "No, you shouldn't have. You inherited Litengård, not me. It's yours to do whatever you want with."

Rob watched the byplay between Kari and Sam with increasing bewilderment. *What were they even talking about?* He glanced at Graham. The younger man's expression was concerned, but he didn't look puzzled.

But now wasn't the time to ask for explanations. The rift between aunt and niece had been well on its way to being repaired and now something else was going on.

"*Bestemor* was your mother," Sam said.

"Yes, and Einar Johannasen was your grandfather. And his brother left the farm to *you*."

"But the Johannasens shouldn't have had it in the first place. It should have been in *Bestemor's* family, not my... grandfather's." She said the last word as if the utterance cost her something. Or as if it left a bad taste in her mouth.

Kari leaned over and grasped Sam's wrist. "I happen to think this is the best outcome. After all, I ended up inheriting everything from *Mor*."

"That wasn't much," Sam said.

"I don't care. You deserve something. Can we drop it?

Enjoy your inheritance? Have something for yourself for once?"

Sam swallowed and nodded, but Rob saw it was with reluctance. And looking at Kari's tense, unhappy face, he couldn't tease out what was misery on her niece's behalf and what might be personal heartache.

Graham held up a hand. "May I ask something?"

Kari leaned back in her chair. "Of course."

"Are you upset that Litengård went to Sam or are you unhappy with how she is disposing of it?"

Kari's face worked. "I don't know." Tears glistened in her eyes but didn't fall.

Rob ached. He looked at Sam, who looked at her aunt with an anguished expression.

"So if I'm understanding this correctly, Sam inherited property in Norway?" Rob asked. Both women nodded.

"Family property," Sam said with a guilty glance at Kari.

"It's a windfall. Take it." Now Kari just seemed weary and resigned.

"Is there any way you could compromise? Do something like sell most of the land and keep the house?" Rob asked.

Sam shook her head. "The attorney in Norway found a buyer who wants to turn it into an agritourism place—kind of like a bed and breakfast, but the guests help out on the farm. For that, they need the house as well as the actual working part of the farm."

"Is that the only possible buyer?" Rob asked.

Graham rested his hand on Sam's, squeezing it a little. "What would be the point of having a house in an expensive, distant foreign country? How would she maintain it? If she hired people to look after it, how would she know they could be trusted? And even if she was able to sell just the farm-land, how long would the money last to keep the house maintained? And all for what? It's a lot to ask."

"Good grief," Kari said, her face going pale. "Graham's right. I can barely handle owning a house I live in. I can't imagine what it would be like to deal with that. I'm sorry, Sam. I should have known you'd sell it. It's logical. I just... didn't think beyond the idea that *Mor* was getting justice."

"It's okay." Sam leaned her head on Graham's shoulder. He wrapped an arm around her and looked down at her drawn face.

"I think it's probably time for us to hit the road," Graham said. "Thanks for a great meal, Kari. Nice to meet you, Rob."

The four of them got to their feet and moved to the foyer where Rob shook Graham's hand and Kari and Sam hugged. Sam gave him a solemn look and pointed her finger at Rob as Graham opened the door.

"Don't be a jackass again," she said.

"I'll try not to be." Rob smiled.

"Okay then." She smiled at Kari, then went out with Graham.

Kari closed the door and leaned back against it. "Well, that went...well? Maybe?"

"Well on some levels, okay on others," Rob said.

"What did you think of Gray?" Concern etched furrows in Kari's brow.

"Solid guy. Besotted with your niece. If he was age-appropriate for Mia and she brought him home and he behaved that way, I'd give him the Dad seal of approval."

Kari's shoulders sagged. "I'm relieved. I thought so too, but he's kind of quiet. Not a lot to go on. And I'm not used to this. I haven't met anyone Sam's dated in years. She had a really bad experience a while ago and was leery about dating. But for a second there I thought they were going to announce they were getting engaged."

"And that would be a bad thing?"

Kari flung up her hands. "It just seems so fast. Like

everything else. That flash flood feeling I was talking about. I feel caught up in too many things I can't control."

Rob reached out, wrapped his fingers around hers and tugged her away from the door. "Come on. There's a little wine left over. Let's build a raft and enjoy the ride."

After dealing with the dishes, Kari allowed Rob to tow her away from the mess and return to the living room, glasses of wine in hand. They sank to the couch and Rob kicked off his shoes, turning to sit sideways and pulling Kari against his chest. She leaned, letting his body heat soak into the tense muscles of her back.

"Tell me what's bugging you." He set his wineglass down on the coffee table and pressed his thumbs into the base of her neck, rubbing in slow, tiny circles.

"You keep doing that and I'm going to lose any ability to speak at all," she said.

"Do your best."

Kari took a breath, then another. The muscles in her shoulders and neck eased a little. "It's just...I'm used to having a small, orderly life. I'm good at that. An expert, in fact."

Rob found a knot a little lower on her back and dug into it. "How so?"

She hissed at the pressure, then dropped her head, succumbing to the massage. The knot softened. "I had a job and an apartment and a car. That was it."

"And now you have a job and a house and a car."

"And a new relationship and a niece who inherited a farm that had belonged to our family."

"The relationship I can see would be a pain. I mean, I've

met the guy. He's a pushy, noisy jackass. Completely beyond the pale. But the rest of it?"

She brought her head up, rocked it side to side, laughing softly, and he stroked his thumbs down the long muscles in the back of her neck. Her breath shuddered in her back, supported by his chest. "Sam's all the family I have."

"Is it just occurring to you that everything seems to be okay with Sam?" His voice was soft, gentle. As if he didn't want to spook her.

"It's just occurring to me that I nearly screwed everything up again with my snit about selling Litengård."

The stroking, probing fingers stilled, then resumed their soothing massage. "What's your connection with the farm?"

"Hardly any. But *Mor* used to tell me stories when I was a little kid."

"Stories? Like fairy tales?"

Kari closed her eyes and let a dreamy smile float across her face. "Pretty much. They did start with 'Once upon a time...' *Mor* would tell me about the cattle they had, the kitchen garden with its vegetables in the summer, the long winter nights when the family would sit and make things in the candlelight."

"It sounds idyllic," Rob said.

"It sounded very *hygge*." Kari's brain was fuzzy now, drifting with the fatigue of a tense, emotional evening and the soothing of Rob's hands.

"More Swedish Chef-speak?" Rob teased, and she could hear the smile in his voice.

"It means...cozy. But more than cozy. I'm not sure I could explain it properly even if I had more than a smattering of Norwegian. It has to do with companionship and creating a congenial space and..." She spread her hands, running out of ways to describe a concept she had only the most tenuous grasp on herself.

"Sounds like what you're trying to create here in this house."

Kari's eyes flew open and the fuzziness vanished as the truth of his statement struck her. "You're right. That's part of the reason why I've always wanted a home of my own. You can really make it yours. You can't paint an entire wall, let alone do that in most rentals." She pointed at the motif over the entrance to the dining room. "And if you can, you know you're going to be moving on eventually. That kind of impermanence made me not want to put the effort in to make a space truly *hygge* in the way I want to."

"Is this...*hygge*," Rob said, the swooping Norwegian vowels going flat in his mouth, "something you can do in a 'small, orderly life' that doesn't include more people? It seems to me that you need people to accomplish it. It seems like you might have gotten there this evening, in fact."

Rob felt the moment when Kari's breath arrested, her back stiffening against his chest. Had he overstepped something, or hit the nail on the head?

"How often are you alone, Kari?"

"A lot," she said, her voice small.

"And yet you seem like someone who naturally loves to have people around. You created a beautiful dinner tonight. You made a lovely evening for Sam and Gray. And me."

She let her head rock back and rest on his shoulder. He transferred his massage to her scalp, fingers threading through her fine hair, and she groaned. "You say that even after my gaffe?" she asked.

He refrained from shrugging, not wanting to disturb her. "We hadn't talked about how open we were going to be with them yet. You were being cautious and I was being an asshole because my blood sugar was low and I have impulse control issues."

"You're being generous."

"No, it's true. I had my daughter in my head berating be for letting what she calls 'hangry' get away from me. But I'm trying. Will you let me?"

She took in a deep breath. It shuddered a little in her chest. "I'll try to."

Rob retraced the thread of their conversation. All roads seemed to lead back to Litengård. "So the farm was a fairy tale to you." He could imagine that fairy tale, with her as the heroine, sitting in a Norwegian farmhouse, her pale skin and hair made luminous by candlelight as she knitted something. It was a beautiful image.

Kari nodded, her head rocking against his collarbone. "For a while. Then the stories dried up. I'd ask *Mor* to tell me more about it and…she'd wave a hand and say, 'Forget about it. It's gone. We're Americans now.' I think now she realized I was idealizing it and she wanted me to be more realistic."

"Or maybe she had hoped the farm would be restored to her family somehow and then lost that hope."

"I don't know how. When she was so sick and told me about her first husband—well, her only husband—she told me she'd written to the Johannasens to notify them of Einar's death, and then again to let them know about Bjorn's birth. That's probably how Sam's great-uncle knew to look for her. But now I wonder if she wanted to shame them into returning Litengård to her family. 'Look! There's an heir! A boy child to work the land and make you proud!'" Her voice went flat and bitter at this last.

"You think your mother didn't value you as a daughter?" The words caught at his throat, made him want to bite.

She shook her head. "No, I think the Johannasens didn't

value *her*. She basically sold herself to them. She married their faithless Einar and he betrayed her. They all did. And then Einar brought her here. A place she never wanted to be. We cremated her, you know." She said this like it was something that should mean something to him.

"Yes?"

"Sam and I scattered her ashes in the Atlantic on the Eastern Shore. She told me she wanted to swim back to Norway. She never wanted to be here."

Rob's fingers flexed on Kari's shoulders. "But it sounds like she made a good life here for you. She found love. She raised children she loved."

"But she always thought of Litengård."

"And now Sam's letting it go."

She nodded. "And Sam *should* let it go. I'm glad she didn't get the same stories that I did. She doesn't have the same fairy tale feeling about it. And she shouldn't. It's not paradise. It's a rugged farm in a cold, harsh country, far from everything she's ever known. Even if she moved to Norway to run it—I can't even finish that sentence. She has no idea how to run a farm. Neither do I. The idea of either of us trying to take it on is ludicrous. We don't even speak Norwegian."

Kari's natural practicality reasserting itself was both reassuring and heartbreaking. She was letting go of a real-life fairy tale in front of his eyes. Rob wrapped his arms around her, resting his cheek against hers, inhaling the light scent of her shampoo, the warmth of her skin.

"Would I be a benefit or a burden in your bed tonight?" he asked.

Kari's eyes fluttered closed. "Benefit. Oh, please be a benefit."

"I'm on it."

Chapter Twenty-One

Rob's arms tightened around Kari. She wished she and Rob could be in two places at once: on this couch, the massage going on far into the night, and in her bed, driving each other wild.

In her bed.

In her house. *Her* house.

Wow. With all the stress she had experienced over purchasing her own home, there was something ground-breaking about this thought. Having sex in her own home for the first time. Like christening it or something. A fresh start. Even the queen-sized bed was new, her previous one being too cheap, too old, and the veteran of too many moves to survive being broken down and reassembled one more time. She still marveled at how solid the new one felt, not swaying and creaking when she got into or out of it.

Yeah, that old bed would never have survived another move, let alone even the thought of what she wanted to do. To have Rob do.

Rob's hands slid down her bare arms, the warmth from them giving her a paradoxical shiver. The shiver was echoed lower, as her body gave a little anticipatory pulse, the nerves of her clit faintly zinging. She got to her feet, Rob following her lead, threading his fingers with hers as they left the living room for the bedroom. Inside, Kari turned on one bedside lamp, its glow illuminating the soft green of the walls.

"Thanks for this," she said, indicating the color as she turned and walked into his open arms.

"Any time."

"Better be careful of how you throw that word around. I have a few more rooms in here."

"Good. Gives me an excuse to be near you more often." The future stretched before her now, more comforting with Rob in it, no longer alone and more than a little apprehensive.

"You need an excuse?"

"Maybe not anymore." His gaze dipped to her mouth. "So, is now the time I tell you I've been thinking about kissing you on and off all evening?"

"On and off, huh?"

A corner of his mouth tugged up a little in a crooked smile that made her heart thump. "Okay, I think the only time I wasn't thinking about kissing you was when we had our little...argument." He smoothed a thumb over her lips as she started to apologize again. "Shh. Not necessary. And I'm just as culpable and just as sorry. Besides, any more talking delays the kissing."

"We couldn't have that," she said, and pressed her lips to his.

Kari's eyes sank closed as she leaned forward, pressing into Rob and deepening the kiss she had started. His breath caught in his chest and his heart started an erratic thump. She traced the edges of his ears with the lightest of touches and it seemed that entirely new nerve endings sprang to life in his body, an electric current running down the back of his neck, through his spine and down his legs, making his knees weak. He tightened his arm around her waist, spearing his fingers into her hair with his other hand. Kari's head tilted at the same time as his did and their mouths met more firmly now, lips parting, tongues teasing, exploring. Rob's hand on her back slid down over her butt and she inhaled as his fingers flexed.

"Mmm. I like it when you gasp like that," he whispered against her mouth.

"You do?" Her voice shivered with laughter. Or arousal. Maybe both.

"Yeah. It makes your breasts press into me. Very nice."

"You like my breasts?" Where had the tinge of doubt in her voice come from?

He rested his forehead against hers, eyes closed. "Why wouldn't I?" Good lord. They were soft and responsive and...well, hell. They were breasts. That alone would be very nice. But *Kari's* breasts? On Kari's body? Was she kidding?

She shrugged, another thing that made her body move in interesting, enticing ways. "They're...not what they once were."

"They're beautiful." He kissed her again. He couldn't conceive of what her breasts must have been once. The idea of younger Kari and younger Rob meeting had the ability to short-circuit his brain entirely. He was glad, in fact, that he hadn't met Kari when Mia was still growing up.

This woman potentially had the power to make him throw away every principle he held dear.

He waited for terror to strike him in the wake of this

realization. Instead, he was swamped with lust. His cock was stirring, hardening. Like Kari's body, his didn't have the same spring and responsiveness it once had had. But it still worked. Oh, yes, it worked.

"This dress…" he mumbled against her mouth. "It's very pretty."

"But you want it off?"

"Yes please."

"Can you do my zipper?" she asked.

"How did you do it up yourself?" He found the tab at the nape of her neck with his fingertips, pulled down, making himself take it slow, tooth by excruciating tooth.

"With much contortion and effort."

"You should have called me. I'd come over and do you up."

"Would you?" She leaned back, a wicked light dancing in her pale eyes.

"Well." His eyes slid to the side. "I might have been tempted to undo you before doing you up."

"Or do me before you…did me up?"

A surprised snort of laughter caught in his throat and the slow descent of the zipper became a rush. His fingers brushed bare skin, warm and soft. A tiny, feral smile flickered across Kari's face and her eyelids sank a little. His cock hardened further and he shifted his weight, trying to ease the constriction of his pants.

"Problem?" she asked.

"Only temporarily. I think."

She nodded. "Yes. Definitely temporary." Her lips nipped at his and then she leaned back, her hands leaving his body to slide the dress over her shoulders, down her arms until it slipped past her hips to the floor. His mouth went dry and he swallowed. Kari was wearing a bra and matching panties in light blue lace, almost the exact color of her eyes. He traced the scalloped edge of one cup, the lace pushing her breast into a plump mound. The edge of one areola was just visible. The entire effect was an unholy combination of innocence and temptation.

"I'm glad I didn't know about this all night," he said, his voice coming out in almost a croak.

"No?" There was a wicked light in her eyes and her mouth curved in a tiny, self-satisfied smile.

"Socializing would have been torture. Dinner would have been torture. Everything would have been torture."

"And what is it now?"

"Whatever the opposite of torture is."

Kari kicked her dress to the side, sending her shoes in the same direction with flicks of her ankles. "Come here. I want some of that opposite torture too."

Kari's fingertips tingled with the desire to get Rob out of his clothes. She popped buttons out of their buttonholes as fast as she could, tugging his shirt free of the waistband of his pants. He caught her wrists, holding them lightly.

"You're in a hurry, speedster." Lines fanned out from his dark eyes, humor glinting from them in the low light.

Her hands clenched into loose fists. "I can't want a little escape after a tense day?"

"Sure. Want away. But let's slow down. We're not kids. We have time."

"I'm sick of adulting." Kari was aware that she was being petulant but she didn't care. "Besides, you got me practically naked in one move. It's not my fault you're wearing more clothes." She leaned into him, letting her head rest on his shoulder. Her wrists slid out of his hands and her hands spread across his chest, pushing his shirt off. Fingers curling into the soft cotton of his undershirt, she dragged it up, letting her touch trail over his sides, relishing how the contact made him shudder. He reached behind his neck and grabbed the shirt, pulling it off. His head emerged, hair mussed, eyes sharp on her.

"Fine. You want to play like we're kids?" His hands slid around her waist, then down past the waistband of her panties, cupping her bare ass and pulling her into his chest.

"Yes," she mumbled into his skin. "I want to be a goddamn adult with a mortgage and a car payment and still *play.*"

"So let's play." His hands skimmed up her back and paused. Her bra's band loosened and she took an unfettered breath. His breath huffed in an almost-laugh. "You really hate those things, don't you?"

"I really do," she said, pulling away so he could remove the hated garment and toss it on the floor.

"It is pretty, though. Matches your eyes."

"Then it has done its job and it can die now," Kari said, her fingers working at Rob's belt buckle, freeing the leather strap and going to work on his fly.

"I don't know how you can wonder that I think your breasts are beautiful," Rob said, his hands cupping them, lifting them back to the plumpness that the bra had given them.

They sag now. They aren't young. Aren't perky. But any more thoughts of this kind fled when he ducked his head and sucked, tongue swirling around the aching nipple. His hand pinched and teased at the other one. His caresses sent an aching desire arrowing through her, her hips swaying toward him eager for contact, friction, connection.

Maybe her middle-aged breasts weren't so bad after all, if they could still make her feel like this. She pushed at his pants, urging them down his legs, limited in what she could do without making Rob pull away, and she didn't want to stop him creating those exquisite sensations.

He did pull away and Kari suppressed a groan. But he pushed his pants down, toeing off his shoes and stumbling a little as he freed his feet.

"Smooth," he said, shooting her a crooked grin that made her heart seem to melt and dribble through her ribcage. She captured his face in her hands, her eyes searching his face.

"I don't want smooth."

"What do you want?"

She swallowed. "Real. I want real."

The crooked grin spread and his hands skimmed up her ribcage, cradled her breasts again. "I want real too."

Kari swallowed, her eyelids fluttered closed.

"I want *you*, Kari." Rob's voice was soft, coaxing. His fingers teased her nipples, his lips traced the side of her neck. "You're real and you're brave and you're...oh. You're so fucking beautiful." His lips met her skin and she gasped. "Yes." He pinched her nipples and her half-lidded eyes closed. "I love that. Your reactions."

She swallowed and closed her eyes. She needed to engage. To act. Not just react. She stroked her hand up the hard ridge of his cock over his boxer briefs. He inhaled, shuddering from the teasing touch. She stepped closer and hooked her fingers into the waistband, pulling his underwear down his legs until they fell around his ankles.

"Time for you to lose the drawers too," he murmured in her ear, his breath fanning her nerves into flame. He bent, dragging the lace slowly down and her eyes flew open as his lips pressed against her clit. Her knees trembled as he brushed her curls aside, the tip of his tongue probing, ever so gently.

"Oh, God." She swallowed, her eyelids fluttering as he

continued to tease. Her knees trembled again and he chuckled, pressing another kiss to her clit.

"Can your knees hold you if I bend you over the bed?"

Kari started to answer, found her voice gone, cleared her throat and tried again. "I think so. Would you like that?"

"I would really like that."

Rob rose from his knees, wincing a bit. Nothing like kneeling on a hardwood floor to remind him of his age. But Kari's hazy, pleasure-ridden expression made him forget all of his discomfort. He took her hand and led her toward the bed, pulling her against him for a long, exploratory kiss. His dick, sandwiched between both of their bellies, throbbed with want. More heat, more contact, more...

He remembered that she'd needed help before. He drew back a little. "Where's your lube?" She wordlessly pointed at the bedside table. He turned and pulled the drawer open.

Interesting. A small blue-green object like a large, silicone covered bullet sat next to a larger purple object shaped a bit like a curved barbell with teardrop-shaped ends. *What the... Oh.* He thought back to their earlier sexual encounter, what she had said about why she needed lube, and comprehension flooded through him. He grabbed the container of lube and the bullet, holding it up.

"You said you wanted to play?"

Her eyes widened and her already pink cheeks flushed a deeper hue, the color spreading down her neck to her collarbones. Her tongue darted out across her lips and she swallowed.

"Your choice," he said, not sure if her reaction was embarrassment, arousal, or some combination of the two.

Her chin dipped twice in a jerky nod, her gaze skimming

from his hand to his dick and then up to his face. Only then did a tiny, feral smile chase over her lips.

"Well then." He wasn't sure how to begin. He'd never even held a vibrator before. All his previous ideas about them had been more...explicitly phallic. Obscene, even. But this little object was almost a cipher of industrial design. The non-business end was silver and had the universal power symbol stamped into it. He pressed his thumb down on it and it jumped to life, emitting a soft buzz as it vibrated. He almost dropped it. "Yikes. This thing is powerful."

Kari nodded. "Be gentle with it. With me." She took it from his hands, turning it off, and led him back to the bed, dropping the vibrator to the coverlet and cupping his jaw in her warm hands. Her lips skimmed across one cheekbone, then the other, then landed warm and sure on his mouth, tongue slipping inside, taking what she wanted and giving him a delicious feeling of being desired. She broke the kiss and breathed in his ear, "How do you want me?"

Dear lord, but this was giving him flashbacks to being a kid, hunched over a skin magazine, reading in a furtive haste. *I never thought it would happen to me, but...* "Turn around," he said, putting his hands on his waist and rotating her toward the bed. Her torso sank forward without his urging, her palms coming to rest flat on the coverlet. The movement made her hips tilt up and Rob drew in a breath. The almost innocent-seeming eroticism of her baring herself to him was going to make his head explode.

He opened the tube, dribbling lube onto his fingers and stroking them over her sex. She hissed.

"Was that bad?"

"Just a little chilly."

"Ah. Sorry."

"Don't be sorry. Just fuck me."

Rob wasn't a guy who needed to be asked to do a thing

224

twice. Especially when it was a thing he was dying to do. "Legs further apart," he said. She shifted and he picked up the bullet before he guided his dick into her. He groaned as he slid home, then groaned again when she clenched around him, just the faintest increase of pressure, but enough to make his nerves almost override his desire to go slow, to give Kari her climax first. He leaned to wrap his arm around her, guiding the humming silicone to her clit.

She hissed again. "Not that hard." And then, "Yes. Oh. Yes," as he moved it, experimenting at the same time as he began to pump his hips. He could feel the vibration faintly, creating an extra delicious shiver in his own body. He forced himself to breathe deeply, to not plunge into her, to not get lost in her.

Not yet.

Not that the limitations forced on him by the application of the vibrator meant he could go crazy. His arm was only so long and he wasn't Stretch Armstrong. He kept his strokes short and circled the vibrator until Kari's body was bowstring-taut and shaking. He pulsed into her and circled the vibrator again. Once, twice. She gave a strained, needy little sound. A third time. As it circled down again, she let out a shuddering cry, pulsing around him so hard it only took a couple of short strokes for him to lose himself entirely, his hips pressing into her as if they were becoming a single being, his dick throbbing, ecstasy and a sharp, warm, needy feeling flooding his body.

He was hardly aware of her taking the still-vibrating bullet from his limp fingers and turning it off. The sudden silence boomed in his ears.

Kari dropped the vibrator and rested her weight on her hands. Rob stroked her back, her rear, and down her thighs before withdrawing slowly.

"God. I didn't want that to end," he said.

Kari straightened and turned, wetness trickling down the insides of her thighs. "Any longer and my knees might have given out."

"I would have caught you," he said, his voice a little rough.

"That's a lot to promise," she said.

"No. No it's not." His eyes were hooded, darker than usual in the soft light. Serious and intense.

"Is something wrong?"

One corner of his mouth kicked up and the serious look was replaced by warmth. The intensity remained, though. "The opposite."

More moisture trickling down her legs. "I…" She hooked a thumb over her shoulder, toward the bathroom.

He nodded. "Yeah."

"I'll be right back."

"I'll be here."

Something about that simple statement hit her square in the chest. She blinked.

"That is, if you want me to be." He half-raised one hand as if to touch her, let it drop.

She reached out, grasped his hand with both of hers. "I do."

His fingers curled around hers, the briefest pressure. "Go get cleaned up."

Kari let go of his hand and cupped Rob's chin, giving him a fast, firm kiss.

"You're a good man, Rob Fox."

Rob watched Kari's retreating back, pale in the low light, feeling stunned.

That electric bolt of…whatever he had felt as he lost himself inside her was entirely new. He felt raw, exposed. Eustace Scrubb from *The Voyage of the Dawn Treader* with his dragon body peeled away, bare and vulnerable as a willow switch.

Okay, nerd. Dial it back.

He rubbed his face. He didn't know what this pounding, needy feeling was, but he knew he should clean himself up a bit. Snatching a few tissues, he dried himself off and dropped the waste in a basket in the corner.

Returning to the bed, he picked up the vibrator and container of lube, setting them down on her bedside table. "I salute you, sir," he whispered to the vibrator. If someone had asked him a few weeks ago if he would have been okay using a device to help get his lover off, he would have been offended. He could do it himself, he would have thought. To do anything else was a failure as a man.

But tonight had turned all that upside down. The vibrator hadn't seemed like a challenge to his masculinity, it had been a way of making Kari keen and shake and lose herself. Of making her feel as good as she could.

And he had certainly reaped the rewards as well. Kari clenching and spasming around his dick was…well. It nearly made his eyeballs roll up into his head just thinking about it.

She returned then, hesitating in the doorway. He held out a hand and she came to him, letting him pull her against his body. This was nice too, the skin to skin contact, her body's softness pressing against him.

"Let's go to bed," he murmured.

Chapter Twenty-Two

Rob wasn't falling asleep.

Kari wanted to sleep so badly. She craved the release into the dark abyss. She loved sleeping. Adored it. But now she lay on her side, her back cuddled to his front, waiting for his breath to deepen, for the arm around her middle to go slack.

It didn't happen. Rob was quite definitely still awake. Her eyes flicked to the clock. They'd been lying here for two hours, neither of them sleeping. Kari was all too aware that the last time they'd made love she had fallen asleep soon after and Rob had spent a mostly sleepless night. This time, knowing that, she was unable to dive off sleep's cliff headlong the way she usually did.

She bit her lip and turned in the circle of his arm. "You can't sleep?" she whispered.

"You neither." Yes. His voice was very clear, very awake.

"I can't sleep because I know you couldn't sleep before. Last time, I mean. I felt bad."

"No reason for you to lose sleep just because I'm being an insomniac."

She thought about this for a minute. "Are you usually an insomniac?"

A long pause. "No."

Kari's throat tightened. "Is this…about me?"

Rob's arm tightened around her. "No. I just can't sleep."

Kari rolled over and reached out in the darkness, carefully letting her hand land on his face, caressing his cheek, running her fingertips through his hair. "Would you… would you feel better if you were sleeping in your own bed?"

"Do you want your bed to yourself?"

"This isn't about me. I want you to get a good night's sleep." Not one hundred percent true. Kari was used to sprawling across her mattress, not needing to worry about crowding anyone else out.

"You're not sleeping either."

"Only because you're not."

He heaved to his elbow, his form more distinct now in the darkness. "I should go. You'd sleep better if I wasn't here."

Kari flopped to her back, looked up into the darkness. "You mean you'd sleep better in your own bed."

A long pause. "Maybe."

"Go. Sleep."

He settled in beside her, his arm wrapping around her waist, his lips pressing her temple. "When will I see you again?" he whispered.

"I'm next door. Whenever you want." Kari was unable to keep the acerbic rasp out of her voice.

"Are you okay? Is it okay if I go back to my place?"

He so clearly didn't want to be here. Kari braced herself for offense, for feelings of rejection to overtake her.

Nothing.

She groped in the darkness until she found his face

again, stroked his cheekbone with her thumb. "Go. Sleep. I'll see you tomorrow. Or whenever."

His lips found hers. A kiss that fired her bloodstream. She cupped his face with her hands and her body torqued with ache as he broke the kiss and got up. She lay and listened to the quiet rustle of him gathering his clothes in the dark. His hand caressed her cheek and his lips found hers again, fastening soft and sweet this time.

"Sleep well, Kari."

"You too."

She listened as he padded out, closing the bedroom door softly behind him, then the whipping cloth sound of his pants being drawn quickly up his legs, then his shod feet treading to the door, then finally the front door's solid thunk as it closed behind him.

With a sigh, Kari sprawled across her mattress, arms and legs splaying towards all four corners and was out within minutes.

Rob's shoulders started to relax as he closed his own front door behind him. He shambled to his room, chucking the shirt and undershirt he hadn't bothered to put back on for his walk home at the laundry hamper in the corner. Toeing off his shoes, he staggered a little and put his hand on the wall to steady himself. Christ, he was tired. He shucked out of his pants and sent them the way of his shirt. He hadn't been able to find his underwear in the dark, but he also hadn't wanted to turn on the light and disturb Kari any more than she already was. Mia could never go back to sleep if he turned on a light when she was a little girl and the knowledge had never left him.

Guilt nagged at him as he stripped back the sheet and

duvet and slid into his bed. His own bed felt right. He'd slept alone for a decade. But he had also loved the feel of Kari's long body snugged up against his own. He had thought that maybe he'd be able to nod off if he felt her relax, her shallow waking breaths turning into deep, slumbrous ones. He had counted on that to soothe him into following her into dreamland.

Instead, she had been looking out for him, worried about him, unable to sleep because he couldn't nod off. He wondered if she was still lying awake like he was, unable to relax.

He lay on his back and pushed his fingers through his hair. What kind of a jerk couldn't sleep in the same bed with the woman he—no. He wouldn't even think it. The feeling or emotion or whatever it was that had ripped through him with his orgasm might be something bigger. But more likely it was a side effect of physical release. Best not to prove Mia right and be impulsive and potentially ruin everything.

Glancing at the clock, he realized that yet again he was wound as tight as he had been in Kari's bed. Tighter, maybe. Monday morning would come all too soon. He needed to sleep, but something nagged at him, as if he had forgotten something.

The heel of his hand crashed into his forehead. He *had* forgotten something. His phone was currently lying on Kari's coffee table.

He would just have to go over there tomorrow morning and retrieve it. And hope Kari had been able to get a good night's sleep.

The sun woke Kari before her alarm did. She rolled to her back, sending her arms and legs in all directions in a languorous stretch. She blinked and relaxed against the mattress, letting the world come back to her slowly. She'd slept soundly but for waking up in the middle of the night, released from a dream about not being able to find a bathroom, her subconscious's way of fighting with her body's desire to remain asleep when she desperately needed to pee.

The lovely, dull ache between her thighs recalled her mind to the previous evening, and when she glanced at the clock, her bullet vibrator and tube of lubricant on the nightstand brought back other memories that sent her lips curving in a smug little smile.

She sat up, surveying the room. Her clothes were scattered around the hardwood floor, her shoes lying at drunken angles where she'd kicked them.

The only thing missing was the man who'd caused the carnage.

She had clung to wakefulness, wanting to delay sleep until he proved to her that he could fall asleep beside her. Instead, he had remained awake and fled for his own bed at the first opportunity.

Another bed he couldn't sleep in if she was in it.

Kari's mouth twisted and she swung her feet out of the bed and onto the floor, standing and stretching again, yawning and blinking.

Well. She hoped he was as well rested as she was. She bent to pick up her dress and laughed as she realized Rob's boxer briefs were resting on top. She tossed his underwear on her bed and gathered up the rest of her clothing from the night before, shoving the dress into the drop-off bag from her dry cleaner and the rest into the laundry basket in her closet. Snagging her robe and wrapping it around her, she grabbed Rob's underwear and folded it into a neat bundle, tucking it into her pocket before she headed for the kitchen.

Passing through the living room, she saw Rob's phone on her coffee table.

Really.

Was the man congenitally forgetful or was he marking his territory?

Going into the kitchen, she started a pot of coffee and leaned on the counter, staring at her backyard, her brain ticking into planning mode. She had hazy ideas about a series of raised beds at one corner of the fence and she let her mind roam over the possibilities as the rich smell of brewing coffee filled the kitchen.

Her doorbell roused her from her gardening trance and she pushed herself off from the counter, fairly sure of who was ringing her bell. Gathering the phone off the coffee table, she walked to the front door and looked through the peephole.

Even distorted by the fisheye lens, Rob looked delicious. Kari opened the door and leaned against the frame, taking in his freshly shaved cheeks, shower-damp hair, and workday wear of khakis and button-down shirt, interchangeable with what he had worn to her little dinner party.

"Looking for these?" Kari offered the phone and produced the underwear from her pocket, pleased to see Rob's cheekbones redden as he opened his hands.

"Thank you," he said, receiving them.

"Coffee?" Kari asked.

"No thanks," Rob said. "I have a staff meeting first thing. But—"

Kari's heart hammered. "But?" He'd dashed out so quickly last night. Had he changed his mind?

He shifted uncomfortably and Kari realized she was holding her breath.

"I know it's probably too much because we've already

spent the entire weekend together, but would you have any interest in doing something tonight?"

"Something?" Her pulse didn't seem to get the message that he wasn't breaking up with her. Or maybe it did.

"Or nothing," he added quickly. "Your place or mine. I just…enjoy your company. If you want to be alone, I get it."

"No," she said, realizing from the way his face fell that he'd misinterpreted her negative. "No, I mean I don't want to be alone."

His face split in an uncertain grin. "Great. I'll see you when I get home, then."

"Do me a favor and put my number in your phone?" she asked.

"Right." His sudden off-kilter manner was adorable. She gave him her number and he typed it in with careful fingers.

"Text me when you get home," she said. "Or during the day. We'll figure out what we want to do."

"Or we could do nothing." He shot her a wicked smile.

Kari smiled. "*Nothing* sounds good too."

Chapter Twenty-Three

"Thanks everyone, let's make this a great week."
Rob closed his laptop and unplugged it from the
conference room projector as his senior staff
gathered their things and rose from the table. "Sandra, do
you think you can give me a minute?"

His help desk manager gave him a look that said she had
an inkling of what was coming. "Sure." She followed Rob to
his office and closed the door behind her without his asking.

He sat at his desk, waving at a guest chair. "I didn't want
to say this in front of the rest of the managers, but apparently your people's reduced response times have something
to do with closing out tickets before they've even addressed
the problem."

Sandra rubbed her forehead and sighed. Her brown
cheeks were flushed with embarrassment. "That batch of
new hires. I've talked to them. I've had more come-to-Jesus
meetings than a revival tent preacher. Two of them seem to
think that they should be interacting with the programmers
all the time and they blow off anyone who isn't directly
involved in making games. I think they think they should

have been hired as game developers or programmers instead of help desk staff."

Rob empathized with Sandra. But he also had a bigger problem on his hands. "One of the people they've blown off is Anna Walter-Venturo. I got a call this morning."

Sandra covered her eyes with her hands. "Tell me that didn't happen."

"Twice." Anna, CFO and Executive Vice President of Operations of Potomac Games, was not someone he wanted to make unhappy. Not least because she was his boss.

Wincing, Sandra put her hands in her lap with a resolute air and asked, "On a scale of one to livid, how livid is she?"

"Angry. I think it's fair that you can tell your staff they close tickets *after* solving problems or they get their own problems. The kind that has security marching them out of the building."

Sandra nodded, running her hand over her short-cropped black curls. "I'll go through the help desk logs, see who is specifically letting us down and put the fear of… something into them."

"Good. These guys need to know that it isn't just programming that writes their paychecks."

"In Anna's case, that's a bit on the nose, considering she manages the people who really do write our paychecks," Sandra said, fingering an earring.

"Exactly. Let me know if I can help."

Sandra sat straighter in her chair. "No. My staff, my problem."

"Yes. Your call. But if you change your mind, let me know. We're a team. I have your back and every faith in you."

"You got it." With a firm little nod, Sandra stood, clasping her tablet to her chest as she left his office.

Rob docked his laptop and turned on his monitor array, muttering. "What else can possibly go wrong today?"

"Oh, thank God."

"Sapna, what are you trying to do?" Kari paused in the break room doorway, a takeout dispenser box of coffee in each hand and a paper carrier bag with cups, cream, sugar, and other items looped over one wrist. Sapna was half on the countertop next to the sink, trying to reach the top shelf of the cupboard on the wall.

"Trying to get the serving stuff for the quarterly afternoon coffee social," Sapna grumbled. "Why it's up here, I can't tell."

"Because I'm the one who organizes it and sets up for it and breaks it down and we don't use the serving stuff at any other time so it makes sense. And yeah, I'm tall," Kari put the coffee and paper bag on one of the break room tables as Sapna scrambled down. "Why are you working on this anyway?" She appreciated the help but some notice would have been nice.

"Assistant to The Man thought you were swamped, asked me to help out." Sapna frowned as Kari stretched to her tiptoes and pulled the tray of serving dishes and utensils down. "And it's not fair that you're vertically gifted."

"No, not fair," Kari agreed, setting the tray down on one of the break room tables. "But it's a fact. And it's a fact that I'm always swamped. But it's also a fact I also always do the setup for the quarterly coffee." *And the breakdown and clean-up afterward.*

Sapna shrugged.

Kari leaned on the table. "Why didn't you let me know you'd been tapped to do this?"

"I figured you must be in a real crunch if Logan's right hand woman asked me to help out." Sapna shrugged again. "I hate to admit it, but I didn't notice how much stuff you seem to do that isn't really work-stuff. Stuff like the quarterly social, the company newsletter, any time there's a wedding or baby shower. You get shit done, Halvorsen. You grease the social wheels of this place. I guess I wanted to contribute."

"That's really nice of you." Kari's eyelids sank closed. "But honestly, it's easier for me to do this myself."

"You sure?" Sapna's voice seemed to come from a long way away. Damn. Kari had thought she'd gotten a good night's sleep. But now she was exhausted.

Kari cracked her eyes open. Nodded. "Yeah. Go edit. Let me set this up. Do you even know who's volunteered to bring stuff?"

Sapna shook her head, her eyes wide. "I feel like I'm being initiated into a secret society."

"Yes, the secret society of flour and vanilla extract. Go. I got this. I know who I need to visit to obtain the baked goods and get this show on the road."

"Okay." Sapna left, the door closing softly behind her. Kari shook her head and laid out the serving items and the coffee on the counter, then went in search of her volunteers.

Who, she realized as she collected a plate of cookies, a coffee cake, and a fruit salad, were all women.

Her shoulders rounded as she finished laying everything out. The first arrival after the clock ticked to two was a cis male editor. And then The Man himself, Logan, came in. As always, he was the only one in the company who wore a suit and tie, and also as always, his suit jacket was in his office, his tie was loosened, and his shirtsleeves were rolled up. Not for the first time, Kari wondered what the point of dressing up was if he was going to essentially dismantle it as soon as he got into his office.

Performance, Kari guessed. Costume. Posturing.

The rest of the employees filtered in, selected snacks, and had the kind of semi-casual, semi-weary, polite conversation that such events seemed to bring out in people. It would all devolve into shop talk by the end of the hour, Kari knew from many years of watching this sort of thing. Logan (or, more probably, his assistant Camille) thought occasional company social events would give the workplace a more "family" atmosphere. But the only real similarity to family was the fact that these people didn't have much of a choice about their association.

"You okay?" Sapna was at Kari's elbow, a slice of cake in one hand, a cup of coffee in the other.

"Fine. Just tired."

"You look more than tired," Sapna said, taking a bite that muffled her next words. "You look pissed."

"Great." Kari made an effort to lighten her expression in case anyone other than Sapna was watching.

"Any reason?" Sapna asked through a mouthful of crumbs.

"Just realizing the sheer amount of stuff the women in this company do day in and day out. And when another woman realizes that a woman is overloaded, what does she do? She sends yet another woman. So yeah. I'm tired." It was all too like her upbringing, being the one who was constantly expected to step up, to do more. To constantly prove her worth in unending labor.

Sapna's mouth twisted and she raised her paper cup to tap against Kari's. "Yeah, don't send a man to do a woman's job. But oh, sister. You're singing my song."

"So yeah. I'm tired. Sick and tired."

Rob's office phone rang, Mia's number on the display. He took a deep breath and held it for a count of five before letting it go with a gust and snatching up the receiver. "Hey kiddo."

"Hi Daddy…"

Shit. Not today. But no, fatherhood wasn't a part-time gig, even now that Mia was grown. "What's the situation?" The words came out sharper than he'd intended. "Sorry. Work today has been a minefield."

"It's just…I've started packing up my place." Mia's tone and the knowledge that her plans were moving forward so quickly twisted Rob's heart.

She'll only be a few hours away. She's an adult. Let go. But it was hard. Mia might be twenty-five, but in his mind her round-cheeked, solemn little face peered at him that first week they spent together alone, after he and Liz had separated. He would probably never get away from that helpless feeling of being fully responsible for her.

"So, what's the matter?" he asked.

"Hugo. He's stressing all over the place. He knows something's up. He's shedding so much there's practically a cloud of fur around him. He whines and paces nonstop. He only eats about half of what he usually does." Mia's voice was strained and thin. "Can I bring him to you early?"

Oh, God. What it must cost the kid to even think about spending her last days before her move without the fuzzball. He rubbed his chest as if he could erase the heartache he felt for her. "Of course. And if you want to come over and sleep in your old room any time before you move so you can be with him, you just do that."

"I might." Mia's voice sounded all too close to tears for Rob's liking.

"You can spend time with your old man while you're at it, you know. Not just the dog."

She gave a watery laugh. Definitely crying now. *Oh, twist the knife, kiddo.* "Of course."

"I'll be home by six. Or do you need me to come by and get him?"

"No, I'll bring him. Thanks, Dad."

Dad. Not Daddy.

"Drive safe, kiddo."

Kari reached up and put the serving utensils back on the top shelf of the cupboard, heaving a big sigh.

"Well, that's done for another three months," Sapna commented from behind her where she was drying the bowl that had held the fruit salad.

Kari made a mental note to return the bowl to its owner before she left for the day, rolled her shoulders, and rocked her head from side to side. "Yeah." Camille, assistant to The Man, was wiping down the last of the tables in the break room. Kari had gotten her quarterly update on Camille's grandkids earlier—*whether I wanted it or not*. She tried to quash the unruly, unworthy thought.

But why was it unworthy?

She was expected to care about someone's grandkids because she was a woman. If she'd been a guy and sort-of wearing a tie—or not wearing a tie at all, for that matter—nobody would expect her to care about kids she'd never met.

Sapna poked Kari in the ribs and she flinched. "What's with the long face?"

"Nothing." Kari waved a tired hand. "Ignore me." She forced a smile for Camille who straightened from her task with a tired grunt and a fist knuckling into the small of her back. Kari reached out a hand for the sponge Camille had been using. "I've got this, Camille. Thanks."

Camille relinquished the sponge, gave a stately wave, and left the break room.

Sapna rolled her eyes. "She sponges down a few tables and is the martyr of the hour."

Kari rinsed the sponge, squeezed it out, and set it beside the sink. "She showed up. She shows up a lot."

"I hear a 'but' behind that statement."

Kari turned and leaned her hips against the counter. "The guys. They're happy enough to show up and *eat*, but do they ever pitch in?" Kari folded her arms across her chest. "No. Hardly ever. And if they do? Oh. It's like they've done something miraculous, turned water into wine. And here we all are doing this shit like it's part of our jobs." Kari waved around the empty break room. Her shoulders were tight. Her jaw was tense. She was so tired.

"Yeah, there aren't a lot of men like your plumber neighbor now, are there?" Sapna asked.

Kari's face went hot. "I told you he's not really a plumber."

"Yeah. Just…good with his hands." Sapna waggled her eyebrows and Kari's face nearly went up in flames. "Oh, wait. Just how good with his hands is he?" Sapna cackled with glee as Kari slapped her hand over her eyes.

"Just…keep it down, Sapna. I don't exactly want the rest of the company to know about my private life." She dropped her hand and glared at her colleague.

Sapna bit her lips together, brown eyes bright with humor. "But back to the point. He sounded like a good guy. Someone who helps out."

Kari fought the urge to let a sappy smile spread across her face. "Yeah. You're right about that. He's…he's kind."

"Don't let that one go, then. He's a keeper." Sapna

snapped her fingers and pointed at Kari. "How long has it been a thing?"

Kari snorted. "Two days, pretty much."

Sapna clasped her hands under her chin and fluttered her eyelashes. "Ah, young love."

"Middle-aged. And not love." The notion scared Kari a little. What if she *did* fall in love with Rob?

And what if he didn't love her back?

Chapter Twenty-Four

Rob unlocked his door and staggered through to the kitchen, laden with cheap cloth grocery bags. Hoisting the bags to the countertop and disentangling his hands, he paused and rubbed his eyes, which felt like they'd been crusted with sand.

Today had felt about a year long. And now he had Mia arriving to drop Hugo off in about ten minutes. His temples throbbed with the headache that had threatened all day. Well. Might as well put away the groceries, since the bottle of painkillers he had purchased was in those bags somewhere.

Christ, being an adult sucked sometimes.

He was just tossing back a glass of water and two tablets when he heard his front door open and canine toenails in the foyer.

"Daddy?"

"In the kitchen, honey." Rob put the glass down and wadded up all but one of the cloth grocery bags, stuffing them into the remaining one. Mia arrived with Hugo hard on her heels and walked straight into Rob. He wrapped his arms around his daughter and she groaned.

"I'm so sorry, Dad. But I'm at the end of my rope."

That makes two of us, he thought. But what he said was, "I got you, kiddo. Don't worry."

Hugo took that moment to try to stuff his nose between their legs, to participate in their hug any way he could. Mia stepped back and dropped to the kitchen floor, wrapping her arms around Hugo's neck. The dog whined and his haunches thumped to the floor.

"It's okay, boy. Your granddad is going to take really good care of you." Mia's voice was choked. Great. She was trying not to cry.

Rob reached down and awkwardly patted his daughter's shoulder. "Maybe you should stay here tonight."

Mia pulled her face out of Hugo's fur and sniffed, scrubbing at her eyes with her hands. "No, but thanks. I have too much to do. As it is, I have to get the rest of his stuff out of the car and get back to packing."

"I told you I'd come get him," Rob said, tamping down his rising irritation.

She shook her head. "No. It's the least I can do when you're taking him for me."

"Well, then. Let's get his stuff." Rob straightened and pulled Mia to her feet. They went to her car and Rob wrestled the dog's crate out while Mia took two bags of paraphernalia out of the little hatchback. "What are you going to do with your car? I imagine having one in New York isn't a great idea."

"Mackenzie — remember her from high school? — needs one to get to her new job, so she's going to buy it from me."

For some reason, this detail made everything seem far more real. Even more real than having Hugo in his house full time. After all, he was used to that, more or less. But Mia was selling her car. The shiny little stripped-down box she had been so proud of being able to afford the down payment and monthly nut on. It had been such a milestone. And she was letting it go. His chest felt tight and uncomfortable.

"Let's get this stuff inside." Rob cleared his throat and hefted the folded-up crate, heading for his house. Mia's car door thumped closed behind him and her footsteps sounded. He was acutely aware of this moment. The last time she would drop Hugo off. Maybe ever.

He set up the crate in his bedroom as usual and Mia laid out the dog's fleecy blanket inside, her shoulders hunched, her motions abrupt. Rob's throat tightened. He knew there was nothing he could do to make this any easier for her, but oh, he wanted to. He wanted to have millions of dollars. To be able to buy her an apartment in Manhattan where she could keep Hugo. For her to have anything else she wanted.

But even if he had been a millionaire, he would have had to let her go, to grow up. To be her own person. His jaw clenched.

"So that's it. All his stuff is here." Mia's voice caught and her eyes squeezed shut. "I have to go. If I draw this out, I'll fall apart."

"Understood, honey." He pulled her in for another quick hug before she drew away, bending to press a kiss to Hugo's head and nearly running from the house.

Rob and Hugo looked at each other.

"Well. Looks like it's just you and me, boy."

To put the cap on Kari's epically shitty day, Rob hadn't texted like he said he would.

At the last stoplight before she turned onto her street,

she grabbed her phone, opened the messaging app, and double-checked. Nope. No texts from anyone today. And since she had only given him her number, she couldn't text him. She should have gotten his number.

Well, she had expected to get it when he texted her. Like he said he would.

Pulling up in front of her house, she saw Rob's car. So, he was home. Great. She had read an article a while back about people who "ghosted" on the people they dated. Just up and disappeared without a word. Was she getting ghosted from next door when she might see him any time? Less a ghosting and more of a haunting.

Kari turned off the car and rested her forehead on the steering wheel. She felt like a teenager again. Not in the energetic, youthful, "I have my whole life ahead of me" way, but in the uncertain, angsty, "why didn't he call?" way.

She took a deep breath, held it for a count of five, then let it go in an explosive whoosh. Time to be an adult again, no matter how adolescent she was feeling. She sat up, grabbed her bag off of the passenger's seat and got out of the car, keeping her eyes fixed on her own front door, resisting the urge to twist her neck and peer at Rob's house. She was going to be a goddamn adult if it goddamn well killed her.

She slammed the door behind her. Okay, maybe she was failing a little on the being an adult mission. But it wasn't like there was anyone on the other side. If a door slammed and nobody was there to hear it, was it really a juvenile thing to do?

Yes, she told herself sternly. *Yes, it was. Knock it off. You had a shitty day. Plenty of people have shitty days and don't manage to turn into absolute brats. Get over yourself.*

Well. That was quite the pep talk. Kari set her bag down on the coffee table and went to her bedroom to change out of her work clothes. Maybe she should eat something and draw. That might make her feel better.

Or drawing might make her think about Rob.

Kari forced herself to slide a drawer shut with care, not slamming it. Okay, so no drawing. She could sit and knit. Maybe watch something on TV. But definitely not home renovation shows or anything Disney. She got a glass of water from the kitchen, not allowing herself to look out the back window which gave her a view of some of his yard, and went back to the living room to sit, picking up the sock she had been working on before faucets and painting and great sex with the impossible man next door seemed to take up all her spare time. She turned on the television and found an old show she'd seen before. Something known and soothing. After a few minutes of knitting and watching, her tight shoulders eased a bit.

Her doorbell ringing sent them straight back up towards her ears. She set the knitting down, turned off the television, and went to answer, peering through the peephole first.

Rob. Opening the door, she leaned against the frame. And then she saw the dog. "What's going on?" she asked, her gaze lifting to his face. He looked as tired as she felt.

"Hugo was getting stressed over Mia's packing, so he's come to live with me a little early."

The dog sat and regarded Kari, head tilting one way and then the other like he was trying to figure something out. Kari, unused to dogs, felt unnerved. "How do you know when a dog is stressed?"

"He wasn't eating well, shedding too much, wandering around and whining all the time."

Kari looked at the dog again. She guessed he did look thinner than when she'd seen him before.

Rob went on. "Anyway, I had a completely shitty day

and only just realized I forgot to text you. So Hugo and I were wondering if you wanted to go for a walk with us."

Some small, petty, irrational part of Kari's brain wanted to hang on to her grievance. He'd had a shitty day? Well, so had she. She wouldn't have forgotten to text, though. As she'd proved today, she was good old *reliable Kari*. She was sick of being reliable. She wanted to be taken care of for once, rather than always having to take care of everyone else. And she'd hoped maybe Rob would take care of her just a little bit tonight.

Instead, he was taking care of a dog.

She sighed. She wasn't being fair. He was also taking care of his kid. And this was one of the things she liked so much about him, the fact that he was such a good dad. She couldn't have it both ways.

"I wondered why you hadn't texted," she said, not yet answering about the walk.

"Yeah, well. Looks like I might have to fire someone. Maybe a couple of someones. And then Mia called and needed bailing out with Hugo and when she dropped him off, she was really upset. I hate seeing her like that."

Kari bit her lip, guilt surging through her. "I'm sorry. I had a shitty day too. Though not on the scale of yours."

"It's not a competition. Come for a walk with us. Let's blow the shitty cobwebs out of the rest of our evening."

Kari clung for one last second to her resentment, then let it go in an exhausted rush. "Okay." She grabbed her phone, a key, and her sneakers, then sat on her front step to put on her shoes after locking up. Rob held out a hand to help her get to her feet.

"Why do you have to fire anyone?" she asked.

Rob rubbed his cheek as they started to move toward the sidewalk. "I got a call before I went into my staff meeting: one of our very senior people—the number two person in the whole company—was getting blown off by my help desk. They were closing out her service tickets without solving her problems."

Kari shot him a sideways glance. "That's a firing offense? Rank has its privileges, I guess. Someone wrongs you and off with his head."

"It's more than that. Anna—our CFO—has been the target of some nasty harassment in the past. Have you heard of Gamergate?"

"I think I read something about it a while ago."

"Yeah, well, the movement against women in gaming didn't end there. The threats against Anna were so vile and frightening that she actually moved. And when my help desk manager investigated the issue of Anna being blown off, she found out that the guy who had been doing it may be a member of the group. She discovered he'd been participating in some online chats using his work computer during business hours. And these so-called people are the worst."

"How so?"

"They've fooled SWAT teams into going to the homes of people they target, saying there's a hostage situation involved. Law enforcement shows up with guns drawn. More than one person has been killed this way."

Kari looked a little green at that. In fact, she looked downright weary. The skin under her eyes looked papery and her cheeks were pale. Rob felt awful. She'd said she had a shitty day too and all he'd done was talk about his own stuff. And he hadn't texted her like he said he would.

His worst expectations about himself were all too true. He was a crappy romantic partner.

Well, he could either wallow or try to do better.

"So how was your day shitty?" he asked.

Kari shrugged. "It wasn't any different from any other day, really. Just some stuff kind of crashing down on me."

"Specifics?" Rob paused at the edge of the neighborhood park and let Hugo sniff a signpost. The dog lifted his leg.

"Just...there's a bunch of things I do at work. None of them are really related to my job in any direct way, but there's nobody else to do it. So, mostly I do. Today was our quarterly coffee social. I get people to volunteer to make things for it, I get it set up, I clean up after. Today the assistant to the President asked another colleague to help out —she didn't ask *me* if I needed or wanted help, but that's another issue."

"Why don't you talk to someone about getting all this stuff reallocated to other people?"

She clipped her lips together for a moment, thinking. "Maybe I will. But the point is, it suddenly struck me that everyone who participates in this thing—actively participates, I'm not talking about just showing up, eating, and leaving—is a woman. And on the rare occasion when a man does participate, people practically throw a parade in his honor because he made a cake. Or, more likely, the guy's wife made a cake and he heroically carried it in on the correct day. Or even worse, he bought something from Safeway and didn't even bother to pop the top off. And it just made me so damn mad."

A wave of defensiveness surged through Rob. Hadn't he been there for Mia her entire life? "Come on. Not every guy is that bad."

Kari stopped and folded her arms. "I don't even know what to do with that statement."

"I mean, some guys step up." Rob gestured at Hugo, who was looking from him to Kari and back. "For crying out loud, I'm taking responsibility for a *life* because my daughter can't."

"Are you really making this about you?"

"Well, you made it about my entire gender. Aren't I included?"

"It's a really interesting leap you're making there. I was talking about every guy in *my* office and you jumped to every guy *on the planet*." She stopped and he did the same. "But yeah, maybe it is about your entire gender. How many times did someone praise you for the weeks you had Mia?" She clutched her hands under her chin. *"Oh, you're doing it all on your own?"*

The unfairness of the statement galled him. "Well, I *was* doing it all on my own."

"And how often do you think her mother got the same sort of praise for doing the exact same thing?"

Rob swallowed. His jaw worked. "Since Liz and I were only minimally civil to each other after the split, I can't say I know. We didn't have a relationship where we exactly shared stuff."

"Well, I can tell you that she probably got none. In fact, she probably got hit with, *Oh, how can you bear to be away from your baby every other week?* The same thing you got cheers for, she got guilt."

He ran his tongue over his teeth, trying to rein in his temper. "You have no idea what you're talking about. You've never even met Liz." *And you don't have kids* he kept himself from saying.

"Actually, I do know what I'm talking about. I've been a woman. I've talked to a lot of women. This is how the world works. Either women nurture or we're evil. Nurturing is expected of us. It's the baseline expectation. But when guys nurture, they're heroes."

"I don't know why I'm the bad guy all of a sudden."

There. He was reasonable. Rational. There was no reason for her to attack him this way.

Kari's hands slapped against her thighs, an abrupt, violent gesture that made Hugo startle and look at her. "You were the one who made a statement about the guys in my office all about you. But if you want to cast yourself as some sort of victim, I'm going to go home. See you around."

Kari's heart hammered so hard it felt like it was trying to escape from her chest. She was lightheaded with fury. Her veneer of calm was closer to cracking than it had been for years. Her stride grew longer and faster until her arms were pumping and her breath rasped in her throat, practically running back to her house.

Reaching her front door, she unlocked it with a shaking hand. *Dammit.* This time, instead of slamming the door, she closed it carefully, shot the deadbolt, and leaned her forehead against the cool painted surface, her breath returning to normal, her hot anger replaced by freezing disappointment. She pushed away from the door, straightened her spine, and swallowed hard. *Time to return to real life.* Rob had been wonderful. And then...he'd just been a guy. Another guy.

Dammit again. She had thought he was different.

Apparently not.

The sound of her doorbell nearly made her jump out of her skin. Her hand slammed to her sternum and she breathed deeply to try to settle her pounding heart. She peered through the peephole and her mouth twisted.

"What do you want?" she yelled through the door.

A long pause. "I want to talk." Rob's raised voice sounded barely controlled.

"What do you want to talk about?"

"Kari, this is ridiculous. Please open the door."

"We have talked. You hurt my feelings. I don't want to talk anymore."

Silence. Maybe he'd gone away. Kari looked through the peephole again. Nope, still there, hands on his hips, face averted from the door as if he was trying to gather himself. While she watched, he turned back, scrubbing his hands across his face. Kari tensed, not sure what she was expecting or dreading. An apology? A goodbye? She wanted both. And neither.

"Kari. I am sorry I hurt your feelings. Now please, can I come in?" His words were slow and deliberate. But there was no trace of sarcasm, no lack of sincerity.

Kari bit her lip. He *would* decide now would be the right time to become reasonable. *Dammit.* Her hand came up, almost of its own accord, turned the deadbolt, and opened the door.

"May I come in?" His careful politeness, Hugo sitting obediently at his side, twisted something inside of her. She nodded, not trusting her voice, and stepped back from the door. He followed her inside, the dog at his heels.

"Can I get you something?" she asked automatically.

"No." He bit out the single syllable.

Okay, not so careful and polite as all that, then. Just careful.

She hovered near an armchair, wondering if she should sit, offer him a seat. Or if this was going to be a short goodbye.

Rob rubbed his hand across his mouth. The dog looked up at him. Kari didn't know much about dogs, but this one seemed worried. He had eyebrow-like markings in his furry face, increasing the effect.

"I'm sorry I hurt your feelings," Rob said.

"You already said that."

He held out a hand, as if containing his own patience and reassuring her at the same time. "I wasn't sure what you could hear through the door. So I'm making sure."

Kari nodded.

He went on. "Can you tell me where it all went wrong? It seemed like we were just sharing our shitty days and then...I was the bad guy."

"No, you were sharing your shitty day but when I tried to share mine you weren't listening to me. I was talking about a specific thing and you made it universal so that it applied to you and got all defensive. I wasn't talking about *you*, Rob. And I wasn't talking about something that applies to all men. But it happens often enough that it's a recogniz-able—and shitty—pattern. You reminding me that not everyone behaves this way isn't news and it doesn't help anything. I still had a shitty day because of it." It felt so clear to her and having to spell it out felt so exasperating that she nearly growled.

Rob blinked and rolled his lips into his mouth. The dog whined. "It's okay, Hugo." He gave the dog's head a distracted pat, then looked at Kari. "So. Where do we go from here?"

"I don't know."

His hand flew up, a frustrated wing, slamming back down on his thigh. The dog flinched but Rob didn't notice this time. "Neither do I. I've always been crap at this, at rela-tionships. Maybe I should just back off. Maybe this was a mistake."

Kari's gut twisted. "So that's it? Just quit?"

Rob shrugged. "I hurt you. I hated hurting you."

"And you think quitting won't hurt me?"

"I don't know. You were pretty mad."

"Yeah. People get mad. People get hurt. And if people..."

255

She swallowed, then forced the next words out. "*Care* about something, they work at it. Even if they're crappy at it at first. If they think the relationship is worth it."

"You think I don't care? Like you're not worth it?"

"If you're not willing to work at it, it seems that way. No relationship is smooth sailing all the time. And not just romantic ones." Which was a cliche, of course. Great. Why didn't she just say something like *relationships are work* and be done with it? Was she going to have to do all the work *here*, too?

"It's not that I'm not willing to work, it's that I think I'm not good at it at all and am going to end up hurting you even more."

Kari suppressed a scream. "Do you have any idea how weak that sounds?"

Chapter Twenty-Five

"Weak?" Jesus, did she have any idea how hard this was for him? "I'm trying to do the right thing, Kari. Or at least figure out what the right thing to do *is* and then do it. That's the opposite of weak. It's damn hard."

She took a deep breath, seeming to gather herself. "Okay, but why are you trying to do it by yourself?"

"What do you mean?"

"If we're a couple…" God, how he hated that *If*. But, at the same time, she was right. "…Don't I get a say? Especially since you seem to be trying to—God forbid—try to protect me. And I've been a grown woman for a long time now. I don't need protecting."

"But I'm just not good at this." He stepped closer to her, as if physical proximity would get her to see, to understand.

"Fine. Were you always good at being a dad?"

That stopped him.

She gave a curt little nod. "I didn't think so. You didn't know what you were doing and you were lost and probably scared out of your mind half the time at first."

Half the time. Hah. She didn't know how terrified he'd been. All the time.

She went on. "But you cared enough to work at it. To get better at it. What hurts isn't so much that you might misunderstand me, but that you don't care enough to try to get better at—" Her jaws clamped together and she didn't finish.

"Better at what?" *Better at loving you?* Because oh, hell. That's what this was. He wasn't afraid of hurting her. Well, he was. But that wasn't the real fear, the big fear.

He was afraid of falling in love with her. Afraid of *her* hurting *him*. But it was too late. His foolish, hammering heart might as well not be in his own chest anymore. It was already halfway to being hers. Maybe more than halfway.

"Why don't you go home and think about it?" she asked, her voice soft, not answering his question, her eyes not meeting his.

He wanted to press her, to force her to answer his question. *Better at what, Kari?* But she was in full Viking Shield Maiden stance, standing with her feet apart, arms folded across her chest, not meeting his eyes. Impermeable.

"Kari. I want—" He stopped. Her hand rested on his chest. She looked at it as if she was memorizing the details of that hand: the long, tapering fingers, the work-roughened cuticles, the thin gold band around her pinky finger.

"Don't be impulsive. Don't just say any old thing. Please. Go home and think. Do some soul-searching. Call a friend if you need to. But don't speak now without thinking." There was no quaver to her voice, no outward display of emotion. But she still wouldn't meet his eyes.

He wasn't sure what it meant that direct, straightforward Kari couldn't meet his gaze. But he knew what he hoped it might mean.

"Okay." Rob's voice was low, almost intense. The dog took that moment to poke his long nose into the back of Rob's knee and he staggered a bit, leaning into her palm. She remembered that first morning in her kitchen, his shirt riding up to show a strip of belly, her wondering what the rest of him might look like. Well, now she knew. And the knowledge made her die a little bit inside, knowing that memory might be all that was left to her.

He straightened, moving away from her a little. "Sorry. Hugo's probably feeling a call of nature. We didn't get to finish our walk."

She nodded, dropping her hand and taking a step back. "Okay. Give me a call or something when you've had a chance to think."

"You can always call me if you need anything." *Oh, God.* That sounded like goodbye. Kari tried to re-freeze the cracking, melting, shattering feeling in her heart. To shore it up with a frosty line of defense.

"No, I can't," she said.

"Sure you can."

She finally met his gaze. His dark eyes were fanned with laugh lines, though his mouth was unsmiling. She tilted her head, irritated. "I don't have your number, so no. I literally can't."

He gave a soft, mirthless laugh. "That's right. I'm sorry." He dug in his pockets, then slapped his thighs in frustration. "I left mine in the house."

You could write it down, she thought. But if this was about him deflecting, not wanting her to call, she was going to let him go. The idea that she might be clingy or needy as he peeled himself out of her grasping hands was too mortifying to think about.

"I'll text you," he said.

She nodded, her chin coming forward as if she believed him. "Sure."

His hand came up, hovered as if to cup her face, then fell as the dog gave a whine and poked him again. "I have to take care of Hugo. I'll talk to you soon."

"Sure," she said again. And with a few strides, he and the dog were at her front door and gone.

Kari's knees were suddenly weak. She dropped to an armchair and sat, the icy defense she had assembled melting away as she took in how empty her little house felt. She supposed she ought to…think about making dinner or something. But she didn't feel like it. The hollow feeling inside her had nothing to do with hunger.

Rising to her feet, she went to the sofa and tucked the knitting project away. Creativity wasn't in her now, not even the mindless creativity of doing something she'd done more than a hundred times. Television didn't appeal. Neither did reading. The only thing that sounded even marginally appealing was going to sleep and waking up after a long enough period that she just forgot that she and Rob had ever had anything. Dragging herself to the bedroom, she flopped down on the bed and rolled over, grabbing a pillow to her. The smell of Rob—his shampoo, his soap, the elusive aroma of his skin—drifted from the pillowcase.

Crap.

Getting up again she started to strip the pillowcase off when her phone chimed from her pocket. She pulled it out and stared at it. On the screen was a text from an unknown number.

This isn't me being impulsive. This is me saying I want to try. It scares me to death, but I want to try. —Rob

Rob breathed as if he had been running and he gripped his phone so hard his hand ached. There. He'd done it. He'd done the scary thing, ripped the band-aid off, put himself out there. Before he could wonder how she'd respond, his phone rang. He looked at the screen.

Liz. *Oh, perfect.*

He raised the phone to his ear. "This is Rob."

"New York, Rob? She's moving to *New York?*" Liz's voice rang in his ear.

"And hello to you, Liz."

"Why didn't you tell me? Why am I the last to know? What the hell is going on?" Liz's voice was low, intense. He could probably count on one hand the number of times Liz had yelled in front of him. Well, *at* him.

Rob closed his eyes and counted to ten. "Last I checked, Mia was an emancipated adult. I didn't know she hadn't told you about her move yet, and it isn't my business to relay her news to you or anyone."

"Adult? Rob, she's a child."

"She's older than we were when she was born."

"Exactly. A child."

Rob rubbed his eyes. In the kitchen, Hugo started noisily lapping water from his bowl. "I'm not going to argue with you about Mia's decisions. If you take issue with them, you're going to have to talk to her."

"I can't. She hung up on me. And now she's not taking my calls."

And you want me *to mediate?* Rob was the last person to be able to navigate this tricky situation. "Give her some time. She's awfully busy right now with packing and settling up her affairs here."

Hugo chose that moment to bellow a powerful *woof* at a squirrel he could see through the sliding glass door that looked out on the patio.

"Is that her dog?" Liz asked.

The question surprised Rob. Her voice sounded flat, like all the previous fight had gone out of her. Rob felt a little sorry for Liz, out in St. Louis. He'd hate to be so far from Mia that he had to fly to see her. And now Mia was moving even further away from her mother. It didn't make a practical or logistical difference, but it was sure to make a psychological one with Liz in the mental state she was in.

"Yeah. Hugo's going to live with me. She can't keep him in the place she's going to be renting up there. With friends. Known friends. College friends. Not people she found at random off the internet."

Liz sighed audibly. "Thank you. I hadn't been able to get that much out of her when we talked."

Translation: *You flew off the handle before she told you anything more than, "I'm moving to New York, Mom."*

"You're welcome," he said. An awkward silence stretched between them. His heart gave a little pang. Silences were hardly ever awkward with Kari. They were purposeful and tactical sometimes, but not awkward.

Liz cleared her throat. "How've you been?"

Rob blinked and resisted the urge to inquire if she'd really just asked him that. He was pretty sure she hadn't asked after him in the twenty years since they divorced. "Fine. Thank you. How are you? How's Hank?"

"He's well. We're well. Did you...did you ever end up with someone?"

Rob sank into a chair. The world was upside down. "Sort of. Just recently. It's a little up in the air right now."

He waited for her to make a snide comment about him fucking it up. Again. Instead, she said, "I hope it works out."

"Liz, are you okay?" This conversation was going places he never thought he'd ever go with her.

She laughed softly. "Yeah."

"So what's with the sudden..." He searched for the words. "Not hating me?"

"Therapy. Anyway, I never hated you. I was mad at you for a lot of years. Jealous of you."

Rob paused and tried to let that sink in. "Jealous? Why?"

A soft sigh sounded in his ear. "Partly because you and Mia seemed to have an easier relationship than she and I did. You always got along more easily. And partly because we split everything fifty/fifty, but when you had Mia, people called it 'babysitting.' And while you were getting pats on the back for 'babysitting,' I was a terrible, unnatural mother for being glad to have a week to catch up with my own life."

Christ. It was almost exactly what Kari had said.

"I'm sorry about that."

"Not your fault. Anyway. I hope this works out however you want it to."

"Thanks. I'm glad you finally found a good husband."

"Did you think you were a bad husband?" Liz sounded genuinely surprised.

"Wasn't I?"

"No. You weren't the right husband for me, but that didn't make you a bad husband. In fact, I'm pretty sure you'd make someone else a great husband."

"A little late for that, even if I wanted to get married again."

"Well. Like I said, I hope it works out for you. Whatever that looks like."

"Thanks." Another pause, but this time it was companionable, not awkward. "Take care of yourself, Liz."

"You too."

Rob sat and stared at the darkened screen of his phone for a long time after that.

Chapter Twenty-Six

Kari pulled into a parking spot at work and took a deep breath, trying to settle her jumping nerves. Overnight, she had decided it was time to do something about what had made yesterday so shitty.

Assembling a list of all the extracurricular tasks and projects she did had been eye-opening, even though she was aware that it cut into her workday on an all-too-frequent basis. Well, now was the time to end it. Kari got out of her car and marched into the office.

After locking her purse in her desk, Kari approached Logan's secretary, sitting at her station outside his office. Most of the available surface was covered with framed photographs of her family, a potted plant looking like it wanted to take a nose dive off the corner. Or maybe that was just Kari's reaction to the crowded scene.

"Good morning, Camille. Does Logan have any time today? Fifteen minutes?"

Camille glanced at her computer screen, then twisted around in her chair, peering into Logan's office. I think he's free now. Mr. Logan?"

Logan looked up from whatever he was reading and waved a hand. "Come on in, Kari."

Crap. She hadn't expected he'd be available right away. She'd figured she would have time to compose herself, think about what she was going to say. But no, that wouldn't be consistent with how her life was working out just about now. She stepped into Logan's office and took the chair he indicated.

"Great work on the social yesterday," he said as she sat.

"Thanks. That was actually what I wanted to talk to you about."

Logan rested his elbows on his desk and steepled his fingers. "What's up?"

Kari folded her hands in her lap, trying to summon up a calm she didn't feel. "Over the years since I started working here, I've taken on a lot of what I might call 'extracurricular' tasks. Like organizing the social. Doing the newsletter. Maintaining the birthday list. Planning the twice-annual potlucks. If someone's having baby or getting married, I'm expected to organize a party for it. I even make sure there's always ice in the break room freezer. That sort of thing."

Logan nodded. "Okay."

"I'm also really swamped with my actual work. But these extracurricular things have their own schedule, and they're time-consuming, so they end up derailing me. I'd like to see if we could get some or all of these tasks reassigned. Or if they aren't important, then let's just stop doing them."

"I wasn't aware that you were doing so much," Logan said, leaning back in his chair.

No, you just didn't bother to think about it. Kari elected not to voice that thought. "Well, I am. And I think it's fair if the load gets spread around, especially to people who never seem to take this kind of thing on. I have had help here and there, but it always comes from the same few people. It wouldn't be right to hand these tasks off to them either."

The corners of Logan's mouth drew down and he nodded. "That sounds fair. Have any ideas of who to assign these things to?"

Kari repressed a smile. "I do."

Rob looked up from the printouts on his desk, the result of Sandra's complete investigation into the help desk specialist's involvement in post-Gamergate activities. "This is ugly," he said to the help desk manager.

Sandra nodded. "I think he's a lone actor, but…"

"But this is bad enough." The posts from an internet chat room contained boasts that the man was *in a position to fuck the bitch up good* and *just wait and see—she'll get what's coming to her*, among other more explicit slurs and threats directed toward Anna. And the boasts and menacing promises only increased in intensity over time. Rob made a face. "This is awful."

"It's pretty pathetic, really." Gloria Yao, Potomac Games' in-house counsel, leaned back in her chair and crossed her legs, leafing through her own set of printouts. "When we look at what he's *actually* done, not helping Anna with her laptop seems to be his idea of all-out warfare, despite his keyboard commando persona online."

Rob shook his head. "Regardless, he's got to go. Anna's history of being targeted by this group makes this especially worrying, but we can't have this kind of attitude from any of our employees toward anyone—let alone any of our other employees. And I shudder to think of what he could do if he decided to up the ante."

Gloria raised her hands. "Not disagreeing. And he's in

his probationary period. We can let him go for any reason or no reason with zero consequences. And I'm also letting law enforcement know. They don't have the best track record on following through on this stuff, but we have to do what we can."

"But even if he's a lone actor, we have to consider the effect he may have had on the rest of my staff," Sandra said, her dark eyes troubled.

"I agree." Rob tapped the printouts to square them and set them aside. "Those are going in his HR file, at any rate. Just in case. What do you want to do about your remaining staff, Sandra?"

"I think we need some emergency training. Sexual harassment, use of company materials, the whole shebang. It's going to create a lot of eye-rolling, but if we can use Anna's experiences as part of the training, it might make the danger more real to them."

"Okay, how can I help?" Rob asked. Reminded of Kari's situation, he wasn't about to have Sandra shoulder the burden of this impossible situation.

"You were going to go to the Los Angeles office next week, right?"

He nodded.

"Brenda's going to need support on this," she said, naming the Los Angeles I.T. team's manager. "I think it would be helpful if we got you out there sooner, organized the training to coincide with your visit. So you can stop in, check in and personally emphasize to Brenda's staff how important this is."

"I think you have an outsized idea of what my presence will do, but okay."

"Well, that's not all…" Sandra trailed off, as if what she was about to ask was going to be too much.

"Out with it."

"Maybe you could stop in Austin on your way home, do the same thing with Trin and their staff there?"

That would mean extending his trip by at least a day. Maybe two. And he had Hugo to think about now. And Kari had so much anxiety about taking care of Hugo already.

But he had to do it. This was too important.

"Yes."

"What did you do?"

Kari looked up from her bookkeeping program to find Sapna staring at her from the doorway, brown eyes bright with glee.

"What do you mean, what did I do?"

"The boys are *pissed*. They've all been assigned to do all the emotional labor crap you've carried on doing for at least five years."

"Oh. That." Kari clipped her lips closed but let her eyebrows lift.

"You look positively *evil*," Sapna said. "I love it." She came into Kari's office, shutting the door behind her and sitting in her guest chair. "Spill."

"I just finally decided I'd go to Logan and show him just how much extracurricular stuff I've been doing. I pointed out that it was interfering with the work that I'm actually paid to do. I suggested he re-allocate those tasks explicitly to people who hadn't ever chipped in before and he agreed."

"Result: a bunch of guys each get one single task off the massive list of stuff you've been carrying almost singlehandedly and each one of them whines like a baby." Sapna twisted a heavy silver ring on her thumb. "I love it. Well, not the whining part. That's annoying as fuck. But the justice of it all. Did Logan say anything about the fact that you've reassigned everything to a list of all men?"

"He didn't. Maybe he didn't notice."

"Regardless. I'll take the win for the time being. Until we end up with events that are badly planned. Because among the whiners there were a few 'but how hard can it be?' guys who've clearly never done anything like this before in their lives." Sapna twirled a strand of glossy black hair around a finger and smirked.

"It isn't that hard," Kari said.

Sapna cackled. "Not hard for you with your knowledge of how to get things done and your organization and your endless lists. These dudes are just going to toss themselves at the problem like birds flying at a plate glass window and wonder why they end up on the ground, stunned."

Kari laughed at the image. "Well, we shall see. This way I at least have time to do my actual job. And with that, shoo. I have some maintenance appointments to make."

Sapna stood, grinning. "You say that like it's something you actually want to do."

"It's my job. And I'm good at it."

That evening, Rob waited for Kari to get home, pacing his living room until she pulled up in front of her house. She emerged from the car with a grocery bag, a bouquet of flowers sprouting from the top.

Huh. He wondered what the occasion was. Picking up his phone, he composed a quick text, asking if he could go over.

Sure, was her almost immediate reply. *Let yourself in.*

Walking the short distance to her front door, he tried to

find the right words to ask what was sounding more and more like a pretty big favor. He opened her door. "Kari?"

"In the kitchen," she called.

He walked to the back of the house and found her arranging the bouquet in a clear glass vase, simple and clean-lined like most of her possessions.

"Do you have a new admirer?" he asked, not proud of the little spurt of jealousy that flared in him.

She gave him a sarcastic look. "No. These are from me to me."

"Celebrating something?"

"A bit. I managed to solve the problem I was telling you about yesterday."

"That's excellent. And—I wanted to talk about yesterday."

She tensed. "Yes?"

"Liz called last night."

"Your ex." Kari's expression shuttered.

"Yes. She was upset about Mia moving to New York. We ended up talking. Really talking about something other than Mia's upbringing, for the first time since before everything went bad."

Kari was looking at him with widened eyes. "Are you… and she…"

Rob realized what she was asking. "What? Oh, God no. Liz lives in Missouri now. With her *husband*. We still don't like each other. But she said something that stopped me in my tracks."

"What was that?"

"She said she had been jealous of me. Of how close I am to Mia, and also, well. She made it clear that you were right about who gets credit for nurturing and who gets taken for granted."

"She did?"

"She did. And I'm sorry I didn't believe you. I also want to thank you for opening my eyes, as little as they wanted to be pried open."

"Oh." Kari threaded the last stem into the vase and stood back to assess her handiwork. She shot him a quick glance. "Thank you for that."

Rob paused, realizing what he had to say now was going to sound like a quid pro quo—not something he wanted. "So, I have something to ask of you. And I don't know where we are."

She looked at him, her expression blank. "Where we are?"

"You and me. Are we okay?"

She nodded, her eyebrows drawing together. "I think we are. Do you?"

"Yes. I'd like us to be, at least."

"So what do you need to ask me about?"

"The situation at work. I need to go out of town for a few days. Which would normally not be a problem at all. But now I have Hugo. He's never been in a kennel. He's already stressed. I—" He cringed at the way this sounded. Transactional. Like he was using her.

Kari held up a hand. "I told you I would take him."

"I know you said you would before. But I also know you're not exactly a pet person."

"You'll tell me what to do, right? How to take care of him?" Kari adjusted a flower.

"Of course. I found a dog walker who will come in and take him for a walk in the middle of the day."

Kari frowned. "You want some stranger to come to my house? To get a *key* to my house?"

Rob blinked. "Oh." He hadn't considered that.

Kari shook her head. "No. This is my first house. It may sound silly, but I'm not ready to have some stranger coming in here."

Rob scrubbed his face with his hands. "Okay…I guess I can…"

"I didn't say I wouldn't do it. I just won't do it that way. Let me see if Sam can stop in and walk him. How many days?" Kari picked up her phone and tapped at it, looking at him expectantly.

"Oh." He should have known she would come up with a plan. Warmth bloomed in his chest. He moved closer to her. Close enough to reach out and touch her. His fingers practically vibrated with the desire to do so. "Three days. Tomorrow through Friday."

"Tomorrow?" Her eyes widened, but she tapped out a brisk message on her phone's screen.

"I had to rearrange my schedule. It's pretty urgent." He finally let his fingertips graze her upper arm, the barest touch. "If Hugo needs to go to a kennel, he can go to a kennel."

She shook her head, looking at her phone. "I got this. And Sam says her schedule is open in the middle of the day. She can come by and walk him."

"Kari." She went still. "Stop. Don't just do something because someone asked it of you."

Kari's head snapped up. "What? No." Not today of all days. Not after what she had accomplished today. She wasn't that person anymore.

"Do you really want to take Hugo for three whole days?"

"Want to? No. I've never been responsible for a pet

before. But Sam's really good with them. She'll help. I'll muddle through. We'll muddle through."

"Okay. I really appreciate it."

"Maybe you should bring him over this evening, get him used to my place a little."

"Good idea. How about I go get us something for dinner and bring him with me?"

"I can make us something."

Rob put his hands on her shoulders, pulling her to him and wrapping his arms around her. "No. Let me take care of you for once."

Her hands slid around his waist and her head came to rest on his shoulder as she remembered her wish to be taken care of. "That sounds nice, actually."

"Excellent. What do you want?"

Kari considered. "I want to not have to choose." Somehow, the idea of not having to make a decision was the most luxurious thing she could think of.

He squeezed her tighter and said, "You got it."

She straightened and leaned back in his arms. "Why don't you bring Hugo over here before you go get the food? That way he and I can get acquainted."

"You sure?"

She nodded. "Does he need anything?"

"What do you mean?"

"Like...food or something?"

"He's been fed for the evening. I'll bring him over with some of his other stuff."

"Dogs have stuff?"

"Toys. Food and water bowls. You know. Stuff."

"Okay, then." She lifted the vase of flowers and put it in the center of the dining room table as Rob left. She moved into the living room to tidy a stack of books on the coffee table.

273

"Silly. You act like you're having a human guest over," she chided herself. "As if the dog is going to notice clutter."

Her front door opened and Rob came in, Hugo on his heels, tags jingling on the dog's collar. Hugo's furry face swung around as he took in these new surroundings and something in Kari melted a little. The poor guy had been passed from person to person lately, his doggy life turned all upside-down. She bent down and extended a hand. Hugo sniffed it, then moved closer to her. She ran her fingertips over the top of his head. The fur there was velvety soft, his ears stiff and springy. "Hey there, guy."

Rob dropped a thick piece of rope knotted at both ends and a hard rubber bone on the floor. "I'll just take this into the kitchen and fill it with water," he said, holding up a red plastic bowl.

"Thanks." Kari didn't look away from the dog, who was regarding her with dark, soulful eyes. She ran her hands down into the coarse, shaggy fur of his shoulders, digging her fingers in, massaging a little. Hugo groaned and slid all the way to the floor, rolling over onto his back. "Does he want me to rub his belly?" Kari called out.

"He loves that." Rob's voice from the kitchen sounded amused.

She crouched down and rubbed the dog's belly while he twisted his long nose this way and that, apparently enjoying the attention, his front paws flopping with abandon. A bubble of pure joy twisted up behind Kari's sternum.

"You have a friend for life." Rob appeared in the doorway, drying his hands on a dish towel and the bubble expanded, threatening to stop her breath. His eyes creased with humor and affection and Kari wanted to cry from the pure perfection of it. His love for his daughter, her dog, all of it.

She scratched the softer fur under Hugo's chin. "We're going to be good friends, aren't we, boy?"

The dog looked at her with eyes half-lidded with plea-sure and his tongue lolled out of his mouth.

Rob laughed softly. "I think that's a yes."

Chapter Twenty-Seven

Rob let himself back into Kari's house a half hour later, the smell from the bags he was carrying making his stomach rumble and the sound of her singing making him grin.

For a moment he hadn't quite realized he wasn't listening to music on her stereo. But no, it was her voice, unaccompanied, singing away to the tune of a Boz Scaggs pop song from the seventies. He laughed outright when he realized she was singing to the dog, modifying the lyrics.

Hugo, who-oh-oh.
He's for the kibble
He's for the toy,
He's just the best boy-yo, boyo...

He let the door thump closed behind him, figuring she might appreciate the warning. But no, she kept singing, apparently unselfconscious, as he walked into the kitchen. Her voice was beautiful, rich and soaring. She was rinsing a glass as she sang, Hugo sitting next to her on the kitchen floor, his brown eyes rapt and pink tongue lolling out of his mouth.

"I see you've made a conquest of the fuzzball," Rob said, putting the takeout bags on the counter.

She inhaled deeply, her eyes fluttering closed. "And you've made a conquest of me with whatever smells that good."

"Peruvian rotisserie chicken. Fried yuca. Black beans and rice. Plantains. Corn. Plenty of sauce at a variety of heat levels."

Kari clutched her belly. "Oh, man. I haven't had that in years. It smells heavenly." She opened an upper cabinet and pulled out a pair of dinner plates, pulling drawers open to get utensils and napkins and setting them out.

"Efficiency. I like it." Rob pulled the takeout containers out of the bags and ferried them to the table, his mouth watering as the rich, savory smells.

Hugo followed them, plopping his haunches on the floor, eyes following the movement of the chicken and side dishes to the plates as Rob and Kari served themselves. "No chicken for you, boy," Rob said.

"Not even a bone?" Kari asked.

Rob blinked. "Absolutely not. Chicken bones are bad for dogs."

Kari's eyes widened. "They are? I mean…dogs. Bones. Isn't that a whole thing?"

"Beef bones. Not chicken. Chicken bones splinter. Bad news for the dog in question. Can even kill a dog if it gets them just right."

She darted a look at Hugo, distress tightening the skin around her eyes. "Are you sure you want to leave him with me? Now I'm afraid I'm going to break your daughter's dog."

"Just only feed him his dog food and you both will be fine."

"If you say so." Kari pulled a morsel of chicken off the

bone and dipped it in the sauce, glancing at Hugo. "None of this for you, Mr. Dog." She popped the bite in her mouth, eyes sinking closed in rapture. "Thank you for this. It's delicious" He felt a little pride at that, silly as it was. He'd only gone to the Peruvian chicken place and bought dinner. But it made her happy.

"You're very welcome." He dipped a yuca fry in sauce and took a bite. "Why didn't you want to choose what we ate?"

She sucked at her fingers. "You've never gotten tired of making decisions?"

"I guess I haven't thought about it."

"Well, take it from me. Sometimes the most exhausting thing you can do is make yet one more decision."

"I'm sorry you're so exhausted." Great. And here he was, loading another thing on her plate. Taking care of Hugo when she'd never owned a pet in her life. "Maybe I can do something for you when I get back from my trip."

"Like what?"

"I'm not sure yet. But I'll think of something." Something bigger than chicken.

The next morning, Rob dropped Hugo off at Kari's house with a quick kiss before heading to the airport. "Let me know if you need anything."

"…And what are you going to be able to do from the other side of the country?"

"Good point. I'll get home as fast as I can."

"Just take care of what you need to take care of," she said.

"Will do." He handed Hugo's leash off to her and she and the dog watched him lope out to his car and drive away.

"Just you and me now, Mr. Dog." Kari closed the door and unclipped the leash. She half expected him to wander off and flop down, but instead, he followed her to her bedroom where she got her shoes. "I'm off to work. Be good," she said, feeling ridiculous, but also somehow unable to not talk to the dog. "Sam will come and take you out in a few hours."

Kari reviewed the long and detailed list of Hugo's schedule, habits, and any other details Rob could think of that might help her spend three days with the dog with as little stress as possible. She had laughed at him as he composed it, trying to impose order on his scattered thoughts. "You're learning, aren't you?"

He had tapped her nose with the butt of his pen. "Always be learning. And if you can, learn from the best. That would be you, in case I wasn't being crystal clear."

Her cheeks warmed now at the remembered compliment. She picked up her handbag and keys and gave Hugo one last pat on the head. "Be a good boy." She wasn't sure if the dog whined as she closed the front door or if the hinges needed oiling. Either way, a flicker of guilt licked through her as she headed for her car. Before she started it, she dug her cell phone out and composed a quick text to Sam:

Let me know how Hugo is after you walk him today, please?

She turned on the car, setting her jaw. She could do this. Millions of people had pets. Her neurotic worrying was silly. Moreover, she *wanted* to do this. Rob could say what he would about her not owing him, but she did. He was in a jam and she could help him.

Sam's reply came just as she was pulling into the parking lot at work.

Sure thing, dog-mommy.

God help her, she was a dog-mommy now. Maybe even a dog-grandmommy.

"Flight sixteen-thirty-five to Los Angeles is now ready for boarding." The gate agent's voice cut through Rob's review of an email from Sandra. So far, none of the rest of the D.C. staff was throwing red flags for potentially harassing behavior and the offender had been fired and escorted off the premises without incident. Investigations were proceeding in the Los Angeles and Austin offices to make sure they weren't harboring any other troublemakers.

Rob rolled his shoulders and rocked his head, standing and picking up his carry-on. Not for the first time he wondered what he'd done to get saddled with everything at once. Mia moving, Hugo, this clusterfuck at work, Kari…

At least Kari was a positive in his life. He rubbed his lips as they curved into a little smile and he joined his boarding group. They had had time for a brief cuddle on the sofa after dinner the evening before, then he dragged himself and Hugo next door, him to pack and prepare for the training session in L.A., Hugo to look soulful and sad, the poor dog all too accustomed to humans putting things in containers and leaving him lately.

Rob would be able to fix that after he got home from this trip. His travel for work was normally minimal—a few visits a year to the other two corporate locations, the occasional conference or training seminar in another state. Maybe when he got home he could take a few days off. Even better, if he could convince Kari to take a few days too—a little staycation to continue exploring what they were starting to have between them…maybe that could fulfill the promise he had made of making it up to her when he got back.

The gate agent scanned the boarding pass on his phone and Rob proceeded to the plane, finding his seat and settling in. His knees nearly touched the seat-back in front of him and he frowned. He knew he wasn't getting taller, so airline seats had to be getting smaller. Yay.

His phone chimed. A text from Mia, a selfie in front of a rental van. *Heading North. Thanks for everything, Dad.*

Rob tried to swallow the enormous lump that had taken residence in his throat and blinked, typing slowly. *Knock 'em dead, kiddo. Let me know if you need anything from your old man.*

Dots pulsed on the screen. *Will do. I'm nervous, but I have the world's best dad in my corner, so I can do anything.*

Rob's eyes squeezed closed and he rubbed his chest over his heart.

He might not be the world's best dad, but he was pretty sure he had the world's best kid.

Kari hurried from her car to her front door. *All seems okay on the doggo front* had been Sam's message around noon, but Kari had been preoccupied and aware that there was a living creature in her house the entire day. Kari opened the door, finding Hugo right behind it.

"Poor Mr. Dog. You want your dinner. And your dad. I want him back too." Kari gave him a distracted pat and strode to the kitchen, putting his food in a bowl and setting it on the floor. He looked at her as if he wasn't sure what he was supposed to do, and Kari remembered Rob telling her that not eating was a sign of stress. She crouched down and tapped the edge of the bowl with her fingertip. "It's okay, Mr. Dog. Eat the food."

Hugo sniffed the mixture and looked at her again. Had she done it wrong? The incorrect combination of kibble and canned food? He took a tentative bite, then another, then steadily ate. Kari sighed and stood, her tense shoulders relaxing as Hugo chomped in earnest.

"You finish all that and I'll go get changed. Then walk."

Hugo's head came up and he looked at her.

"You understand words? Like walk?" Kari felt ridiculous, but also felt like she was having an actual conversation of some kind. Hugo looked from her face to the bowl. "Keep eating. We'll...w-a-l-k after," she said, spelling the word that seemed to distract him so easily.

She left Hugo wolfing his dinner to change into shorts and a tee shirt. The dog came clicking and jingling into her room as she was tying her sneakers, blowing dog-food-breath into her face. Kari screwed up her eyes and twisted her head away. "Ugh. Thanks for that."

Hugo merely sat and thudded his tail against the floor in a steady rhythm.

"Okay. Fine. Walk." Was it her imagination or were his eyes brighter at the sound of that word? The dog followed her to the front door where she collected his leash, clipping it to his collar and looping the handle around her wrist. Sam had told a story at the dinner party about losing Graham's dog Honey when she was jumped by another dog. Kari didn't think another dog would be stupid enough to attack Hugo, but then again, what did she know about dogs?

Rob had told her that Hugo was very well trained, and she had to admit she appreciated the way the big dog stayed at her side, not ranging around or—God forbid—pulling at the leash like she'd seen around the neighborhood. In contrast, his trotting stride next to her was a light, graceful float.

This was nice. She'd never seriously considered getting a pet before, but there was something soothing about Hugo's solid bulk and furry, watchful presence. They reached a little area that wasn't quite park, wasn't quite woodland—kind of a borderland between a house and the little neighborhood park. Hugo paused to sniff and then looked back at her.

"You're fine, do what you need to do." Hugo nosed around some more, then squatted.

Oh. Yeah. Thanks to Rob's extensive notes, Kari had remembered to bring a plastic bag with her, but she hadn't been quite prepared for the sheer size of what Hugo left behind. She pulled the bag out of her pocket as he stood, peeling it back over her hand and squatting. Best to get this over fast. But Hugo kicked his hind legs backward, as if to cover his poo with debris. Kari closed her eyes and stood, waiting for the sounds to stop, cautiously cracking one eye open to see Hugo sitting on his haunches again, tongue lolling as if he was proud of his accomplishment.

Kari gulped and wrapped her plastic-shrouded fingers around the mass. It was squishy. And warm. And utterly disgusting. Holding her breath, she inverted the bag around it and tied it off, swallowing down a spurt of nausea. Holding the bag with her fingertips, she stood and looked at Hugo.

"If I was in any doubt about my feelings for Rob, this would end them. Guess we better finish your walk, Mr. Dog."

If she didn't know any better, she would have sworn he winked at her.

Rob pushed his key card into the hotel room lock for the third time before he got the blessed green light. His neck was tight, his eyeballs felt like they'd been sandpapered. The day with the Los Angeles I.T. team had not exactly gone swimmingly. While there had been some earnest faces in the training room, there had also been some accusatory stares.

He hated surveilling staff. For the most part, his attitude towards staff internet use was: keep it clean, keep it safe and as long as you do the job we pay you to do, I don't care. He knew the more you clamped down on a bunch of smart geeks, the more they would waste time figuring ways around the surveillance technology and the less time actually doing their jobs. But there was a line to walk there, and he was worried he'd fallen too far on the lenient side.

His job now was to not compound the problem by falling too far on the hard-ass side.

The door thudded behind him as he found the light switch. His shoulder, supporting the strap of his carryon, was shrugged up near his ear. It ached. Just about everything ached. He dropped the bag on a little padded bench and flopped backwards onto the bed, the springy surface bouncing underneath him. He rubbed his eyes and imagined it was Kari's cool fingers, not his rough, blunt ones, that caressed his face. The thought eased the tension in his neck and shoulder, though a sharp emotion spiked through him at the same time. His hands slid away from his face and he stared up at the ceiling, the sprinkler head an unexpected focal point.

He missed her.

He hadn't even been away from her for a day, but he missed her.

His phone chimed. "What," he muttered, twisting his hips so he could retrieve the infernal device from his back pocket. Pulling his reading glasses out of his shirt pocket he slid them on and looked at the screen with Kari's name on it. It took him a moment to register he was looking at a photo of a sketch of Hugo, the dog's eyes watchful and solemn. Another chime, another sketch, this time of Hugo in motion, presumably bounding after some toy. He had that ready-to-pounce look. Next, the dog lying down, eyes closed, head resting on his front paws.

The sweet ache of missing Kari intensified and then

flared when the next message came in. This one wasn't a sketch. Instead, it was a selfie. Kari and Hugo, with a message:

Sitting on the floor with him because he wouldn't hop on the sofa with me.

Rob smiled and typed. *Mia would be proud. She's worked hard to train him.*

A chagrined-looking emoji popped on his screen. *I take it he won't sleep in my bed either?*

Rob shuddered at the idea of the huge dog in his bed. He had yet to be able to get a good night's sleep next to Kari. Hugo, with his fur and his dog-breath and his pointy nails, would be a nightmare. *Yeah. NO. Please don't undo his training. I don't want him hopping in my bed.*

She called then, and he brought the phone to his ear. "This is Rob."

"I know."

"Don't ding me for old habits. I've been answering the phone like that for at least twenty years."

Her voice softened. "No dinging. It's very…you."

"I'm not sure how to take that."

"It's the whole Rob Fox package. Taking care of people. Dorky dad-jokes. Being proud of your daughter. Answering your personal phone like it might be a business call, even though you know it's me."

He shifted his shoulders on the mattress, took off the reading glasses he didn't need now. "I'm still not sure how to take it."

"I like it. I like the Rob Fox package." She paused. Coughed. "I mean…"

He resisted the urge to make a joke about the double entendre. "Thanks. I like the Kari Halvorsen package an awful lot too." The gorgeous, creative, generous package that was Kari.

"You do?"

"Yeah. The totally organized yet spontaneous artist. The maker of great food. The creator of that Norwegian cozy thing you told me about."

"*Hygge.*"

"Yeah. That. I think she's pretty special. In fact, before you texted me, I was thinking how much I missed her."

"You saw me this morning."

"Yeah. For two seconds. And I'm not going to see you for another two days. And I can usually trot out my front door and see you in less than a minute. So, I miss you."

Silence. Maybe the sound of her swallowing. It was hard to tell. "Yeah. I miss you too. It's weird seeing your house all dark, knowing you're not there."

"I'll be home Friday."

Exhaustion washed over him. He had to get on another plane early tomorrow morning, fly to Austin, do the whole depressing dog and pony show yet again with that staff. Introduce the trainer who came at an exorbitant price due to the last-minute booking, make it clear that he was personally invested in the message the trainer was going to hammer home, be the bad guy even though some shithead in his own office had tried to victimize someone. He liked his job. He was good at it.

But if he could transport himself home right this minute and be with Kari, he'd be home faster than he could say, "Landing party to beam aboard."

Chapter Twenty-Eight

Kari woke with a gasp, her pulse spiking, eyes flying open.

Someone is in the house.

She whipped to her side and saw brown eyes in a furry face regarding her. Hugo's mouth opened, long pink tongue lolling out.

"Shit." Kari rolled to her back, her hand on her chest as if the pressure could ease the hammering of her heart. She squeezed her eyes closed and tried to take a deep breath, but her body was still convinced that Hugo was some sort of intruder, her fight-or-flight reaction slow to exit the field of battle.

A huff of warm air in her ear and a swipe of wetness on the side of her face made her squeeze her eyes tighter, but it also made her laugh, the tightness in her chest easing. "Thanks, Mr. Dog. I think I'm good here. I take it someone wants his morning routine."

Hugo, no surprise, had nothing to say to this. Kari levered herself to a sitting position and blinked in the morning sunlight, taking stock.

First night with dog, and all is well. She nodded. Last night, she had retreated into what she knew—drawing. Hugo had seemed to appreciate the attention, even if it wasn't outright stroking his coat or playing with him. Then the texting and conversation with Rob. Her heart skipped a little at the memory.

So, I miss you.

There was that teenage feeling again. But instead of angsty and anxious, this time it was the bloom of young infatuation, the thrill of knowing your feelings are returned. She squeezed her eyes shut for a moment, her hands clenching as if she could physically contain the emotion.

Something cold and wet poked her bare hip. She looked down and saw Hugo, looking at her with an expectant gleam in his eyes.

"Sorry. I'm on it." She got out of bed and pulled out some clothes, padding to the bathroom to pee and run a brush through her pillow-ruffled hair before dressing. The dog followed her, watching with interest as she went through her routine.

"Kind of creepy to watch someone urinate," she muttered as she walked to the front door, Hugo hard on her heels. "Though I don't suppose you really have opinions on the subject." She collected a plastic bag, snapped his leash to his collar, and let them out the door. Hugo seemed bouncier this morning, swinging his head around to look at a robin hopping across Rob's lawn and to track a squirrel spiraling up a tree a little further down. This time, when he squatted, Kari was prepared. She waited for him to stop kicking before holding her breath and squatting to clean up.

"I guess I have to apologize for judging you watching me pee," she said as she straightened and tied the bag off. "Though you don't have to participate in quite the same way I do. Ready for breakfast?"

The dog's ears pricked a little higher and his tongue disappeared inside his mouth. Kari had noticed this behavior before: a lolling tongue seemed to indicate waiting or contentment, whereas a closed mouth signaled attention. Interesting.

"I think I'm getting this dog thing," she told Hugo as they went inside. Rob would be proud of her.

The idea made her smile.

⁂

"So, how's the team, Trin?" Rob asked the Austin help desk manager.

Trin, fingering the gauges stretching their earlobes into half-inch voids, ran their top teeth over the hoop that pierced their lower lip. They looked like a combination of walking pin-board and billboard, but also had the respect of the team and knew their stuff. Rob, weary from travel and a bad night of little sleep, braced himself for bad news.

"I don't *think* we have a problem here," Trin said.

"But?"

Trin shrugged. "Almost impossible to tell for sure." Their thick, dark brows were drawn together, muscled shoulders hunched under a tight superhero tee shirt. Rob wasn't quite sure which superhero the shirt represented—the design was a little abstract. He bit back a wry grin, realizing that he would have instantly known which Disney Princess was on a piece of media. Comic books, not so much.

"We're not expected to do the impossible," Rob said. "If our employees are haunting the nastier corners of the internet in their off hours and that's it, there's nothing we can or even should do about that. But if the audits of our internal network traffic are more or less clean, then I feel we've done what we could.

289

"I hate feeling like Big Brother," Trin said, tugging at a silver barbell that ran through their ear in two places. Rob repressed a flinch. He knew the piercing couldn't possibly hurt now—he'd known Trin for three years and they had already had most of the array of metalwork when they met, barbell included. But Rob marveled at Trin's capacity to endure pain.

"Yeah, well. I do too. You know my philosophy," Rob responded. "But we have to take this seriously."

Trin nodded and ran a hand over their hair, an array of tiny twists springing out from their dark scalp. "Yeah. Didn't mean to say you enjoyed it."

"I know. You're doing a great job here, Trin. Sandra thinks the world of you. She asked me specifically to come out here as a show of support for you."

"Really?" Trin's dark eyes were uncertain. "Because it kind of feels like…a vote of no confidence."

"I'm sorry it feels that way." Rob's eyelids felt heavy. His limbs felt heavy. Everything felt heavy. Exhaustion flowed like lead through his veins. "I know this might feel like corporate coming down on everyone because of something one person did. But what we're trying to do is make sure we have good people focused on making good games in a good environment." Great. Could he say the word "good" one more time, just to hammer home how out of his depth he felt about everything? "I don't care about Nerf gun wars in the cubicles or gif battles in Slack or non-pornographic surfing when the workload is light. I do care when we've got toxic people. I care even more when those toxic people are using our resources to act on their toxicity, especially against our people. Because it's not about Anna being powerful or important. It's because she's one of our own."

Trin nodded, but the tense lines around their eyes remained. "What about the rest of the staff?"

Rob nodded. "We're moving to address that. The entire staff of the company is going to get the same training. We're focusing here first because it's where the problem started."

"Okay. You might want to tell our people that. They're feeling singled out."

"I will." The lead in Rob's veins redoubled. This was above his pay grade. He didn't want to be here. He wanted to be back home with Kari. He slapped his hands on his thighs, faking an energy he didn't feel. "So. Let's get to the training."

Kari pulled up to her house, a smile already tugging at the corners of her lips. "Hugo, we're going to have a great evening," she murmured as she turned off the car. Then she saw Sam sitting on her front step, the dog next to her. A hundred scenarios ran through her mind, freezing her ability to think.

Her motions stiff, she got out of the car and walked toward Sam. "Have you been here long?"

Sam shook her head. She stroked Hugo from the top of his head down his back. "No. I came at noon, walked him, and went to class. But I got a weird vibe from him at lunch, so I came back about an hour ago. And he's been a busy guy."

"How?" Kari's brain spun. Had he gotten into something toxic for dogs? She cringed internally, remembering her ignorant comment about bones. Chocolate was on Rob's list as something dogs shouldn't eat. Was there something else? Had she left something out that he'd gotten into? "Is he okay?"

Sam thumped Hugo, who was panting, his ears at half-mast. "I think he's fine. Your dining room...kind of isn't."

Kari blinked, her stomach swooping. "How?"

Sam stood, dusting the seat of her shorts with a hand. Hugo tracked her movements, mouth closed and eyes alert, seemingly oblivious to Kari's presence. Sam opened the door and Kari and Hugo followed her inside, through the living room into the dining room. Sam pointed, but Kari already saw. Her eyes widened, hand coming up to cover her mouth. A section of baseboard and part of the wall were destroyed, the edges a ragged mess.

Kari sank to her knees, taking the dog's face in her hands and looking at him. "Is he okay?"

"Well, not if he did this," Sam said, her tone dry. "He's young and his routine's been interrupted too much and he's stressed out."

"No, I mean is he full of wood splinters?" Kari scanned the dog's body in helpless worry. He looked the same as he always did. Maybe a little sheepish. But how soon might he have symptoms of something?

"I cleaned up. He may have ingested a few bits of wood, but probably not enough to make him sick. It was a mess in here." Sam looked at the damage. "Well, a bigger mess."

Kari rose to her feet and all but ran into the kitchen. She grabbed Rob's list off the counter, digging in her purse with her free hand. Oh, god. Rob wasn't going to be proud of her at all. She'd screwed everything up.

"What are you doing?" Sam asked.

"I need to call the vet. I'm not taking any chances." Good grief. Why had he entrusted the dog to her? She didn't have a clue what she was doing. Dialing the number with shaking fingers, she explained what had happened to the woman who answered the phone.

"Bring him in," the woman said, her voice calm and soothing. "But this isn't unusual."

"It isn't?" Kari's voice sounded hysterical to her own ears.

"No. We see this kind of thing a lot. But the doctor should make sure he doesn't have something wrong with his mouth and check for intestinal blockage."

Kari's knees wobbled. "Okay. Thanks. I'll be right there." She hung up and shoved the phone back in her bag. "I've got to get him to the vet."

"I'll come with you." Sam patted her thigh and the dog followed her to the front door, Kari hard on their heels. Sam attached Hugo's leash, then looked at Kari and held her hand out. "Give me your keys."

"Why?"

"Because you're a mess. And we won't fit comfortably with the dog in the cab of my truck, so I'm driving your car."

"Oh." Normally, Kari would argue. But she felt like her muscles were simultaneously vibrating with tension and turning to water from exhaustion and stress. She handed the keys off to her niece and took Hugo's leash in return.

"It'll be okay," Sam said.

"Let's just get him checked out," Kari said.

✿

"Well, that's done." Rob rubbed his temples, his head throbbing. In truth, the session had gone better with the Austin crew than the L.A. staff. He didn't sense anything more negative than resigned tolerance of a boring day of training from this group.

"At least they'll be glad to get back to network connectivity issues and scrubbing malware tomorrow," Trin said, looking around the empty training room.

"Small mercies." Rob flinched, his phone buzzing in his

back pocket. He tugged it out and looked at the screen, a throb in his head making him wince. It took him a moment to comprehend the message. "Oh, no."

"Something wrong?" Trin asked.

"My daughter's dog—well, my dog now, I guess—he's been staying at my…" He shied away from using the term *girlfriend*. It sounded as absurd to apply to a forty-two year old woman as *boyfriend* sounded applied to his forty-eight year old self. "Next-door neighbor's house. Apparently, he chewed up her baseboards. They just got back from the vet."

"Sucks." Trin said. "Is the dog okay?"

"The dog is apparently fine." Kari had led with, *Hugo's okay* in her text.

"That's a relief, right?" Trin asked.

"Yeah." Rob's jaw was stiff. *Dammit*. He should have *known* something like this would happen. Why hadn't he even thought to bring Hugo's crate over? Mia told him that the dog was going through a stressed period. He'd seen the evidence with his own eyes. Hell, he'd cleaned up the toy Hugo destroyed with his own hands, a blizzard of white stuffing and scraps of cloth.

And, of course Hugo hadn't destroyed one of his own toys this time. No, he had to damage Kari's *home*. The home that was simultaneously her greatest achievement and greatest source of stress already. Kari must be going through hell right now. A sickening wave of guilt rolled through him.

"Hang on, Trin. I should give her a call." Rob tapped Kari's contact information and moved to a corner of the training room. Trin mouthed *I'll be in my office* and left.

Kari answered on the first ring. "You didn't have to call," she said.

"Of course I did."

"Aren't you doing training?"

"It just finished. How are you?"

"Hugo's fine." Her voice sounded exhausted.

"No, how are *you*?" The waves of guilt were rolling breakers now. Give him a long board and he could have surfed them.

"I'm okay. We—Sam and I—got him checked out. The vet says nothing wrong with his mouth, no mass of wood in his abdomen."

"Sam's with you. Good." Somehow, knowing her niece was there supporting her made him feel even more guilty. He should have been the one to pick up the pieces. He made the mess, after all. Or his dog did.

"Yeah. She's been great."

"How are you holding up?"

"I'll survive," she said.

"I'll be home by noon tomorrow if nothing goes wrong. Well, if nothing else goes wrong."

"It's okay. We're doing fine. Hugo seems calm now. I'm going to take tomorrow off to be with him. To make sure."

"Oh—" He was about to say "You don't have to do that," but he was sickeningly aware that she probably did feel she had to, for the sake of her house and her sanity. "Send me a photo of the damage. I'll fix it." That was at least something he could do.

"Why do you want a picture? You'll see it soon enough."

"I don't know. To prepare myself, I guess? If it was bad enough for you to take Hugo to the vet, it must be a lot of damage." He made a mental note to find out how much the visit had cost and pay her back for that too. "I'm sorry he's been such a problem."

"He hasn't been a problem. Well, except for this."

"That's a pretty big 'except.'"

"Please don't blow this up even bigger than it is. I'm going to go now. Sam and I are going to order a pizza and binge some Netflix."

"Send me that photo."

"Okay." And she was gone, leaving Rob stewing in guilt, frustration, and helplessness.

"...And so that's how it all happened." Sam tipped the dregs of her beer down her throat. The pizza was gone. Hugo had watched every bite as it traveled from plate to mouth. Sam had finally told Kari the whole story of how she met Graham and, if Kari was any judge, fallen deeply in love. Sam was a private person and she wasn't explicitly forthcoming to that degree, but it was pretty clear to Kari that her loner niece and Graham were serious about each other.

Plus, Rob had pronounced the younger man "smitten" with Sam, and Kari couldn't disagree with that assessment based on what she'd seen.

Kari twisted the neck of her own beer bottle between her fingers, wondering what to say next. Changing the subject might make Sam think she didn't care. Inquiring further into the new relationship might be taken as invasive.

"I'm moving in with him," Sam blurted.

Kari blinked. "You...you mean, like, *living* with him?"

Sam nodded, her brown ponytail swinging, dark blue eyes flicking up to meet Kari's gaze, then scudding away. "We get along really well. It seems silly for me to go home in the evening when I just want to be with him and he wants to be with me. He's got a nice little house. Something like this, actually." She waved at the living room. "And a great dog." She beaned Hugo on the head with a gentle finger. "Though she, like this dude, has had her moments."

"And you're in love with him." Kari couldn't believe how steady her voice was. This was momentous. Her stoic Sam had not only fallen in love, but she was *talking* about it.

Sam swallowed hard. "Yeah. I am." Her voice was so low it was almost a whisper, almost like she couldn't quite take in the enormity of what she was saying, what she was feeling.

"Well, for what it's worth, Rob said that Graham was 'smitten.'"

Sam laughed and her shoulders retreated from where they had been lifting toward her ears. "Do guys have a sense about that sort of thing?"

"He said he had expertise in such things having had young men brought home for his inspection by his daughter."

"That's right. He's got a kid."

"Hardly a kid. She's out on her own and moved to New York. That's why we have Mr. Dog." Kari waved at Hugo, who had been looking from Kari to Sam and back again as the conversation progressed, as if it was a tennis match.

Then the impact of the *we* she had used hit her.

Sam didn't miss it either. "And by *we,* you don't mean you and me. You mean you and Rob."

Kari took a sip of beer. It had gotten warm in her hands and the liquid tasted faintly disgusting at that temperature. She tugged a magazine forward on the coffee table and set the bottle on it. "Yeah. I guess I do."

Sam looked from the dog to Kari. "Do you think you'll... take it further?"

"Further how?" Heat prickled the back of her neck, even though she knew Sam wasn't talking about sex.

Sam waved at the living room again. "You think he'll move in with you? Or you with him?"

The idea of Rob in her house all the time felt funny. This house was *hers.* That was the whole point. She loved having him over, but...always? They hadn't even successfully shared a bed overnight without him spending the majority of it staring at the ceiling.

By the same token, the idea of moving into his house seemed wrong. She'd finally accomplished something she'd wanted all her life: a home of her own. To give that up now? No.

"I don't know, Sammie. I really don't know."

Chapter Twenty-Nine

Rob's jaw ached as the jet finally touched down. The beginning of the Texas summer storms had delayed his departure, then his plane had dodged additional weather cells as it flew East. All told, he was landing an hour later than he had expected.

He pulled his phone out and powered it on, tapping the screen as it came to life. When he could finally text, he typed out a message to Kari: *Flight was late. Sorry. Home in about an hour.*

He hadn't expected a response, but it came almost immediately. *No hurry. We're here. Front door is unlocked. Let yourself in when you get here.*

She had typed *here*. He had specified *home*.

He massaged the muscles at the hinges of his jaw. He shouldn't be trying to play house with the woman whose... house his dog had eaten. But *dammit*. Hugo's little cellulose and sheetrock snack couldn't have been more ill-timed. The bottom edge of the photo she had texted him yesterday was still visible in the texting app and he drew it into full view on the screen.

It was ugly. He had expected…less damage. He hadn't known Hugo's jaws were capable of that kind of destruction. An entire piece of baseboard would have to be cut, and the hole in the drywall would need to be patched. He'd need to repaint the entire wall when everything was repaired. And the newly fitted-in piece of baseboard would always be visible unless she elected to paint those as well.

Maybe he should just replace the entire length of baseboard. Hadn't she said one of the things she loved was the natural, unpainted wood?

His brain hummed with lists and plans as the crew opened the cabin door and people started to get to their feet, retrieve their luggage. Text notifications chimed from various areas of the cabin. Rob got up, careful not to hit his head on the underside of the overhead bin, and retrieved his briefcase and carry-on.

Once he was free of the slow mass of his fellow passengers shuffling up the jet bridge, he strode through the airport at top speed, eager to get home.

Eager to make it up to her.

Kari sat on the rug in the living room, legs stretched out, back resting against the sofa. Hugo's back was plastered against her leg, nose pointing toward her hip, fast asleep. He woofed softly and twitched. Kari put her sketch pad aside and watched him, fascinated. His paws flicked, the woofs puffing his doggy cheeks, his eyes darting behind closed lids.

He must be dreaming. She smoothed her hand over his shoulder, keeping her touch light on the coarse fur. He sighed, groaning a little, legs stretching, tail giving one heavy thump against her shin.

Kari was beginning to see the appeal of pets, despite the

damage done to her dining room. Hell, she was sitting on the floor because of his training not to get on the furniture.

Sam had smiled last night when Kari related this fact to her. "It's probably for the best. Less wear and tear on your stuff. But if you want to come over and cuddle a dog on the sofa, Graham lets Honey get on the furniture."

So, here she was on the floor. There was something so incredibly satisfying about Hugo's warm, furry body pressed against her. The need, the trust. So she'd elected to sit on the floor and sketch out some ideas for a painting for her bedroom. The pale green walls still delighted her, but Rob was right. The room needed more. She picked up the pad again, flipping back through the sketches she'd started and abandoned. An abstract idea, riffing on the ideas off the traditional Scandinavian motifs seemed interesting but somehow flat and unappealing in execution. A realistic representation of her backyard was laughable. Why would she want her own drawing of a thing she could see by looking out the window?

She flipped to a fresh page and let her hand just sweep across the page, the pencil laying down a faint line. *Hm.* It reminded her of something. She continued to riff with her pencil, humming a pop song from AM radio when she was a kid. The shape of what she was creating was familiar, the composition reminding her of something.

Continuing to let her pencil drift, building the composition, Kari's eyes widened. *Oh.* It was the lake shore, where Rob had taken her to draw while he fished. But this time there were no people at all. No people in kayaks and canoes, no Rob standing on the shore, no little Mia beside him. Her pencil seemed to dart up of its own accord, sketching the outline of a heron slicing through the air, the only living, moving thing in the landscape.

Kari's chest tightened. Was this lonely scene what she

wanted? Was this a message from her subconscious or just something she'd drawn recently and looked to recreate without the details?

But no, there were details there. Trees, the riffling of the water against the shoreline, the lone heron. Just no people.

Kari swallowed. Her throat felt thick. She rested her hand on Hugo's ribcage, the rise and fall of his breathing soothing. A tiny smile curved her lips. Yeah, this pet thing was something she could get behind. She snorted at her own fanciful thoughts. It didn't have to be all or nothing. Turning over her conversation with Sam the night before she wondered why things had to change. Why did they have to "go further"? What they had was nice. Balanced. Comfortable.

Hugo's eyes snapped open and he scrambled to his feet, the abrupt motion making Kari gasp, her hand withdrawing from his fur to slam to her chest. At the same time, she heard her door open. She was on her feet before she knew what she was doing, her heart hammering.

"Kari?" Rob's voice called from the entryway.

"In here." Kari took a shuddering breath, then another, looking to slow her rabbiting pulse. Hugo was already trotting to meet Rob, ears pricked, tail swinging.

"Are you okay?" Rob came into the room, looking rumpled and worried.

"Yeah. Hugo spooked when he heard you and that startled me, and..." Kari waved a hand to indicate the rest and bent to retrieve her sketch pad, which had landed on the floor when she jumped up.

"Oh." Rob's eyes traveled to the dining room. The damage was invisible from where he was standing and he took a restless step toward it before he seemed to remember that this wasn't his house. "May I?"

Kari nodded, irritated for reasons she couldn't define,

and Rob strode to where Hugo had done his destruction, Kari following.

Rob rubbed the side of his face, his eyes wide. "Holy shit."

The photograph hadn't done justice to the damage Hugo had wreaked. Rob blinked, revising his earlier shopping lists of repair materials. He wondered if the dog had somehow done more damage in the interim, despite Kari being here. Crouching, he touched the edges of the hole in the drywall, noting with some relief that the dog had, at least, had the dumb luck not to do his damage near an electrical outlet.

The idea that Hugo could have electrocuted himself and he would have to tell Mia was sickening. The idea Kari would come home to an electrocuted Hugo was equally horrifying. Guilt sat like lead in his gut.

"Okay. I need to get to the home center and pick up a few things, then I can get started fixing this." Rising to his feet, he noticed a crease between Kari's brows. Hugo was sitting at her feet, panting, and she was leaning sideways to fiddle with one of his ears. "And I'll get this beast out of your hair."

"He's not a beast," Kari said, smoothing her hand over Hugo's head.

"He did this," Rob said, waving at the hole, "so he's in the metaphorical doghouse as far as I'm concerned." Hugo had caused her stress and worry and had *eaten her beloved house*.

But the bigger problem was that Rob was responsible for Hugo being there at all.

He was responsible for this hole and he was going to fix it. He could do this. He could fix the damage that Hugo had made. He could make Kari's beloved, anxiety-inducing house whole.

Kari's eyelids sank closed. There were dark smudges under those lovely blue eyes and her skin looked tightly stretched across the high cheekbones. *Dammit.*

Rob slapped his thigh. "Come on, boy. Let's get your stuff and get you next door. Then I can get the things I need to get started on the repairs."

"Do you need to..." Kari trailed off, her hands flapping.

"Need to what?"

"Need to do everything *now*?" Now she just seemed exasperated.

Of course he had to do everything now. The faster he could get Hugo out of here, the faster he could get to work, the faster he could smooth this whole thing over, make it like it never happened. They could keep building the precious thing they'd started. It was so obvious, he didn't know what to say.

"I need to fix this. And I need to pay you for the vet bill."

The groove between Kari's eyebrows deepened. "Okay, I get that. It's just..."

"It's just *what*?" It was just glaring, that was what it was. Clear as day. He'd fucked up, he'd fix it, they'd move on.

"Nothing." Kari's hand stilled on Hugo's head. "You want to get started. Okay. Is there anything I can do to help?"

"No." God forbid. He'd made the mess, he'd clean it up.

Kari's teeth ground as Rob collected Hugo's things and took the dog next door, promising to return in an hour or so once he'd made a run to the home center. The house seemed hollow without Hugo there, emptier. She had gotten used to his watchful, furry presence so quickly. But the restless, frustrated thread of emotion simmering in Kari had little to do with the dog not being there anymore. She paced from dining room to kitchen, turning on her heel and returning through the dining room to the living room, realization lighting inside her.

It was the way Rob charged in and took over that unsettled her, leaving her restless and almost angry.

No, not almost angry. Furious. She paced across the living room. This was *her* house. Her space. Did she want her wall repaired? Of course she did. But the way he had rammed in—without so much as a hello—taking stock, making decisions, it made the hair on the back of her neck stand on end. The whole point of her purchasing a house was that it was *hers*. Hers to decide when and how the hole in her wall would be repaired. How dare he come in here all abrupt and take-charge? And why was he in such a *hurry*?

A new thought intruded: maybe Rob wanted to do this so quickly because he wanted everything to be over.

Kari dropped to the sofa and rested her forehead in her hand. That made sense. He had so much going on in his life. His daughter moving, his workplace drama, the acquisition of a dog, maybe other stuff she didn't have any clue about. It would make sense that he might try to simplify, to cut away any dead weight.

The thought sliced through her like a serrated blade, jagged and rough. Her breath hitched and she pressed her knuckles to her mouth.

Wait. Think. Wasn't it just two days ago he told her he missed her?

But that was before The Hole. Maybe now she was just one more mess to be dealt with. One more obligation. Her shoulders went tight at the thought. It was hideous. She was craving closeness, connection. She'd had a little of it, there on the floor with Hugo. And then Rob had come stomping in and…*dammit*. He hadn't even kissed her cheek. Just rampaged around, making decisions and then even taking the dog away.

Kari stood, her arms folded tight across her chest. It was her house. And it was time she stood up for herself.

"I can't believe you did that," Rob muttered to Hugo as he got his suitcase and briefcase out of the car. The dog, docile and calm, nosed at his leash. "How can you be such a great dog ninety-nine percent of the time and then turn around and literally eat a hole in Kari's house?"

But, of course, Hugo didn't have answers for him. He was a dog.

"Let's get you inside. Or better yet, back yard where you won't cause any damage. Any more damage." He hustled Hugo through the house and let him out back, where the dog promptly pounced on his half-deflated football, tossing it in the air with his teeth and looking at Rob, panting as if he should come and play. "Not today, boy. I have to atone for your crimes."

Rob shut the door and went to his room to change into clothes he could get dirty in. He went over his mental list again, realizing he needed to cut out a sample of the base-board in order to match it with the stock at the home center. He also needed to measure the hole in the drywall and get the chip for the paint color so he could have the home center mix up some more. He checked his watch. Two o'clock. If he got supplies and got set up, he could do the cutting and dry-fitting before the day was out, then complete the repair tomorrow and paint on Sunday. By the end of the weekend, Kari's home should be back to normal.

There was a sharp rap at his door. Frowning, Rob went to open it, surprised to see Kari on his doorstep. "I was just going to go over and get a sample of the baseboard, measure the hole," he said.

"Can we forget about the damn hole for a minute?" She sounded peeved. She had a right to be. But if she was peeved about the destruction in her house, why did she want to forget about it?

"I don't understand."

"You just...you come into my house, taking charge and making decisions and..." She waved over at her house. "It's *my house.*"

"Of course it's your house."

She folded her arms and glared at him. "So stop acting as if it's yours."

He blinked, speechless for a moment. "How was I doing that?"

She looked at him as if he was exceptionally stupid. "I just told you. Storm in, take over, make decisions—"

"Do you know what needs to be done to fix it?" he broke in.

"No."

"Well then, what decisions are there for you to make?"

"I don't know. Maybe I *want* a hole in my wall." Her hands flew out, excess energy seeming to spark off of her.

"That's absurd." Anger started to simmer in Rob's gut. He just wanted to make everything right. Why was she being so goddamned *difficult* about it?

"Okay, so maybe I want an absurd house. Maybe I don't care that the hole is there for now. Maybe all this hurry makes it feel like you're just trying to speed through this because I'm just one more obligation for you. But I'm not an obligation."

"Of course you're not." But his denial was a little too quick. There *was* a sliver of truth in what she said.

"Two nights ago, you said you missed me."

His head spun with the sudden change of topic. "I did. I did miss you."

"So what's changed? Why am I getting punished?"

"How am I punishing you by wanting to fix what the dog did?" In his stew of confusion and rising anger, his voice was almost a shout. He squeezed his eyes shut and pinched the bridge of his nose. "What the hell is going on here, Kari?" he said in a softer voice.

"It *feels* like punishment." Her voice was tight, choked. "Two days ago you miss me and now you want to…get past me? Get this over with?"

He opened his eyes and looked at her. "Get what over with?"

"Us?"

"Why would you think that?"

"Oh, I don't know. You race into my house without even a hello…" She gave a bleak little laugh. "And now I'm standing on your front step, Rob. You don't even want me inside your *home*."

Chapter Thirty

Kari struggled to keep her breath deep and even. Her *feelings* were so clear. Why couldn't she put words together to express them?

Rob stepped back from the doorway. "Why don't you come in," he said, his voice stern. His eyes had dark shadows and lines of tension fanned out from the corners.

She followed him in, the door closing behind her sounding all too final. But then his fingertips skimmed her bare arm as he passed her, leading her into the living room. The touch was momentary but intimate. Reassuring and confusing all at once.

"Have a seat," he said, dropping to the sofa and indicating the cushion next to him. Unsure, she sat, her fingers entwined in her lap, twisting together so hard they hurt. Rob rested his hand on top of her clasped fingers, no demand in his simple gesture. Kari swallowed and pulled her hands apart, turning her palm upward. Rob covered it with his own, his skin warming hers. "What's going on, Kari? Start from the beginning."

Kari scanned his face. The shadows under his eyes and

the stress lines were still there, but there was also a sort of guarded, patient watchfulness. It was a look that picked at Kari's anxiety, peeled it away in tiny strips, like a label from a beer bottle. She swallowed again, gathering her flying thoughts.

"So…from the beginning. Before you came in—into my house. I was sitting on the floor with Hugo. I was having a nice time. Hugo was having a nice time. Well, he was sleeping. If he's anything like me, that constitutes a nice time."

"Why were you sitting on the floor?"

"Because Hugo doesn't get on the couch. And he's companionable."

Rob nodded and squeezed her fingers.

"So I was sitting there, sketching and enjoying his company. He's kind of funny when he's sleeping, you know? And I was looking forward to you coming home."

Something shifted in Rob's expression at that, a minuscule relaxation that made Kari squeeze his hand. After a moment, his fingers tightened on hers in response. He nodded for her to continue.

"…And I was sketching and Hugo was sleeping and then suddenly you were *there* and charging around and taking stock and making decisions and taking Hugo away…" She heaved a shuddering sigh. "It felt very…abrupt. And isolating. Lonely. Like you wanted to put me behind you."

Rob licked his lips and Kari noticed his normally clean-shaven cheeks were rough with stubble. "I only wanted to put everything back the way it was. So we could go forward. Not to put you behind me." His dark eyes flicked toward the ceiling and his chest heaved. "I would never want to remove anything that gave you comfort. I thought Hugo would be a source of stress and aggravation. I thought the hole in your wall would be a source of stress and aggravation."

Kari shook her head. "I don't know why, but I wasn't

mad at Hugo. I know the hole can be fixed. There's no huge hurry. I didn't miss having an unblemished wall, I missed *you*."

Rob nodded. "And—maybe this is silly, but I texted you that I was coming *home* and you texted back that you were *here* and...I maybe over-interpreted that as you putting me at a distance."

"Ah." Kari's head rocked back, comprehension flooding her. Moments ago, when she had told him she looked forward to him coming *home*, he had relaxed. "You know how weak that is, don't you?"

"Yeah." He ducked his head, a sheepish smile curving his lips. "So...maybe we should talk a little more. 'Use our words,' as I would have said to Mia when she was...well, two."

Kari's lovely mouth tightened at that. "Kind of like 'Are You Smarter Than a Fifth Grader' but even worse. 'Are You Half As Emotionally Intelligent As a Toddler'?"

Rob shook the hand he grasped. Kari's fingers still gripped his, a reassuring sign. "Not quite as bad as that." But he worried that he'd insulted her.

Kari closed her eyes and Rob braced for impact. For rejection. Instead, Kari's eyes opened, the light blue sending a laser of conflicting emotion through him.

"How was your trip, dear?" she asked.

He laughed. "Kind of horrible. My staff hates training and maybe me. How have you been?"

"Well, my boyfriend's dog ate a hole in my house and then when he came home, instead of cuddling me he tried to be a home renovation genius."

"What a jerk."

"He's not so bad."

"Boyfriend, huh?" The hated word now seemed… normal. Benign. Welcome, even.

"Well, he's kind of…"

"Old?"

"I was going to say a silver fox, but you do you."

A bubble of laughter was trapped under his sternum. "Rob Fox, silver fox?"

"You know it, baby." Kari's pale eyebrows waggled.

The bubble popped and Rob collapsed back onto the sofa, helpless with laughter.

"You never made that connection?" Kari asked.

"The connection between my last name and…"

"And you being a total silver fox. Yes." Kari's expression was a combination of sardonic and *∂uh*.

Rob swallowed. "Um. Thanks. Very flattering. Yes." He rubbed a hand across his face, palm rasping across his rough cheeks. "Okay. Of all the admittedly limited number of ways I thought today would go… This wasn't one of them."

Kari settled beside him, her head resting on the back of the sofa next to his. "How did you think it would go?"

He folded his lips into his mouth, thinking. Kari squeezed his hand, the barest pressure. He kept his eyes on the ceiling and said, "I'd swoop home. I'd take the evil canine sorcerer who destroyed your drywall—" He cut his eyes to her, checking to see if she was on board with him making light of what he had thought of as a total disaster. Her calm was undisturbed. "I'd take that evil sorcerer away. I'd fix the destruction the evil sorcerer had wrought. I'd be the hero."

"Hm." Kari's free hand toyed with the hair at the nape of his neck, somehow making him realize how tired he was. Relaxation and fatigue flooded through him. "So I'm the damsel in distress in this scenario?"

Rob chuckled. "Honey, I can't imagine you as a damsel. Distressed, maybe. But Viking Shield Maidens don't do damsel." He pulled his hand out of hers and wrapped it around the back of her neck, giving it a gentle squeeze. "Anyway. You know I wouldn't think of you that way. Have pity on a poor, broken down old man."

She shifted against him, leaning her head on his shoulder and he slid his arm around her, pulling her tight against his side. "This is nice," she murmured.

"More what you had in mind?"

"Yes. I had been hoping for quiet and cuddles, not power tools, noise, and dust."

"Fair enough. Are we going to do this for the rest of the afternoon?"

"Or until one of us gets a crick in the neck."

"Solid plan."

A thump and a scrape from the back door told Rob Hugo had had enough of playing by himself in the back yard and was pawing to be let in. Kari lifted her head, allowing Rob to stand and drag himself up to the door. He wondered where all the driving energy he had had not an hour before had gone. Now, he felt all the events of the last week like liquid lead in his veins.

"Come on in, boy." He held the door as the dog came in, pausing to slurp some water out of his bowl in the corner. Dragging back to the living room, he held a hand out to Kari. "Come nap with me."

"Nap?" She arched an eyebrow as she placed her hand in his and let him pull her to her feet. "Is that slang for something else?"

He shook his head, huffing a soft laugh. "I'm too tired to even think about a double entendre. Just come sleep."

"But you can't sleep when I'm in the same bed with you."

He thought of how badly he had slept while he was on the road. How much he had missed her. "Try me."

Hugo followed them to Rob's bedroom, settling into a wire crate in the corner with a thump and a groan. Kari toed her sneakers off and sat on the bed.

"Come here." The mattress dipped as Rob sat on the other side and Kari lay down, scooting backwards until her back was tucked up against his front and his arm slid around her waist. She tried to let her mind drift, but was still aware of Rob behind her. Would he fall asleep? Or would she have to slink home after an hour of tense waiting and leave him alone to finally get some rest?

Little by little, Rob's arm grew slack and his breathing deepened. Kari wanted to turn over and see if he was faking it. But if he wasn't faking, she would only wake him, and it was plain the man needed sleep. She was still keyed up from the argument and the uncertainty, sure she wouldn't fall asleep herself.

Until she awoke to warm lips pressing against the side of her neck. "Morning, sleepyhead," Rob murmured in her ear.

"Mmm. How long did we nap?" Kari cleared her throat, surprised at the roughness in her voice.

"About two hours. That is, if you fell asleep around the time I did."

"You actually slept?" It felt more like a blink than a nap. She didn't remember dreaming or sliding into sleep, but sticky cobwebs of slumber stuck to Kari's consciousness, keeping her from clear thinking.

"I actually did." His voice vibrated with suppressed humor. He sounded far too awake. Smug, even. His hips shifted, hardness pressing against her bottom. Her eyelids lowered in a languid blink as the arm circling her waist started to move, his hand sweeping down across her belly, skating over the front of her thigh, then back up the side of her leg to her hip, soothing and comforting and erotic all at the same time. He pressed his lips to the back of her neck, sending shivers radiating down her spine. She shifted, restless, her body and brain waking up in tandem as he stroked her, avoiding her most sensitive places, her breasts and the throbbing need between her legs, yet still somehow stoking her desire higher.

She turned in the circle of his arm. "Rob—"

"I want to taste you. Can I?"

Kari laughed, an inadvertent explosion of disbelief. "*Can* you? Of course."

"Hm." His big brown eyes creased with humor, pupils blown wide with desire. "Well then." Moving with speed that made her sleep-addled mind dizzy, he sat up and popped the button on her shorts, dragging down the zipper and stripping her bare before kneeling between her legs, hands warming her thighs, thumbs stroking circles and nearly making her weep with the desire to be touched more intimately. To have his hands or his mouth or *anything* on the hectic flesh that waited, crying out for contact.

Rob rubbed his cheek, grimacing. "I haven't shaved in two days," he said.

"Are you trying to back out of this?"

"No! In fact, it's something I've been thinking about for a while. Since before I got that first little taste the other night."

"Trust me, it will not be a problem."

"Well, then." Shooting her a wolfish grin, he bent and pressed a kiss...to her belly button.

Kari groaned. "Tease."

"Patience, woman," he mumbled against her belly, stimulating the sensitive skin with soft lips and light brushes of his rough cheeks. Kari twisted the coverlet in her fists, her entire being focused on the unsatisfied throbbing between her legs. When he shifted back, parting her thighs further with gentle hands, she inhaled sharply, her eyes squeezed shut. The next thing she felt was his lips on the inside of her knee.

This time she didn't bother to protest. He was determined to torture her and she was just going to woman up and take it.

Enjoy it, even.

Rob used lips, tongue, stubble, even teeth to tease at the insides of her thighs, moving ever closer to the part of her that was ready to incinerate. Finally, after what felt like a year, his tongue skimmed up between her lips, reaching and circling her clit with a soft, warm touch that made her shiver.

"Oh. *Oh.*" Kari's own voice sounded far away. Rob moved again, settling closer to her, shoulders spreading her legs wide the touch of his mouth and tongue more sure against her, no longer toying, but firing her up in earnest. Warmth licked all through her, the pleasure both intense and languid. She came with a suddenness that surprised her, like fireworks across the night sky. Rob held his tongue against her as she writhed and shuddered through the aftermath, his hands sliding under her thighs to clasp her fingers.

"Mmm." His final hum gave her a miniature quake that shivered up her spine. Kari opened her eyes and stared at the ceiling, blinking, her entire body blasted clean.

Rob pressed himself up, gratified by the hazy, sex-drunk look on Kari's face. The taste of her, the feel of her losing control, still vibrated through his own unsatisfied desire. Pulling his tee shirt over his head, he scrubbed his mouth with it and tossed it aside, moving to stretch out next to Kari. She rolled to face him, her cheek in her hand, her breath evening and her gaze becoming sharp.

"You've been holding out on me. I didn't know you could do that."

Rob shrugged, his face heating.

"You're *blushing*?" Kari's fingertips skimmed across his cheekbone. "After doing that to me in broad daylight. You're a marvel."

She leaned forward, capturing his lips with her own, throwing a leg over his hips and pulling them together. He groaned as his dick ground against her, trapped by the fabric of his shorts. The pressure felt so good, but it wasn't enough.

As if she could hear his thoughts, Kari rolled herself on top of him, pulling away from the kiss to kneel and strip his shorts and underwear off. Climbing back on, she rode the length of him, slick and warm.

"Are you...wet enough?" he asked, his voice a strangled, twisted thing. He realized her shirt was still on, the soft fabric swaying as she undulated. Skating his hands under the hem, he lifted the cotton. She ducked forward, letting him drag the shirt over her head, shaking her hair back from her face. "Oh. Bra. Bad, evil bra." He unhooked the offending garment, pulling it off. Faint pink marks marred her skin where the elastic had pressed. He trailed his fingertips along the lines. "Bad." He pulled her down to him, capturing her breast with his mouth, teasing the nipple with his tongue. "Evil." He transferred his attention to her other breast as she rocked on him, slick and hot. The groan from deep in his throat vibrated in his lips, making Kari gasp.

Kari's hand wrapped around his dick, angling it up and into her. His hands cupped her hips as she slid down, enveloping him. He bucked off the bed, ass clenching, pushing further into that sweet heat. Kari bent over him, the tips of her hair trailing across his chest, tickling. A strange joy bubbled up in him, suffusing his body, his mind.

I love you, Kari Halvorsen.

The thought shocked him.

But it made perfect sense.

He wrapped his hands around her neck, pulling her flush against him, hips rolling up to meet hers, lips pressing, tongues tangling.

I love Kari Halvorsen.

Some tiny shred of self-control kept him from saying the words out loud. Not now. Not while she was moaning into his mouth, fingers tangling in his hair. Not while there was no space between them, joined like a single being. The position left barely any leverage to move, but he didn't want any separation between them, so he pulsed up into her. The tiny motions made her groan and cling tighter.

"Good?" he asked.

"Oh, God. So good. Don't stop."

"Don't worry." He redoubled his efforts, moving faster, and was rewarded with a stuttering cry from Kari, and a warm, pulsating sensation that sent him over the edge after her with a hoarse groan, pushing up into her as hard as he could, his orgasm radiating through his entire body.

When he recovered, Kari's panting breath puffed hot against his neck. He smoothed his hand down her back, tracing the bumps of her spine. "You okay?"

"Broken," she mumbled into his neck. "You broke me."

He tried to tamp down the adolescent swell of pride her words gave him. "What do you think you did to me?"

"You did it to me twice."

"You're saying it like it's a bad thing."

318

Kari lifted up, resting her forehead on his. "Not a bad thing. Just. Wow."

Yup, the battle against feeling like a cocky teenager was lost now. Over. He cupped her cheeks and kissed her. "Can I tell you something?"

She didn't move. "Sure."

"I don't want to scare you, but I think I might be falling in love with you." It was a half-truth. He didn't think anything. He was one hundred percent sure he was in love with her. But it felt safer to edge over to the truth, rather than confront it boldly.

It was still terrifying, though.

More terrifying was how still she'd gone. *Shit.* He was still half inside her, his softening dick sliding out of her by degrees. This was not the way to do this.

"I'm sorry. I shouldn't have—" He stopped, her finger landing on his lips.

"Shh." She took her finger away and kissed him, the briefest press of her lips, somehow seeming like a promise.

"I think that makes two of us," she whispered.

Kari's blood had turned to champagne. That was the only explanation for the feeling that fizzed through her, energizing all the nerves, overriding the lassitude that had flooded her after her second orgasm. Rob rolled them so they lay on their sides, face to face, his breath still coming a little fast, his hand warm on her hip.

"So this is...exciting." He said, his eyes searching her face. Whatever he was looking for, he didn't seem to find, as a crease appeared between his brows.

"What's the matter?" Kari stroked the indentation with a fingertip.

"You seem so calm," he said.

"Calm?" What she was feeling must have shown on her face. How could it not? "Anything but. I feel like I swallowed a truck full of firecrackers."

His face eased at that, but a trace of wariness remained. "You're hard to read sometimes, you know that?"

She shrugged. "I live in my body. I look at my face in the mirror every day. It's hard to know what comes across and what doesn't."

"So tell me."

"I thought I already did."

"I said I thought I was falling in love with you. You said you 'think' that makes two of us. That's pretty vague."

"Ah." She scratched her nose, searching for the words. "I guess…it was having you gone. I was lonely. I'm used to being *alone*, but it was different this time. It wasn't just that I was alone. I missed you. Specifically you. I couldn't wait for you to get home."

His hand slid from her hip to the dip of her waist. "I know what you mean. Hotels don't usually faze me. I can usually sleep anywhere. Well—"

She grimaced. "Yeah. Until you couldn't sleep with me in the bed."

"Two times. Only two times. And I hadn't slept with anyone else in ten years. More. I wasn't into sleepovers even when I was dating. That's a long time and I'm an old, set in my ways kind of guy."

"Bullshit." Kari gave his shoulder a little push and he rolled onto his back, laughing. She squirmed closer and rested her head on his chest, his arm curling around her shoulders. "You're a forty-eight year old hottie who sometimes has a little too much energy and restlessness for your own good. You need to settle down a little."

"Settle down, old man."

"You seriously need to stop it with the old man thing. Especially after you've given a woman two orgasms."

"Give a nice old man a sexy younger girlfriend and see what he can do," Rob said. That made Kari laugh in earnest, her stomach cramping. "You think I'm kidding."

Kari lifted her head so she could see his face. His eyes were closed, a smug smile curving his lips, creases fanning from the corners of his eyes. "No," she said, "I think you're impossible."

"Nah. Merely improbable."

"So, I was thinking." Rob popped a piece of popcorn in his mouth and chewed, distracted by Kari shifting next to him on the sofa. He'd managed to convince her to forego the bra when they got dressed again. An excellent idea in theory, but in practice it tended to derail his brain.

"Hm?" She elbowed him in the ribs before digging into the bowl on his lap for her own handful of popcorn and pointed at her face with her other hand. "Eyes are up here, bud."

"'Sorry, not sorry,' as the kids say. One of my best ideas ever."

"Speaking of which, you're sure Mia's safely in New York, right? I'm still traumatized from last time."

"Absolutely. Her Instagram feed is full of photos of her new digs, roommates, cardboard boxes, the whole shebang. Unless she invents a *Star Trek* transporter, she's in Queens."

"Okay, so what were you thinking?"

He paused, trying to gather his scattered thoughts. "Oh. Your kitchen."

She gave him a slow blink. "From my boobs to my kitchen. Your brain is an interesting place."

"You have no idea. Anyway, have you considered doing a DIY renovation?"

"Me? The woman with no skills whatsoever in that area?"

"No experience. That's different. And besides, you have me."

Kari looked at him, twisting her mouth sideways. "You want to redo my kitchen? I thought you said kitchen renovation was hell."

"It is if you're trying to live in the house and prepare anything close to a meal. Even making coffee gets fraught pretty fast. But you've got a fully-functioning kitchen right here." He waved toward his own kitchen. "And maybe we can…" He paused, the idea forming a little too big for him to wrap his brain around.

"Maybe we can what?"

"Experiment with spending even more time together," he hedged.

She paused, popcorn halfway to her mouth. "Playing house?"

Damn, she was sharp. And how he loved it. "Pretty much."

She chewed slowly. Swallowed. "How much money would this run me?"

"A fraction of what you were thinking, I'm pretty sure. The Swedish flat-pack store has sales a couple of times a year."

"Swedish. Really." She gave him an arched-eyebrow look then laughed. "Okay, fine. I'm intrigued."

"Good. When I redid my kitchen I was pretty shocked by how the upper cabinets were attached to the walls. It seemed like a miracle that they hadn't come crashing down before."

She gave him a horrified look. "Do I need to go take all my plates out now?"

"No. If they've stayed up this long, they'll stay up for a few more months."

"You're really all in, aren't you?"

"Didn't I say I was?"

"Yeah." She paused, her eyes going unfocused. "I'm getting used to the idea. I feel like a teenager."

"Acne and angst?"

"No. The rarest of rare experience for a teenage girl: the boy I like likes me back."

"I feel like I should give you my letter jacket."

"You have a letter jacket?"

"No. Mathletes weren't given letter jackets."

"Awww. You were a mathlete." She tilted her head and batted her eyes. "That's so perfect."

"Far from perfect." He kissed her softly.

"Perfect for me, then," she murmured against his lips.

Epilogue

You sure you don't need anything else? Kari texted, her hip resting against the handle of her grocery cart, eyeing the lines stretching from the minimally-staffed checkout stations into the aisles.

Nope. We're good.

"The man wants to do Thanksgiving and he can't even plan properly," Kari muttered, stuffing the phone in her back pocket and pushing the cart to the self-checkout, mentally crossing her fingers that the finicky scanners would actually work. "Who plans to make pumpkin pie and doesn't think to check to make sure there's enough sugar?" Not to mention the five obscure but necessary ingredients he'd realized he didn't have for the very special stuffing. And the other random things.

The grocery gods smiled on her. She only waited twenty minutes for a checkout station and didn't have to get one of the harried-looking grocery employees to come over and help her with a scanning failure or other issue with the stupid machines. She stuffed her purchases into cloth bags and left, shoving her cart into the corral with a sigh of relief.

A grocery store on Thanksgiving afternoon was not exactly a low-stress environment.

A short drive home and she was pushing through her front door, the smell of roasting turkey floating from the kitchen. "Everything okay back there?"

"Fine." The word was closer to a grunt, but somehow it made her smile. She lugged her purchases to the kitchen, finding Rob elbow deep in bread crumbs, sausage, cranberry, and she didn't know what else.

"Your leeks, sir. And all the other stuff."

"Perfect timing. You mind washing and chopping them? I need them for the stuffing." He nodded at the big bowl in front of him.

"Not at all." The gleaming, modernized kitchen was still enough of a novelty that mundane tasks seemed like a pleasure. And having an actual dishwasher was pure heaven. "Step aside, Mr. Dog." Hugo moved from his position in front of the new, huge farmhouse sink, circling to the other side of Rob, alert for any sign of something dropping from the counter.

"He's so attentive. He really loves you," Kari teased as she rinsed the leeks, shaking them out and putting them on a cutting board.

"He loves sausage."

Kari pulled a knife from the block. "He'll be excited to see Mia in an hour or so. Won't you, boy?"

The dog's attention didn't waver but his tail thumped once. Kari shook her head and chopped the leeks, dumping them into the bowl for Rob to mix in with the rest of the stuffing. Leaving him to finish preparing that dish, she went into the dining room, picking up the tablecloth she'd ironed earlier in the day off the chest and floating it over the table, replacing candlesticks after she'd squared the cloth off. Returning to the kitchen to get silverware, Rob was just

325

closing the oven door on the stuffing and turkey. He straightened, rolling his shoulders and she fitted herself behind him, wrapping her arms around his waist and resting her cheek against the back of his head. His hands ran over her arms, coming to rest over her clasped fingers, squeezing gently. They stood there like that for a few breaths, a lovely, quiet moment to add to the chain of lovely moments since she had first let Rob into this room all those months ago to look at her faucet.

She took one more breath, enjoying, then straightened, pulling away from the warmth and solidity of Rob's body. "Okay. Table setting."

"No." Rob turned, his fingers capturing hers, pulling her to him. "Kiss first."

"Mmm. Okay." The familiar, joyful heat that hadn't faded in their time together bloomed in her chest as their lips met, first teasing, then settling into angled heads, pressure, and languor. She pulled back again. "They're going to be here any minute. I got a text a few minutes ago that Sam and Graham were on their way to pick up Mia from the Metro."

Rob rested his forehead against hers. "Okay. Rain check."

"Definitely."

The sound of the door opening and a clamor of voices made Hugo's head whip around, his jaws shutting with an audible *clop*.

"She's here, boy," Rob said to the dog and Hugo took off at a run for the entryway. Rob dried his hands on a dish towel and walked to the living room where Mia, Sam, and Graham were taking turns hugging Kari. Mia dropped to her knees to receive a tongue bath from Hugo, who was making anxious little whining noises. She laughed and wiped her face on the sleeve of her coat, getting to her feet to wrap her arms around Rob's middle. Hugo tried to join the hug, stuffing his face in between their legs.

"Glad you could make it, kiddo." Rob stroked his daughter's curly hair, his heart threatening to burst out of his chest.

"Glad to be here, Dad." Mia grinned up at him, releasing him from her tight hug. "I see you have implemented your plan."

"Yeah, we noticed the For Sale sign next door," Sam said. "You have some splainin' to do, Auntie dearest." She poked her finger at Kari, who gasped and grabbed Sam's hand.

"*I* have explaining? What is *this*?" She looked from the sapphire ring on Sam's left hand to Graham, who was sporting a smug grin. "I guess I don't have to ask if you guys had a nice time in Norway."

Rob had wondered if Graham was going to use their vacation to pop the question. The younger man had been oddly keyed up prior to their trip. Well, as keyed up as quiet, pensive Graham seemed to get.

"He asked me to marry him almost as soon as we were in Norway. Well. After several hours on the train and an hour in a car. Then he asked me. At the hotel." Sam turned to Rob, a sly smile on her face. "You're selling your house, huh? That's *interesting*. I wonder where you're going to move to?" She tapped her chin with her index finger looking from Rob to Kari and back again.

"He's pretty much been living here for a while now," Kari said, shooting Rob a quick smile. "After a while it just seemed silly to have two houses." It was true. While they worked on her kitchen, she had all but moved into his house after a week of traipsing back and forth for meals. That had worked so well and been so surprisingly easy that when her kitchen was finished, he found himself working on more improvement projects and spending more nights at Kari's than he did at his own house. Eventually they had decided to run a full experiment: live in her house for a month and see what happened. And it had been glorious. After more discussion, he had decided to put his house on the market and move in completely.

"It's okay, though. I have an excellent landlady to rent from." Rob winked at Kari and she laughed.

"From being the person who called the landlady to solve problems to being the landlady herself, all in less than a year," Kari said. "Let's go finish off the meal and we can all get caught up."

Rob trailed the group back to the kitchen, the room humming with happy chatter and laughter. He might be about to sell his house, but home was where Kari was.

Enjoyed Handy for You?

Sign up for my newsletter for news about new books, sales, and more!

https://adelebuck.com/sign-up-for-my-newsletter/

And if you're so inclined, please leave a review on your favorite book vendor's site, Goodreads, or wherever you review books. Even a sentence can help a reader find a book. Thank you for reading, and keep reading for a sneak peek of the last book in the All for You series: *Willing for You.*

Chapter 1 of Willing for You

Gina took a deep breath and tried to control her trembling fingers as she ripped open the envelope. She shouldn't be doing this here. Should've waited until she was upstairs in the privacy of her apartment. Instead, here she was, standing at the bank of mailboxes, tearing open her fall grade report. She unfolded the paper, her eyes skimming past the two A grades, the 4.0 average, to rest on the detail she dreaded.

Yes, there it was. Three credits — one class to go — and she was done. Possessor of a Master's in Business Administration. And if she didn't have her own business up and running and most importantly *successful* before graduation day, she was going to have to go back to Boston.

The glass door of her condo complex opened and Gina glanced up, suppressing a groan when she saw who it was. She kept her voice neutral as she said, "Hi, Chad."

The grin on Chad's ruddy face was broad and confident. He wasn't a bad-looking guy if a big, Irish former pride of the University of Maryland football defensive end was your thing.

Yeah. Most decidedly *not* Gina's thing.

"What'cha got there?" he asked, nodding at the paper in her hand.

"My grad school grades," she said, folding the paper and putting it back in its envelope.

Chad made a face. "Always dreaded that when I was in college. Had to keep my grades up or no more football." His eyebrows drew together sympathetically. "Bad news?"

Yes, but not the kind you mean. Gina shook her head, a welling of pride warring with the latent panic. "No. I'm still four-point-oh."

Chad's eyes widened. "Really?" She nodded. "I didn't think that was even possible. You must be really super-smart."

"Not really." Gina shook her head. Organized, yep. Diligent, check. Hardworking, hell yeah. But she'd never classify herself as exceptionally smart.

"Anyway…" Chad shifted from foot to foot, his face getting redder. Oh, no. He was going to ask her out. Again. She should never have gone out with him, not even once. That had to have been the most boring night of her life. If he wasn't so *nice* she might be able to give him the *Hell no, not on your life, not even in this lifetime* speech his persistence needed. But while she could be brash and bold and sarcastic this far from home, she could never be mean.

Her phone rang in her bag. *Thank God. Literally saved by the bell.* She grabbed it and glanced at the screen.

Mom.

Maybe she'd picked the wrong cliché. More like out of the frying pan and into the fire.

"I have to take this," she said as she swiped to answer. Her spine automatically straightened as if her mother could see her slouching, her guarded, proper, home-Gina armor settling around her. *Go ahead* she mouthed at Chad, nodding to the elevator. An all-too familiar pang of guilt shot through her as his hopeful expression collapsed into chagrin and he turned to go.

"Hi Ma."

"Gina, sweetheart. What's this I hear about you not coming home for Christmas until the twenty-second?" Boom, right out of the gate. If she thought she'd felt guilty about Chad, now she was really in for it.

"I have things to do down here," she said, rubbing her forehead, the beginning of a headache stirring behind her eyes.

"What's more important than coming home to your family?"

My independence. My ability to be myself. She didn't dare say that. "I have some projects to finish up." Client presentations for her fledgling business, but she hoped her mother would assume incorrectly that she had additional schoolwork to do. The lie of omission stuck in her throat as her mother sighed.

"I'm not mad, Gina, I'm…" Gina silently mouthed her mother's next words, "…just very disappointed." The Catholic mother's version of a sniper-shot. Another pang of guilt spiked through Gina, making her headache pulse.

"Maybe you don't really need that degree after all," her mother said. "We want you back home so much. We miss you."

Panic combined with the guilt, and Gina's pulse accelerated. "No, Ma. I'm so close to graduating. It would be ridiculous to quit now."

"How close?"

Gina closed her eyes. *Damn.* Backed into a corner. "One more class."

"Oh, that's *wonderful.*" The warmth in her mother's voice caused the pang to double in size, the pain in her head a steady drumbeat now. "Your father will be thrilled to have you home. He's told me he's going to create a very special job for you. At least until you get married…"

Now Gina just wanted to curl up and cry. After all her planning and scheming, she was running out of time.

"Oh, and you know who your father ran into at Knights of Columbus last week?" her mother went on as Gina pinched the bridge of her nose and squeezed her eyes shut. "Tony DiSchino." *Of course. Dad just* happened *to run into him.* Only the last guy in the world Gina wanted to see. Smooth, suave Tony DiSchino, ruiner of lives and her parents' dream son-in-law.

"You know how highly your father thinks of Tony, so we're going to have him over for dinner while you're home…" Again. Gina swallowed a scream of frustration.

Of course Dad loved Tony. Born into wealth—in a complementary industry to her father's own property development business, even. Handsome. The guy who had everything handed to him on a silver platter while Gina worked like a dog. Everybody just *loved* Tony.

Everybody but Gina.

#

Tony hitched his shoulder, trying to shrug up the leather briefcase strap that threatened to slide down his arm, and broke into a run.

This is the final boarding call for flight one-twelve to Washington's Reagan National Airport, the PA system announced.

"Shit. Shitshitshitshit." He gripped the briefcase strap with one hand, tightened his hold on his wheelie bag, and sprinted for the gate. A trickle of sweat ran down his temple, gaining speed with every footfall until it slithered under his collar. When he reached the gate agent, breathing hard and aware of his sweaty brow and the unpleasant dampness in his armpits, he did his best to summon up his usual outward calm as he dug in his pocket for his phone. "One second," he

334

huffed, pulling up his boarding pass. Yeah. Totally failing on that calm thing. What an auspicious beginning to one of the most important trips of his entire life.

"Take your time," the agent responded, a cute little smirk on her face that Tony might have appreciated had he not been so flustered. He held the phone under the red light to scan it, the authenticating beep soothing his hammering pulse. He strode down the jetway, gathering his usual calm around him and smiling automatically at the flight attendant as he stowed his wheelie over seat 2C, then settling into the wide leather seat and shoving his briefcase under the seat in front of him. He ran a hand over his brow, then wiped his fingers on his pants.

He'd made it.

Well, he'd made it this far. The rest of what he had to accomplish? A whole hell of a lot more work.

The flight crew sealed up the plane and they were pulling away from the gate and rolling down the runway so soon, his pulse kicked a little.

He'd cut it close this time, even for him.

Keeping Tony time. His mother's fondly amused voice rang in his head. *You were even born two weeks past your due date.*

And his dad's habitual rejoinder. *Late and disrespectful.*

Tony shrugged his shoulders, trying to settle the ache in the one that had supported the briefcase strap. He was uncharacteristically tense and tight all over, but the shoulder was particularly tweaked. He massaged the muscle, stretching his neck away from the tightness, teeth clamping at the shooting pain.

"Can I get you anything?" The flight attendant, impeccable in her uniform, addressed the older white businessman type in a wrinkled suit in the window seat next to Tony. The guy ordered a Scotch. Going by the stale smell wafting off the guy, it wasn't his first of the day.

"And for you?" The woman transferred her attention to Tony, a purely professional smile on her face.

On a short flight, Tony would normally order water. Or, if he was feeling daring, a Bloody Mary mix. Not with actual vodka. No. Just something with flavor.

"Gin and tonic," he said, his smile as reflexive as the one on the flight attendant's face. What the hell. It was after four in the afternoon. Maybe it would take the edge off this unfamiliar off-kilter feeling. He could nurse the watered-down drink for the brief flight, wait for his luggage, pick up his rental, and be right as rain to drive into D.C. and take up his temporary new life.

Tony nodded, his jaw set, and pulled his briefcase from under the seat in front of him. Drawing out the dossier his father's staff had pulled together, he settled back, accepting the drink the flight attendant handed him with absent thanks.

"Gina Romano, we meet again," he mouthed to himself.

Come on. He might feel like a secret agent with this assignment, but there was no way he was going to make Business Drone in 2D think he was crazy by talking to a woman who wasn't there.

Even though he had to be crazy to be setting himself up for a year of unrelieved boredom. For what had to be the hundredth time in the last few months, he barely kept himself from cursing out his grandfather, the author of this whole screwed-up situation. But there was no point in that. Better to be bored than lose control of the company to his walking disaster of a cousin. And for his plan to work, proper Gina Romano was absolutely perfect.

He just had to convince her of that.

\#

"You know I'm right." Gina shot her best toothy smile at Laura.

336

It wasn't fair, she knew it. She knew she could eventually get camera-shy, introverted Laura into agreeing with her by sheer confidence and force of will. Laura knew nothing about marketing or public relations. Nothing about a business plan.

But dammit, Gina *was* right. Just two weeks ago there'd been an article in the freaking *New York Times* about female rock climbers and instructors. The fact that Laura hadn't been included in it made Gina want to kick herself, even though she only had the barest experience with media and had no advance knowledge the paper had been working on the piece.

You're not a public relations expert, she reminded herself. *But you can be an awesome small business consultant.*

Look at how she'd helped build Laura's climbing business. A website, a targeted advertising and marketing plan, a full roster of clients during the season. Gina's initial plan had resulted in an A grade for her small business marketing class and her advisor was encouraging her to think about using it for the capstone project of her MBA. It was also the proof of concept she needed to actually build her dream business and live on her own terms instead of fretting over commercial leases or whatever other godawful tasks her father had planned for her.

Now it was December first, the regular climbing season was over, and other female climbers were getting play in the New York fucking *Times*. So, the opportunity for Laura to get more exposure was ripe. And Gina needed to get some media experience to flesh out her business offerings. Win-win. But only if she could get Laura to see things her way before the opportunity slipped away.

Laura glared at her, her dark blue eyes accusatory. "You want me to be on *television?*"

Gina waved a hand. "Local news. Just the D.C. market. It would be good for you!"

"How?" Laura rested her elbows on the kitchen table in the little house she shared with her fiancé, Simon, her fingers spearing into her brown hair. The sapphire on her left ring finger glinted through the strands.

"This will be good for the LTA," Gina said. "You can help get the word out." Laura's new full-time job was as an advocate for the Land Trust Alliance, an environmental group focused on cleaning up natural areas. The organization had hired her largely because she was a rock-climbing instructor and could speak eloquently about the practical ramifications of protecting the environment.

Laura glared. "If you're going to want me to bring the Land Trust into this, I need to clear it with them."

Gina waved her hands. "No. This isn't about them specifically. This is total local news puff piece. You take the reporter to a climbing area and talk about..." *What was the term?* "Climbing when it's stupidly cold?"

"Ice climbing."

"Really? That's what I'm looking for? I was thinking there'd be a fancier word for it."

Laura's hands thudded back to the table. "No. Really. But it's not usually cold enough around D.C. for ice climbing. And even if I wanted to do this—which I don't—it wouldn't be exciting television."

"Why not?"

"It's cold. Even without much ice around, there are some slick patches. You have to be even more patient than usual." Laura gave her a pointed look and she made a face.

So Gina wasn't known for her patience—at least not when she wasn't performing for her parents? So what?

"You have to move slowly," Laura said. "Not exciting stuff."

338

"That's okay," Gina said. "The angle isn't flash or excitement—I want to capitalize on that *Times* story. Show people around here that you don't have to go all the way to Wyoming or Colorado or wherever to hire a female instructor. Maybe even encourage more women to think about not just climbing but becoming instructors."

Laura gave her a sideways look, eyes slits. "Low blow."

"But it's true." Gina knew that Laura couldn't resist the idea of bringing more women into the sport. Far from wanting to remain one of the few female instructors in the area, she'd told Gina she'd welcomed the respite. She had spent the summer and fall booked solid with trips and clinics. "Just let me pitch it to a reporter. Or two. Maybe it won't work."

"Maybe it will." Laura managed to make that sound like a fate worse than death.

If it did? A huge feather in her cap. Something to show potential clients. Another selling point that would help her build her business. Gina clasped her hands under her chin and let her eyes go wide. "Please? For me? For my business? And can you imagine how great it would be for my capstone project?" Her grade would be in the stratosphere. "Just imagine how pissed those two assholes at Altitude will be to see you get media attention." Earlier in the year, the two owners of the climbing gym Laura had booked trips from had not only treated her like the sexist pieces of shit they were, but they'd basically tried to run her out of the business. Gina would relish the chance to rub their noses in Laura's success.

Laura let out a burst of air and her elbows slid out until her forehead rested on her hands. "Okay, fine. Give it a try."

"Yesss." Gina shot a fist into the air. Step one in the journey to independence. If only she could get there in time.

Acknowledgments

John Jacobson, it was a delight to be edited by you again. You're such a great partner and publishing ally. Thank you for pushing me to put in all the feelings!

As always, thank you to all of my friends, no matter if we've met or gotten together online or off. I get so much support and love from my writing community and I appreciate all of you.

Author's Note

The shipwreck in this book is loosely based on the facts of the *Andrea Doria*, an Italian liner that collided with the Swedish American Line vessel *Stockholm* in 1956.

About the Author

When not writing, Adele is a librarian at a Washington, D.C. law school. Prior to that, she had a short stint as an index editor and over a dozen years in corporate communications and executive relationship management. Even prior to that, she was an actress and stage manager.

She holds a theatre degree from Syracuse University and graduate degrees from the University of Maine School of Law and the University of Maryland's iSchool.

A New Hampshire native, Adele has lived in the D.C. area for over 20 years with her fantastic husband and the requisite number of neurotic cats.

Sign up for Adele's newsletter on her website, adelebuck.com.